**Praise for *New York Times* bestselling author
Diana Palmer**

"Palmer proves that love and passion can be found even in the most dangerous situations."
—*Publishers Weekly* on *Untamed*

"The popular Palmer has penned another winning novel, a perfect blend of romance and suspense."
—*Booklist* on *Lawman*

**Praise for *New York Times* bestselling author
Maisey Yates**

"Yates's thrilling…contemporary proves that friendship can evolve into scintillating romance.… This is a surefire winner not to be missed."
—*Publishers Weekly* on *Slow Burn Cowboy*
(starred review)

"Her characters excel at defying the norms and providing readers with…an emotional investment."
—*RT Book Reviews* on *Claim Me, Cowboy* (Top Pick)

A prolific author of more than one hundred books, **Diana Palmer** got her start as a newspaper reporter. A *New York Times* bestselling author and voted one of the top ten romance writers in America, she has a gift for telling the most sensual tales with charm and humor. Diana lives with her family in Cornelia, Georgia. Visit her website at DianaPalmer.com.

Maisey Yates is a *New York Times* bestselling author of more than seventy-five romance novels. She has a coffee habit she has no interest in kicking, and a slight Pinterest addiction. She lives with her husband and children in the Pacific Northwest. When Maisey isn't writing, she can be found singing in the grocery store, shopping for shoes online and probably not doing dishes. Check out her website, maiseyyates.com.

New York Times Bestselling Author

DIANA PALMER

ROGUE STALLION

**HARLEQUIN®
BESTSELLING
AUTHOR
COLLECTION**

Recycling programs
for this product may
not exist in your area.

ISBN-13: 978-1-335-91529-0

Rogue Stallion

First published in 1994. This edition published in 2020.

Copyright © 1994 by Harlequin Books S.A.

Need Me, Cowboy
First published in 2019. This edition published in 2020.
Copyright © 2019 by Maisey Yates

This edition published by arrangement with Harlequin Books S.A.

For questions and comments about the quality of this book, please contact us at CustomerService@Harlequin.com.

Harlequin Enterprises ULC
22 Adelaide St. West, 40th Floor
Toronto, Ontario M5H 4E3, Canada
www.Harlequin.com

Printed in U.S.A.

CONTENTS

Books by Diana Palmer

Long, Tall Texans

Fearless
Heartless
Dangerous
Merciless
Courageous
Protector
Invincible
Untamed
Defender
Undaunted

Wyoming Men

Wyoming Tough
Wyoming Fierce
Wyoming Bold
Wyoming Strong
Wyoming Rugged
Wyoming Brave

Visit the Author Profile page
at Harlequin.com for more titles.

ROGUE STALLION

Diana Palmer

Chapter 1

There was a lull in Sheriff Judd Hensley's office, broken only by the soft whir of the fan. It sometimes amused visitors from back East that springtime in Whitehorn, Montana, was every bit as unpredictable as spring in the southeastern part of America, and that the weather could be quite warm. But the man sitting across the desk from Hensley was neither visitor nor was he amused. His dark, handsome face was wearing a brooding scowl, and he was glaring at his superior.

"Why can't the city police investigate? They have two detectives. I'm the only special investigator in the sheriff's department, and I'm overworked as it is," Sterling McCallum said, trying once more.

Hensley toyed with a pen, twirling it on the desk absently while he thought. He was about the same build as McCallum, rugged and quiet. He didn't say much. When he did, the words meant something.

He looked up from the desk. "I know that," he said. "But right now, you're the one who deserves a little aggravation."

McCallum crossed his long legs and leaned back with a rough sigh. His black boots had a flawless shine, a legacy from his years in the U.S. Navy as a career officer. He had an ex-military mind-set that often put him at odds with his boss, especially since he'd mustered out with the rank of captain. He was much more used to giving orders than to taking them.

In the navy, the expected answer to any charge of dereliction of duty, regardless of innocence or guilt, was, "No excuse, sir." It was still hard for McCallum to get used to defending his actions. "I did what the situation called for," he said tersely. "When someone tries to pull a gun on me, I get twitchy."

"That was only bravado," Hensley pointed out, "and you knocked out one of his teeth. The department has to pay for it. The county commission climbed all over me and I didn't like it." He leaned forward with his hands clasped and gave the younger man a steady look. "Now you're the one with the problems. Dugin Kincaid found an abandoned baby on his doorstep."

"Maybe it's his," McCallum said with smiling sarcasm. Dugin was a pale imitation of his rancher father, Jeremiah. The thought of him with a woman amused McCallum.

"As I was saying," the sheriff continued without reacting to the comment, "the baby was found outside the city limits—hence our involvement—and its parents have to be found. You're not working on anything that pressing. You can take this case. I want you to talk with Jessica Larson at the social-welfare office."

McCallum groaned. "Why don't you just shoot me?"

"Now, there's no need to be like that," Hensley said, surprised. "She's a nice woman," he said. "Why, her dad was a fine doctor...."

His voice trailed off abruptly. McCallum remembered that Hensley's son had died in a hunting accident. Jessica's father had tried everything to save the boy, but it had been impossible. Hensley's wife, Tracy, divorced him a year after the funeral. That had happened years ago, long before McCallum left the service.

"Anyway, Jessica is one of the best social workers in the department," Hensley continued.

"She's the head of the department now, and a royal pain in the neck since her promotion," McCallum shot right back. "She's Little Miss Sunshine, spreading smiles of joy wherever she goes." His black eyes, a legacy from a Crow ancestor, glittered angrily. "She can't separate governmental responsibility from bleeding-heart activism."

"I wonder if it's fair to punish her by sticking her with you?" Hensley asked himself aloud. He threw up his hands. "Well, you'll just have to grin and bear it. I can't sit here arguing with you all day. This is my department. I'm the sheriff. See this?" He pointed at the badge on his uniform.

"Needs polishing," McCallum noted.

Hensley's eyes narrowed. He stood up. "Get out of here before I forget you work for me."

McCallum unfolded his six-foot-plus length from the chair and stood up. He was just a hair taller than the sheriff, and he looked casual in his jeans and knit shirt and denim jacket. But when the jacket fell open, the butt of his .45 automatic was revealed, giving bystanders a hint of the sort of work he did. He was a plainclothes detective, although only outsiders were fooled by his casual attire. Most everyone in Whitehorn knew that McCallum was as conservative and military as the shine on his black boots indicated.

"Don't shoot anybody," Hensley told him. "And next time a man threatens to shoot you, check for a gun and disarm him before you hit him, please?" Hensley's eyes went to the huge silver-and-turquoise ring that McCallum wore on the middle finger of his right hand. "That ring is so heavy it's a miracle you didn't break his jaw."

McCallum held up his left hand, which was ringless. "This is the hand I hit him with."

"He said it felt like a baseball bat."

"I won't tell you where he hit *me* before he started ranting about shooting," the detective replied, turning to the door. "And if I didn't work for you, a loose tooth would have been the least of his complaints."

"Jessica Larson is expecting you over at the social-services office," Hensley called.

McCallum, to his credit, didn't slam the door.

Jessica Larson was fielding paperwork and phone calls with a calmness that she didn't feel at all. She'd become adept at presenting an unflappable appearance while having hysterics. Since her promotion to social-services director, she'd learned that she could eat at her desk during the day and forgo any private life after work at night. She also realized why her predecessor had taken an early retirement. A lot of people came into this office to get help.

Like most of the rest of the country, Montana was having a hard time with the economy. Even though gambling had been legalized, adding a little more money to the state's strained coffers, it was harder and harder for many local citizens to make ends meet. Ranches went under all the time these days, forced into receivership or eaten up by big corporations. Manual labor, once a valuable commodity in the agricultural sector, was now a burden on the system when those workers lost jobs. They were unskilled and unemployable in any of the new, high-tech markets. Even secretaries had to use computers these days. So did policemen.

The perfunctory knock on her office door was emphasized by her secretary's high-pitched, "But she's busy…!"

"It's all right, Candy," Jessica called to the harassed young blonde. "I'm expecting McCallum." She didn't add that she hadn't expected him a half hour early. She tried to think of Sterling McCallum as a force of nature. He was like a wild stallion, a rogue stallion who traveled alone and made his own rules. Secretly, she was awed by him. He made her wish that she was a gorgeous model with curves in all the right places and a beautiful face—maybe with blond hair instead of brown. At least she was able to replace her big-rimmed glasses with contacts, which helped her appearance. But when she had allergies, she had to wear the glasses…like right now.

McCallum didn't wait for her to ask him to sit down. He took the chair beside her desk and crossed one long leg over the other.

"Let's have it," he said without preamble, looking unutterably bored.

Her eyes slid over his thick dark hair, so conventionally cut, down to his equally dark eyebrows and eyes in an olive-tan face. He had big ears and big hands and big feet, although there was nothing remotely clumsy about him. He had a nose with a crook in it, probably from being broken, and a mouth that she dreamed about: very wide and sexy and definite. Broad shoulders tapered to a broad chest and narrow hips like a rodeo rider's. His stomach was flat and he had long, muscular legs. He was so masculine that he made her ache. She was twenty-five, a mature woman and only about ten years younger than he was, but he made her feel childish sometimes, and inadequate—as a professional and as a woman.

"Hero worship again, Jessica?" he chided, amused by her soft blush.

"Don't tease. This is serious," she chided gently in turn.

He shrugged and sighed. "Okay. What have you done with the child?"

"Jennifer," she told him.

He glowered. "The abandoned baby."

She gave up. He wouldn't allow anyone to become personalized in his company. Boys he had to pick up were juvenile delinquents. Abandoned babies were exactly that. No names. No identity. No complications in his ordered, uncluttered life. He let no one close to him. He had no friends, no family, no connections. Jessica felt painfully sorry for him, although she tried not to let it show. He was so alone and so vulnerable under that tough exterior that he must imagine was his best protection from being wounded. His childhood was no secret to anyone in Whitehorn. Everyone knew that his mother had been an alcoholic and that, after her arrest and subsequent death, he had been shunted from foster home to foster home. His only real value had been as an extra hand on one ranch or another, an outsider always looking in through a cloudy window at what home life might have been under other circumstances.

"You're doing it again," he muttered irritably.

Her slender eyebrows lifted over soft brown eyes. "What?" she asked.

"Pigeonholing me," he said. "Poor orphan, tossed from pillar to post..."

"I wish you'd stop reading my mind," she told him. "It's very disconcerting."

"I wish you'd stop bleeding all over me," he returned. "I don't need pity. I'm content with my life, just as it is. I had a rough time. So what? Plenty of people do. I'm here to talk about a case, Jessica, and it isn't mine."

She smiled self-consciously. "All right, McCallum," she said agreeably, reaching for a file. "The baby was taken to Whitehorn Memorial and checked over. She's perfectly healthy, clean and well-cared for, barely two weeks old. They're keeping her for observation overnight and then it will be up to the juvenile authorities to make arrangements about her care until her parents are located. I'm going over to see her in the morning. I'd like you to come with me."

"I don't need to see it—"

"Her," she corrected. "Baby Jennifer."

"—to start searching for its parents," he concluded without missing a beat.

"Her parents," Jessica corrected calmly.

His dark eyes didn't blink. "Was there anything else?"

"I'll leave here about nine," Jessica continued. "You can ride with me."

His eyes widened. "In that glorified yellow tank you drive?"

"It's a pickup truck!" she exclaimed defensively. "And it's very necessary, considering where I live!"

He refused to think about her cabin in the middle of nowhere, across a creek that flooded with every cloudburst. It wasn't his place to worry about her just because she had no family. In that aspect of their lives they were very much alike. In other ways...

He stood up. "You can ride with me," he said, giving in with noticeable impatience.

"I hate riding around in a patrol car," she muttered.

"It doesn't have a sign on it. It's a plainclothes car."

"Of course it is, with those plain hubcaps, no white sidewalls, fifteen antennas sticking out of it and a spotlight. It doesn't need a sign, does it? Anyone who isn't blind would recognize it as an unmarked patrol car!"

"It beats driving a yellow tank," he pointed out.

She stood up, too, feeling at a disadvantage when she didn't. But he was still much taller than she was. She pushed at a wisp of brown hair that had escaped from the bun on top of her head. Her beige suit emphasized her slender build, devoid as it was of any really noticeable curves.

"Why do you screw your hair up like that?" he asked curiously.

"It falls in my face when I'm trying to work," she said, indicating the stack of files on her desk. "Besides Candy, I only have two caseworkers, and they're trying to take away one of them because of new budget cuts. I'm already working Saturdays trying to catch up, and they've just complained about the amount of overtime I do."

"That sounds familiar."

"I know," she said cheerily. "Everyone has to work around tight budgets these days. It's one of the joys of public service."

"Why don't you get married and let some strong man support you?" he taunted.

She tilted her chin saucily. "Are you proposing to

me, Deputy?" she asked with a wicked smile. "Has someone been tantalizing you with stories of my home-made bread?"

He'd meant it sarcastically, but she'd turned the tables on him neatly. He gave in with a reluctant grin.

"I'm not the marrying kind," he said. "I don't want a wife and kids."

Her bright expression dimmed a little, but remnants of the smile lingered. "Not everyone does," she said agreeably. The loud interruption of the telephone ringing in the outer office caught her attention, followed by the insistent buzz of the intercom. She turned back to her desk. "Thanks for stopping by. I'll see you in the morning, then," she added as she lifted the receiver. "Yes, Candy," she said.

McCallum's eyes slid quietly over her bowed head. After a minute, he turned and walked out, closing the door gently behind him. He did it without a goodbye. Early in his life, he'd learned not to look back.

The house where McCallum lived was at the end of a wide, dead-end street. His neighbors never intruded, but it got back to him that they felt more secure having a law-enforcement officer in the neighborhood. He sat on his front porch sometimes with a beer and looked at the beauty of his surroundings while watching the children ride by on bicycles. He watched as a stranger watches, learning which children belonged at which houses. He saw affection from some parents and amazing indifference from others. He saw sadness and joy. But he saw it from a distance. His own life held no highs or lows. He was answerable to no one, free to do whatever he pleased with no interference.

He'd had the flu last winter. He'd lain in his bed for

over twenty-four hours, burning with fever, unable to cook or even get into the kitchen. Not until he missed work did anyone come looking for him. The incident had punctuated how alone he really was.

He hadn't been alone long. Jessica had hotfooted it over to look after him, ignoring his ranting and raving about not wanting any woman cluttering up his house. She'd fed him and cleaned for him in between doing her own job, and only left when he proved to her that he could get out of bed. Because of the experience, he'd been ruder than ever to her. When he'd gone back to work, she'd taken a pot of chicken soup to the office, enough that he could share it with the other men on his shift. It had been uncomfortable when they'd teased him about Jessica's nurturing, and he'd taken out that irritation on her.

He hadn't even thanked her for her trouble, he recalled. No matter how rude he was she kept coming back, like a friendly little elf who only wanted to make him happy. She was his one soft spot, although, thank God, she didn't know it. He was curt with her because he had to keep her from knowing about his weakness for her. He had been doing a good job; when she looked at him these days, she never met his eyes.

He sipped his beer, glowering at the memories. His free hand dropped to the head of his big brown-and-black Doberman. He'd had the dog for almost a year. He'd found Mack tied in a croker sack, yipping helplessly in the shallows of a nearby river. Having rescued the dog, he couldn't find anyone who was willing to take it, and he hadn't had the heart to shoot it. There was no agency in Whitehorn to care for abandoned or stray animals. The only alternative was to adopt the pup, and he had.

At first Mack had been a trial to him. But once he housebroke the dog and it began to follow him around the house—and later, to work—he grew reluctantly fond of it. Now Mack was part of his life. They were inseparable, especially on hunting and fishing trips. If he had a family at all, McCallum thought, it was Mack.

He sat back, just enjoying the beauty of Whitehorn. The sun set; the children went inside. And still McCallum sat, thinking and listening to the hum of the quiet springtime night.

Finally, he got up. It was after eleven. He'd just gone inside and was turning out the lights when the phone rang.

"It's Hensley," the sheriff announced over the phone. "We've got a 10-16 at the Miles place, a real hummer. It's outside the city police's jurisdiction, so it either has to be you or a deputy."

"It won't do any good to go, you know," McCallum said. "Jerry Miles beats Ellen up twice a month, but she never presses charges. Last time he beat up their twelve-year-old son, and even then—"

"I know."

"I'll go anyway," McCallum said. "It's a hell of a shame we can't lock him up without her having to press charges. She's afraid of him. If she left him, he'd probably go after her, and God knows what he'd do. I've seen it happen. So have you. Everybody says leave him. Nobody says they'll take care of her when he comes looking for her with a gun."

"We have to keep hoping that she'll get help."

"Jessica has tried," McCallum admitted, "but nothing changes. You can't help people until they're ready to accept it, and the consequences of accepting it."

"I heard that."

McCallum drove out to the Miles home. It was three miles out of Whitehorn, in the rolling, wide-open countryside.

He didn't put on the siren. He drove up into the yard and cut the lights. Then he got out, unfastening the loop that held his pistol in place in the holster on his hip, just in case. One of Whitehorn's policemen had been shot and killed trying to break up a domestic dispute some years ago.

There was no noise coming from inside. The night was ominously quiet. McCallum's keen eyes scanned the area and suddenly noticed a yellow truck parked just behind the house, on a dirt road that ran behind it and parallel to the main highway.

Jessica was in there!

He quickened his steps, went up on the front porch and knocked at the door.

"Police," he announced. "Open up!"

There was a pause. His hand went to the pistol and he stood just to the side of the doorway, waiting.

The main door opened quite suddenly, and a tired-looking Jessica Larson smiled at him through a torn screen. "It's all right," she said, opening the screen door for him. "He's passed out on the bed. Ellen and Chad are all right."

McCallum walked into the living room, feeling uncomfortable as he looked at the two people whose lives were as much in ruin as the broken, cheap lamp on the floor. The sofa was stained and the rug on the wood floor had frayed edges. There were old, faded curtains at the windows and a small television still blaring out a game show. Ellen sat on the sofa with red-rimmed eyes, her arm around Chad, who was crying. He had a bruise on one cheek.

"How much longer are you going to let the boy suffer like this, Ellen?" McCallum asked quietly.

She stared at him from dull eyes. "Mister, if I send my husband to jail, he says he'll kill me," she announced. "I think he will. Last time I tried to run away, he shot our dog."

"He's sick, Ellen," Jessica added gently. Her glance in the direction of the bedroom had an odd, frightened edge to it. "He's very sick. Alcoholism can destroy his body, you know. It can kill him."

"Yes, ma'am, I know that. He's a big man, though," the woman continued in a lackluster voice, absently smoothing her son's hair. "He loves me. He says so. He's always sorry, after."

"He's not sorry," McCallum said, his voice deep and steady. "He enjoys watching you cry. He likes making you afraid of him. He gets off on it."

"McCallum!" Jessica said sharply.

He ignored her. He knelt in front of Ellen and stared at her levelly. "Listen to me. My mother was an alcoholic. She used a bottle on me once, and laughed when she broke my arm with it. She said she was sorry, too, after she sobered up, but the day she broke my arm, I stopped believing it. I called the police and they locked her up. And the beatings stopped. For good."

Ellen wiped at her eyes. "Weren't you sorry? I mean, she was your mother. You're supposed to love your mother."

"You don't beat the hell out of people you love," he said coldly. "And you know that. Are you going to keep making excuses for him until he kills your son?"

She gasped, clasping the boy close. "But he won't!" she said huskily. "Oh, no, I know he won't! He loves

Chad. He loves me, too. He just drinks so much that he forgets he loves us, that's all."

"If he hurts the child, you'll go to jail as an accessory," McCallum told her. He said it without feeling, without remorse. He said it deliberately. "I swear to God you will. I'll arrest you myself."

Ellen paled. The hands holding her son contracted. "Chad doesn't want to see his daddy go to jail," she said firmly. "Do you, son?"

Chad lifted his head from her shoulder and looked straight at McCallum. "Yes, sir, I do," he said in a choked voice. "I don't want him to hit my mama anymore. I tried to stop him and he did this." He pointed to his eye.

McCallum looked back at Ellen. There was accusation and cold anger in his dark eyes. They seemed to see right through her.

She shivered. "He'll hurt us if I let you take him to jail," she said, admitting the truth at last. "I'm scared of him. I'm so scared!"

Jessica stepped forward. "There's a shelter for battered women," she replied. "I'll make sure you get there. You'll be protected. He won't come after you or Chad, and even if he tries, he can be arrested for that, too."

Ellen bit her lower lip. "He's my *husband*," she said with emphasis. "The good book says that when you take a vow, you don't ever break it."

McCallum's chin lifted. "The same book says that when a man marries a woman, he cherishes her. It doesn't say one damned thing about being permitted to beat her, does it?"

She hesitated, but only for a minute. "I have an aunt in Lexington, Kentucky. She'd let me and Chad live with her, I know she would. I could go there. He doesn't know about my aunt. He'd never find us."

"Is that what you want?" Jessica asked.

The woman hesitated. Her weary eyes glanced around the room, taking measure of the destruction. She felt as abused as the broken lamp, as the sagging sofa with its torn fabric. Her gaze rested finally on her son and she looked, really looked, at him. No child of twelve should have eyes like that. She'd been thinking only of her own safety, of her vows to her husband, not of the one person whose future should have mattered to her. She touched Chad's hair gently.

"It's all right, son," she said. "It's gonna be all right. I'll get you out of here." She glanced away from his wet eyes to McCallum. Her head jerked toward the bedroom. "I have to get away. I can't press charges against him…."

"Don't worry about it," McCallum said. "He'll sleep for a long time and then he won't know where to look for you. By the time he thinks about trying, he'll be drunk again. The minute he gets behind a wheel, I'll have him before a judge. With three prior DWI convictions, he'll spend some time in jail."

"All right." She got uneasily to her feet. "I'll have to get my things…." Her eyes darted nervously to the bedroom.

McCallum walked to the doorway and stood there. He didn't say a word, but she knew what his actions meant. If her husband woke up while she was packing, McCallum would deal with him.

She smiled gratefully and went hesitantly into the dimly lit bedroom, where her husband was passed out on the bed. Jessica didn't offer to go with her. She sat very still on the sofa, looking around her with a kind of subdued fear that piqued McCallum's curiosity.

Jessica drove her own truck to the bus station, parking it next to the unmarked car in which McCallum had put Chad and his mother. It was acting up again, and she tried to recrank it but it refused to start.

They saw the mother and son onto the bus and stood together until it vanished into the distance.

McCallum glanced at his watch. It was after midnight, but he was wound up and not at all sleepy.

Jessica mistook the obvious gesture for an indication that he wanted to get going. "Thanks for your help," she told him. "I'd better get back home. Could you take me? My truck's on the blink again."

"Sure. I'll send someone over in the morning to fix the truck and deliver it to your office. I'm sure you can get a ride to work."

"Yes, I can. Thanks," she said, relieved.

He caught her arm and shepherded her into the depot, which was open all night. There was a small coffee concession, where an old man sold coffee and doughnuts and soft drinks.

Jessica was dumbfounded. Usually McCallum couldn't wait to get away from her. His wanting to have coffee with her was an historic occasion, and she didn't quite know what to expect.

Chapter 2

McCallum helped her into a small booth and came back with two mugs of steaming coffee.

"What if I didn't drink coffee?" she asked.

He smiled faintly. "I've never seen you without a cup at your elbow," he remarked. "No cream, either. Sugar?"

She shook her head. "I live on the caffeine, not the taste." She cupped her hands around the hot cup and looked at him across the table. "You don't like my company enough to take me out for coffee unless you want something. What is it?"

He was shocked. Did she really have such a low self-image? His dark eyes narrowed on her face, and he couldn't decide why she looked so different. She wasn't wearing makeup—probably she'd been in too big a hurry to get to Ellen's house to bother. And her infrequently worn, big-lensed glasses were perched jauntily on her nose. But it was more than that. Then he realized what the difference was. Her hair—her long, glorious, sable-colored hair—was falling in thick waves around her shoulders and halfway down her back. His fingers itched to bury themselves in it, and the very idea made his eyebrows fly up in surprise.

"I don't read minds," she said politely.

"What?" He frowned, then remembered her question. "I wanted to ask you something."

She nodded resignedly and sipped at her coffee.

He leaned back against the dark red vinyl of the booth, studying her oval face and her big brown eyes behind the round lenses for longer than he meant to. "How is it you wound up in that house during a domestic dispute?"

"Oh. That."

He glared at her. "Don't make light of it," he said shortly. "More cops have been hurt during family quarrels than in shoot-outs."

"Yes, I know, I do read statistics. Ellen called me and I went. That's all."

One eye narrowed. "Next time," he said slowly, "you phone me first, before you walk into something like that. Do you understand me?"

"But I was in no danger," she began.

"The man weighs two-fifty if he weighs a pound," he said shortly. "You're what—a hundred and twenty sopping wet?"

"I'm not helpless!" She laughed nervously. It wouldn't do to let him know the terror she'd felt when Ellen had called her, crying hysterically, begging her to come. It had taken all her courage to walk into that house.

"Do you have martial-arts training?"

She hesitated and then shook her head irritably.

"Do you carry a piece?"

"What would I do with a loaded gun?" she exclaimed. "I'd shoot my leg off!"

The scowl got worse. "Then how did you expect to handle a drunken man who outweighs you by over a hundred pounds and was bent on proving his strength to anyone who came within swinging range?"

She nibbled her lower lip and stared into her coffee. "Because Ellen begged me to. It's my job."

"No, it's not," he said firmly. "Your job is to help people who are down on their luck and to rescue kids from abusive environments. It doesn't include trying to do a policeman's work."

His eyes were unblinking. He had a stare that made her want to back up two steps. She imagined it worked very well on lawbreakers.

She let out a weary breath. "Okay," she said, holding up a slender, ringless hand. "I let my emotions get the best of me. I did something stupid and, fortunately, I didn't get hurt."

"Big of you to admit it," he drawled.

"You're a pain, McCallum," she told him bluntly.

"Funny you should mention it," he replied. "I made the same complaint about you to Hensley only this morning."

"Oh, I know you don't approve of me," she agreed. "You think social workers should be like you—all-business, treating people as though they were statistics, not getting emotionally involved—"

"Bingo!" he said immediately.

She put her coffee cup down gently. "A hundred years ago, most of the country south of here belonged to the Crow," she said, looking pointedly at him, because she knew about his ancestry. "They had a social system that was one of the most efficient ever devised. No one valued personal property above the needs of the group. Gifts were given annually among the whole tribe. When a man killed a deer, regardless of his own need, the meat was given away. To claim it for himself was unthinkable. Arguments were settled by gift giving. Each person cared about every other person in the village, and people were accepted for what they were. And no one was so solitary that he or she didn't belong, in some way, to every family."

He leaned forward. "With the pointed exception of Crazy Horse, who kept to himself almost exclusively."

She nodded. "With his exception."

"Someone told you that I had a Crow ancestor," he guessed accurately.

She shrugged. "In Whitehorn, everyone knows everyone else's business. Well, mostly, anyway," she added, because she was pretty sure that he didn't know about her own emotional scars. The incident had been hushed up because of the nature of the crime, and because there'd been a minor involved. It was just as well. Jessica couldn't have a permanent relationship with a man, even if she would have given most of a leg to have one with McCallum. He was perfect for her in every way.

"I'm more French Canadian in my ancestry than Crow." He studied her own face with quiet curiosity. She had a pretty mouth, like a little bow, and her nose was straight. Her big, dark eyes with their long, curly lashes were her finest feature. Even glasses didn't disguise their beauty.

"Are you nearsighted or farsighted?" he asked abruptly.

"Nearsighted." She adjusted her glasses self-consciously. "I usually wear contacts, but my eyes itch lately from all the grass cuttings. I'm blind as a bat without these. I couldn't even cross a street if I lost them."

His eyes fell to her hands. They were slightly tanned, long-fingered, with oval nails. Very pretty.

"Are you going to arrest Ellen's husband?" she asked suddenly.

He pursed his lips. "Now what do you think?"

"We didn't get Ellen to press charges," she reminded him.

"We couldn't have. If she had, she'd have to come back and face him in court. She's afraid that he might kill her. He's threatened to," he reminded her. "But as it is, he won't know where to look for her, and even if he did, it won't matter."

"What do you mean?" she asked curiously.

His eyes took on a faint glitter, like a stormy night sky. "He gets drunk every night. He's got three previous convictions on DWI and he likes to mix it up in taverns. He'll step over the line and I'll have him behind bars, without Ellen's help. This time I'll make sure the charges stick. Drunkenness is no excuse for brutality."

She was remembering what he'd said to Ellen about his own mother breaking his arm with a bottle when he was a little boy.

She reached out without thinking and gently touched the long sleeve of his blue-patterned Western shirt. "Which arm was it?" she asked quietly.

The compassion in her voice hurt him. He'd never known it in his youth. Even now, he wasn't used to people caring about him in any way. Jessica did, and he didn't want her to. He didn't trust anyone close to him. Years of abuse had made him suspicious of any overture, no matter how well meant.

He jerked his arm away. "What you heard wasn't something you were meant to hear," he said icily. "You had no business being in the house in the first place."

She cupped her mug in her hands and smiled. The words didn't sting her. She'd learned long ago not to take verbal abuse personally. Most children who'd been hurt reacted that way to kindness. They couldn't trust anymore, because the people they loved most had betrayed them in one way or another. His was the same story she'd heard a hundred times before. It never got easier to listen to.

But there was a big difference between anger and hostility. Anger was normal, healthy. Hostility was more habit than anything else, and it stemmed from low esteem, feelings of inadequacy. It was impersonal, unlike aggression, which was intended to hurt. A good social worker quickly learned the difference, and how not to take verbal outpourings seriously. McCallum was something of a psychologist himself. He probably understood himself very well by now.

"I didn't mean to snap," he said curtly.

She only smiled at him, her eyes warm and gentle. "I know. I've spent the past three years working with abused children."

He cursed under his breath. He was overly defensive with her because she knew too much about people like him, and it made him feel naked. He knew that he must hurt her sometimes with his roughness, but damn it, she never fought back or made sarcastic comments. She just sat there with that serene expression on her face. He wondered if she ever gave way to blazing temper or passion. Both were part and parcel of his tempestuous nature, although he usually managed to control them. Years of self-discipline had helped.

"You don't like being touched, do you?" she asked suddenly.

"Don't presume, ever, to psychoanalyze me," he replied bluntly. "I'm not one of your clients."

"Wasn't there any social worker who tried to help you?" she asked.

"They helped me," he retorted. "I had homes. Several of them, in fact, mostly on ranches."

Her hands tightened on the cup. "Weren't you loved?"

His eyes flashed like glowing coals. "If you mean have I had women, yes," he said with deliberate cruelty. "Plenty of them!"

Jessica surrendered the field. She should have known better than to pry. She didn't want to hear anything about his intimate conquests. The thought of him... like that...was too disturbing. She finished her coffee and dragged a dollar bill out of her pocket to pay for it.

"I'll take care of it," he said carelessly.

She looked at him. "No, you won't," she said quietly. "I pay my own way. Always."

She got up and paid the old man behind the counter, and walked out of the concession ahead of McCallum.

She was already unlocking her pickup truck when he got outside. Even if it wouldn't start, she needed her sweater. She got it out and locked it up again.

"You actually lock that thing?" he asked sarcastically. "My God, anyone who stole it would be doing you a favor."

"I can't afford theft insurance," she said simply. "Keeping my family home takes all my spare cash."

He remembered where she lived, across the creek on the outskirts of town, with a huge tract of land—hundreds of acres. She played at raising cattle on it, and she had a hired hand who looked after things for her. Jessica loved cattle, although she knew nothing about raising them. But prices were down and it wasn't easy. He knew that she was fighting a losing battle, trying to keep the place.

"Why not just sell out and move into one of the new apartment complexes?"

She turned and looked up at him. He was taller up close. "Why, because it's my home. My heritage," she said. "It was one of the first homes built in Whitehorn, over a hundred years ago. I can't sell it."

"Heritage is right here," he said abruptly, placing his hand against her shoulder and collarbone, in the general area of her heart.

The contact shocked her. She moved back, but the truck was in the way.

He smiled quizzically. "What are you so nervous about?" he asked lazily. "This isn't intimate."

She was flushed. The dark eyes that looked up into his were a little frightened.

He stared at her until images began to suggest themselves, and still he didn't move his hand. "You've had to go a lot of places alone, to interview people who wanted assistance," he began. "At least one or two of those places must have had men very much like Ellen's husband—men who were drunk or who thought that a woman coming into a house alone must be asking for it. And when you were younger, you wouldn't have expected…" She caught her breath and his chin lifted. "Yes," he said slowly, almost to himself. "That's it. That's why you're so jumpy around men. I noticed it at Ellen's house. You were concerned for her, but that wasn't altogether why you kept staring so nervously toward the bedroom."

She bit her lower lip and looked at his chest instead of his eyes. His pearl-button shirt was open down past his collarbone, and she could see a thick, black mat of curling hair inside. He was the most aggressively masculine man she'd ever known, and God only knew why she wasn't afraid of him when most men frightened her.

"You won't talk, will you?" he asked above her head.

"McCallum…" She caught his big hand, feeling its strength and warmth. She told herself to push it away, but her fingers couldn't seem to do what her brain was telling them.

His breathing changed, suddenly and audibly. His warm breath stirred the hair at her temple. "But despite whatever happened to you," he continued as if she hadn't spoken, "you're not afraid of me."

"You must let me go now." She spoke quietly. Her hand went flat against his shirtfront. She knew at once that it was a mistake when she felt the warm strength of his body and the cushy softness of the thick hair under the shirt. The feel of him shocked her. "My…goodness, you're—you're furry," she said with a nervous laugh.

"Furry." He deliberately unsnapped two pearly buttons and drew the fabric from under her flattened hand. He guided her cold fingers over the thick pelt that covered him from his collarbone down, and pressed them over the hard nipple.

She opened her mouth to protest, but his body fascinated her. She'd never seen a man like this at close range, much less touched one. He smelled of soap and faint cologne. He drowned her in images, in sensations, in smells. Her fascinated eyes widened as she gave way to her curiosity and began to stroke him hesitantly.

He shivered. Her gaze shot up to his hard face, but his expression was unreadable—except for the faint, unnerving glitter of his eyes.

"A man's nipple is as sensitive as a woman's," he explained quietly. "It excites me when you trace it like that."

The soft words brought her abruptly to her senses. She was making love to a man on a public street in front of the bus depot. With a soft groan, she dragged her hand away from him and bit her lower lip until she tasted blood.

"What a horrified expression," he murmured as he refastened his shirt. "Does it shock you that you can feel like a woman? Or don't you think I know that you hide your own emotions in the job? All this empathy you pour out on your clients is no more than a shield behind which you hide your own needs, your own desires."

Her face tightened. "Don't *you* psychoanalyze *me!*" she gasped, throwing his earlier words right back at him.

"If I'm locked up inside, so are you, honey," he drawled, watching her react to the blunt remark.

"My personal life is my own business, and don't you call me honey!"

She started to turn, but he caught her by the upper arms and turned her back around. His eyes were merciless, predatory.

"Were you raped?" he asked bluntly.

"No!" she said angrily, glaring at him. "And that's all you need to know, McCallum!"

His hands on her arms relaxed, became caressing. He scowled down at her, searching for the right words.

"Let me go!"

"No."

He reached around her and relocked the truck. He helped her into his car without asking if she was ready to come with him, started it and drove straight to his house.

She was numb with surprise. But she came out of her stupor when he pulled the car into his driveway and turned off the engine and lights. "Oh, I can't," she began quickly. "I have to go home!"

Ignoring her protest, he got out and opened the door for her. She let him extricate her and lead her up onto his porch. Mack barked from inside, but once Sterling let them in and turned on the lights, he calmed the big dog easily.

"You know Mack," he told Jessica. "While you're getting reacquainted, I'll make another pot of coffee. If you need to wash your face, bathroom's there," he added, gesturing toward a room between the living room and the kitchen.

Mack growled at Jessica. She would try becoming his friend later, but right now she wanted to bathe her hot face. She couldn't really imagine why she'd allowed McCallum to bring her here, when it was certainly going to destroy her reputation if anyone saw her alone with him after midnight.

By the time she got back to the living room, he had hot coffee on the coffee table, in fairly disreputable black mugs with faded emblems on them.

"I don't have china," he said when she tried to read the writing on hers.

"Neither do I," she confessed. "Except, I do have two place settings of Havilland, but they're cracked. They were my great-aunt's." She looked at him over her coffee cup. "I shouldn't be here."

"Because it's late and we're alone?"

She nodded.

"I'm a cop."

"Well...yes."

"Your reputation won't suffer," he said, leaning back to cross his long legs. "If there's one thing I'm not, it's a womanizer, and everyone knows it. I don't have women."

"You said you did," she muttered.

He looked toward her with wise, amused eyes. "*Did,* yes. Not since I came back here. Small towns are hot-beds of gossip, and I've been the subject of it enough in my life. I won't risk becoming a household word again just to satisfy an infrequent ache."

She drank her coffee quickly, trying to hide how much his words embarrassed her, as well as the reference to gossip. She had her own skeletons, about which he apparently knew nothing. It had been a long time ago, after all, and most of the people who knew about Jessica's past had moved away or died. Sheriff Judd Hensley knew, but he wasn't likely to volunteer information to McCallum. Judd was tight-lipped, and he'd been Jessica's foremost ally at a time when she'd needed one desperately.

After a minute, Sterling put down his coffee cup and took hers away from her, setting it neatly in line with his. He leaned back on the sofa, his body turned toward hers.

"Tell me."

She clasped her hands tightly in her lap. "I've never talked about it," she said shortly. "He's dead, anyway, so what good would it do now?"

"I want to know."

"Why?"

His broad shoulders rose and fell. "Who else is there? You don't have any family, Jessica, and I know for a fact you don't have even one friend. Who do you talk to?"

"I talk to God!"

He smiled. "Well, He's probably pretty busy right now, so why don't you tell me?"

She pushed back her long hair. Her eyes sought the framed print of a stag in an autumn forest on the opposite wall. "I can't."

"Have you told anyone?"

Her slender shoulders hunched forward and she dropped her face into her hands with a heavy sigh. "I told my supervisor. My parents were dead by then, and I was living alone."

"Come on," he coaxed. "I may not be your idea of the perfect confidant, but I'll never repeat a word of it. Talking is therapeutic, or so they tell me."

His tone was unexpectedly tender. She glanced at him, grimaced at the patience she saw there—as if he were willing to wait all night if he had to. She might as well tell him a little of what had happened, she supposed.

"I was twenty," she said. "Grass green and sheltered. I knew nothing about men. I was sent out as a caseworker to a house where a man had badly beaten his wife and little daughter. I was going to question his wife one more time after she suddenly withdrew the charges. I went there to find out why, but she wasn't at home and he blamed me for his having been accused. I'd encouraged his wife and daughter to report what happened. He hit me until I couldn't stand up, and then he stripped me...." She paused, then forced the rest of it out. "He didn't rape me, although I suppose he would have if his brother-in-law hadn't driven up. He was arrested and charged, but he plea-bargained his way to a reduced sentence."

"He wasn't charged with attempted rape?"

"One of the more powerful city councilmen was his brother," she told him. She left out the black torment of those weeks. "He was killed in a car wreck after being paroled, and the councilman moved away."

"So he got away with it," McCallum murmured angrily. He smoothed his hand over his hair and stared out the dark window. "I thought you'd led a sheltered, pampered life."

"I did. Up to a point. My best friend had parents who drank too much. There were never any charges, and she hid her bruises really well. She's the reason I went into social work." She smiled bitterly. "It's amazing how much damage liquor does in our society, isn't it?"

He couldn't deny that. "Does your friend live here?"

She shook her head. "She lives in England with her husband. We lost touch years ago."

"Why in God's name didn't you give up your job when you were attacked?"

"Because I do a lot of good," she replied quietly. "After it happened, I thought about quitting. It was only when the man's wife came to me and apologized for what he'd done, and thanked me for trying to help, that I realized I had at least accomplished something. She took her daughter and went to live with her mother.

"I cared too much about the children to quit. I still do. It taught me a lesson. Now, when I send caseworkers out, I always send them in pairs, even if it takes more time to work cases. Some children have no advocates except us."

"God knows, someone needs to care about them," he replied quietly. "Kids get a rough shake in this world."

She nodded and finished her coffee. Her eyes were curious, roaming around the room. There were hunting prints on the walls, but no photographs, no mementos. Everything that was personal had something military or work-related stamped on it. Like the mugs with the police insignias.

"What are you looking for? Sentiment?" he chided. "You won't find it here. I'm not a sentimental man."

"You're a caring one, in your way," she returned. "You were kind to Ellen and Chad."

"Taking care of emotionally wounded people goes with the job," he reminded her. He picked up his coffee cup and sipped the black liquid. His dark eyes searched hers. "I'll remind you again that I don't need hero worship from a social worker with a stunted libido."

"Why, McCallum, I didn't know you knew such big words," she murmured demurely. "Do you read dictionaries in your spare time? I thought you spent it polishing your pistol."

He chuckled with reserved pleasure. His deep voice sounded different when he laughed, probably because the sound was so rare, she mused.

"What do you do with yours?" he asked.

"I do housework," she said. "And read over case files. I can't sit around and do nothing. I have to stay busy."

He finished his coffee and got up. "Want another cup?" he asked.

She shook her head and stood up, too. "I have to get home. Tomorrow's another workday."

"Let me open the latch for Mack so that he has access to the backyard and I'll take you over there."

"Won't he run off?" she asked.

"He's got a fenced-in area and his own entrance," he replied. "I keep it latched to make sure the neighbor's damned cat stays out of the house. It walks in and helps itself to his dog food when I'm not home. It climbs right over the fence!"

Jessica had to smother a laugh, he sounded so disgusted. She moved toward the dog, who suddenly growled up at her.

She stopped dead. He was a big dog, and pretty menacing at close range.

"Sorry," McCallum said, tugging Mack toward his exit in the door. "He's not used to women."

"He's big, isn't he?" she asked, avoiding any further comment.

"Big enough. He eats like a horse." He took his keys out of his pocket and locked up behind her while she got into the car.

They drove back toward her place. The night sky was dark, but full of stars. The sky went on forever in this part of the country, and Jessica could understand how McCallum would return here. She herself could never really leave. Her heart would always yearn for home in Montana.

When they got to her cabin, there was a single lighted window, and her big tomcat was outlined in it.

"That's Meriwether," she told him. "He wandered up here a couple of years ago and I let him stay. He's an orange tabby with battle-scarred ears."

"I hate cats," he murmured as he stopped the car at her front door.

"That doesn't surprise me, McCallum. What surprises me is that you have a pet at all—and that you even allow a stray cat on your property."

"Sarcasm is not your style, Miss Larson," he chided.

"How do you know? Other than the time you were sick, you only see me at work."

He pursed his lips and smiled faintly. "It's safer that way. You lonely spinsters are dangerous."

"Not me. I intend to be a lonely spinster for life," she said firmly. "Marriage isn't in my plans."

He scowled. "Don't you want kids?"

She opened her purse and took out her house key. "I like my life exactly as it is. Thanks for the lift. And the shoulder." She glanced at him a little selfconsciously.

"I'm a clam," he said. "I don't broadcast secrets; my own or anyone else's."

"That must be why you're still working for Judd Hensley. He's the same way."

"He knew about your problem, I gather?"

She nodded. "He's been sheriff here for a long time. He and his wife were good friends of my parents. I'm sorry about their divorce. He's a lonely man these days."

"Loneliness isn't a disease," he muttered. "Despite the fact that you women like to treat it like one."

"Still upset about my bringing you that pot of soup, aren't you?" she asked him. "Well, you were sick and nobody else was going to feed and look after you. I'm a social worker. I like taking care of the underprivileged."

"I am *not* underprivileged."

"You were sick and alone."

"I wouldn't have starved."

"You didn't have any food in the house," she countered. "What did you plan to do, eat your dog?"

He made a face. "Considering some of the things *he* eats, God forbid!"

"Well, I wouldn't eat Meriwether even if I really were starving."

He glanced at the cat in the window. "I don't blame you. Anything that ugly should be buried, not eaten."

She made a sound deep in her throat and opened the car door.

"Go ahead," he invited. "Tell me he's not ugly."

"I wouldn't give you the satisfaction of arguing," she said smugly. "Good night."

"Lock that door."

She glowered at him. "I'm twenty-five years old." She pointed at her head. "This works."

"No kidding!"

She made a dismissive gesture with her hand and walked up onto the porch. She didn't look back, even when he beeped the horn as he drove away.

Chapter 3

Jessica unlocked her front door and walked into the familiar confines of the big cabin. A long hall led to the kitchen, past a spare bedroom. The floor, heart of pine, was scattered with worn throw rugs. The living and dining areas were in one room at the front. At the end of the hall near the kitchen was an elegant old bathroom. The plumbing drove her crazy in the winters—which were almost unsurvivable in this house—and the summers were hotter than blazes. She had no air-conditioning and the heating system was unreliable. She had to supplement it with fireplaces and scattered kerosene heaters. Probably one day she'd burn the whole place down around her ears trying to keep warm, but except for the infrequent cold, she remained healthy. She dreamed of a house that was livable year-round.

A soft meow came from the parlor, and Meriwether

came trotting out to greet her. The huge tabby was marmalade colored. He'd been a stray when she found him, a pitiful half-grown scrap of fur with fleas and a stubby tail. She'd cleaned him up and brought him in, and they'd been inseparable ever since. But he hated men. He was a particularly big cat, with sharp claws, and he had to be locked up when the infrequent repairman was called to the house. He spat and hissed at them, and he'd even attacked the man who read the water meter. Now the poor fellow wouldn't come into the yard unless he knew Meriwether was safely locked in the house.

"Well, hello," she said, smiling as he wrapped himself around her ankle. "Want to hear all about the time I had?"

He made a soft sound. She scooped him up under one arm and started up the staircase. "Let me tell you, I've had better nights."

Later, with Meriwether curled up beside her, his big head on her shoulder, she slept, but the old nightmare came back, resurrected probably by the violence she'd seen and heard. She woke in a cold sweat, crying out in the darkness. It was a relief to find herself safe, here in her own house. Meriwether opened his eyes and looked at her when she turned on the light.

"Never mind. Go back to sleep," she told him gently. "I think I'll just read for a while."

She picked up a favorite romance novel from her shelf and settled back to read it. She liked these old ones best, the ones that belonged to a different world and always delivered a happy ending. Soon she was caught up in the novel and reality thankfully vanished for a little while.

* * *

At nine o'clock sharp the next morning, McCallum showed up in Jessica's office. He was wearing beige jeans and a sports jacket over his short-sleeved shirt this morning. No tie. He seemed to hate them; at least, Jessica had yet to see him dressed in one.

She was wearing a gray suit with a loose jacket. Her hair was severely confined on top of her head and she had on just a light touch of makeup. Watching her gather her briefcase, McCallum thought absently that he much preferred the tired woman of the night before, with her glorious hair loose around her shoulders.

"We'll go in my car," he said when they reached the parking lot, putting his sunglasses over his eyes. They gave him an even more threatening demeanor.

"I have to go on to another appointment, so I'll take my truck, now that it's been fixed, thanks to you...."

He opened the passenger door of the patrol car and stood there without saying a word.

She hesitated for a minute, then let him help her into the car. "Are you deliberately intimidating, or does it just come naturally?" she asked when they were on the way to the hospital.

"I spent years ordering noncoms around," he said easily. "Old habits are hard to break. Plays hell at work sometimes. I keep forgetting that Hensley outranks me."

That sounded like humor, but she'd had no sleep to speak of and she felt out of sorts. She clasped her briefcase closer, glancing out the window at the landscape. Montana was beautiful in spring. The area around Whitehorn was uncluttered, with rolling hills that ran forever to the horizon and that later in the year would be rich with grain crops. Occasional herds of cattle dotted the horizon. There were cottonwood and willow trees along the streams, but mostly the country was wide open. It was home. She loved it.

She especially loved Whitehorn. With its wide streets and multitude of trees, the town reminded her of Billings—which had quiet neighborhoods and a spread-out city center, with a refinery right within the city limits. The railroad cut through Billings, just as it did here in Whitehorn. It was necessary for transportation, because mining was big business in southern Montana.

The Whitehorn hospital was surrounded by cottonwood trees. Its grounds were nicely landscaped and there was a statue of Lewis and Clark out front. William Clark's autograph in stone at Pompey's Pillar, near Hardin, Montana, still drew photographers. The Lewis and Clark expedition had come right through Whitehorn.

Jessica introduced herself and McCallum to the ward nurse, and they were taken to the nursery.

Baby Jennifer, or Jenny as she was called, was in a crib there. She looked very pretty, with big blue eyes and a tiny tuft of blond hair on top of her head. She looked up at her visitors without a change of expression, although her eyes were alert and intelligent.

Jessica looked at her hungrily. She put down her briefcase and with a questioning glance at the nurse, who nodded, she picked the baby up and held her close.

"Little angel," she whispered, smiling so sadly that the man at her side scowled. She touched the tiny hand and felt it curl around her finger. She blinked back tears. She would never have a baby. She would never know the joy of feeling it grow in her body, watching its birth, nourishing it at her breast....

She made a sound and McCallum moved between her

and the nurse with magnificent carelessness. "I want to see any articles of clothing that were found on or with the child," he said courteously.

The nurse, diverted, produced a small bundle. He unfastened it. There was one blanket, a worn pink one—probably homemade, judging by the hand-sewn border—with no label. There was a tiny gown, a pretty lacy thing with a foreign label, the sort that might be found at a fancy garage sale. There were some hand-knitted booties and a bottle. The bottle was a common plastic one with nothing outstanding about it. He sighed angrily. No clues here.

"Oh, yes, there's one more thing, Detective," the nurse said suddenly. She produced a small brooch, a pink cameo. "This was attached to the gown. Odd, isn't it, to put something so valuable on a baby? This looks like real gold."

McCallum touched it, turned it over. It was gold, all right, and very old. That was someone's heirloom. It might be the very clue he needed to track down the baby's parents.

He fished out a plastic bag and dropped the cameo into it, fastening it and sticking it in his inside jacket pocket. It was too small to search for prints, and it had been handled by too many people to be of value in that respect. Hensley had checked all these things yesterday when the baby was found. The bottle had been wiped clean of prints, although not by anybody at the Kincaid home. Apparently the child's parents weren't anxious to be found. The puzzling thing was that brooch. Why wipe fingerprints off and then include a probably identifiable piece of heirloom jewelry?

He was still frowning when he turned back to Jessica. She was just putting the child into its crib and straightening. The look on her face was all too easy to read, but she quickly concealed her thoughts with a businesslike expression.

"We'll have to settle her with a child-care provider until the court determines placement," Jessica told the nurse. "I'll take care of that immediately when I get back to the office. I'll need to speak to the attending physician, as well."

"Of course, Miss Larson. If you'll come with me?"

McCallum fell into step beside her, down the long hall to Dr. Henderson's office. They spoke with him about the child's condition and were satisfied that she could be released the next morning.

"I'll send over the necessary forms," Jessica assured him, shaking hands.

"Pity, isn't it?" the doctor said sadly. "Throwing away a baby, like a used paper plate."

"She wasn't exactly thrown away," Jessica reminded him. "At least she was left where people would find her. We've had babies who weren't so fortunate."

McCallum pursed his lips. "Has anyone called to check on the baby?" he asked suddenly.

"Why, yes," the doctor replied curiously. "As a matter of fact, a woman from the *Whitehorn Journal* office called. She wanted to do a story, but I said she must first check with you."

McCallum lifted an eyebrow. "The *Whitehorn Journal* doesn't have a woman reporter."

He frowned. "I understood her to say the *Journal*. I may have been mistaken."

"I doubt it," McCallum said thoughtfully. "It was

probably the child's mother, making sure the baby had been found."

"If she calls again, I'll get in touch with you."

"Thanks," McCallum said.

He and Jessica walked back down the hall toward the hospital exit. He glanced down at her. "How old are you?"

She started. "I'm twenty-five," she said. "Why?"

He looked ahead instead of at her, his hands stuck deep in his jean pockets. "These modern attitudes may work for some women, but they won't work for you. Why don't you get married and have babies of your own, instead of mooning over someone else's?"

She didn't answer him. Rage boiled up inside her, quickening her steps as she made her way out the door toward his car.

He held the door open for her. She didn't even bother to comment on the courtesy or question it, she was so angry. He had no right to make such remarks to her. Her private life was none of his business!

He got in beside her, but he didn't start the engine. He turned toward her, his keen eyes cutting into her face. "You cried," he said shortly.

She grasped her briefcase like a lifeline, staring straight ahead, ignoring him.

He hit the steering wheel with his hand in impotent anger. He shouldn't let her get to him this way.

"How can you be in law enforcement with a temper like that?" she demanded icily.

He stared at her levelly. "I don't hit people."

"You do, too!" she raged. "You hit that man who threatened to pull a gun on you. I heard all about it!"

"Did you hear that *he* kicked me in the… Well, never

mind, but he damned near unmanned me before I laid a finger on him!" he said harshly.

She clutched the briefcase like a shield. "McCallum, you are crude! Crude and absolutely insensitive!"

"Crude? Insensitive?" he exclaimed shortly. He glared at her. "If you think that's crude, suppose I give you the slang term for it then?" he added with a cold smile, and he told her, graphically, what the man had done.

She was breathing through her nostrils. Her eyes were like brown coals, and she was livid.

"Your hand is itching, isn't it?" he taunted. "You want to slap me, but you can't quite work up the nerve."

"You have no right to talk to me like this!"

"How did you ever get into this line of work?" he demanded. "You're a bleeding-heart liberal with more pity than purpose in your life. If you'd take down that hair—" he pulled some pins from her bun "—and keep on those contact lenses, you might even find a man who'd marry you. Then you wouldn't have to spend your life burying your own needs in a job that's little more than a substitute for an adult relationship with a man!"

"You…!" The impact of the briefcase hitting his shoulder shocked him speechless. She hit him again before he could recover. The leather briefcase was heavy, but it was the shock of the attack that left him frozen in his seat when she tumbled out of the car and slammed the door furiously behind her.

She started off down the street with her hair hanging in unruly strands from its once-neat bun and her jacket askew. She looked dignified even in her pathetic state, and she didn't look back once.

Chapter 4

She made it two blocks before her feet gave out. Thank goodness for the Chamber of Commerce, she thought, taking advantage of the strategically placed bench near the curb bearing that agency's compliments. The late April sun was hot, and her suit, though light, was smothering her. The high heels she was wearing with it were killing her. She took off the right one, grimaced and rubbed her hose-clad foot.

She was suddenly aware of the unmarked patrol car that cruised to the curb and stopped.

McCallum got out without any rush and sat down beside her on the bench.

"You are the most difficult man I've ever met," she told him bluntly. "I don't understand why you feel compelled to make me so miserable, when all I've ever wanted to do was be kind to you!"

He leaned back, his eyes hidden behind dark sunglasses, and crossed his long legs. "I don't need kindness and I don't like your kind of woman."

"I know that," she said. "It shows. But I haven't done a thing to you."

He took off his sunglasses and turned his face toward her. It was as unreadable as stone, and about that warm. How could he tell her that her nurturing attitude made him want to scream? He needed a woman and she had a delectable body, but despite her response to him that night in front of the bus station, she backed away from him the minute he came too close. He wasn't conceited, yet he knew he was a physically dynamic, handsome man. Women usually ran after him, not the reverse. Jessica was the exception, and perhaps it was just as well. He wasn't a man with commitment on his mind.

"We're supposed to be working on a case together," he reminded her.

"I don't work on cases with men who talk to me as if I were a hooker," she shot back with cold dark eyes. "I don't have to take that sort of language from you. And I'll remind you that you're supposed to be upholding the law, not verbally breaking it. Or is using foul language in front of a woman no longer on the books as a misdemeanor in Whitehorn?"

He moved uncomfortably on the bench, because it *was* a misdemeanor. She'd knocked him off balance and he'd reacted like an idiot. He didn't like admitting it. "It wasn't foul language. It was explicit," he defended himself.

"Splitting hairs!"

"All right, I was out of line!" He shifted his long legs.

"You get under my skin," he said irritably. "Haven't you noticed?"

"It's hard to miss," she conceded. "If I'm such a trial to you, Detective, there are other caseworkers in my office...."

He turned his head toward her. "Hensley said I work with you. So I work with you."

She reached down and put her shoe back on, unwittingly calling his attention to her long, elegant legs in silky hose.

"That doesn't mean we have to hang out together," she informed him. "We can talk over the phone when necessary."

"I don't like telephones."

Her eyes met his, exasperated. "Have you ever thought of making a list of your dislikes and just handing it to people?" she asked. "Better yet, you might consider a list of things you *do* like. It would be shorter."

He glowered at her. "I never planned to wind up being a hick cop in a hick town working with a woman who thinks a meaningful relationship has something to do with owning a cat."

"I can't imagine why you don't go back into the service, where you felt at home!"

"Made too many enemies." He bit off the words. "I don't fit in there, either, anymore. Everything's changing. New regulations, policies..."

"Did you ever think of becoming a diplomat?" she said with veiled sarcasm.

"No chance of that," he murmured heavily, then sighed. "I should have studied anthropology, I guess."

Her bad temper dissipated like clouds in sunlight. She could picture it. She laughed.

"Oh, hell, don't do that," he said shortly. "I didn't mean to be funny."

"I don't imagine so. Is your lack of diplomacy why you're not in the service anymore?"

He shook his head. "It didn't help my career. But the real problem was the new political climate. I'm no bigot, but I'm not politically correct when it comes to bending over backwards to please special-interest groups. If I don't like something, I can't pretend that I do. I didn't want to end up stationed in a microwavable room in Moscow, listening to people's conversations."

She frowned. "I thought you were in the navy? You know...sailing around in ships and stuff."

His dark eyes narrowed. "I didn't serve on a ship. I was in Naval Intelligence."

"Oh." She hadn't realized that. His past took on a whole new dimension in her eyes. "Then how in the world did you end up here?"

"I had to live someplace. I hate cities, and this is as close to a home as I've ever known," he said simply. "The last place I lived was with an elderly couple over near the county line. They're dead now, but they left me a little property in the Bighorn Mountains. Who knows, I may build a house there one day. Just for me and Mack."

"I don't think I like dogs."

"And I hate cats," he said at once.

"Why doesn't that surprise me?"

His eyebrow jumped. He put his sunglasses back on and got to his feet. He looked marvelously fit, all muscular strength and height, a man in the prime of his life. "I'll run you back to your office. I want to go out to the Kincaid place and have a talk with Jeremiah."

She stood up, holding her briefcase beside her. "I can walk. It's only another block or so."

"Five blocks, and it's midday," he reminded her. "Come on. I won't make any more questionable remarks."

"I'd like that sworn to," she muttered as she let him open the door for her.

"You're a hot-tempered little thing, aren't you?" he asked abruptly.

"I defend myself," she conceded. "I don't know about the 'little' part."

He got in beside her and started the engine. Five minutes later she was back in the parking lot at her office. She was strangely reluctant to get out of the car, though. It was as though something had shifted between them, after weeks of working fairly comfortably with each other. He'd said "the last place he lived," and he'd mentioned an elderly couple, not parents.

"May I ask you something personal?" she said.

He looked straight at her, without removing his sunglasses. "No."

She was used to abruptness and even verbal abuse from clients, but McCallum set new records for it. He was the touchiest man she'd ever met.

"Okay," she said, clutching her briefcase as she opened the door. She looked over her shoulder. "Oh, I'm, uh, sorry about hitting you with this thing. I didn't hurt you, did I?"

"I've been shot a couple of times," he mentioned, just to make sure she got the idea that a bash with a briefcase wasn't going to do much damage.

"Poor old bullets," she muttered.

His face went clean of all expression, but his chest convulsed a time or two.

She got out of the car and slammed the door. She walked around to the driver's side and bent down. "I accept your apology."

"I didn't make any damned apology," he shot right back.

"I'm sure you meant to. I expect you were raised to be a gentleman, it's just that you've forgotten how."

The sunglasses glittered. She moved back a little.

"Don't you have anything to do? What the hell do they pay you for, and don't tell me it's for stand-up comedy."

"Actually, I'm doing a brain-surgery-by-mail course," she said pertly. "You're first on my list of potential patients."

"God forbid." He slipped the car into gear.

"Wait a minute," she said. "Are you going to tell anyone about the brooch you found?"

"No," he replied impatiently. "That brooch is my ace in the hole. I don't want it publicized in case someone comes to claim the baby. I'll mention it to selected people when it comes in useful."

"Oh, I see," she said at once. "You can rule out impostors. If they don't know about the brooch, they're not the baby's mother."

"Smart lady. Don't mention it to anyone."

"I wouldn't think of it. You'll let me know what you find out at the Kincaids', won't you?" she asked.

"Sure. But don't expect miracles. I don't think Dugin's the father, and I don't think we're going to find the baby's mother or any other relatives."

"The baby is blond," she said thoughtfully. "And so is Dugin."

"A lot of men in this community are blond. Besides, have you forgotten that Dugin is engaged to Mary Jo Plummer? With a dish like that wearing his ring, he isn't likely to be running around making other women pregnant."

"And he could afford to send it away if it was his, or have it adopted," she agreed. "Funny, though, isn't it, for someone to leave a baby on his doorstep? What did his father say?"

"Jeremiah wasn't there, according to Hensley. He'd been away and so Dugin called the law."

"That isn't like the Jeremiah Kincaid I know," she mused. "It would be more in character for him to start yelling his head off and accusing Dugin of fathering it."

"So I've heard."

He didn't say another word. Under that rough exterior, there had to be a heart somewhere. She kept thinking she might excavate it one day, but he was a hard case.

He gave her a curt nod, his mind already on the chore ahead. Dismissing her from his mind, he picked up the mike from his police radio and gave his position and his call letters and signed off. Without even a wave, he sped out of the parking lot.

She watched him until he was out of sight. She was feeling oddly vulnerable. There was a curious warm glow inside her as she went back into the office. She wished she understood her own reactions to the man. McCallum confused and delighted her. Of course, he also made her homicidal.

* * *

McCallum went out to the Kincaid ranch the next day, with the brooch in hand. He had some suspicions about that brooch, and it would be just as well to find out if anyone at the ranch recognized it.

When he drove up, the door was opened by Jeremiah himself. He was tall and silver haired, a handsome man in his late sixties. His son was nothing like him, in temperament or looks. Jeremiah had a face that a movie star would have envied.

"Come on in, McCallum, I've been expecting you," Jeremiah said cordially. "Can I pour you a whiskey?"

Characteristically, the man thought everyone shared his own fondness for Old Grandad. McCallum, when he drank, which was rarely, liked the smoothness of scotch whiskey.

"No, thanks. I'm working," McCallum replied.

"You cops." Jeremiah shook his head and poured himself a drink. "Now," he said, when they were seated on the elegant living room furniture, "how can I help you?"

McCallum pulled the brooch, in its plastic bag, out of his pocket and tossed it to the older man. Jeremiah stared at it for a long moment, one finger touching it lightly, reflectively. Then his head lifted.

"Nope," he told McCallum without any expression. "Never saw this before. If it was something that belonged to anyone in this family, you'd better believe I'd recognize it," he added.

He tossed it back to McCallum and lifted his glass to his lips. "What else can I tell you?"

"Was there anything on the baby that wasn't turned in when Sheriff Hensley came?" McCallum persisted.

"Not that I'm aware of," the other man said pleasantly. "Of course, I wasn't home at the time, you know. I didn't find out what had happened until the baby had been taken away. Hell of a thing, isn't it, for a mother to desert her child like that!"

"I didn't say it was deserted by its mother," McCallum replied slowly.

Jeremiah laughed, a little too loudly. "Well, it's hardly likely that the baby's father would have custody, is it? Even in these modern times, most men don't know what to do with a baby!"

"Apparently, some men still don't know how to prevent one, either."

Jeremiah grunted. "Maybe so." He glanced at the younger man. "It isn't Dugin's. I know there's been talk, but I asked the boy straight out. He said that since he got engaged to Mary Jo last year, there hasn't been any other woman."

"And you believe him?"

Jeremiah cleared his throat. "Dugin's sort of slow in that department. Takes a real woman to, uh, help him. That's why he's waited so late in life to marry. Mary Jo's a sweet little thing, but she's a firecracker, too. Caught her kissing him one afternoon out in the barn, and by God if they didn't almost go at it right there, standing up, in front of the whole world! She's something, isn't she, for a children's librarian."

McCallum's eyes were on the lean hands holding the glass of whiskey. They were restless, nervous. Jeremiah was edgy. He hid it well, but not with complete success.

"It sounds as though they'll have a good marriage."

"I think so. She's close to his age, and they sure enjoy being together. Pity about your boss's marriage," he

added with a shrug, "but his wife always was too brainy
for a man like that. I mean, after all, a cop isn't exactly
an Ivy League boy." He noticed the look on McCallum's
face and cleared his throat. "Sorry. No offense meant."

"None taken," Sterling replied. He got to his feet.
"If you think of anything that might help us, don't hes-
itate to call."

"Sure, sure. Look, that crack I made about cops not
having much education…"

"I took my baccalaureate degree in science while
I was in the navy," he told Jeremiah evenly. "The last
few years before I mustered out, I worked in Naval Intelligence."

Jeremiah was surprised. "With that sort of background,
why are you working for the sheriff's department?"

"Maybe I just like small towns. And I did grow up
here."

"But, man, you could starve on what you make in
law enforcement!"

"Do you think so?" McCallum asked with a smile.
"Thanks for your time, Mr. Kincaid."

He shook hands with the man and left, thinking
privately that he'd rather work for peanuts in law enforcement than live the sort of aimless existence that
Jeremiah Kincaid did. The man might have silver hair,
but he was a playboy of the first order. He was hardly
ever at home, and Dugin certainly wasn't up to the chore
of taking care of a spread that size.

Speaking of Dugin… McCallum spotted him near
the toolshed, talking to a younger man, and walked toward him.

Dugin shaded his eyes against the sun. He was tall
and fair, in his forties, and he was mild-mannered and

unassuming. He'd always seemed younger than he was. Perhaps it was because his father had always overshadowed him. Dugin still lived at home and did most everything his father told him to. He smiled and held out his hand when McCallum reached him.

"Nice day, isn't it?" Dugin asked. "What can I do for you, Deputy? And how's the kid?"

"She's fine. They're placing her in care until the case comes up. Listen, do you know anything that you haven't told the sheriff? Was there anything else with the baby that wasn't turned in?"

Dugin thought for a minute and shook his head. "Not a thing. It isn't my kid," he added solemnly. "I hear there's been some talk around Whitehorn about my being the father, but I'm telling you, I don't know anything. I wouldn't risk losing Mary Jo for any other woman, Deputy. Just between us," he added wryly, "I wouldn't have the energy."

McCallum chuckled. "Okay. Thanks."

"Keep in touch with us about the case, will you?" Dugin asked. "Even though it's not my child, I'd still like to know how things come out."

"Sure."

McCallum walked slowly back to his patrol car, wondering all the way why the baby had been left here, and with Dugin. There had to be a clue. He should have shown that cameo to Dugin, but if Jeremiah didn't recognize it, there was little point in showing it to his son. As Jeremiah had suggested, if it were a family heirloom, he would have recognized it immediately.

It was a lazy day, after that. McCallum was drinking coffee in the Hip Hop Café with his mind only vaguely on baby Jennifer and her missing parents. He was aware of faint interest from some of the other diners when his portable walkie-talkie made static as it picked up a call. Even though most people in Whitehorn knew him, he still drew some curiosity from tourists passing through. He was a good-looking man with a solid, muscular physique that wasn't overdone or exaggerated. He looked powerful, especially with the gun in its holster visible under his lightweight summer jacket.

The call that came over the radio made him scowl. He'd had enough of Jessica Larson the day before, but here she was after him again. Apparently there was a domestic disturbance at the Colson home, where a young boy lived with his father and grandmother.

Sterling went out to the car to answer the call, muttering all the way as he sat down and jerked up the mike.

"Why is Miss Larson going?" he demanded.

"I don't know, K-236," the dispatcher drawled, using his call letters instead of his name. "And even if I did, I wouldn't tell you on an open channel."

"I'll see that you get a Christmas present for being such a good boy," McCallum drawled back.

There was an unidentified laugh as McCallum hung up and drove to the small cottagelike Colson house on a dirt road just out of town.

He got there before Jessica did. If there was a fight going on here, it wasn't anything obvious. Terrance Colson was sitting on the porch cleaning his rifle while his mother fed her chickens out back in the fenced-in compound. The boy, Keith, was nowhere in sight. Terrance was red-faced and seemed to have trouble holding the rifle still.

"Afternoon, McCallum!" Terrance called pleasantly. "What can I do for you?"

McCallum walked up on the porch, shook hands with the man and sat down on one of the chairs. "We had a report, but it must have been some crank," he said, looking around.

"Report of what?" Terrance asked curiously.

Before McCallum could answer, Jessica came driving up in her rickety yellow truck. She shut it off, but it kept running for a few seconds, knocking like crazy. That fan belt sounded as if it were still slipping, too. He'd noticed it the night at the bus station.

She got out, almost dropping her shoulder bag in the dirt, and approached the house. McCallum wondered just how many of those shapeless suits she owned. This one was green, and just as unnoticeable as the others. Her hair was up in a bun again. She looked the soul of business.

"Well, hello, Miss Larson," Terrance called. "We seem to be having a party today!"

She stopped at the steps and glanced around, frowning. "We had a call at the office—" she faltered for a moment "—about a terrible fight going on out here. I was requested to come and talk to you."

Terrance looked around pointedly, calling her attention to the peaceful surroundings. "What fight?"

She sighed. "An unnecessary call, I suppose," she said with a smile. "I'm sorry. But as I'm here already, do you think I might talk to Keith for a minute? He told his counselor at school that he'd like to talk to me when I had time."

Terrance stared at her without blinking. "Funny, he

never said anything to me about it. And he's not here right now. He's out fishing."

"Do you think I could find him?" she asked persistently.

"He goes way back in the woods," he said quickly. "It's not a good time. He came home in a real bad mood. Best to leave him alone until he cools down."

She shrugged. "As you wish. But do tell him that I'll be glad to listen anytime he wants to talk about those school problems." She didn't add that she wondered why he couldn't tell them to the counselor, who was a good psychologist.

"I'll tell him," Terrance said curtly.

"Good day then." She smiled at Terrance, nodded at McCallum and went to climb back into her truck.

McCallum said his own goodbye, wondering why Mrs. Colson never came out of the chicken pen to say hello the whole time he was there. And Terrance's expression had hardened when he'd mentioned the boy. Odd.

He climbed into the patrol car and gave his call sign and location, announcing that he was back in service again. He followed after Jessica's sluggish truck and wondered if she was going to make it back into town.

When she parked her car at the office, he drove in behind her. The squealing of her fan belt was louder than ever. She really would have to do something about it when she had time.

"Your fan belt is loose," he told her firmly. "It's going to break one day and you'll be stranded."

"I know. I'm not totally stupid."

He got out of the car and walked with her to the office, not making a comment back, as he usually did. He seemed deep in thought. "Something funny's going on out at that place," he said suddenly. "Old Mrs. Colson hiding out with the chickens, Keith nowhere in sight, Terrance cleaning his gun, but without any gun oil…."

"You have a very suspicious mind," she accused gently. "For heaven's sake, do you always go looking for trouble? I'm delighted that there wasn't anything to it. I know the family, and they're good people. It's Keith who gives them fits. He's been into one bout of trouble after another at school since he was in the fifth grade. He's a junior now, and still getting into fights and breaking rules. He was picked up with another boy for shoplifting, although Keith swore he was innocent and the officers involved believed him. I've been trying to help the family as much as possible. Terrance lost his job at the manufacturing company that shut down last fall, and Milly is trying to make a little money by taking in ironing and doing alterations for the dry cleaners. The Colsons are hurting, but they're too proud to let me help much."

He frowned thoughtfully. "Isn't that the way of it?" he asked quietly. "The people who need help most never ask for it. On the other hand, plenty who don't deserve it get it."

She glowered up at him. "You're so cynical, McCallum! Don't you believe anybody can be basically good?"

"No."

She laughed and shook her head. "I give up. You're a hopeless case."

"I'm in law enforcement," he pointed out. "What we see doesn't lead us to look for the best in people."

"Neither does what I see, but I still try to believe in basic goodness," she replied.

He looked down at her for a long moment, letting his eyes linger on her soft mouth and straight nose before they lifted to catch her eyes.

"No, you don't," he said abruptly. "How can you still believe? What happens is that you just close your eyes to the ugliness. That's what most people do. They don't want to know that human beings can do such hideous things. Murder and robbery and beatings are so unthinkable that people pretend it can't occur. Then some terrible crime happens to them personally, and they have to believe it."

"You don't close your eyes to it," she said earnestly. "In fact, you look for it everywhere, even when you have to dig to find it. You have to try to rise above the ugliness."

His eyes darkened. He turned away. "I work for a living," he said lazily. "I haven't got time to stand around here socializing with you. Get that fan belt seen to."

She looked after him. "My goodness, do I really need a big, strong man to tell me how to take care of myself?"

"Yes."

He got into his car, leaving her aghast, and drove off.

Chapter 5

For several days, McCallum scoured the area for any clues as to the identity of the baby called Jennifer. He checked at every clinic and doctor's office in the area, as well as the local hospital and those in the surrounding counties. But every child's parents were accounted for. There were no leftover babies at any of the medical facilities. Which meant that the baby had probably been born at home, and a midwife had attended the birth. There were plenty of old women in the community who knew how to deliver a baby, and McCallum knew that he could spend years searching for the right person. Prospects looked dismal.

He was just leaving the office for lunch when Jessica Larson walked up to him on the street.

"I need to get your opinion on something," she said, and without preamble, caught his big, lean hand in hers and began to drag him off toward a parked car nearby.

"Now, hold it," he growled, hating and loving the feel of her soft hand in his.

"Don't grumble," she chided. "It won't hurt a bit. I just want you to talk to these young people for me before they make a big mistake." She paused at the beat-up old Chevy, where two teenagers sat guiltily in the front seat. They didn't look old enough to be out of school.

"This is Deputy McCallum," Jessica told the teens. "Ben and Amy want to get married," she explained to him. "Their parents are against it. Ben is seventeen and Amy is sixteen. I've told them that any marriage they make can be legally annulled by her parents because she's under age. Will you tell them that, too?"

He wasn't sure about the statutes on marriageable age in Montana, having never had occasion or reason to look them up. But he was pretty sure the girl was under the age of consent, and he knew what Jessica wanted him to say. He could bluff when he had to.

"She's absolutely right," he told them. "A minor can't legally marry without written permission from a parent. It would be terrible for you to have to—"

"She's pregnant," Ben mumbled, red-faced, and looked away. "I tried to get her to have it… Well, to not have it, really. She won't listen. She says we have to get married or her folks'll kill her."

Jessica hadn't counted on that complication. She stood there, stunned.

McCallum squatted down beside the car and looked at Amy, who was obviously upset. "Why don't we start at the beginning?" he asked her gently. "These are big decisions that need thought."

While Jessica looked on, stunned by the tenderness in McCallum's deep voice, Amy began to warm to him.

"I don't know if I'm pregnant, really," she confessed slowly. "I think I am."

"Shouldn't you find out for sure, before you wind up in a marriage neither of you is ready for?" he asked evenly.

"Yes, sir."

"Then the obvious next step is to see a doctor, isn't it?"

She grimaced. "My dad'll kill me."

"I'll speak to your parents," Jessica promised her. "They won't kill you. They're good people, and they love you. You're their only child."

"I'd just love to have a baby," Amy said dreamily, looking at Ben with fantasy-filled eyes that didn't even see his desperation, his fear. "We can have a house of our own, and I can get a job...."

McCallum looked hard at Jessica.

"Let's go over to your parents' house, Amy," she said. She had McCallum firmly by the hand again, and she wasn't about to let go. "I'm sure Deputy McCallum won't mind coming with us," she added, daring him to say no.

He gave up plans for a hamburger and fries and told his stomach to shut up. Resignedly, he helped Jessica into his car, and they followed the teens to Amy's house.

"It wasn't so bad, was it?" Jessica commented after the ordeal was finally over. "She'll see a doctor and then get counseling if she needs it. And there won't be a rushed marriage with no hope of success. They didn't even blame Ben too much."

"Why should they?" he muttered as he negotiated a right turn. "She's the one with dreams of babies and happy ever after, not him. He just wants to finish high school and go on to veterinary college."

"Ah, the man's eternal argument. 'Eve tempted me with the apple.'"

He glanced at her musingly. "Most women can lead a man straight to bed with very little conscious effort. Especially a young man."

She lifted her eyebrows. "Don't look at me. I've never led anyone to my bed with conscious effort or without it." She stemmed the memories that thoughts of intimacy resurrected.

"Have you wanted to?"

The question, coming from such an impersonal sort of man, surprised her. "Why…no."

"Have you let the opportunity present itself?" he persisted.

She straightened her skirt unnecessarily. "I'm sorry I made you miss your lunch."

He let the subject go. "How do you know you did?"

"Oh, you always go to lunch at eleven-thirty," she remarked. "I see you crossing over to the café from my office."

He chuckled softly, and it wasn't until she saw the speculation on his face that she realized why.

"I wasn't…watching you, for God's sake!" she blurted out, reddening.

"Really?" he teased. "You mean I've mistaken that hero worship in your eyes all this time?"

Her dark eyes glared at him. "You are very conceited."

"Made so by a very expressive young face," he countered. He glanced at her while they paused at a stop sign. "Don't build a pedestal under me, Jessie," he said, using a nickname for her for the first time. "I'm not tame enough for a woman like you."

She gaped at him. "If you think that I...!"

Incredibly, he caught the back of her head with a steely hand and leaned over her with slow, quiet intent. His dark eyes fell to her shocked mouth and he tugged gently until her mouth was a fraction below his. She could taste his minty breath, feel the heat of his mouth threatening her lips. She could feel the restrained passion in his long, fit body as it loomed over hers.

"You're afraid of me," he whispered into her mouth. "And it has nothing to do with that bad experience you had. It isn't the kind of fear that causes nightmares. It's the kind that makes your body swell hard with desire."

While she was absorbing the muted shock the words produced, his mouth lowered to touch and tease her soft lips in tender, biting kisses that made her muscles go rigid with sensation. Her hand caught at his shirt, searching for something to hold on to while she spun out of reality altogether. Her nails bit into his chest.

He groaned under his breath. "You'd be a handful," he whispered. "And if you were a different sort of woman, I'd accept with open arms the invitation you're making me right now."

"What...invitation?"

His nose rubbed against hers. "This one."

He brought his mouth down over her parted lips with real intent, feeling them open and shiver convulsively as he deepened the pressure. She whimpered, and the sound shot through him like fire. He abruptly drew back.

His breathing was a little quick, but his expression showed none of the turmoil that kissing her had aroused in him.

She was slower to recover. Her face was flushed, and her mouth was red, swollen from the hard pressure of his lips. She looked at him with wide-eyed surprise.

"You're like a little violet under a doorstep," he commented quietly. "A lovely surprise waiting to be discovered."

She couldn't find the words to express what she felt.

He touched her soft mouth. "Don't worry about it. Someday the right man will come along. I'm not him."

"Why did you do that?" she whispered in a choked voice.

"Because you wanted me to, Jessica," he drawled. "You've watched me for months, wondering how it would feel if I kissed you. Okay. Now you know."

Her eyes darkened with something like pain. She averted them.

"What did you expect?" he mused, pulling the car back out into the road. "I'm not a teenager on his first date. I know exactly what to do with a woman. But you're off-limits, sweetheart. I don't make promises I can't keep."

"I haven't asked you to marry me, have I?" she asked, bouncing back.

He smiled appreciatively. "Not yet."

"And you can hold your breath until I do." She pushed back a disheveled strand of hair. "I'm not getting mixed up with you."

"You like kissing me."

She glared at him. "I like kissing my cat, too, McCallum," she said maliciously.

"Ouch!"

She nodded her head curtly. "Now how arrogant do you feel?"

He chuckled. "Well, as one of my history professors

was fond of saying, 'I've always felt that arrogance was a very admirable quality in a man.'"

She rolled her eyes.

He drove back into town, but he didn't stop at her office. He kept going until he reached the Hip Hop Café, a small restaurant on the southeast corner of Amity Lane and Center.

She glanced at him uncertainly.

"If I haven't eaten, I know you haven't," he explained.

"All right. But I pay for my own food."

His eyes slowly wandered over her face. "I like independence," he said unexpectedly.

"Do I care?" she asked with mock surprise.

He smiled. "Fix your lipstick before we go inside, or everyone's going to know what we've been doing."

She wouldn't blush, she wouldn't blush, she wouldn't…!

All the same, her cheeks were pink in the compact mirror she used as she reapplied her lipstick and powdered her nose.

McCallum had taken the time to wipe the traces of pink off his own firm mouth with his handkerchief.

"Next time, I'll get rid of that lipstick before I start," he murmured.

"Oh, you'd be so lucky!" she hissed.

He lifted an eyebrow over wise, soft eyes. "Or you would. It gets better, the deeper you go. You cried out, and I hadn't even touched you. Imagine, Jessica, how it would feel if I did."

She was out of the car before he finished speaking. She should go back to her office and leave him standing there. He was wicked to tease her about something she couldn't control. It didn't occur to her that he might be overcompensating for the desire he'd felt with her. Experienced he might be, but it had been a while since he'd had a woman and Jessica went right to his head. He hadn't realized it was going to be so fulfilling to kiss her. And it seemed to be addictive, because it was all he could think about.

"I won't let you torment me," she said, walking ahead of him to the door. "And before we go any farther, you'd better remember that Whitehorn isn't that big. Everybody knows everybody else's business. If I go in there with you, people are going to talk about us."

He had one hand in his pocket, the other on the door handle. He searched her eyes. "I know," he said quietly. He opened the door deliberately.

It was a quiet, companionable lunch. There were a few interested looks, including a sad one from a young waitress who had a hopeless crush on McCallum. But people were discreet enough not to stare at them.

"After all, we could be talking over a case," Jessica said.

He frowned at her. "Does it really matter?" he asked. "You're very sensitive to gossip. Why?"

She shrugged, averting her eyes. "Nobody likes being talked about."

"I don't know that I ever have been since I've come back," he said idly. He sipped his coffee. "And with your spotless reputation, it's hardly likely to think that you have," he added with a chuckle.

She picked up her coffee cup, steadying it with her other hand. "Thank you for helping me with Amy and Ben."

"Did I have a choice? I wonder if there isn't a law against deputy sheriffs being kidnapped by overconscientious social workers. And while we're on the subject of laws, that one about underage marriages is one I'll have to look up or ask Hensley about. I've never had cause to use it before."

"You may again. We've had several cases like Amy and Ben over the years."

"What if she is pregnant?" he asked.

"Then she'll have choices and people to help her make them."

He glared at her.

"I know that look," she said softly. "I even understand it. But you have to consider that sometimes what's best for a young girl isn't necessarily what you feel is right."

"What if I lost my head one dark night and got you pregnant, Jessica?" He leaned back, his eyes narrowed. "What would you do in Amy's place?"

The color that rushed into her face was a revelation. She spilled a bit of coffee onto the table.

"Well, well," he murmured softly.

She put the cup down and mopped up the coffee with napkins. "You love shocking me, don't you?"

"Never mind the shock. Answer me. What would you do?"

She bit her lower lip. "The correct thing…"

He caught her hand and held it tight in his. "Not the correct thing, or the sensible thing, or even the decent thing. What would *you* do?" he asked evenly.

"Oh, I'd keep it," she said, angry at being pushed into answering a question that would not, could not, ever arise. It hurt her to remember how barren she was. "I'm just brimming over with motherly instincts, old-fashioned morality and an overworked sense of duty.

But what I'm trying to make you see is that regardless of my opinion, I have no right to force my personal sense of right and wrong on the rest of the world!"

He forgot the social issue in the heat of the moment, as he allowed himself to wonder how it would feel to create a child with Jessica. It made him feel…odd.

Jessica saw the speculation in his eyes and all her old inadequacies came rushing back. "McCallum," she began, wondering whether or not to tell him about her condition.

His fingers linked with hers, his thumb smoothing over them. "You're twenty-five, aren't you? I'm ten years older."

"Yes, I know. McCallum…"

His eyes lifted to catch hers. "My first name is Sterling," he said.

"That's an unusual name. Was it in your family?"

He shrugged. "My mother never said." Memories of his mother filled his mind. He withdrew, mentally and physically. He pulled his hand slowly away from Jessica's. "Maybe it was the name of her favorite brand of gin, who knows?"

She grimaced, hating that pain in his eyes. She wanted to soothe him, to comfort him.

He looked up and saw the expression on her face. It made him furious.

"I don't need pity," he said through gritted teeth.

"Is that how I looked? I'm sorry. It disturbs me to see how badly your past has affected you, that's all." She smiled. "I know. I'm a hopeless do-gooder. But think, McCallum—if you'd had someone who really cared what happened to you, wouldn't it have changed your whole life?"

He averted his eyes. "Facts are facts. We can't go back and change the past."

"I know that. If we could, think how many people would leap at the chance."

"True," he agreed.

She studied him over her cup. "This town must hold some bad memories for you. Why did you come back after all these years?"

"I got tired of my job," he replied. "I can't even talk about it, do you know? It was all classified. Let's just say that I got into a situation I couldn't handle for the first time in my life, and I got out. I don't regret it. I manage better here than I ever dreamed I would. I'm not rich, but I'm comfortable, and I like my job and the people I work with. Besides," he added, "the memories weren't all bad. I have a few good ones tucked away. They keep me going when I need them."

"And was there ever a special woman?" she asked, deliberately not looking at him.

He cocked an eyebrow. "*Women,* plural," he replied. "Not just one woman. They all knew the score. I made sure of it and I'm a loner. I don't want to change."

Jessica felt a vague disappointment.

"Were you hoping?" he taunted.

She glared at him. "For what? You, with a bow around your neck on Christmas morning? It's a long time until Christmas, McCallum, and you'd look silly in gift wrapping."

"Probably so." He studied her. "I wonder how you'd look in a long red stocking?"

"Dead, because that's the only way I'd ever end up in one. Heavens, look at the time! I've got my desk stacked halfway to the ceiling. I have to go!"

"So do I," he agreed. "The days are never long enough to cope with all the paperwork, even in my job."

"In everyone's job. God knows how many trees die every day to satisfy bureaucrats. Know what I think they do with all those triplicate copies? I think they make confetti and store it for parades."

"I wouldn't doubt it." He pushed away his empty cup, stood up, laid a bill on the table, picked up the check and walked to the counter with it.

Jessica dug out a five dollar bill and paid her share.

"Late lunch, huh, McCallum?" the waitress asked with an inviting smile.

"Yeah." He smiled back at her. "Thanks, Daisy."

She colored prettily. She was barely twenty, red-headed, cute and totally infatuated with McCallum.

He opened the door for Jessica and walked her back to his car.

"Thanks for your help," she told him with genuine appreciation. "Those kids needed more of a talking to than I could give them. There's something about a uniform…" she added with a gleam in her eyes. Of course she was kidding; McCallum, a plainclothesman, wasn't wearing a uniform.

"Tell me about it." He'd already discovered that uniforms attracted women. It was something most career law-enforcement officers learned how to deal with early.

"Have you found out anything about Jennifer?" she asked on the way back to her office.

He detailed the bits and pieces he'd been following up. "But with no luck. Do you know any midwives around the community?" he asked. "Someone who would be able to deliver a child and could do it without telling half the world?"

Jessica pursed her lips. "One or two women come to mind. I'll look into it."

"Thanks."

He stopped at her office and waited, with the car idling, for her to get out.

"I'll let you know how things go with Amy," she offered.

He looked at her with an expression that bordered on dislike. It had flattered him that she kept asking for his help, and she seemed to like his company. But he liked kissing her too much, and that made him irritable. He didn't want a social worker to move into his life. He was weakening toward her, and he couldn't afford that. "I don't remember asking for a follow-up report," he said, deliberately being difficult.

It didn't faze Jessica, who was used to him. His bad humor bounced off her. That kiss hadn't, of course, but she had to remember that he was a loner and keep things in perspective. She could mark that lapse down to experience. She knew she wouldn't forget it anytime soon, but she had to keep her eyes off McCallum.

"You're so cynical, McCallum," she said heavily. "Haven't you ever heard that old saying about no man being an island?"

"I read John Donne in college," he replied. "I can be an island if I please."

She pursed her lips again, surveying him with marked interest. "If you really were an island, you'd have barbed wire strung around the trees and land mines on the beaches."

She went inside, aware of the deep masculine laughter she left behind her.

* * *

The abandoned baby, Jennifer, had been placed in care, and Jessica couldn't help going to see her. She was living temporarily as a ward of the court with a local family that seemed to thrive on anyone's needful children.

"We can't have any of our own, you see," Mabel Darren said with a grin. She was in her mid-thirties, dark and bubbly, and it didn't take a clairvoyant to know that she loved children. She had six of them, all from broken homes or orphaned, ranging in age from a toddler to a teen.

The house was littered, but clean. The social-services office had to check it out periodically to comply with various regulations, but there had never been any question of the Darrens' ability to provide for their charges. And if ever children were loved, these underprivileged ones were.

"Isn't she a little angel?" Mabel asked when Jessica had the sweet-smelling infant in her arms.

"Oh, yes," Jessica said, feeling a terrible pain as she cuddled the child. She would never know the joy of childbirth, much less that of watching a baby grow to adulthood. She would be alone all her life.

Mabel would have understood, but Jessica could never bring herself to discuss her anguish with anyone. She carried Jennifer to the rocking chair and sat down with her, oblivious to the many other duties that were supposed to be demanding her attention.

The older woman just smiled. "It's time for her bottle. Would you like to feed her while you're here? Then I could get on with my dirty dishes," she added. She knew already that if she could make Jessica think she was helping, the social worker was much more likely to do what she really wanted to.

"If it would help," Jessica said. Her soft, dark eyes were on the baby's face and she touched the tiny head, the hands, the face with fingers that trembled. She'd never known such a profound hunger in her life, and tears stung her eyes.

As if the baby sensed her pain, her big eyes opened and she stared up at Jessica, unblinking. She made a soft gurgling noise in her throat. With a muffled cry, Jessica cuddled Jennifer close and started the chair rocking. At that moment, she would have given anything—anything!—for this tiny precious thing to be her very own.

Mabel's footsteps signaled her approach. Jessica composed herself just before the other woman reappeared with a bottle. She managed to feed the baby and carry on a pleasant conversation with Mabel, apparently unruffled by the experience. But deep inside, she was devastated. Something about Jennifer accentuated all the terrible feelings of inadequacy and made her child hungry. She'd never wanted anything as much as she wanted the abandoned infant.

After she fed the baby, she went back to the office, where she was broody and quiet for the rest of the day. She was so silent that Bess, who worked in the outer office, stuck her auburn head in the door to inquire if her boss was sick.

"No, I'm all right, but thanks," Jessica said dully. "It's been a long day, that's all."

"Well, you got to have lunch with Sterling McCallum," Bess mused. "I wouldn't call that tedious. I dress up, I wear sexy perfume, but he never gives me a second look. Is he really that formidable and businesslike *all* the time?" she asked with a keen stare.

Jessica's well-schooled features gave nothing away.

She smiled serenely. "If I ever find out, you'll be the first to know. It was a business lunch, Bess, not a date," she added.

"Oh, you stick-in-the-mud," she muttered. "A gorgeous man like that, and all you want to talk about is work! I'd have him on his back in the front seat so fast…!"

Shocking images presented themselves, but with Jessica, not Bess, imprisoning Sterling McCallum on the seat of his car. She had to stop thinking of him in those terms! "Really, Bess!" she muttered.

"Jessica, you do know what century this is?" Bess asked gently. "You know, women's liberation, uninhibited sex?"

"AIDS? STDs?" Jessica added.

Bess made a soft sound. "Well, I didn't mean that you don't have to be careful. But McCallum strikes me as the sort of man who would be. I'll bet he's always properly equipped."

Jessica's face had gone scarlet and she stood up abruptly.

"I'm just leaving for home!" Bess said quickly, all too aware that she'd overstepped the mark. "See you tomorrow!"

She closed the door and ran for it. Jessica was even-tempered most of the time, but she, too, could be formidable when she lost her cool.

Jessica restrained a laugh at the speed with which Bess took to her heels. It was just as well not to let employees get too complacent, she decided, as she opened another file and went back to work.

It was after dark and pouring rain when she decided to go home. Meriwether would be wanting his supper, and she was hungry enough herself. The work would still be here, waiting, in the morning. But it had taken her mind off Baby Jennifer, which was a good thing.

She locked up the office and got into her yellow pickup as quickly as possible. Her umbrella, as usual, was at home. She had one in the office, too, but she'd forgotten it. She was wet enough without trying to go back and get it. She fumbled the key into the ignition, locked her door and started the vehicle.

The engine made the most ghastly squealing noise. It didn't help to remember McCallum's grim warning about trouble ahead if she didn't get it seen to.

But the mechanic's shop was closed, and so were all the service stations. The convenience store was open, and it had self-service gas pumps, but nobody who worked inside would know how to replace a fan belt. In fact, Tammie Jane was working the counter tonight, and the most complicated thing she knew how to do was change her nail polish.

With a long sigh, Jessica pulled the truck out onto the highway and said a silent prayer that she would be able to make it home before the belt broke. The squeal that usually vanished when she went faster only got worse tonight.

The windshield wipers were inadequate, too. A big leaf had gotten caught in the one on the driver's side, smearing the water rather than removing it. Jessica groaned out loud at her bad luck. It had been a horrible day altogether, and not just because of the predicament she was in now.

She pulled onto the dirt road that led to her home. The rain was coming down harder. She had no idea how long it had been pouring, because she'd been so engrossed in her work. Now she saw the creek ahead and wondered if she'd even be able to get across it. The water was very high. This was an old and worrying problem.

She gunned the engine and shot across, barely missing another struggling motorist, her elderly CB-radio-fanatic neighbor. He waved to her as he went past, but she was too occupied with trying to see ahead to really look at him. She almost made it up the hill, but at that very moment, the fan belt decided to give up the ghost. It snapped and the engine raced, but nothing happened. The truck slid back to the bottom of the hill beside the wide, rising creek, and the engine went dead.

Chapter 6

Jessica sat in the truck without moving, muttering under her breath. She hoped that her eccentric neighbor had noticed her plight and alerted someone in town on his CB radio, but whether or not he'd seen her slide back down the hill was anyone's guess.

She decided after a few minutes that she was going to be stranded unless she did something. The creek was rising steadily. She was terrified of floods. If she didn't get up that hill, God only knew what might happen to her when the water rose higher. The rain showed no sign of slackening.

She opened the door and got out, becoming soaked within the first couple of minutes. She made a rough sound in her throat and let out an equally rough word to go with it. Stupid old truck! She should have listened to McCallum.

She managed to get the hood up, but it did no good. There was no source of light except the few patches of sky on the horizon that weren't black as thunder. She didn't even have a flashlight. Well, she had one—but the battery was dead. She'd meant to replace it....

The deep drone of an engine caught her attention. She turned, blinded by headlights, hoping against hope that it was her elderly neighbor. He could give her a ride home, at least.

A huge red-and-black Bronco with antennas all over it and a bar of lights on top swept up beside her and stopped. She recognized it from McCallum's house. It had been sitting in the garage next to the patrol car he used when he was on call at night. He got out of it, wearing a yellow rain slicker. The rain seemed to slacken as he approached her.

"Nice wheels," she commented.

"I like it," he replied. "Fan belt broke, huh?"

She glowered, shivering in the rain. "Terrific guess."

"No help here, until I can get a new belt and put it on for you. Nothing's open this late." He closed the hood and marched her around to the passenger side of the Bronco. "Climb in."

He helped her into the big vehicle and she sat, shivering, on the vinyl seat while, with the four-wheel drive in operation, he drove effortlessly up the muddy hill and on to her cabin.

"What were you doing out at this time of night anyway?" he asked.

"Trying to get stranded in the rain," she told him.

He glared at her.

"I was working late." She sneezed.

"Get in there and take a bath."

"I had planned to. Have you…had supper?" she added, without looking at him.

"Not yet."

She touched the door handle. "I have a pot of soup in the refrigerator. I could make some corn bread to go with it."

"If you could make some coffee, I'd be delighted to join you. I'd just got off duty when I monitored a call about a stranded motorist."

She grinned, because she knew which motorist he meant. "Done." She got out and left him to follow.

The minute he walked in the door, Meriwether, having come to meet his mistress, bristled and began spitting viciously at the newcomer.

"I like you, too, pal," McCallum muttered as he and the cat had a glaring contest.

"Meri, behave yourself!" Jessica fussed.

"If you'll show me what the soup's in, I'll start heating it while you're in the shower," he offered.

She led him into the kitchen, dripping everywhere, and got out the big pot of soup while he hung up his drenched slicker.

"I'll make the corn bread when I get back. You could preheat the oven," she added, and told him what temperature to set it.

"Okay. Where's the coffee?"

She showed him the filters and coffee and how to work the pot. Then she rushed down the hall to the bathroom.

Ten minutes later, clean and presentable in a sweatshirt and jeans, with her hair hanging in damp strands down her back, she joined him in the kitchen.

"You'll catch a cold," he murmured, glancing at her

from his seat at the table with a steaming cup of black coffee. "Sit down for a minute and I'll pour you a cup."

"I'll make the corn bread first," she said. "It won't take a minute."

And it didn't. She put it in the preheated oven to bake and then sat down across from McCallum to sip her coffee. He was wearing a brown plaid shirt, with jeans and boots. He always looked clean and neat, even when he was drenched, she thought, and wondered if his military training had a lot to do with it.

"Do you always keep your house this hot?" he asked, unfastening the top buttons of his shirt.

"I don't have air-conditioning," she explained apologetically. "But I can turn on the fan."

"Are you cool?"

She shook her head. "I'm rather cold-blooded, I'm afraid. But if you're too hot…"

"Leave it. It's probably the coffee." He leaned back. The action pulled his shirt away from his chest and she got a glimpse of the thick mat of curling black hair that covered it.

She averted her eyes in the direction of the stove and watched it fanatically, not daring to look at him again. He was devastating like that, so attractive physically that he made her toes curl.

He saw the look he was getting. It made his heart race. She was certainly less sophisticated than most women he knew, but she still made him hungry in a new and odd sort of way.

"You said you monitored a stranded motorist's call?" she asked curiously.

"Yes. Your neighbor called the office on his mobile unit, and when I heard where the stranded motorist was,

I told Dispatch that I'd respond." He grinned at her. "I knew who it was and what was wrong before I got here."

She took an audible breath. "Well, it might have been something besides the fan belt," she said.

"You're stubborn."

"I meant to have it checked," she defended herself. "I got busy."

"Next time you'll know better, won't you?"

"I hate it when you use that tone," she muttered. "I'm not brain dead just because I'm a woman!"

His eyebrows raised. "Did I imply that you were?"

"You have an attitude…."

"So do you," he shot back. "Defensive and standoffish. I'd have told a man no differently than I told you that your fan belt needed replacing. The difference is that a man would have listened."

She put her coffee cup down hard and opened her mouth to speak just as the beeper on the oven's timer went off.

He got up with her and took the soup off the burner while she checked the corn bread in the oven. It was nicely browned, just right.

She was silent while she dished up the abbreviated meal, and while they ate it.

"You're a good cook, Jessie," he commented when he'd finished his second helping. "Who taught you?"

"My grandmother," she said. "My mother was not a good cook. She tried, God bless her, but we never gained weight around here." She pushed back her bowl. "You're handy enough in a kitchen yourself."

"Had to be," he said simply. "My mother was never sober enough to cook. If I hadn't learned, we'd both have starved. Not that she ate much. She drank most of her meals."

"You sound so bitter," she said gently.

"I *am* bitter," he shot back. He crossed his long legs, brushing at a smudge of mud on one polished black boot. "She robbed me of my childhood." His eyes sought her. "Isn't that what most victims of child abuse tell you—that what they mourn most is the loss of childhood?"

She nodded. "That's the worst of it. The pain and bitterness go on for a long time, even after therapy. You can't remake the past, McCallum. The scars don't go away, even if the patient can be made to restructure the way he or she thinks about the experience."

He turned his coffee cup around, his eyes on the white china soup bowl, now empty. "I never did what young boys usually get to do—play sports, join the Boy Scouts, go on trips, go to parties... From the time I was old enough, I did nothing except look after my mother, night after drunken night." His lean hand contacted absently on the bowl. "I used to hope she'd die."

"That's very normal," she assured him.

His broad shoulders rose and fell. "She did die, though in jail. I had her arrested when it all got too much after she attacked me one night. She was convicted of child abuse, sent to jail, and she died there when I was in my early teens. I was put to work as a hired hand for any family that would take me in. I had a room in a bunkhouse or in the barn, never with the family. I spent most of my life as an outsider looking in, until I was old enough to join the service. The uniform gave me a little self-esteem. As I grew older, I learned that my situation wasn't all that rare."

"Sadly, it isn't," she told him. "Sterling, what about your father?"

Her use of his first name made him feel warm inside. He smiled at her. "What about him?"

"Did he die?"

"Beats me," he said quietly. "I never found out who he was. I'm not sure she knew."

The implications of that statement were devastating. She winced.

"Feeling sorry for me all over again?" he murmured gently. "I don't need pity, Jessie. I've come to grips with it over the years. Plenty of people had it worse."

She traced the rim of her coffee cup soberly. "I'm sorry that it was that way for you."

"Different from your childhood, I imagine."

"Oh, yes. I was loved and wanted, and petted. I don't suppose I had a single bad experience in my whole childhood."

"They say we carry our childhood around with us, like luggage. I'll have to worry about not being too rough on my kids. You'll be just the opposite."

She felt sick inside, and tried not to show it. "Have you managed to find out anything else about little Jenny?" she asked, changing the subject.

"Nothing except dead ends," he had to admit. "I did find one new lead, but it didn't work out. How about you? Anything on the midwives?"

"I've spoken to two, but they say they don't know anything." She twirled her spoon on the tablecloth. "I'm not sure they'd tell me if they did," she added, looking up. "Sometimes they get in trouble for helping with deliveries, especially if something goes wrong. What if the mother died giving birth, Sterling?"

"That's a thought." His lips pursed. "I might check into any recent deaths involving childbirth."

"It might not lead to anything at all, but someone has to know about her. I mean, she didn't come from under a cabbage leaf."

He chuckled. "I don't think so."

She liked the sound of his laughter. She smiled as she got up to put the dishes in the sink.

"No dishwasher?" he teased as he helped.

"Of course I have a dishwasher—myself." She smiled at him. "I'll put these in to soak and do them later."

"Do them now, while I'm here to help you."

She did, because it would keep him here that much longer. She enjoyed his company far too much. She filled the sink with soapy water, while outside the rain continued steadily, broken occasionally by a rumble of thunder. "Were you always so bossy?" she asked as she washed a plate and handed it to him to be rinsed.

"I suppose so," he confessed. "That's force of habit. I was the highest-ranking officer in my group."

"What did you do in Naval Intelligence?"

He put the plate in the dish drainer and leaned toward her. "That's classified," he whispered.

"Well, excuse me for asking!" she teased.

His dark eyes searched hers. "I like the way you look when you smile," he commented absently. "It lights up your whole face."

"You hardly ever smile."

"I do when I'm with you. Haven't you noticed?"

She laughed self-consciously. "Yes, but I thought it was because you find me tedious." She washed another few dishes and passed them to him.

He rinsed them and then began drying, because there

were none left to be washed. "I find you disturbing," he corrected quietly.

She let the water out of the sink and took a second cloth, helping to dry the few dishes. "Because I'm forever dragging you into awkward situations?"

"Not quite."

They finished drying the dishes and Jessica put them away. She hung up the kitchen towels. Lightning flashed outside the window, followed by a renewal of pelting rain and a deep, vibrating rumble of thunder.

"Are you afraid of thunderstorms?" he asked her.

"A little."

He moved closer, his face filling her whole line of vision. "Are you afraid of me?" he continued.

Her eyes slid over his face, lingering on his firm mouth and chin. "That would depend on what you wanted from me," she countered bluntly.

"That's forthright enough," he said. "All right, cards on the table. Suppose I want you sexually?"

She didn't drop her eyes. "I don't want sex."

His gaze narrowed. "Because of what happened to you?" he guessed.

"Not entirely." She stared at the opening in his shirt, feeling her heartbeat increase as the clean cologne-and-soap scent of his body drifted into her nostrils. "It's mainly a matter of morality, I guess. And I'm not equipped for casual affairs, either. This is a small town. I…don't like gossip. I've always tried to live in such a way that people wouldn't think less of me."

"I see," he said slowly.

She shifted her shoulders. "No, you don't. You've been away so long maybe you've forgotten what it's really like." Her eyes were faintly pleading. "I like my life the way it is. I don't want to complicate it. I'm sorry."

His lean hands caught her waist gently and brought her against the length of his body. He stopped her instinctive withdrawal.

"Hush," he whispered. "Be still."

"What are...you doing?"

"I'm showing you that it's too late," he replied. His big hands smoothed her back up to her shoulder blades. "You want me. I want you. We can slow it down, but we can't stop it. Deep inside, you don't want to stop me." His gaze dropped to her soft mouth, and he watched her lips part. "You've been handled brutally. But you've never been touched with tenderness. I'm going to show you how it feels."

"I'm not sure that I want to know," she whispered.

He bent toward her. "Let's see."

Her fingers went up to touch his lips, staying their downward movement. Her eyes were wide and soft and faintly pleading. "Don't...hurt me," she said.

He moved her hand to his shirtfront and scowled. "Do you think I want to?"

"No, I don't mean physically. I mean..." She searched for words. "Sterling, I can't play games. I'm much too intense. It would be better if we were just friends."

He tilted her chin up and held her eyes. "Think about what you're saying," he said gently. "I know about your past. I know that you've been assaulted, that you don't date anyone. I even know that you're half-afraid of me. Considering all that, do you think I'm the sort of man who would tease you?"

She looked perplexed. Her hand had moved somehow into the opening where the buttons were unfastened. She felt the curly tangle of thick chest hair over warm, hard muscle. It was difficult to concentrate when all she wanted to do was touch him, test his maleness.

"Well, no," she confessed.

"I don't play games with women," he said flatly. "I'm straightforward. Sometimes too much so. I want you, but I'd never force you or put you in a position where you couldn't say no." He laughed mirthlessly. "Or don't you realize that I've been in that position myself?"

Her brows jerked together as she tried to puzzle out what he was saying.

"When one of my foster mothers got drunk enough," he said slowly, bitterly, "anything male would do. She tried to seduce me one night."

Her heart ached for him. What a distasteful, sickening experience it would have been for a young boy. "Oh, Sterling!" she said sadly.

The distaste dominated his expression. "I knocked her out of the bed and left the house. The next morning, we had it out. I told her exactly what would happen if she ever tried it again. I was almost as big then as I am now, you see. She couldn't force me." His hands let her go and he moved away.

She'd come across the same situation so many times, with so many families. It was amazing how many children suffered such traumas and never told, because of the shock and shame.

She moved closer to him, but she didn't touch him. She knew very well that abused children had real problems about being touched by other people sometimes—especially when something reminded them of the episodes—unless it was through their own choice. The scars were long lasting.

"You never told anyone," she guessed.

He wouldn't look at her. "No."

"Not even your caseworker?"

He shrugged. "He was the sort who wouldn't have believed me. And I had too much pride to beg for credibility."

She mourned the help he could have gotten from someone with a little more compassion.

"I've never told anyone," he continued, glancing down at her. "Amazing that I could tell you."

"Not really," she said, smiling. "I think you could tell me anything."

His face tautened. It was true. He would never balk at divulging his darkest secrets to this woman, because she had an open, loving heart. She wouldn't ridicule or judge, and she wouldn't repeat anything he said.

"I think I must have that sort of face," she continued, tongue-in-cheek, "because total strangers come up and talk to me about the most shocking things. I actually had a man ask me what to do about impotence."

He chuckled, his bad memories temporarily driven away. "And what did you tell him?"

"That a doctor would be a more sensible choice for asking advice," she returned. Her eyes searched his dark, hard face. "Sex was really hard for you the first time, wasn't it?" she asked bluntly.

Again his face tautened. "Yes."

She glanced away, folding her arms over her breasts. "I wasn't a child when I had my bad experience, but it made the thought of intimacy frightening to me. I'm realistic enough to know that it would be different with someone I cared about, but all I can see is the way he was. He reminded me of an animal."

"Do I?"

She turned quickly. "Don't be absurd!"

One eyebrow quirked. "Well, that's something."

She went back to him, looking up solemnly into his face. "I find *you* very disturbing," she confessed. "Physically, I mean. I guess that's why I shy away from you sometimes."

He traced her smooth cheek with a steely forefinger. "I don't think I've ever known anyone as honest as you."

"I hate lies. Don't you?"

"I hear enough of them. Nobody I've ever arrested has been guilty. It was a frame-up, or they didn't mean to, or somebody talked them into it."

"I know what you mean."

The exploring finger reached her mouth and traced its soft bow shape gently. His jaw tightened. She could hear the heavy breath that passed through his nostrils as his eyes began to darken and narrow.

"Why don't you unfasten my shirt and put your hands on me?" he asked huskily.

Her face colored vividly. "I don't know if that would be a good idea."

"It's the best one I've had tonight," he assured her. "No games. Honest. I want to make love to you a little, that's all. I won't let it get too far."

She put her hands against his shirtfront, torn between what she wanted to do and what was sensible.

"It's hard for me, with women," he said roughly. "Does that reassure you any?"

She smiled gently. "Will it make you angry if I confess that it does?"

He bent and his smiling mouth brushed against hers. "Probably. Open your mouth."

She obeyed him like a sleepwalker, but he soon brought every single nerve she had singing to life. Her hands slid under the shirt and over the thick tangle of hair that covered him, past male nipples that hardened at her touch. He moaned softly and pulled her closer. She sighed into his mouth as he deepened the kiss and made her knees go weak with the passion he kindled in her slender body.

"It isn't enough," he said in a strained tone. He bent and lifted her, his gaze reassuring as she opened startled eyes. "I want to lie down with you," he whispered as he carried her to the sofa. "I have to get closer, Jessie. Closer than this."

"It's dangerous," she managed through swollen lips.

"Life is dangerous." He put her down on the sofa, full length, and stretched out alongside her. "I won't hurt you. I swear to God, I won't. All it will take is one word, when you want me to stop."

His mouth traced hers. "And what…if I can't say it?" she whispered brokenly.

"I'll say it for you…."

He kissed her until she trembled, but even then he didn't touch her intimately or attempt to carry their lovemaking to greater depths. He lifted his head and looked down at her with tenderness and bridled passion. With her long hair loose around her face and her lips swollen from his kisses, her dark eyes wide and soft and dazed, he thought he'd never seen anything so beautiful in all his life.

"Are you stopping?" she whispered unsteadily.

"I think I should," he mused, managing to project a self-assurance he didn't really feel. His lower body ached.

"But we haven't done anything except kiss each other…." She stopped abruptly when she realized what she was saying.

He chuckled wickedly. "Jessie, if I push up that sweatshirt, we're both going to be in trouble. Because, frankly, it shows that you aren't wearing anything under it."

She followed his interested gaze and saw two hard peaks outlined vividly against the soft material. Scarlet faced, she got to her feet. "Well!"

He sat back on the sofa, watching her with smug, delighted eyes. She aroused an odd protectiveness in him that he'd never felt with another woman. She was unique in his shattered life. He wanted her, but it went far beyond desire.

"Don't be embarrassed," he said gently. "I didn't say it with any cruel intent. It delights me that you can want me, Jessie." He hesitated. "It delights me that I can want you. I wasn't sure…"

She searched his hard face. "Yes?" she prompted gently.

He got up and went to her slowly, secrets in his eyes.

She pushed back the glorious cloud of her hair and then reached up to touch his sculptured cheek. "Tell me," she coaxed.

He brought her hand to his lips. "I exaggerated when I told you there had been a parade of women through my bed," he said quietly.

Her eyes were solemn, steady, questioning.

His shoulders moved restlessly. He looked tormented. He tried to tell her, but the words wouldn't come.

Her fingers traced his hard mouth. "It's all right." She pulled his head down and kissed his eyes closed. He shivered. "My dear," she whispered. Her mouth traced his and softly kissed his lips, feeling them open and press down, responding with a sudden feverish need. He pulled her close and increased the pressure, groaning as she gave in to him without a single protest.

He let her go slowly, his tall, fit body taut with desire and need as he looked down at her hungrily.

"I've never been with anyone like you," he said flatly. "Because of the way I grew up, I always equated sex with a certain kind of woman," he said huskily. "So that's where I went, when I had to have it." He sighed heavily. "Not that I was ever careless, Jessie."

She bit her lip, trying not to remember Bess's taunt.

"What is it?" he asked suspiciously.

"I can't tell you. You'll get conceited."

His eyebrows arched. He cocked his head. "Come on."

"A girl I know made the comment that she thought you'd be absolute heaven to make love with, and that she'd bet you were always prepared."

He chuckled softly. "Did she? Who?"

"I'll never tell!"

He pursed his lips, amused. "As it happens, she was right." He bent and brushed her mouth with his. "On both counts," he whispered and nipped her lower lip.

She smiled under his lips. "I know. About the first count, anyway."

"You can take my word for the other. How about supper tomorrow night?"

She stared at him blankly. "What?"

"I want to take you out on a date," he explained. "One of those things where a man and woman spend time together, and at the end of the evening, do what we've already done."

"Oh."

His eyebrow lifted as he fastened his shirt. "Well?"

Her face lit up. "I'd love to!"

He smiled. "So would I. Thanks for supper." He moved to the door and glanced back. She was ruffled and flustered. He liked knowing that he'd made her that way. "I'll send the mechanic over first thing in the morning to see about that fan belt. And I'll come and drive you to work."

"You don't have to," she declared breathlessly.

"I want to." The way he said it projected other images, exciting ones. She laughed inanely, captivated by the look on his dark face.

"I'd better go," he murmured dryly. "Good night, Jessie."

"Good night."

He closed the door gently behind him. "Lock it!" he added from outside.

She rushed forward and threw the lock into place. A minute later she heard deep laughter and the sound of his booted feet going down the steps.

Chapter 7

The restaurant was crowded, and heads turned from all directions when Jessica, in a neat-fitting burgundy dress with her hair loose around her shoulders, walked in with McCallum, who was wearing slacks and a sports coat.

"I told you people would notice that we're together," she said under her breath as they were seated.

"I didn't mind the last time, and I don't mind now," he murmured, smiling. "Do you?"

She smiled back. "Not at all."

The waitress brought menus, poured water into glasses and went away to give them time to decide what to order.

"Why... Miss Larson!"

Jessica looked up. Bess, one of her caseworkers, and a good-looking young man who worked in the bank had paused by their table.

"Hello, Bess," Jessica said, smiling. "How are you?"

"Fine! Don't you look nice? Hi, McCallum," she added, letting her blue eyes sweep over him in pure flirtation. "You look nice, too!"

"Thanks."

"Bess, the waitress is gesturing to us," the young man prompted. He was giving McCallum a nervous look. Probably it was the fact that McCallum was in law enforcement that disturbed him. Lawmen were set apart from the rest of the world, Jessica had discovered over the years. But it could have been the way Bess was looking at the older man. Jessica had to admit that McCallum was sensuous and handsome enough to fit any woman's dream. Compared to him, Bess's date seemed very young, and he was undoubtedly jealous.

"Oh, sure, Steve. Good to see you both!" she said breezily, leading him away.

"She thinks you're a hunk," Jessica said without thinking, then bit her lip.

His eyebrows lifted. "So?" Now he knew who'd made the comment she'd related at her cabin.

"She's very young, of course," she added mischievously.

"No, she isn't," he countered. "In fact, she's only a year younger than you. Nice figure, too."

Jessica fought down an unfamiliar twinge of jealousy. She fumbled with her silverware. Nobody disturbed her like McCallum did.

He reached across the table and caught her hand in his, sending thrills of pleasure up her arm that made her heart race. "I didn't mean it like that. Jessie, if I were interested in your co-worker, why would I spend half my free time thinking about you?"

She smiled at him, thrown off balance by the look in his dark eyes. "Do you?" she asked. Her hand slipped and almost overturned her water glass. He righted it quickly, smiling patiently at her clumsiness. It wasn't like her to do such things.

"Hold tight, and I'll protect you from overturning things," he said, clasping her cold fingers in his. "We'll muddle through together. In my own way, I've got as many hang-ups and inhibitions as you have. But if we try, we can sort it out."

"Sort what out?" she echoed curiously.

He frowned. "Do you think I make a habit of taking women out? I'm thirty-five years old, and since I've been back here, I've lived like a hermit. I'm hungry for a woman...."

This time the glass went over. He called the waitress, who managed to clear away the water with no effort at all. She smiled indulgently at an embarrassed Jessica, who was abjectly apologetic.

She took their order and left. Across the restaurant, Bess was giggling. Jessica looked at Sterling McCallum and knew in that moment that she loved him. She also knew that she could never marry him. He might not realize it now, but he'd want children one day. He was the sort of man who needed children to love and take care of. He'd make a good husband. Of course, marriage was obviously the last thing on his mind at the moment.

"Good God, woman," he muttered, shaking his head with indulgent amusement. "Will you just let me finish a sentence before you react like that? I don't have plans to ravish you. Okay? Now, move that glass aside before we have another mishap."

"I'm sorry. I'm just all thumbs."

"And I keep putting my foot in my mouth," he said ruefully. "What I was going to say, before the great water glass flood," he added with a grin at her flush, "was that it's time I started going out more. I like you. We'll keep it low-key."

She looked at the big, lean hand holding hers so gently. Her fingers moved over the back of it, tracing, savoring its strength and masculinity. "I like your hands," she said absently. "They're very sensitive, for such masculine ones." She thought about how they might feel on bare, soft skin and her lips parted as she exhaled with unexpected force.

His thumb eased into the damp palm of her hand and began to caress it, making her heart race all over again. "Yours are beautiful," he said, and the memory of how her hands felt on his chest was still in his gaze when he looked up.

She was holding her breath. She looked into his eyes, and neither of them smiled. It was like lightning striking. She could see what he was thinking. It was all there in his dark gaze—the need and the hunger and the ardent passion he felt for her.

"Uh, excuse me?"

They both looked up blankly as the waitress, smiling wryly, waited for them to move their hands so she could put the plates down.

"Sorry," Sterling mumbled.

The waitress didn't say a word, but her expression spoke volumes.

"I think we're becoming obvious," he remarked to Jessica as he picked up his fork, trying not to look around at the interested glances they were getting from Bess and Steve.

"Yes." She sounded pained, and looked even more uncomfortable.

"Jessie?"

"Hmm?" She looked up.

He leaned forward. "I'm dying of frustrated passion here. Eat fast, could you?"

She burst out laughing. It broke the tension and got them through the rest of the meal.

But once he paid the check and they went out to the parking lot and got into the Bronco, he didn't take her straight home. He drove a little way past the cabin and pulled down a long, dark trail into the woods.

He locked his door, unfastened his seat belt and then reached across her wordlessly to lock her own door and release her seat belt, as well.

His eyes in the darkness held a faint glitter. She could feel the quick, harsh rush of his breath on her forehead. She didn't protest. Her arms reached around his neck as he pulled her across his lap. When his mouth lowered, hers was ready, waiting.

They melted together, so hungry for each other that nothing else seemed to matter.

She'd never experienced kisses that weren't complete in themselves. He made her want more, much more. Every soft stroke of his hands against her back was arousing, even through the layers of fabric. The brush of his lips on hers didn't satisfy, it taunted and teased. He nibbled at the outside curves of her mouth with brief little touches that made her heart run wild. She clung to him, hoping that he might deepen the kiss on his own account, but he seemed to be waiting.

She reached up, finally, driven to the outskirts of

desperation by the teasing that went on and on until she was taut as drawn rope with unsatisfied needs.

"Please!" she whispered brokenly, trying to pull his head down.

"It isn't enough, is it?" he asked calmly. "I hoped it might not be. Open your mouth, Jessica," he whispered against her lips as he shifted her even closer to his broad, warm chest. "And I'll show you just how hungry a kiss can make you feel."

It was devastating. She felt her breath become suspended, like her mind, as his lips fitted themselves to hers and began to move in slow, teasing touches that quickly grew harder and rougher and deeper. By the time his tongue probed at her lips, they opened eagerly for him. When his tongue went deep into her mouth, she arched up against him and groaned out loud.

Her response kindled a growing hunger in him. It had been a long time for him, and the helpless twisting motions of her breasts against him made him want to rip open her dress and take them in his hands and his mouth.

Without thinking of consequences, he made her open her mouth even farther under the crush of his, and his lean hand dropped to her bodice, teasing her breasts through the cloth until he felt the nipples become hard. Only then did he smooth the firm warmth of one and begin to caress it with his fingertips. When he caught the nipple deliberately in his thumb and forefinger, she cried out. He lifted his head to see why. As he'd suspected, it wasn't out of fear or pain.

She lay there, just watching him as he caressed her. He increased the gentle pressure of his fingers and she gasped as she looked into his eyes. A slow flush spread over her high cheekbones in the dimly lit interior.

He didn't say a word. He simply sat there, holding her and looking down into her shadowed eyes. It was hard to breathe. Her body was soft in his arms and that pretty burgundy dress had buttons down the front. His eyes went past the hand that now lay possessively on her breast and he calculated how easy it would be to open the buttons and bare her breasts to his hungry mouth. But she was trembling, and his body was getting quickly out of control. Besides that, it was too soon for that sort of intimacy. He had to give her time to get used to the idea before he tried to further their relationship. It was important not to frighten her so that she backed away from him.

He moved his hand up and pushed back her disheveled hair with a soft smile. "Sorry," he murmured dryly. "I guess I let it go a little too far."

"It was my fault, too. You're…you're very potent," she said after a minute, feeling the swelling of her mouth from his hard kisses and the tingling of her breast where his hand had toyed with it. She still couldn't imagine that she'd really let him do that. But, oddly, she didn't feel embarrassed about it. It seemed somehow proper for McCallum to touch her like that, as if she belonged to him already.

He grinned at her expression. "You're potent yourself. And that being the case, I think I'd better get you home."

She fingered his collar. "Okay." Her hands traced down to his tie and the top button of his shirt.

"No," he said gently, staying her fingers. "I like having you touch me there too much," he murmured dryly. "Let's not tempt fate twice in one night."

She was a little disappointed, even though she knew he was right. It *was* too soon. But her eyes mirrored more than one emotion.

He watched those expressions chase across her face, his eyes tender, full of secrets. "How did you get under my skin?" he wondered absently.

She glowed with pleasure. "Have I?"

"Right down to the bone, when I wasn't looking. I don't know if I like it." He studied her for a long moment. "Trust comes hard to me. Don't ever lie to me, Jessica," he said unexpectedly. "I can forgive anything except that. I've been sold out once too often in the past. The scars go deep and they came from painful lessons. I can't bear lies."

She thought about being barren, and wondered if this would be the right time to tell him. But it wasn't a lie, was it? It was a secret, one she would get around to, if it ever became necessary to tell him. But right now they were just dating, just friends. She was over-reacting. She smiled. "Okay. I promise that I'll never deliberately lie to you." That got her around the difficult hurdle of her condition. She wasn't lying. She just wasn't confessing. It was middle ground, and not really dishonest. Of course it wasn't.

He let go of her hand and started the vehicle, turning on the lights. He glanced sideways at her as he pulled the Bronco out into the road and drove back to her cabin. She might be afraid, but there was desire in her, as well. She wanted him. He had to keep that in mind and not give up hope.

He stopped at her front steps. "I want to take you out

from time to time," he said firmly. "We can go out to eat—as my budget allows," he added with a grin, "and to movies. And I'd like to take you fishing and deer tracking with me this fall."

"Oh, I'd enjoy that." She looked surprised and delighted. The radiance of her face made her so stunning that he lost his train of thought for a minute.

He frowned. "Just don't go shopping for wedding bands and putting announcements in the local paper," he said firmly. He held up a hand when she started, flustered, to protest. "There's no use arguing about it, my mind's made up. I do know that you make wonderful homemade bread, and that's a point in your favor, but you mustn't rush me."

Her eyes brightened with wicked pleasure. "Oh, I wouldn't dream of it," she said, entering into the spirit of the thing. "I never try to rush men into marriage."

He chuckled. "Okay. Now you stick to that. I don't like most people," he mused. "But I like you."

"I like you, too."

"In between hero-worshipping me," he added outrageously.

She looked him over with a long sigh. "Can I help it if you're the stuff dreams are made of?"

"Pull the other one. I'll see you tomorrow."

"That reminds me, there's a young man in juvenile detention that I'd like you to talk to for me," she said. "He's on a rocky path. Maybe you can turn him around."

He rolled his eyes upward. "Not again!"

"You know you don't mind," she chided. "I'll phone you from the office tomorrow."

"All right." He watched her get out of the Bronco. "Lock your doors."

His concern made her tingle. She grinned at him over her shoulder. "I always do. Thanks for supper."

"I enjoyed it."

"So did I." She wanted to, but she didn't look back as she unlocked the door. She was inside before she heard him drive off. She was sure that her feet didn't touch the floor for the rest of the night. And her dreams were sweet.

In the days and weeks that followed, Jessica and Mc-Callum saw a lot of one another. He kissed her, but it was always absently, tenderly. He'd drawn back from the intensity of the kisses they'd shared the first night he took her out. Now, they talked about things. They discovered much that they had in common, and life took on a new beauty for Jessica.

Just when she thought things couldn't get any better, she walked into the Hip Hop Café and came face-to-face with a nightmare—Sam Jackson.

The sandy-haired man turned and looked at her with cold, contemptuous eyes. He was the brother of the man who'd attacked her and who had later been killed. He was shorter and stockier, but the heavy facial features and small eyes were much the same.

"Hello, Jessica Larson," he said, blocking her path so that she was trapped between the wall and him. "I was passing through and thought I might look you up while I was in town. I wanted to see how my brother's murderer was getting along."

She clutched her purse in hands that trembled. She knew her face was white. Her eyes were huge as she looked at him with terror. He had been the most vocal person in court during the trial, making remarks about her and to her that still hurt.

"I didn't kill your brother. It wasn't my fault," she insisted.

"If you hadn't gone out there and meddled, it never would have happened," he accused. His voice, like his eyes, was full of hate. "You killed him, all right."

"He died in a car wreck," she reminded him with as much poise as she could manage. "It was not my fault that he attacked me!" She carefully kept her voice down so that she wouldn't be overheard.

"You went out there alone, knowing he'd be on his own because you'd tried to get his wife to leave him," he returned. "A woman who goes to a man's house by herself when he's alone is asking for it."

"I didn't know that he was alone!"

"You wanted him. That's why you convinced his wife to leave him."

The man's attitude hadn't changed, it had only intensified. He'd been unable from the beginning to believe his brother could have beaten not only his wife, but his little girl, as well. To keep from accepting the truth, he'd blamed it all on Jessica. His brother had been the most repulsive human being she'd ever known. She looked at him levelly. "That's not true," she corrected. "And you know it. You won't admit it, but you know that your brother was on drugs and you know what he did because of it. You also know that I had nothing to do with his death."

"Like hell you didn't," he said with venom. "You had him arrested! That damned trial destroyed my family, humiliated us beyond belief. Then you just walked away. You walked off and forgot the tragedy you'd caused!"

Her whole body clenched at the remembered agony. "I felt for all of you," she argued. "I didn't want to hurt you, but nothing I did was strictly on my own behalf. I wanted to help his daughter, your niece! Didn't any of you think about her?"

He couldn't speak for a minute. "He never meant to hurt her. He said so. Anyway, she's all right," he muttered. "Kids get over things."

Her eyes looked straight into his. "No, they don't get over things like that. Even I never got over what your brother did to me. I paid and I'm still paying."

"Women like you are trash," he said scornfully. "And before I'm through, everyone around here is going to know it."

"What do you mean?"

He smiled. "I mean I'm going to stick around for a few days and let people know just what sort of social worker they've got here. Maybe during the last few years, some of them have forgotten...."

"If you try to start trouble—" she began.

"You'll what?" he asked smugly. "Sue me for defamation of character? Go ahead. It took everything we had in legal fees to defend my brother. I don't have any money. Sue me. You can't get blood out of a rock."

She tried to breathe normally, but couldn't. "How is Clarisse?" she asked, mentioning the daughter of the man who'd assaulted her so many years before.

"She's in college," he said, "working her way through."

"Is she all right?"

He shifted irritably. "I guess. We hear about her through a mutual cousin. She and her mother washed their hands of us years ago."

Jessica didn't say another word. She'd been planning to eat, but her appetite was gone.

"Excuse me, I have to get back to work," she said. She turned around and left the café. She hardly felt anything all the way to her office. She'd honestly thought the past was dead. Now here it was again, staring her in the face. She'd done nothing wrong, but it seemed that she was doomed to pay over and over again for a crime that had been committed against her, not by her.

It was a cruel wind that had blown Sam Jackson into town, she thought bitterly. But if he was only passing through, perhaps he wouldn't stay long. She'd stick close to the office for a couple of days, she decided, and not make a target of herself.

But that was easier said than done. Apparently Sam had found out where her office was, because he passed by it three times that day. The next morning, when Jessica went into work, it was to find him sitting in the Hip Hop Café where she usually had coffee. She went on to the office and asked Bess if she'd mind bringing her a coffee when she went across the street.

"Who is that fat man?" Bess asked when she came back. "Does he really know you?"

Jessica's heart stopped. "Did he ask you about me?"

"Oh, no," Bess said carelessly. She put a plastic cup of coffee in front of Jessica. "He didn't say anything to me, but he was talking to some other people about you." She hesitated, wondering if she should continue.

"Some people?" Jessica prompted.

"Sterling McCallum was one of them," the caseworker added slowly.

Jessica didn't have to ask if what the man had said

was derogatory. It was obvious from the expression on her face that it was.

"He said his brother died because of you," Bess continued reluctantly. "That you led him on and then threw him over after you'd gotten his wife out of the way."

Jessica sat down heavily. "I see. So I'm a femme fatale."

"Nobody who knows you would believe such a thing!" Bess scoffed. "He was a client, wasn't he? Or rather, his brother was. Honest to God, Jessica, I knew there had to be some reason why you always insist that Candy and Brenda go out on cases together instead of alone. His brother was the reason, wasn't he?"

Jessica nodded. "But that isn't how he's telling it. New people in the community might believe him, though," she added, trying not to remember that several old-timers still believed that Jessica had been running after the man, too.

"Tell him to get lost," the other woman said. "Or threaten to have him arrested for slander. I'll bet McCallum would do it for you. After all, you two are looking cozy these days."

"We're just friends," Jessica said with emphasis. "Nothing more. And Sterling might believe him. He's been away from Whitehorn for a long time, and he doesn't really know me very well." She didn't add that McCallum had such bad experiences in the past that it might be all too easy for him to believe what Sam Jackson was telling him. She was afraid of the damage that might be done to their fragile relationship.

"Don't worry," Bess was saying. "McCallum will give him his walking papers."

"Do you think so?" Jessica took a sip of her coffee. "We'd better get to work."

She half expected McCallum to come storming into the office demanding explanations. But he didn't. Nothing was said at all, by him or by anyone else. Life went on as usual, and by the end of the day, she'd relaxed. She'd overreacted to Sam's presence in Whitehorn. It would be all right. He was probably on his way out of town even now.

McCallum was drinking a beer. He hardly ever had anything even slightly alcoholic. His mother had taught him well what alcohol could do. Therefore, he was always on guard against overindulgence.

That being the case, it was only one beer. He was off duty and not on call. Before he'd met the newcomer in the café that morning, he might have taken Jessica to a movie. Now he felt sick inside. She'd never told him the things he'd learned from Sam Jackson.

Jessica was a pretty woman when she dressed up. She'd been interning at the social-services office, Sam Jackson had told him, when she'd gone out to see his brother Fred. Fred's wife had become jealous of the way Jessica was out there all the time, and she'd left him. Jessica teased and flirted with him, and then, when things got out of hand and the poor man was maddened with passion, she'd yelled rape and had him arrested. The man had hardly touched her. He'd gone to jail for attempted rape, got out on parole six months later and was killed in a horrible car wreck. His wife and child had been lost to him, he was disgraced and it was all Jessica's fault. Everybody believed her wild lies.

Sam Jackson was no fly-by-night con man. He'd

been a respected councilman in Whitehorn for many years and was still known locally. McCallum had asked another old-timer, who'd verified that Jessica had had Jackson's brother arrested for sexual assault. It had been a closed hearing, very hushed up, and a bit of gossip was all that managed to escape the tight-lipped sheriff, Judd Hensley, and the attorneys and judge in the case. But people knew it was Jessica who had been involved, and the rumors had flown for weeks, even after Fred Jackson's family left town and he was sent to jail for attempted rape.

The old man had shaken his head as he recalled the incident. Women always said no when they meant yes, he assured McCallum, and several people thought that Jessica had only gotten what she'd asked for, going out to a man's house alone. Women had too goldarned much freedom, the old-timer said. If they'd never gotten the vote, life would have been better all around.

McCallum didn't hear the sexism in the remark; he was too outraged over what he'd learned about Jessica. So that shy, retiring pose was just that—an act. She'd played him for an absolute fool. No woman could be trusted. Hadn't he learned from his mother how treacherous they could be? His mother had smiled so sweetly when people came, infrequently, to the house. She'd lied with a straight face when a neighbor had asked questions about all the yelling and smashing of glass the night before. Nothing had happened except that she'd dropped a vase, she'd insisted, and she'd cried out because it startled her.

Actually, she'd been raving mad from too much alcohol and had been chasing her son around the house with an empty gin bottle. That was the night she'd broken his arm. She'd managed to convince the local doctor, the elderly practitioner who'd preceeded Jessica's father, that he'd slipped and fallen on a rain-wet porch. She'd tried to coax him to set it and say nothing out of loyalty to the family. But Sterling had told. His mother had hurt him. She'd lied deliberately about their home life. She'd pretended to love him, until she drank. And then she was like another person, a brutal and unfeeling one who only wanted to hurt him. He'd never trusted another woman since.

Until Jessica. She was the one exception. He'd grown close to her during their meetings, and he wanted her in every way there was. He valued her friendship, her company. But she'd lied to him, by omission. She hadn't told him the truth about her past.

There was one other truth Sam Jackson had imparted to him, an even worse one. In the course of the trial, it had come out that the doctor who had examined Jessica found a blockage in her fallopian tubes that would make it difficult, if not impossible, for her to get pregnant.

She knew that Sterling was interested in her, that he would probably want children. Yet she'd made sure that she never told him that one terrible fact about herself. She could not give him a child. Yet she'd never stopped going out with him, and she knew that he was growing involved with her. It was a lie by omission, but still a lie. It was the one thing, he confessed to himself, that he could never forgive.

He was only grateful that he'd found her out in time, before he'd made an utter fool of himself.

Chapter 8

Unfortunately, it was impossible for Jessica not to notice that McCallum's attitude toward her had changed since Sam Jackson's advent into town. He didn't call her that evening or the next day. And when she was contacted by the sheriff's office because the child of one of her client families—Keith Colson—was picked up for shoplifting, she wondered if he would have.

She went to the sheriff's office as quickly as she could. McCallum was there as arresting officer. He was polite and not hateful, but he was so distant that Jessica hardly knew what to say to him.

She sat down in a chair beside the lanky boy in the interrogation room and laid her purse on the table.

"Why did you do it, Keith?" she asked gently.

He shrugged and averted his eyes. "I don't know."

"You were caught in the act," she pressed, aware of

McCallum standing quietly behind her, waiting. "The store owner saw you pick up several packages of cigarettes and stick them in your pockets. He said you even looked into the camera while you were doing it. You didn't try to hide what you were doing."

Keith moved restlessly in the chair. "I did it, okay? How about locking me up now?" he added to McCallum. "This time I wasn't an accomplice. This time I'm the—what do you call it?—the perpetrator. That means I do time, right? When are you going to lock me up?"

McCallum was scowling. Something wasn't right here. The boy looked hunted, afraid, but not because he'd been caught shoplifting. He'd waited patiently for McCallum to show up and arrest him, and he'd climbed into the back of the patrol car almost eagerly. There was one other disturbing thing: a fading bruise, a big one, was visible beside his eye.

"I can't do that yet," McCallum said. "We've called the juvenile authorities. You're underage, so you'll have to be turned over to them."

"Juvenile? Not *again!* But I wasn't an accomplice, you know I did it. I did it all by myself! I shouldn't have to go back home this time!"

McCallum hitched up his slacks and sat down on the edge of the table, facing the boy. "Why don't you tell me the truth?" he invited quietly. "I can't help you if I don't know what's going on."

Keith looked as if he wanted to say something, as if it was eating him up inside not to. But at the last minute, his eyes lowered and he shrugged.

"Nothing to tell," he said gruffly. He glanced at McCallum. "There's a chance that they might keep me, isn't there? At the juvenile hall, I mean?"

McCallum scowled. "No. You'll be sent home after they've done the paperwork and your hearing's scheduled."

Keith's face fell. He sighed and wouldn't say another word. McCallum could remember seeing that particular expression on a youngster's face only once before. It had been on his own face, the night the doctor set the arm his mother had broken. He had to get to the bottom of Keith's situation, and he knew he couldn't do that by talking to Keith or any of his family. There had to be another way, a better way. Perhaps he could talk to some people at Keith's school. Someone there might know more than he did and be able to shed some light on the situation for him.

Jessica went out to see Keith's father and grandmother. She'd hoped McCallum might offer to go with her, but he left as soon as Keith was delivered to the juvenile officer. It was all too obvious that he found Jessica's company distasteful, probably because Sam Jackson had been filling his head full of half-truths. If he'd only come out and accuse her of something, she could defend herself. But how could she make any sort of defense against words that were left unspoken?

Terrance Colson was not surprised to hear that his son was in trouble with the law.

"I knew the boy was up to no good," he told Jessica blithely. "Takes after his mother, you know. She ran off with a salesman and dumped him on me and his grandmother years ago. Never wanted him in the first place." He sounded as if he felt the same way. "God knows I've done my best for him, but he never appreciates anything at all. He's always talking back, making trouble. I'm not surprised that he stole things, no, sir."

"Did you know that he smoked?" Jessica asked deliberately, curious because the boy's grandmother stayed conspicuously out of sight and never even came out to the porch, when Jessica knew she'd heard the truck drive up.

"Sure I knew he smoked," Terrance said evenly. "I won't give him money to throw away on cigarettes. That's probably why he stole them."

That was a lie. Jessica knew it was, because McCallum had offered the boy a cigarette in the sheriff's office and he'd refused it with a grimace. He'd said that he didn't like cigarettes, although he quickly corrected that and said that he just didn't want one at the moment. But there were no nicotine stains on his fingers, and he certainly didn't smell of tobacco.

"You tell them to send him home, now, as soon as they get finished with him," Terrance told Jessica firmly. "I got work to do around here and he's needed. They can't lock him up."

"They won't," she assured him. "But he won't tell us anything. Not even why he did it."

"Because he needed cigarettes, that's why," the man said unconvincingly.

Jessica understood why McCallum had been suspicious. The longer she talked to the boy's father, the more curious she became about the situation. She asked a few more questions, but he was as unforthcoming as Keith himself had been. Eventually, she got up to leave.

"I'd like to say hello to Mrs. Colson," she began.

"Oh, she's too busy to come out," he said with careful indifference. "I'll give her your regards, though."

"Yes. You do that." Jessica smiled and held out her hand deliberately. As Terrance reluctantly took it, she saw small bruises on his knuckles. He was righthanded. If he hit someone, it would be with the hand she was holding.

She didn't remark on the bruises. She left the porch, forming a theory that was very disturbing. She wished that she and McCallum were on better terms, because she was going to need his help. She was sorry she hadn't listened to him sooner. If she had, perhaps Keith wouldn't have another shoplifting charge on his record.

When she got back to her office, she called the sheriff's office and asked them to have McCallum drop by. Once, he would have stopped in the middle of whatever he was doing to oblige her. But today it was almost quitting time before he put in a belated appearance. And he didn't look happy about being summoned, either.

She had to pretend that it didn't matter, that she wasn't bothered that he was staring holes through her with those angry dark eyes. She forced a cool smile to her lips and invited him to sit down.

"I've had a long talk with Keith's father," she said at once. "He says that Keith smokes and that's why he took the cigarettes."

"Bull," he said curtly.

"I know. I didn't notice any nicotine stains on Keith's fingers. But I did notice some bruises on Terrance's knuckles and a fading bruise near Keith's eye," she added.

He lifted an eyebrow. "Observant, aren't you?" he asked with thinly veiled sarcasm. "You were the one who said there was nothing wrong at Keith's home, as I recall."

She sat back heavily in her chair. "Yes, I was. I should have listened to you. The thing is, what can we do about it? His father isn't going to admit that he's hitting him, and Keith is too loyal to tell anyone about it. I even thought about talking to old Mrs. Colson, but Terrance won't let me near her."

"Unless Keith volunteers the information, we have no case," McCallum replied. "The district attorney isn't likely to ask a judge to issue an arrest warrant on anyone's hunch."

She grimaced. "I know." She laced her fingers together. "Meanwhile, Keith's desperate to get away from home, even to the extent of landing himself in jail to accomplish it. He won't stop until he does."

"I know that."

"Then do something!" she insisted.

"What do you have in mind?"

She threw up her hands. "How do I know? I'm not in law enforcement."

His dark eyes narrowed accusingly on her face. "No. You're in social work. And you take your job very seriously, don't you?"

It was a pointed remark, unmistakable. She sat up straight, with her hands locked together on her cluttered desk, and stared at him levelly. "Go ahead," she invited. "Get it off your chest."

"All right," he said without raising his voice. "You can't have a child of your own."

She'd expected to be confronted with some of the old gossip, with anything except this. Her face paled. She couldn't even explain it to him. Her eyes fell.

The guilt told him all he needed to know. "Did you

ever plan to tell me?" he asked icily. "Or wasn't it any of my business?"

She stared at the small print on a bottle of correction fluid until she had it memorized. "I thought...we weren't serious about each other, so it...wasn't necessary to tell you."

He didn't want her to know how serious he'd started to feel about her. It made him too vulnerable. He crossed one long leg over the other.

"And how about the court trial?" he added. "Weren't you going to mention anything about it, either?"

Her weary eyes lifted to his. "You must surely realize that Sam Jackson isn't anyone's idea of an unbiased observer. It was his brother. Naturally, he'd think it was all my fault."

"Wasn't it?" he asked coldly. "You did go out to the man's house all alone, didn't you?"

That remark was a slap in the face. She got to her feet, her eyes glittering. "I don't have to defend a decision I made years ago to you," she said coolly. "You have no right to accuse me of anything."

"I wasn't aware that I had," he returned. "Do you feel guilty about what happened to Jackson's brother?"

Her expression hardened to steel. "I have nothing to feel guilty about," she said with as much pride as she could manage. "Given the same circumstances, I'd do exactly what I did again and I'd take the consequences."

He scowled at her. "Including costing a man his family, subjecting him to public humiliation and eventually to what amounted to suicide?"

So that was what Sam had been telling people. That Jessica had driven the man to his death.

She sat back down. "If you care about people," she

said quietly, "you believe them. If you don't, all the words in the world won't change anything. Sam should have been a lawyer. He really has a gift for influencing opinion. He's certainly tarred and feathered me in only two days."

"The truth usually comes out, doesn't it?" he countered.

She didn't flinch. "You don't know the truth. Not that it matters anymore." She was heartsick. She pulled her files toward her. "If you'll excuse me, Deputy McCallum, I've already got a day's work left to finish. I'll have another talk with Keith when the juvenile officers bring him back to the sheriff's office."

"You do that." He got up, furious because she wouldn't offer him any explanation, any apology for keeping him in the dark. "You might have told me the truth in the beginning," he added angrily.

She opened a file. "We all have our scars. Mine are such that it hurts to take them out and look at them." She lifted wounded dark eyes to his. "I can't ever have babies," she said stiffly. "Now you know. Ordinarily, you wouldn't have, because I never had any intention of letting our relationship go that far. You were the one who kept pushing your way into my life. If you had just let me alone…!" She stopped, biting her lower lip to stifle the painful words. She turned a sheet of paper over deftly. "Sam Jackson's brother got what he deserved, McCallum. And that's the last thing I'll ever say about it."

He stood watching her for a minute before he finally turned and went out. He walked aimlessly into the outer office. She was right. He was the one who'd pursued her, not the reverse. All the same, she might have told him the truth.

"Hi, McCallum," Bess called to him from her desk, smiling sweetly.

He paused on his way out and smiled back. "Hi, yourself."

She gave him a look that could have melted ice. "I guess you and Jessica are too thick for me to try my luck, hmm?" she asked with a mock sigh.

He lifted his chin and his dark eyes shimmered as he looked at her. "Jessica and I are friends," he said, refusing to admit that they were hardly even that anymore. "That's all."

"Well, in that case, why don't you come over for supper tonight and I'll feed you some of my homemade spaghetti?" she asked softly. "Then we can watch that new movie on cable. You know, the one with all the warnings on it?" she added suggestively.

She was pretty and young and obviously had no hang-ups about being a woman. He pursed his lips. It had been a long, dry spell, although something in him resisted dating a woman so close to Jessica. On the other hand, he told himself, Jessica had lied to him, and what was it to her if he dated one of her employees?

"What time?" he asked gruffly.

She brightened. "Six sharp. I live next door to Truman Haynes. You know where his house is, don't you?" He nodded. "Well, I rent his furnished cottage. It's very cozy, and old Truman goes to bed real early."

"Does he, now?" he mused.

She grinned. "Yes, indeed!"

"Then I'll see you at six." He winked and walked out, still feeling a twinge of guilt.

Bess stuck her head into Jessica's office just before she left. "McCallum said that you and he were just good friends, and you keep saying the same thing," she began, "so is it all right if I try my luck with him?"

Jessica was dumbfounded, but she was adept at hiding her deepest feelings. She forced a smile. "Why, of course."

Bess let out a sigh of relief. "Thank goodness! I invited him over for supper. I didn't want to step on your toes, but he is so sexy! Thanks, Jessica! See you tomorrow!"

She closed the door quickly, and a minute later, Jessica heard her go out. It was like a door closing on life itself. She hesitated just briefly before she turned her eyes back to the file she was working on. The print was so blurred that she could hardly read it.

Whitehorn was small and, as in most small towns, everyone knew immediately about McCallum's supper with Bess. They didn't know that nothing had happened, however, because Bess made enough innuendos to suggest that it had been the hottest date of her life. Jessica was hard-pressed not to snap at her employee, but she couldn't let anyone know how humiliating and painful the experience was to her. She had her pride, if nothing else.

Sam Jackson heard about the date and laughed heartily. Originally he'd planned to spend only one night in Whitehorn, but he was enjoying himself too much to leave in a rush. A week later, he was still in residence at the small motel and having breakfast every morning at the café across from Jessica's office.

Jessica was near breaking point. People were gossiping about her all over again. She became impatient with her caseworkers and even with clients, which was unlike her. She couldn't do anything about Sam Jackson, and certainly McCallum wasn't going to. He seemed to like the man. And he seemed to like Bess as well, because he began to stop by the office every day to take her to lunch.

"I'm leaving now," Bess said at noon on Friday. She hesitated, and from the corner of her eye, Jessica saw her looking at her in concern. No wonder since even to her own eyes she looked pale and drawn. In fact, she was hardly eating anything and was on the verge of moving out of town. Desperation had cost her the cool reason she'd always prided herself on.

"Have a nice lunch," she told Bess, refusing to look up because she knew Sterling McCallum was standing in the outer office, waiting.

Bess still hesitated. She felt so guilty she couldn't stand herself lately. It was painfully obvious how her boss felt about Sterling McCallum. It was even more obvious now that McCallum was taking Bess out. She hated being caught between the two of them, and it was shocking to see how Jessica was being affected by it. Bess had a few bad moments remembering how she'd embroidered those dates with McCallum to make everyone in the office think they had a hot relationship going.

Jessica was unfailingly polite, but she treated Bess like a stranger now. It was painful to have the old, pleasant friendliness apparently gone for good. Jessica never looked into her eyes. She treated her like a piece of furniture, and it really hurt. Bess couldn't even blame her. She asked for permission to go out with McCallum, but she'd known even when Jessica gave it that the other woman cared deeply about him. She was ashamed of herself for putting her own infatuation with McCallum over Jessica's feelings. Not that it had done her any good. McCallum was fine company, and once he'd kissed her with absent affection, but he couldn't have made it more obvious that he enjoyed being with her only in a casual way. On the other hand, when he looked at Jessica there was real pain in his eyes.

"Can't I bring you back something?" Bess asked abruptly. "Jessica, you look so—"

"I'm fine," Jessica said shortly. "I have a virus and I've lost my appetite, that's all. Please go ahead."

Bess grimaced as she closed the door, and the concern was still on her face when she joined McCallum.

He'd seen Jessica, too, in that brief time while her office door was open. He'd wanted to show her that he didn't care, that he could date other women with complete indifference to her feelings. But it was backfiring on him. He felt sick as he realized how humiliated she must be, to have him dating one of her own coworkers. It wasn't her fault that she couldn't bear a child, after all, and she was right—he'd never acted as if he had any kind of permanent relationship in mind for the two of them. He was still trying to find reasons to keep her at arm's length, he admitted finally. He was afraid to trust her, afraid of being hurt if he gave his heart completely. He'd believed Sam Jackson because he'd wanted to. But now, as he thought about it rationally, he wondered at his own gullibility. Was he really so desperate to have Jessica out of his life that he'd believe a total stranger, a biased total stranger, before he'd even ask Jessica for her version of what had happened?

Sam Jackson had been having lunch in the café, too,

and stopped by McCallum's table to exchange pleas-
antries with him and Bess. Sheriff Hensley drove by
in the patrol car and saw them in the window. Later
that afternoon, he invited McCallum into his office and
closed the door.

"I heard Sam Jackson's been in town six days," he
said quietly. "What's his business here?"

"He's just passing through," McCallum said.

"And...?"

McCallum was puzzled. It wasn't like his boss to be
so interested in strangers who visited town. "And he's
just passing the time of day as well, I guess."

Hensley folded his hands together on his desk
and toyed with a paper clip. "He's the sort who holds
grudges." He looked up. "I've heard some talk I don't
like. It was a closed trial, but a lot of gossip got out anyway. Fred's wife and daughter left town as soon as the
verdict was read, but Jessica had nowhere to go except
here. Fred, of course, gave her a rough time of it."

"Maybe he had reason to," McCallum ventured
curtly.

Hensley put the paper clip down deliberately. "You
listen to me," he said coldly. "Jessica did nothing except
try to help his wife and child. Fred was a cocaine addict.
He liked to bring his friends home at night while his
wife was working at the hospital. One night he was so
high that he beat his daughter and she ran away. It was
Jessica who took her in and comforted her. It was Jessica
who made her mother face the fact that she was married to an addict and that she had to get help for them.
Jessica was told—probably by your buddy Sam—that
Fred had forced Clarisse, his daughter, to go back home

with him. That's why she went out there that day. He at-tacked Jessica instead, and she barely got away in time."

McCallum didn't say a word. His complexion paled, just a little.

"For her pains, because the court trial was in the judge's chambers, and not publicized for Clarisse's sake, Jessica took the brunt of the gossip. All anyone heard was that Jessica had almost gotten raped. It was the talk of the town. Everywhere she went, thanks to Sam Jackson, she was pointed out and ridiculed as the girl who'd led poor Fred on and then yelled rape. She took it, for Clarisse's sake, until her mother could get another job and they could leave town while Fred was safely in jail."

"He didn't tell me that," McCallum said dully.

"Sam Jackson hated Jessica. He was on the city coun-cil. He had influence and he used it. But time passed and Sam left town. It didn't end there, however. Fred got out of jail in six months and came after Jessica. He was killed in a wreck, all right," the sheriff stated. "He was out for vengeance the day he was paroled and was chasing Jessica in his car, high as a March kite, until he ran off a cliff in the process. He would have killed her if he hadn't."

McCallum felt cold chills down his spine. He could picture the scene all too easily.

"Jessica survived," Hensley continued curtly, and McCallum barely registered the odd phrasing. "She held her head up, and those of us who knew the truth couldn't have admired her more. She's suffered enough. I didn't realize Sam Jackson was even in town until I happened to see him this morning, but he won't be here any longer. I'm going to give him a personal escort to the county line right now." He stood up, grabbing his hat. "And for what it's worth, I think you're petty to start dating Bess right under Jessica's nose, on top of everything else. She doesn't deserve that."

McCallum got to his feet, too. "I'd like a word with Jackson before you boot him out of town."

Hensley recognized the deputy's expression too well to agree to what McCallum was really suggesting.

"You believed him without questioning what he said," Hensley reminded him. "If there's fault, it's as much yours as his. You aren't to go near him."

McCallum's thin lips pressed together angrily. "He had no business coming here to spread more lies about her."

"You had no business listening to them," came the merciless reply. "Learn from the experience. There are always two sides to every story. You've got enough work to do. Why don't you go out there and act like a deputy sheriff?"

McCallum reached for his own hat. "I don't feel much like one right now," he said. "I've been a fool."

"Hard times teach hard lessons, but they stay with us. Jessica isn't judgmental, even if you are."

McCallum didn't say another word, but he had his reservations. He'd hurt her too much. He knew before he even asked that she might forgive him, but that she'd never forget the things he'd said to her.

Chapter 9

Sam Jackson left town with the sheriff's car following him every inch of the way to the county line. He'd had to do some fast talking just to keep an irritated Hensley from arresting him for vagrancy. But his bitter hatred of Jessica hadn't abated, and he hoped he'd done her some damage. His poor brother, he told himself, had deserved some sort of revenge. Perhaps now he could rest in peace.

McCallum didn't go near Jessica's office, for fear that Bess might make another play for him and complicate things all over again. He did go to Jessica's house the next afternoon, hat in hand, to apologize.

She met him at the door in a pair of worn jeans and a T-shirt, her hair in a ponytail and her glasses perched on her nose. It was a beautiful day, and the Montana air sparkled. The world was in bloom, and the Whitehorn area had never been more beautiful under the wide blue sky.

"Yes?" Jessica asked politely, as if he were a stranger.

He felt uncomfortable. He wasn't used to making apologies. "I suppose you know why I'm here," he said stiffly.

She stripped off her gardening gloves. "It's about Keith, I guess," she replied matter-of-factly, without any attempt at dissembling.

He frowned. "No. We persuaded the authorities to keep Keith for a few days at the juvenile hall while we did some investigating. I haven't come about that."

"Oh." Her eyes held no expression at all. "Then what do you want?"

He propped one foot on the lowest step and stared at the spotless shine of his black boot. "I came to apologize."

"I can't imagine why."

He looked up in time to catch the bitterness that touched her face just for an instant. "What?"

"I'm a liar and a temptress and a murderess, according to Sam Jackson," she said heavily. "From what everyone says, you were hanging on to every word he said. So why should you want to apologize to me?"

He drew in a breath and shifted his hat from one hand to the other. "Hensley told me all of it."

"And that's why you're here." She sounded weary, resigned. "I might have known it wasn't because you came to your senses," she said without inflection in her voice. "You preferred Sam Jackson's version of the truth, even after I reminded you that he was biased."

"You told me a half-truth from the beginning!"

"Don't you raise your voice to me!" she said angrily,

punching her glasses up onto her nose when they started to slip down. "I didn't want to remember it, can't you understand? I hate having to remember. Clarisse was the real victim, a lot more than I was. I just happened to be stupid enough to go out there alone, trying to protect her. And believe me, it wasn't to tempt Fred! The only thing I was thinking about was how to spare Clarisse any more anguish!"

"I know that now." He groaned silently. "Why didn't you tell me?"

"Why should you have expected me to?" she replied, puzzled. "I don't know very much about you, except that your mother drank and was cruel to you and that you had a very nasty time of it in foster care."

He hesitated, searching her eyes.

"You've told me very little about yourself," she said. "I only know bits and pieces, mostly what I've heard from other people. But you expected me to tell you things I haven't told anyone my whole life. Why should you expect something from me that you're not willing to give in return?"

That gave him food for thought. He ran a hand through his hair. "I don't suppose I should have."

"And it's all past history now," she added. "You're dating Bess. I don't trespass on other women's territory. Not ever. Bess even asked if I had anything going with you before she invited you to supper. I told her no," she added firmly.

There was a sudden faint flush high on his cheekbones, because he remembered telling Bess the same thing. But it wasn't true, then or now. "Listen—" he began.

"No, you listen. I appreciate the meals we had together and the help you gave me on cases. I hope we can work together amicably in the future. But as you have reason to know, I have nothing to offer a man on any permanent basis."

He moved closer, his eyes narrowed with concern. "Being barren isn't the end of the world," he said quietly.

She moved back and folded her arms over her chest, stopping him where he stood. "You thought so. You even said so," she reminded him.

His teeth ground together. "I was half out of my mind! It upset me that you could keep something so important to yourself. That was why I got uptight. It isn't that I couldn't learn to live with it...."

"But you don't have to. Nobody has to live with it except me," she said quietly. "I'm sure that Bess has no such drawbacks, and she has the advantage of being completely without inhibitions. She's sweet and young, and she adores you," she said through tight lips. "You're a very lucky man."

"Lucky," he echoed with growing bitterness.

"Now, if you'll excuse me," she said with a bright smile, pulling her gloves back on, "I have to finish weeding my garden. Thanks for stopping by."

"Just like that?" he burst out angrily. "I hadn't finished."

She brushed dirt off the palm of one glove. "What is there left to say?" she asked with calm curiosity.

He studied her impassive face. She had her emotions under impeccable control, but beneath the surface, he perceived pain and a deep wounding that wasn't likely to be assuaged by any apology, however well meant. He was going to have to win back her trust and respect. That wasn't going to happen overnight. And he didn't expect her to make it easy for him.

He rammed his hat back onto his head. "Nothing, I guess," he agreed, nodding. "I said it all, one way or another, when I jumped down your throat without knowing the truth."

"Sam can be very convincing," she replied. She averted her face. "He turned the whole town against me for a while. You can't imagine how vicious the gossip was," she added involuntarily. "I still hate being talked about."

Jessica didn't add that he'd helped gossip along by dating Bess, so that his rejection of her was made public. But he knew that already. It must have added insult to injury to have his new romantic interest and Sam's renewed accusations being discussed at every lunch counter in town. He understood now, as he hadn't before, why she'd worried so much about being seen in public with him.

"How about Jennifer?" she added suddenly, interrupting his gloomy thoughts. "Any news on her parents?"

"No luck yet," he replied. "But I think I may be on to something with Keith."

"I hope so," she said. "I feel terrible that I didn't suspect something before this."

"None of us is perfect, Jessica," he said, his voice deep and slow and full of regret. His dark eyes searched hers in silence, until she averted her own to ward off the flash of electricity that persisted between the two of them. "I'll let you know what I find out."

She nodded, but didn't reply. She just walked away from him.

He talked to a school official about Keith, and discovered that the boy had been an excellent student until about the time his father lost his job.

"He was never a problem," the counselor told him. "But he let slip something once about his father liking liquor a little too much when he was upset. Things seemed to go badly for Terrance after his wife left, you know. Losing his job must be the last straw."

"I'm sure it's unpleasant for him to have to depend on public assistance," McCallum agreed. "But taking it out on his child isn't the answer."

"People drink and lose control," the counselor said. "More and more of them, in these pressured economic times. They're usually sorry, too late. I'll try to talk to Keith again, if you like. But I can't promise anything. He's very loyal to his father."

"Most kids are," McCallum said curtly. He was remembering how he'd protected his brutal mother, right up until the night she'd broken his arm with the bottle. He'd made excuse after excuse for her behavior, just as Keith was probably doing now.

He contacted the juvenile officer and had a long conversation with him, but the man couldn't tell him any more than he already knew. Keith hadn't reached the end of his rope yet, and until he did, there was little anyone could do for him.

McCallum did get a break, a small one, in the abandoned-baby case. It seemed that a local midwife did remember hearing an old woman from out of town talk about delivering a child in a clandestine manner for a frightened young woman. It wasn't much to go on, but anything would help.

McCallum decided that it might be a good idea to share that tidbit with Jessica. He dreaded having to see Bess again, after the way he'd led her on.

But it turned out not to be the ordeal he'd expected.

Bess was just coming back from the small kitchen with a cup of coffee when he walked into the office. She moved closer and grinned at him.

"Hi, stranger!" she said with a friendly smile. "How about some coffee?"

"Not just now, thanks." He smiled ruefully. "Bess, there's something I need to tell you."

"No, there isn't," she said with a sigh. "I'd already figured it all out, you know. I never meant to step on Jessica's toes, but I had a major crush on you that I had to get out of my system." She gave him a sheepish glance. "I didn't realize how painful it was going to be, trying to work here after I'd all but stabbed Jessica in the back. No one in the office will speak to me, and Jessica's very polite, but she isn't friendly like she used to be. Nothing is the same anymore."

"I'm sorry about that," he said, knowing it was as much his fault as hers.

She shrugged and moved a little closer. "Still friends?" she asked hesitantly.

"Of course," he replied gently. He bent and kissed her lightly on the cheek.

Jessica, who'd come into the outer office to ask Bess to make a phone call for her, got an eyeful of what looked like a tender scene and froze in place.

"Jessica," McCallum said roughly as he lifted his head and saw her.

Bess turned in time to watch her boss disappear back into her own office, her back straight and dignified.

"Well, that was probably the last straw," Bess groaned. "I was going to talk to her today and apologize."

"So was I," he replied. "She didn't deserve to be hurt any more, after what Sam Jackson did to her."

"I hope it's not too late to undo the damage," Bess added. Then she realized how false a picture she'd given everyone about her dates with McCallum, and she felt even worse. She'd embroidered them to make herself look like a femme fatale, because McCallum hadn't been at all loverlike. But her wild stories had backfired in the worst way. In admitting that she'd lied, she'd make herself look like a conceited idiot. Jessica was cool enough to her already. She hated the thought of compounding the problem with confessions of guilt.

"There's nothing to undo," McCallum replied innocently. "I did enjoy your cooking," he added gently.

"I'm glad." She hesitated nervously. She might as well tell him how she'd blown up their friendship, while there was still time. "McCallum, there's just one little thing—"

"Later," he said, patting her absently on the shoulder. "I've got to talk to Jessica about a case."

"Okay." She was glad of the reprieve. Not that she didn't still have to confess her half-truths to Jessica.

He knocked briefly on Jessica's door and walked in. She looked up from her paperwork. Nothing of her inner torment showed on her unlined face, and she even smiled pleasantly at him.

"Come in, Deputy," she invited. "What can I do for you?"

He closed the door and sat down across from her. "You can tell me that I haven't ruined everything between us," he said bluntly.

She looked at him with studied curiosity. "We're still friends," she assured him. "I don't hold grudges."

His jaw clenched. "You know that wasn't what I meant."

She put down the file she'd been reading and crossed her hands on it. "What can I do for you?" she asked pleasantly.

Her bland expression told him that he couldn't force his way back into her life. He couldn't make her want him, as she might have before things went wrong between them. She was going to draw back into her shell for protection, and it would take dynamite to get her out of it this time. He doubted if he could even get her to go out for a meal with him ever again, because she wouldn't want gossip about them to start up a second time. He'd never felt so helpless. Trust, once sacrificed, was hard to regain.

"What about Keith?" she asked. "I presume that's why you came?"

"Yes," he confirmed untruthfully. He sat back in the chair and told her about the talk he'd had with the school counselor. "But there's nothing we can do until I have some concrete reason to bring his father in for questioning. And Keith is holding out. The juvenile authorities can't dig anything out of him." He crossed his long legs. "On the other hand, we may have a break in the Baby Jennifer case."

She started. It wasn't pleasant to hear him say that. She'd become so involved with the tiny infant that a part of her hoped the mother would never be found. She was shocked at her own wild thoughts.

"Have you?" she asked numbly.

"A midwife knows of an old woman who helped a frightened young woman give birth. I'm trying to track her down. It may be our first real lead to the mother."

"And if you find her, then what?" she asked intently. "She deserted her own little baby. What sort of mother would do that? Surely to God the courts won't want to give the child back to her!"

He'd never seen Jessica so visibly upset. He knew she'd allowed herself to become attached to the infant, but he hadn't realized to what extent until now.

"I'm sure it won't come to that," he said slowly. "Jessica, you aren't having any ideas about taking the baby yourself?" he added abruptly.

She glared at him. "What if I do? What can a court-appointed guardian do that I can't? I can manage free time to devote to a child, I make a good salary—"

"You can't offer her a settled, secure home with two parents," he said curtly. "This isn't the big city. Here in Whitehorn the judge will give prior consideration to a married couple, not a single parent."

"That's unfair!"

"I'm not arguing with that," he said. "I'm just telling you what to expect. You know the judges around here as well as I do—probably better, because you have more dealings with them. Most of them have pretty fixed ideas about family life."

"The world is changing."

"Not here, it isn't," he reminded her. "Here we're in a time capsule and nothing very much changes."

She started to argue again and stopped on a held breath. He was right. She might not like it, but she had to accept it. A single woman wasn't going to get custody of an abandoned baby in Whitehorn, Montana, no matter how great a character she had.

She faced the loss of little Jennifer with quiet desperation. Fate was unfair, she was thinking. Her whole life seemed to be one tragedy after another. She put her head in her hands and sighed wearily.

"She'll be better off in a settled home," he mumbled. He hated seeing her suffer. "You know she will."

She sat up again after a minute, resignation in her demeanor. "Well, I won't stop seeing her until they place her," she said doggedly.

"No one's asked you to."

She glared at him. "She wouldn't get to you, would she, Deputy?" she asked with bitter anger. "You can walk away from anyone and never look back. No one touches you."

"You did," he said gruffly.

"Oh, I'm sure Bess got a lot further than I did," she said, her jealousy rising to the surface. "After all, she doesn't have any hang-ups and she thinks you're God's gift to women."

"You don't understand."

"I understand everything," she said bluntly. "You wanted to make sure that no one in town connected you with the object of so much scandal. Didn't you tell me once that you hated gossip because people talked about you so much when you were a boy? That's really why you started taking Bess out, isn't it? The fact that she was infatuated with you was just a bonus."

He scowled. "That wasn't why—"

She stood up, looking totally unapproachable. "Everyone knows now that Bess is your girlfriend. You're safe, McCallum," she added proudly. "No one is going to pair you off with me ever again. So let well enough alone, please."

He stood up, too, feeling frustrated and half-mad with restrained anger. "I'd been lied to one time too many," he said harshly. "Trust comes hard to me."

"It does to me, too," she replied in a restrained tone.

"You betrayed mine by turning your back on me the first chance you got. You believed Sam instead of me. You wouldn't even come to me for an explanation."

His face tautened to steel. He had no defense. There simply was none.

"You needn't look so torn, McCallum. It doesn't matter anyway. We both know it was a flash in the pan and nothing more. You can't trust women and I'm not casual enough for affairs. Neither of us would have considered marriage. What was left?"

His dark eyes swept over her with quiet appreciation of her slender, graceful body. "I might have shown you, if you'd given me half a chance."

She lifted her chin. "I told you, I'm not the type for casual affairs."

"It wouldn't have been casual, or an affair," he returned. "I'm not a loner by choice. I'm by myself because I never found a woman I liked. Wanted, sure. But there has to be more to a relationship than a few nights in bed. I felt…more than desire for you."

"But not enough," she said, almost choking on the words. "Not nearly enough to make up for what I…am."

His face contracted. "For God's sake, you're a woman! Being barren doesn't change anything!"

She turned away. The pain was almost physical. "Please go," she said in a choked tone. She sat back down behind her desk with the air of an exhausted runner. She looked older, totally drained. "Please, just go."

He rammed his hands into his pockets and glared at her. "You won't give an inch. How do you expect to go through life in that sewn-up mental state? I made a mistake, okay? I'm not perfect. I don't walk around with a halo above my head. Why can't you forget?"

Her eyes were vulnerable for just an instant. "Because it hurt so much to have you turn away from me," she confessed huskily. "I'm not going to let you hurt me again."

His firm lips parted. "Jessica, we learn from our mistakes. That's what life is all about."

"Mistakes are what *my* life is all about," she said, laughing harshly. She rubbed her hand over her forehead. "And there are still things you don't know. I was a fool, McCallum, and it was your fault because you wouldn't take no for an answer. Why did you have to interfere? I was happy alone, I was resigned to it...."

"Why did you keep trying to take care of me?" he shot back.

She had to admit she'd gone out of her way in that respect. She glanced up and then quickly back down to her desk. "Temporary insanity," she pleaded. "You had no one, and neither did I. I wanted to be your friend."

"Friends forgive each other."

She gnawed her lower lip. She couldn't tell him that it was far more than friendship she'd wanted from him. But she had secrets, still, that she could never share with him. She couldn't tell him the rest, even now. His fling with Bess had spared her the fatal weakness of giving in to him, of yielding to a hopeless affair. If it had gone that far, she corrected. Because it was highly doubtful that it would have.

"What are you keeping back?" he asked. "What other dark skeletons are hiding in your closet?"

She pushed her hair back from her wan face. "None that you need to know about, McCallum," she said, leaning back. She forced a smile. "Why don't you take Bess to lunch?"

"Bess and I are friends," he said. "That's all. And I've caused enough trouble around here. I understand that you're barely speaking to her. That's my fault, not hers."

She glared at him. "Bess is a professional who reports to me, and how I treat her is my business."

"I know that," he replied. "But she's feeling guilty enough. So am I."

Her eyebrows lifted. "About what?"

"Neither of us made your life any easier," he said. "I didn't know what happened to you. But even if you'd been all that Sam Jackson accused you of being, I had no right to subject you to even more gossip. Bess knows why I took her out. I could have caused her as much pain as I caused you. I have to live with that, too. Fortunately, she was no more serious than I was."

"That isn't what she told us," Jessica said through her teeth.

He stared at her with dawning horror. What stories had Bess told to produce such antagonism from Jessica, to make her look so outraged?

He scowled. "Jessica, nothing happened. We had a few meals together and I kissed her, once. That's all."

"It's gentlemanly of you to defend her," she said, stone faced. "But I'm not a child. You don't have to lie to protect her."

"I'm not lying!"

She pulled the file open and spread out the papers in it. "I'd like to know what you find out about that midwife," she said. "And about Keith, if the juvenile authorities get any results."

He stared at her for a long moment. "Tit for tat, Jessica?" he asked quietly. "I wouldn't believe you, so now you won't believe me?"

She met his eyes evenly. "That has nothing to do with it. I think you're being gallant, for Bess's sake," she replied. "It's kind of you, but unnecessary. Nothing you do with Bess or anyone else is my business."

He wouldn't have touched that line with a gloved hand. He stared at her for a long moment, searching for the right words. But he couldn't find any that would fit the situation.

He found plenty, however, when he closed Jessica's door and stood over Bess, who'd been waiting for him to finish.

"What did you tell her?" he asked bluntly.

She grimaced. "I embroidered it a little, to save face," she protested. "I thought we were going to be a hot item and it hurt my feelings that you didn't even want to kiss me. I'm sorry! I didn't know how hard Jessica was going to take it, or I'd never have made up those terrible lies about us."

He grimaced. "How terrible?"

She flushed. She couldn't, she just couldn't, admit that! "I'll tell her the truth," she promised. "I'll tell her all of it, honest I will. Please don't be mad."

"Mad." He shook his head, walking toward the door. "I must be mad," he said to himself, "to have painted myself into this sort of corner. Or maybe I just have a talent for creating my own selfdestruction."

He kept walking.

Chapter 10

The last words McCallum spoke to Bess might have been prophetic. He was thinking about Jessica when he shouldn't have been, and he walked into a convenience store outside town not noticing the ominous silence in the place and the frightened look on the young female clerk's face.

It seemed to happen in slow motion. A man in a faded denim jacket turned with a revolver in his hand. As McCallum reached for his own gun, the man fired. There was an impact, as if he'd been hit with a fist on his upper arm. It spun him backwards. A fraction of a second later, he heard the loud pop, like a firecracker going off. In that one long minute while he tried to react, the perpetrator forgot his quarry—Tammie Jane, the terrified young clerk—and ran out the door like a wild man.

"You've been shot! Oh, my goodness, what shall I do?" Tammie Jane burst out. She ran to McCallum, her own danger forgotten in her concern for him.

"It's not so bad," he said, gritting his teeth as he pulled out a handkerchief to stem the surging, rhythmic flow of blood. "Nothing broken, at least, but it looks as if the bullet may have…clipped an artery." He wound the handkerchief tighter and put pressure over the wound despite the pain it caused. "Are you all right?"

"Sure! He came in and asked for some cigarettes, and when I turned to get them, he pulled out that gun. Gosh, I was scared! He'd just told me to empty the cash register when you walked in."

"I walked in on it like a raw recruit," he added ruefully. "My God, I don't know where my mind was. I didn't even get off a shot."

"You're losing a lot of blood. I'd better call for an ambulance—"

"No need. I'll call the dispatcher on my radio." He made his way out to his patrol car, weaving a little. He was losing blood at a rapid rate and his head was spinning. He raised the dispatcher, gave his location and succinctly outlined the situation, adding a terse description of the suspect and asking for an all-points bulletin.

"Stay put. We'll send the ambulance," the dispatcher said, and signed off. The radio blared with sudden activity as she first called an ambulance and then broadcast a BOLO—a "be on the lookout for" bulletin—on the municipal frequency.

The clerk came out of the store with a hand towel and passed it to McCallum. His handkerchief was already soaked.

"I don't know how to make a tourniquet, but I'll try if you'll tell me how," Tammie Jane volunteered worriedly. Blood from his wound was pooling on the pavement, as McCallum was holding his arm outside the car.

He leaned back against the seat, his hand still pressing hard on the wound. "Thanks, but the ambulance will be here any minute. I can hear the siren."

It was fortunate that Whitehorn was a small town. Barely two minutes later, the ambulance sped up and two paramedics got out, assessed the situation and efficiently loaded a dazed McCallum onto a stretcher and into the ambulance.

He was still conscious when they got to the hospital, but weak from loss of blood. They had him stabilized and the blood flow stemmed before they pulled up at the emergency-room entrance.

He grinned sheepishly as they unloaded him and rolled him into the hospital. "Hell of a thing to happen to a law-enforcement officer. I got caught with my eyes closed, I guess."

"Thank your lucky stars he was a bad shot," one of them said with an answering smile. "That's only a flesh wound, but it hit an artery. You'd have bled to death if you'd taken your time about calling us."

"I'm beginning to believe it."

They wheeled him into a cubicle and called for the resident physician who was covering the emergency room.

Jessica had had a long morning, and her calendar was full of return calls to make. McCallum had shaken her pretty badly about Baby Jennifer. She hadn't been facing facts at all while she was spinning cozy daydreams about herself and the baby together in her cozy cottage.

Now she was looking into a cold, lonely future with nothing except old age at the end of it. From the bright, flaming promise of her good times with McCallum, all that was left were ashes.

She took off her glasses and rubbed her tired eyes. She'd just about given up wearing the contact lenses now that she wasn't seeing McCallum anymore. She didn't care how she looked, except in a business sense. She dressed for the job, but there was no reason to dress up for a man now. She couldn't remember ever in her life feeling so low, and there had been plenty of heartaches before this one. It seemed as if nothing would go right for her.

The telephone in the outer office rang noisily, but Jessica paid it very little attention. She was halfheartedly going through her calendar when Bess suddenly opened Jessica's office door and came in, pale and unsettled.

"Sterling McCallum's been shot," she blurted out, and was immediately sorry when she saw the impact the words had on Jessica, who stumbled to her feet, aghast.

"Shot?" she echoed helplessly. "McCallum? Is he all right?"

"That was Sandy. She's a friend of mine who works at the hospital. She just went on duty. She said he was in the recovery room when she got to the hospital. Apparently it happened a couple of hours ago. Goodness, wouldn't you think *someone* would have called us before now? Or that it would have been on the radio? Oh, what am I saying? We don't even listen to the local station."

"Does Sandy know how bad he is?" Jessica asked, shaken.

"She didn't take time to find out. She called me first." She didn't add that it was because Sandy thought, like most people did, that McCallum and Bess were a couple. "All she knew was that he'd been shot and had just come out of emergency surgery."

"Cancel my afternoon appointments," Jessica said as she gathered up her purse. "I'll finish this paperwork when I get back, but I don't know when that will be."

"Do you want me to drive you?" Bess offered.

Jessica was fumbling in her purse for the keys to her truck. "No. I can drive myself."

Bess got in front of her in time to prevent her from rushing out the door. "I lied about Sterling and me," she said bluntly, flushing. "It wasn't true. He didn't want anything to do with me and I was piqued, so I made up a lot of stuff. Don't blame him. He didn't even know I did it."

Jessica hesitated. She wanted to believe it, oh, so much! But did she dare?

"Honest," Bess said, and her eyes met Jessica's evenly, with no trace of subterfuge. "Nothing happened."

"Thanks," Jessica said, and forced a smile. Then she was out the door, running. If he died... But she wouldn't think about that. She had to remember that to stay calm, and that they hadn't said he was in critical condition. She had to believe that he would be all right.

It seemed to take forever to get to the hospital, and when she did, she couldn't find a parking space. She had to drive around, wasting precious time, until someone left the small parking area reserved for visitors. There had been a flu outbreak and the hospital was unusually crowded.

She ran, breathless, into the emergency room. She paused at the desk to ask the clerk where McCallum was.

"Deputy McCallum is in the recovery room three doors down," the clerk told her. "Wait, you can't go in there…!"

Jessica got past a nurse who tried to stop her and pushed into the room, stopping at the sight of a pale, drawn McCallum lying flat on his back, his chest bare and a thick bandage wrapped around his upper arm. There were tubes leading to both forearms, blood being pumped through one and some sort of clear liquid through the other.

The medical team looked up, surprised at Jessica's sudden entrance and white face.

"Are you a relative?" one of them—probably the doctor—asked.

"No," McCallum said drowsily.

"Yes," Jessica said, at the same time.

The man blinked.

"He hasn't got anyone else to look after him," Jessica said stubbornly, moving to McCallum's side. She put her hand over one of his on the table.

"I don't need looking after," he muttered, hating having Jessica see him in such a vulnerable position. He was groggy from the aftereffects of the anesthetic they'd given him while they removed the bullet and repaired the damage it had done.

"Well, actually, you do, for twenty-four hours at least," the doctor replied with a grin. "We're going to admit him overnight," he told Jessica. "He's lost a lot of blood and he's weak. We want to pump some antibiotics into him, too, to prevent infection in that wound. He's going to have a sore arm and some fever for a few days."

"And he can't work, right?" she prompted.

McCallum muttered something.

"Right," the doctor agreed.

"I'll stay with him tonight in case he needs anything," Jessica volunteered.

McCallum turned his head and looked up at her with narrow, drowsy dark eyes. "Sackcloth and ashes, is it?" he asked in a rough approximation of his usual forceful tones.

"I'm not doing penance," she countered. "I'm helping out a friend."

For the first time, his eyes focused enough to allow him to see her face clearly. She was shaken, and there was genuine fear in her eyes when she looked at him. Probably someone had mentioned the shooting without telling her that it was relatively minor. She looked as if she'd expected to find him dead or shot to pieces.

"I'm all right," he told her. "I've been shot before, and worse than this. It's nothing."

"Nothing!" she scoffed.

"A little bitty flesh wound," he agreed.

"Torn ligament, severed artery that we had to sew up, extensive loss of blood…" the doctor was saying.

"Compared to the last time I was shot, it's nothing," McCallum insisted drowsily. "God, what did you give me? I can't keep my eyes open."

"No need to," the doctor agreed, patting him gently on his good shoulder. "You rest now, Deputy. You'll sleep for a while and then you'll have the great-grandfather of a painful arm. But we can give you something to counteract that."

"Don't need any more…painkillers." He yawned and his eyes closed. "Go home, Jessica. I don't need you, either."

"Yes, you do," she said stubbornly. She looked around her, realizing how crazy she'd been to push her way in. She flushed. "Sorry about this," she said, backing toward the door. "I didn't know how badly he was hurt. I was afraid it was a lot worse than this."

"It's all right," the doctor said gently. He smiled. "We'll take him to his room and you can sit with him there, if you like. He'll be fine."

She nodded gratefully, clutching her purse like a life jacket. She slipped out of the room and went to sit down heavily in a chair in the waiting room. Her heart was still racing and she felt sick. Just that quickly, McCallum could have been dead. She'd forgotten how uncertain life was, how risky his job was. Now she was face-to-face with her own insecurities and she was handling them badly.

When they wheeled him to a semiprivate room, she went along. The other half of the room was temporarily empty, so she wouldn't have to contend with another patient and a roomful of visitors. That was a relief.

She noticed that there was a telephone, and when McCallum had been settled properly and the medical team had left, she dialed her office and told Candy his condition and that she wouldn't be back, before asking to be transferred to Bess.

"Can I bring you anything?" Bess offered.

"No, thank you. I'm fine." She didn't want Bess here. She wanted McCallum all to herself, with no intrusions.

It was selfish, but she'd had a bad fright. She wanted time to reassure herself that he was all right, that he wasn't going to die.

"Then call us if you need us," Bess said. "I talked to Sandy again and told her the truth, so she won't, well, say anything to you about me and Sterling McCallum. I'm glad he's going to be okay, Jessica."

"So am I," she agreed. She hung up and pulled a chair near the bed. She'd noticed a strange look from one of the nurses earlier. That had probably been Bess's friend.

McCallum was sleeping now, his expression clear of its usual scowl. He looked younger, vulnerable. She grimaced as she looked at his poor arm and thought how painful it must have been. She didn't even know if they'd caught the man who'd shot him. Presumably they were combing the area for him.

A few minutes later, Sheriff Hensley and one of the other deputies stopped by the room to see him. Hensley had gone by McCallum's house to feed Mack and get McCallum a change of clothing. The shirt he'd been wearing earlier was torn and covered in blood. McCallum was still sleeping off the anesthesia.

"Have you caught the man who did it?" Jessica asked.

Hensley shook his head irritably. "Not yet. But we will," he said gruffly. "I wouldn't have had this happen for the world. McCallum's a good man. On the salary the job pays, we don't get a lot of men of his caliber."

Jessica had never questioned a man of McCallum's education and background working in such a notoriously low-paying job. "I wonder why he does a lot of things," she mused, watching the still, quiet face of the unconscious man. "He's very secretive."

"So are you."

She grimaced. "Well, everyone's entitled to a skeleton or two," she reminded him.

He shrugged. "Plenty of us have them. Tell him I fed his dog, and brought those things by for him. I'll be back tomorrow. Are they going to try to keep him overnight?"

"Yes," she said definitely. "I'll stay with him. He won't leave unless he knocks me out."

"Harris here can stay with you if you think you'll need him," Hensley said with a rare smile.

Jessica glanced at the pleasant young deputy. "Thanks, but the doctor has this big hypodermic syringe...."

"Good point." Hensley took another look at McCallum, who was sleeping peacefully. "Tell him we're on the trail of his assailant. We're pretty sure who it is, from the description. We're watching the suspect's grandmother's house. It's the one place he's sure to run when he thinks it's safe."

Jessica nodded. "That's one advantage of small towns, isn't it?" she mused. "At least we generally know who the scoundrels are and where to find them."

"It makes police work a little easier. The police are helping us. McCallum's well liked."

"Yes." She looked up. "Thanks for getting Sam Jackson off my back."

He smiled. "Neighbors help each other. Maybe you'll do me a favor one day."

"You just ask."

"Well, a loaf of that homemade raisin bread wouldn't exactly insult me," he volunteered.

"When I get McCallum out of here, raisin bread will be my first priority," she promised him.

The way she worded it amused him, but it shocked her that she should feel proprietorial about McCallum, who'd given her no rights over him at all. She'd simply walked in and taken charge, and he wasn't going to like it. But she knew what he'd do if she left—go home this very night and back to work in the morning. He didn't believe in mollycoddling himself. No, she couldn't leave. She had to keep him here overnight and then make sure that he rested as the doctor had told him to. But how was she going to accomplish that?

She was still worrying about the problem when he woke up, after dark, and winced when he tried to stretch. They had a hospital gown on him, and the touch of the soft cotton fabric seemed to irritate him. He tried to pull it off.

Jessica got up and restrained his hand. They still had tubes in him, the steady drips going at a lazy speed.

"No, you mustn't," she said gently, bending over him.

His eyes opened. He stared at her and then looked around and frowned. "I'm still here?"

She nodded. "They want you to stay until tomorrow. You're very weak and they haven't finished the transfusion."

He let out a long, drowsy breath. "I feel terrible. What have they done to me?"

"They stitched you up, I think," she said. "Then they gave you something to make you rest."

He looked up at her again, puzzled. "What are you doing here? It's dark."

"I'm staying tonight, too," she said flatly. Her eyes dared him to argue with her.

"What for?"

"In case you need anything. Especially in case you try to leave," she added. "You're staying right there, McCallum. If you make one move to get up, I'll call the nurse and she'll call the doctor, and they'll fill you so full of painkillers that you'll sleep until Sunday."

He glared at her. "Threats," he said, "will not affect me."

"These aren't threats," she replied calmly. "I asked the doctor, and he said he'd be glad to knock you out anytime I asked him to if you tried to leave."

"Damn!" He lifted both hands and glared at the needles. "How did I get into this mess?"

"You let a man shoot you," she reminded him.

"I didn't let him," he said gruffly. "I walked in without looking while he was trying to rob the store. I didn't even see the gun until the bullet hit me. A police special, no less!" he added furiously. "It was a .38. No wonder it did so much damage!"

"I'm very glad he can't shoot straight," she said.

"Yes. So am I. He was scared—that's probably why he missed any vital areas. He fired wildly." His eyes closed and his face tightened as he moved. "I hope I get five minutes alone with him when they catch him. Have you heard from Hensley?"

"He and Deputy Harris came by to see you while you were asleep. They think they know who it was. They're staking out one of his relative's houses."

"Good."

"Didn't you know the place was being robbed? Wasn't that why you went in?" she persisted.

"I went in because I wanted a cup of coffee," he said

with a rueful smile. "I don't think I'll ever want another one after this. Or if I do, I'll make it at home."

"I could ask the nurse if you can have one now," she offered.

"No, thanks. I'll manage." He hesitated. "Do they have a male nurse on this floor?"

"Yes."

"Could you ask him to step in here, please?"

She didn't have to ask why. She went out to find the nurse and sent him in. She waited until she saw him come out again before she rejoined McCallum.

"Damned tubes and poles and machines," he was muttering. He looked exhausted, lying there among the paraphernalia around the bed. He turned his head and looked at her, seeing the lines in her face, the lack of makeup, the pallor. "Go home."

"I won't," she said firmly. She sat back down in the chair beside his bed. "I'll leave the hospital when you do. Not before."

His eyebrows lifted. "Have I asked you to be responsible for me?" he asked irritably.

"Somebody has to," she told him. "You don't have anybody else."

"Hensley would sit with me if I asked him, or any of the deputies."

"But you wouldn't ask them," she replied. "And the minute I walk out the door, you'll discharge yourself and go home."

"I need to go home. What about Mack?" He groaned. "He'll have to go without his supper."

"Sheriff Hensley has already fed him. He also brought you a change of clothing."

That seemed to relax him. "Nice of him," he commented. "Who'll feed Mack tomorrow morning and let him out?"

"I guess we'll have to ask the sheriff to go again. I'd offer, but that dog doesn't like women. I don't really want to go into your house when you aren't there. He growls at me."

"Your cat growls at me. It didn't stop me from going to your house."

"Meriwether couldn't do too much damage to you. But Mack is a big dog with very sharp teeth."

His eyes searched hers. "Afraid of him?"

"I guess maybe I'm afraid of being chewed up," she said evasively.

"Okay. Hand me the phone."

She did, and helped him push the right buttons. He phoned Hensley and thanked him, then asked him about feeding Mack in the morning. Hensley already knew McCallum kept a spare key in his desk and had used it once already. He readily agreed to take care of Mack.

"That's a load off my mind," McCallum said when he finished and lay back against the pillows. He flexed his shoulder and then frowned. "Do I smell something?"

As he said that, the door opened and a nurse came in bearing two trays. "Dinnertime," she said cheerfully, arranging them on the table. "I brought one for you, too, Miss Larson," she added. "You haven't even had coffee since you've been here."

"That's so nice of you!" Jessica said. "Thank you!"

"It's our pleasure. Make sure he eats," she added to Jessica on her way out. "He'll need all the protein he can get to help replenish that lost blood."

"I'll do that," Jessica promised.

She lifted the tops off the dishes on one tray while McCallum made terrible faces.

"I hate liver," he told her. "I'm not eating it."

She didn't answer him. She cut the meat into small, bite-size pieces and proceeded to present them at his lips. He glared at her, but after a minute of stubborn resistance, opened his mouth and let her put the morsels in, one at a time.

"Outrageous, treating a grown man like this," he muttered. But she noticed that he didn't refuse to eat, as he easily could have. In fact, he didn't lodge a single protest even when she followed the liver with vegetables and, finally, vanilla pudding.

It was intimate, doing this for him. She hadn't considered her actions at all, but now she realized that they could be misconstrued by a large number of people, starting with McCallum. She was acting like a lovesick idiot. What must he have thought when she came bursting into the recovery room where he was lying, forcing her way into his life like this?

She fed him the last of the pudding and, with a worried look, moved the tray to the other table.

"Now eat your own dinner before it gets cold," he insisted. "If you're determined to stay here all night, you need something to keep you going."

"I'm not really hungry...."

"Neither was I," he said with a cutting smile. "But *I* didn't have any choice. Now do you pick up that fork, or do I climb out of this bed and pick it up for you?"

His hand went to the sheet. With a resigned sigh, she uncovered her own plate and took it, and her fork, back to her chair. She didn't like liver any more than he did, but she ate it. At least it was filling.

He watched her until she cleared her plate and finished the last drop of her coffee. "Wasn't that good?" he taunted.

"I hate liver," she muttered.

"So do I, but that didn't save me." He grinned at her. "Turnabout is fair play."

She sighed, standing to replace her plate on the tray. She hadn't touched her pudding.

"Aren't you going to eat that?" he asked.

"I like chocolate," she muttered. "I hate vanilla."

"I don't." His eyes twinkled. "Want to feed it to me?"

Her blush was caused more by the silky soft tone of his voice than by the words. She couldn't help it.

"If you like," she said hesitantly.

"Come on, then."

She got the pudding and approached the bed. But when she started to open the lid, he caught her hand and tugged until she bent forward.

"Sterling!" she protested weakly.

"Humor me," he whispered, reaching up to cup her chin in his lean hand and pull her face down. "I'm a sick man. I need pampering."

"But—"

"I want to kiss you," he whispered at her lips. "You can't imagine how much. Just a little closer, Jessie. Just another inch…"

She sighed against his hard mouth as she moved that tiny distance and let her lips cover his. He made a soft sound and, despite the tubes attached to his arm, his hand snaked behind her head to increase the pressure of his mouth. She stiffened, but it was already too late to save herself. The warm insistence of the kiss worked its way through all her doubts, fears and reservations and touched her very soul. She sighed and gave in to the need to reassure herself that he was alive. Her own mouth opened without coyness and she felt the shock that ran through him before he groaned and deepened the kiss.

The sound of a tray rattling outside the room brought her head up. He looked somber and his eyes were narrow and hot.

"Coward," he taunted.

Her lips felt swollen. She pulled gently back from him and stood up, her knees threatening to give way. He had an effect on her body that no other man ever had. There were so many reasons why she shouldn't allow this feeling between them to grow. But other than disappointment, there was no other emotion left in her at the moment. That, and a raging pleasure that turned quickly to frustration.

Chapter 11

The nurse came in to remove the dishes, and some-how Jessica managed to look calm and pleasant. But inside, her whole being was churning with sensation. She looked at Sterling and her mouth tingled in memory.

She was wondering how she was going to manage the situation, but then the doctor came in on his rounds and ordered a sedative for the patient. It was administered at once, and McCallum glowered as the nurse finished checking his vital signs and the technicians came back to get some samples they needed for the lab. It was fif-teen minutes before they left him alone with Jessica. And by then, the shot was beginning to take effect.

"Hell of a thing, the way they treat people here," he murmured as his eyelids began to droop. "I wanted to talk to you."

"You can talk tomorrow. Now go to sleep. You'll feel better in the morning."

"Think so?" he asked drowsily. "I'm not sure about that."

He shifted and a long sigh passed his lips. Only seconds later, he was dozing. Jessica settled in her chair with a new paperback she'd tucked into her purse after a brief stop at the bookstore on her way to lunch. She must have had some sort of premonition, she mused. And unlike McCallum, she didn't have to worry about her pet. Meriwether had plenty of water and cat food waiting for him, and a litter box when he needed it. He might be lonely, but he wouldn't need looking after. She opened the book.

But the book wasn't half as interesting as McCallum. She finally put it aside and sat looking at him, wishing that her life had been different, that she had something to offer such a man. He was a delight to her eyes, to her mind, her heart, her body. She couldn't have imagined anyone more perfect. He liked her, that was obvious, and he was attracted to her. But for his own sake, she had to stop things from progressing any further than liking. Her own weakness was going to be her worst enemy, especially while he was briefly vulnerable and needed her. She had to be sure that she didn't let his depleted state go to her head. Above all, she had to keep her longings under control.

Eventually, she tried to sleep. But the night was long and uncomfortable as she tried to curl up in the padded chair. In the morning, McCallum was awake before she was, and she opened her eyes to find him propped up in bed watching her.

"You don't snore," he commented with a gentle smile.

"Neither do you," she returned.

"Fortunate for us both, isn't it?"

She sat up, winced and stretched. Her hair had come down in the night and it fell around her shoulders in a thick cloud. She pushed it back from her face and re-adjusted her glasses.

"Why don't you wear your contact lenses?" he asked curiously. "And before you fly at me, I don't mean you look better with them or anything. I just wondered why you'd stopped putting them in."

She stood up. "It didn't seem worth the effort any-more," she said. "And they're not as comfortable as these." She touched the big frames with her forefinger. She smiled. "And they're a lot of trouble. Maybe I'm just lazy."

He smiled. "Not you, Jessie."

"How do you feel?"

"Sore." He moved his shoulder with a groan. "It's going to be a few days before I feel like much, I guess."

"Good! That means you won't try to go back to work!"

He glowered at her. "I didn't say that."

"But you meant it, didn't you?" she pressed with a wicked grin.

He laid his head back against the pillow. "I guess so." He studied her possessively. "Are you coming home with me?"

Her heart jumped up into her throat. "What?"

"How do you expect to keep me at home if you don't?" he asked persuasively. "Left on my own, I'm sure I'd go right back to the office."

There was a hint of cunning in his eyes, and she didn't trust the innocent expression on his face. He had something in mind, and she didn't want to explore any possibilities just now.

"You could promise not to," she offered.

"I could lie, too."

"I have a job," she protested.

"Today is Friday. Tomorrow is Saturday. What do you do that someone else can't do as well for one day?"

"Well, nothing, really," she said. She hesitated. "People might talk...."

"Who gives a damn?" he said flatly. "We've both weathered our share of gossip. To hell with it. Come home with me. I need you."

Those three words made her whole body tingle with delight. She stared at him with darkening eyes, with a faint flush on her cheekbones that betrayed how much the statement affected her.

"I need you," he repeated quietly.

"All right."

"Just like that?"

She smiled. "Just like that. But only for today," she added.

His eyebrows rose. "Why, Jessica, did you think I was inviting you to spend the night with me?"

She glowered back. "You stop that. I'm just going to take care of you."

He beamed. "What a delightful prospect."

Her jaws tightened. "You know what I mean, and it isn't that!"

"I know what I wish you meant," he teased softly.

"You're going to be a handful, aren't you?" she asked with resignation.

"I'll try not to cause you a lot of trouble." He studied her long and intently. "Besides, how difficult can it be?" He indicated his shoulder. "I'm not in any shape for what you're most concerned about. Long, intimate sessions on my sofa will have to wait until I'm properly fit again, Jessica," he added in a soft, wicked tone. "Sorry if that disappoints you."

She turned away to keep him from seeing the flush on her cheeks. "Well, if you're going to leave today, I'd better see if the doctor agrees that you can. I'll go and check at the nurses' station."

"You tell them that even if he says I can't, I'm going home," he informed her.

She didn't argue. It wouldn't really do any good.

By noon, they'd discharged him, and Jessica, after stopping by her house to change clothes and feed her cat, drove him to his house. It disturbed her a little to have her pickup truck sitting in his driveway, but there wasn't a lot she could do about it. He wasn't able to cook or clean, and there was no one else she could ask to do it—except possibly Bess, and that was out of the question.

She hesitated when he unlocked the door and Mack growled at the sight of her.

"Stop that," McCallum snapped at the dog.

Mack stopped at once, eagerly greeting his master.

McCallum petted him and motioned Jessica into the house before he dropped heavily into his favorite armchair.

"It's good to be home," he remarked.

"How about something to eat?" she asked. "You didn't stay long enough to have lunch."

"I wasn't hungry then. There's a pizza in the freezer and some bacon and eggs in the fridge."

"Any flour?"

He glared at her. "What the hell would I want with flour?"

She threw up her hands. It wasn't a question she should have asked a bachelor who liked frozen pizza.

"So much for hopes of quiche," she said half to herself as she put down her purse and walked toward the kitchen.

"Real men don't eat quiche," he called after her.

"You would if you had any flour," she muttered. "But I guess it's going to be bacon and eggs."

"We could order a pizza from the place downtown."

"I don't want pizza. And you need something healthy."

"I won't eat tofu and bean sprouts."

She was searching through the refrigerator and vegetable bins. There were three potatoes and a frozen pizza, four eggs of doubtful age, a slice of moldy bacon and a loaf of green bread.

"Don't you ever clean things out in here?" she called.

He shrugged, then winced as the movement hurt his shoulder. "When I get time," he told her.

She came back and reached for her purse. "Please don't try to go to work while I'm gone."

"Where, exactly, are you going?"

"To get some provisions," she said. "Some *edible* provisions. You couldn't feed a dedicated buzzard on what's in your kitchen."

He chuckled and reached for his wallet. He handed her a twenty-dollar bill. "All right. If you're determined, go spend that."

"I'll need to stop by my office, too."

"Whatever."

She hesitated in the doorway, indecision on her face. "If you'd rather I sent Bess over—"

"Bess was a pleasant companion," he replied. "She

was never anything more, regardless of what she might have told you."

"Okay." She went out and closed the door behind her.

She stopped by the office just long enough to delegate some chores and answer everyone's concerns about McCallum. Bess was interested, but not overly so, and she smiled reassuringly at Jessica before she told her to wish him well.

After that, Jessica went shopping. When she got back to McCallum's house, he was sprawled on the sofa in his sock feet with a can of beer in his hand, watching a movie.

"What did you buy?" he asked as she carried two plastic sacks into the kitchen.

"Everything you were out of." She handed him back two dollars and some change.

He glanced at the grocery bags. "What are you going to cook me?"

"Country-fried cubed steak, gravy, biscuits and mashed potatoes."

"Feel my pulse. I think I've just died and gone to heaven. Did I hear you right? I haven't had that since it was a special at the café last month."

"I hope it's something you like."

"'Like' doesn't begin to describe how I feel about it. Try 'overwhelmed with delight.' But to answer your question, yes, I like it."

"It's loaded with cholesterol and calories," she added, "but I can cut down on the grease."

"Not on my account." He chuckled. "I love unwholesome food."

She prepared the meal in between glimpses of the movie he was watching. It was a thriller, an old police drama set back in the thirties, and she enjoyed it as much as he did. Later, they ate in front of the television and watched a nature special about the rain forest.

"That's a good omen," he said when they'd finished and she was collecting the plates.

"What is?"

"We like the same television programs. Not to mention the same food."

"Most people like nature specials."

"One woman I dated only watched wrestling," he commented.

She stacked the plates and picked them up. "I don't want to hear about your other dates."

"Why not?" he asked calculatingly. "I thought you only wanted to be friends with me."

She stopped, searching for words. But she couldn't quite find the right ones, so she beat it back to the kitchen and busied herself washing dishes. Mack sat near her on the floor, watching her without hostility. It was the first time since she'd been in the house that he didn't growl at her.

She put away the dishcloth and cleaned up the kitchen. There was enough food left for McCallum to have for supper. She put it on a platter and covered it, so that he could heat it up later.

He'd turned off the television when she came back into the living room. He was lying full length on the sofa with his eyes closed, but he opened them when he heard her step. His dark eyes slid up and down her body, over the simple blue dress that clung to her slender body. The expression in them made her pulse race.

"I should…go home." Her voice faltered.

He didn't say a word. His hand went to his shirt and

slowly, sensually, unfastened it. He moved it aside, giving her a provocative view of his broad, hair-roughened chest.

"I have things to do," she continued. She couldn't quite drag her eyes away from those hard, bronzed muscles.

He held out his good arm, watching her in a silence that promised pleasures beyond description.

She knew the risks. She'd known them from the first time she saw him. Up until now, they'd weighed against her. But the realization of how close he'd come to death shifted the scales.

She went to him, letting him draw her down against him, so that she was stretched out beside him on the long sofa, pressed close against his hard, warm body.

"Relax," he said gently, easing her onto her back and grimacing as he moved to loom over her. "I'm not stupid enough to start something I can't finish."

"Are you sure?" she asked a little worriedly, because the minute her hips tilted into his, she felt the instant response of his body.

"Not really." He groaned and laughed softly in the same breath, shifting her away slightly. "But let's pretend that I am. I like you in this dress, Jessie. It fits in all the right places. But I don't like the way it fastens. Too damned many buttons and hooks in back.... Ah, that's better."

"McCallum!" she cried as the bodice began to slip. She made a grab for it, but his fingers intercepted the wild movement.

"What are you afraid of?" he murmured softly, smiling down at her. "It won't hurt."

She bit her lower lip. "I...can't let you look at me,"

she said, lowering her eyes to the hard throbbing of his pulse in his neck.

He frowned. "Now, or ever?" he asked with a patience he didn't feel.

"E-ever," she clarified. She pulled the bodice closer. "Let me up, please, I want to... McCallum!"

Even with a bullet wound, he was stronger and quicker than she was. The dress was suddenly around her waist, and he was looking at her body in the wispy nylon bra with its strategically placed lace. But it wasn't her breasts that had his attention.

She closed her eyes and shivered with pain. "I tried to stop you," she said harshly, biting back tears. "Now, will you let me go!"

"My God." The way he spoke was reverent. But there was no revulsion, either in the words or in his face. There was only pain, for what she must have suffered.

"Oh, please," she whispered, humiliated.

"There's no need to look like that," he said quietly. "Lie still. I'm going to take you out of this dress."

"No...!"

He caught her flailing hand and brought it to his mouth, kissing the palm gently. His dark eyes met her wild ones. "You need to be made love to," he said softly. "More than you realize. You're not hideous, Jessica. The scars aren't that bad."

She fought tears and lost. They fell, hot and profuse, pouring down her cheeks. Her hand relaxed its hold on her dress and she lay still, letting him smooth away it and her half-slip and panty hose until she lay there in only her briefs and bra.

He bent and she felt with wonder the touch of his mouth as it traced the thin white lines from her breasts down her belly to where they intersected just below her naval.

His big, lean hand held her hip while he caressed her with his mouth, his thumb edging under the lace of the briefs to touch her almost, but not quite, intimately. She caught her breath at the sensations he was teaching her and arched involuntarily toward the pleasure.

"You crazy woman," he breathed as he lifted his head and looked down into her dazed, hungry eyes. "Why didn't you tell me?"

"I thought… They're so ugly."

He only smiled. He bent and his mouth brushed lazily over hers, parting her lips, teasing, tasting. And while he held her in thrall, his hand went behind her to find the single catch. He freed it and lazily tugged the bra away from her firm, high breasts.

She didn't protest. His eyes on her gave her the purest delight she'd ever known. She gazed up at him with rapt wonder while he looked and looked until her nipples grew hard and began to ache.

Then, finally, he began to touch them, and she shivered with sensations she'd never known. Her lips parted as she tried to catch her breath.

He chuckled with appreciation and triumph. "All that time wasted," he murmured. "They're very sensitive, aren't they?" he added when she jerked at the faint brush of his fingertips. He took the hardness between his thumb and forefinger and pressed it gently, and she cried out. But it wasn't because he was hurting her. She was responsive to a shocking degree. That embarrassed her, because he was watching her like a hawk, and she tried to push his hand away.

"Shh," he whispered gently. "Don't fight it. This is

for you. But when you're a little more confident, I'm going to let you do the same thing to me and watch how it excites me. I'm just as susceptible as you are, just as hungry."

"You're...watching me," she got out.

"Oh, yes," he agreed quietly. "Can you imagine how it makes me feel, to see the pleasure my touch gives you?" His fingers contracted and she shivered. "My God, I couldn't get my head through a doorway right now, do you know that? You make me feel like ten times the man I am."

He bent and put his mouth where his fingers had been. She whimpered at first and pushed against him frantically.

He lifted his head and looked into her eyes, seeing the fear.

"Tell me," he said softly.

"He...bit me there," she managed hoarsely.

He scowled. His eyes went to her body and found the tiny scars. His expression hardened to steel as he touched them lightly.

"I won't bite you," he said deeply. "I promise you, it won't hurt. Can you trust me enough to let me put my mouth on you here?"

She searched his face. He wasn't a cruel man. She knew already that he was protective toward her. She let herself relax into the soft cushions of the sofa and her hands dropped to his shoulders, lingering there, tremulous.

"Good," he whispered. He bent again, slowly. This time it was his tongue she felt, soothing and warm, and then the whispery press of his lips moving on soft skin. The sensations were a little frightening, because they seemed to come out of nowhere and cause reactions not only in her breasts, but much lower.

His hand slid down her body and slowly trespassed under the elastic.

She should protest this, she should tell him to...stop!

He felt her nails bite into him, heard her moans grow, felt her body tauten almost to pain.

He lifted his head and stopped. Her face was gloriously flushed, her eyes shy and hungry and frustrated. She looked at him with wonder.

"Your body is capable of more pleasure than you know," he said gently. "I won't hurt you."

She arched back faintly, involuntarily asking for more, but he moved away. He wasn't touching her now. He was propped just over her, watching her face, her body.

"Why did you stop?" she whispered helplessly.

"Because it's like shooting fish in a barrel," he said simply. "You've just discovered passion for the first time in your life. I want to be sure that it's me, and not just new sensations, that are motivating you. The next step isn't so easy to pull back from, Jessie," he added solemnly. "And I don't know if I can make love completely with my shoulder in this fix."

She blinked, as if she hadn't actually realized how involved they were becoming.

His eyes dropped to her taut breasts and down her long, elegant legs before they moved back up to meet her shy gaze. He didn't smile even then. "I didn't really understand before," he said. "You were involved in the crash that killed Fred, weren't you? You were damaged internally in the wreck."

She nodded. "Fred was released because of a technicality six months after he went to prison. He blamed me for all his trouble, so he got drunk and laid in wait for me one night when I was working late. He chased me and ran me off the road. I was hurt. But he was killed." She shivered, remembering that nightmare ride. "They had to remove an ovary and one of my fallopian tubes. Even before the accident the doctors thought I'd be unlikely to get pregnant, and now... Well, it would be a long shot."

His face didn't change, his expression didn't waver. He didn't say a word.

She grimaced. "You need children, Sterling," she said in a raw whisper, her eyes mirroring the pain in the words. "A wife who loves you, and a home." Her gaze fell to his broad, bare chest and her hands itched to touch him.

"And you think that puts you out of the running?" he asked.

"Doesn't it?"

His fingers pressed down gently over her belly, and his hand was so big that it almost covered her stomach completely. "You're empty here," he said, holding her gaze. "But I'm empty here."

His hand moved to his chest, where his heart was, before it dropped back down beside her to support him. "I've never been loved," he said flatly. "I've been wanted, for various reasons. But my life has been conspicuously lacking in anyone who wanted to look after me."

"Bess did," Jessica recalled painfully.

He touched her mouth with his fingertips. "Bess is young and unsettled and looking for something that she hasn't found yet. I'm fond of her. But I never felt desire for her. It's hard to explain," he added with a humorless laugh, "but for me, desire and friendship don't usually go together."

She searched his face. "They didn't, with Bess?"

"That's right. Not with *Bess*."

He emphasized the name, looking at her with more than idle curiosity.

"With…anyone else?"

He nodded.

Obviously, she was going to have to drag it out of him, but she had to know. "With…me?" she asked, throwing caution to the winds.

"Yes," he said quietly. "With you."

She didn't know how to answer him. Her body felt hot all over at the look he was giving her. She'd never known passion until now, and it was overwhelming her. She wanted him, desired him, ached for him. She wanted to solve all the mysteries with him. The inhibitions she'd always felt before were conspicuously absent.

She felt her breasts tightening as she stared at the hair-matted expanse of his muscular chest.

"Are you surprised that you can feel desire, after all you've been through?" he asked gently.

"Yes."

"But then, strong emotions can overcome fear, can't they?" He bent, nuzzling his face against her bare breasts, savoring the softness of her skin against his. "Jessie, if my arm didn't throb like blazing hell, I'd have you right here," he breathed. "I ache all over from wanting you."

"So do I," she confessed. She slid her arms around his neck and pressed her body completely against his, shivering a little when she felt the extent of his arousal.

He felt her stiffen and his hands were gentle at her

back. "Lie still," he whispered. "It's all right. You're in no danger at all."

"I never dreamed that I could feel like this," she whispered into his throat, where her face was pressed. "That I could want like this." Her breasts moved against the thick hair that covered his chest and she moaned at the sensations she felt.

His lean hand slipped to the base of her spine and one long leg moved, so that he could draw her intimately close, letting her feel him in an embrace they'd never shared.

Her intake of breath was audible and she moaned harshly. So did he, pushing against her roughly for one long, exquisite minute until he came to his senses and rolled away from her. He got unsteadily to his feet with a rough groan.

"Good God, I'm losing it!" he growled. He made it to the window and stared out, gripping the sash. He fought to breathe, straining against the throbbing pain of his need for her.

She lay still for a minute, catching her own breath, before she sat up and quickly got back into her clothes. Her long hair fell all around her shoulders in tangles, but she couldn't find the pins he'd removed that had held it in place.

He turned finally and stared at her with his hands deep in his pockets. He was pale and his shoulder hurt.

"They're in my pocket," he told her, smiling gently at her flush. "Embarrassed, now that we've come to our senses?"

She lifted her eyes to his. "No," she said. "I don't really think I can be embarrassed with you. I—" she smiled gently "—I loved what you did to me."

Chapter 12

For a minute, he didn't seem to breathe at all. Then his eyes began to soften and a faint smile tugged at the corners of his mouth.

"In that case," he said, "we might do it again from time to time."

She smiled, too. "Yes."

He couldn't remember when he'd felt so warm and safe and happy. Just looking at Jessica produced those feelings. Touching her made him feel whole.

"I should go," she said reluctantly. "Meriwether will need his food and water changed, and I have other chores to do."

He thought about how the house was going to feel when she left, and it wasn't very pleasant. He'd been alone all his life and he was used to it. It had never bothered him before, but suddenly, it did. He frowned as he studied her, wondering at the depth of his feelings, at his need to be near her all the time. Once he would have fought that, but something had rearranged his priorities…perhaps getting shot.

"Okay," he said after a minute. "Let me feed Mack and we'll go."

Her heart flew up. "*We'll* go…. You're coming home with me?"

He nodded.

Her lips parted as she looked at him and realized that he didn't want to be separated from her any more than she wanted to be apart from him.

"Did you think it was one-sided?" he asked, moving toward her. "Didn't it occur to you that in order for something to be this explosive, it has to be shared?"

Her expression mirrored her sense of wonder. So did his. He pulled her against him, wincing a little when the movement tugged at his stitches, and bent his head. He kissed her with slow, aching hunger, feeling her instant response with delight.

"If I go home with you, people will really talk about us," he whispered against her mouth. "Aren't you worried?"

"No," she said with a smile. "Kiss me…."

He did, thoroughly, and she returned it with the same hunger. After a minute, he had to step back from her. His chest rose and fell heavily as he searched her eyes.

"Do you have a double bed?" he asked.

"Yes." She flushed and then laughed at her own embarrassment. That part of their relationship was something she'd have to adjust to, but she wasn't too worried about being able to accomplish it.

He touched her mouth with aching tenderness. "I was

teasing," he chided. "I can't stay, as much as I want to. But I'll stay until bedtime."

"You could sleep on the sofa," she offered.

"I know that. I'll have one of the guys pick me up and drive me home. I don't want you alone on the roads late at night." He gently touched her cheek, which was flushed at his concern for her. "It's going to be rough. I don't want to be apart from you anymore, even at night. Especially at night," he said with a rough laugh.

"Yes, I know. I feel the same way." With her fingertips, she traced his thick eyebrows and then his closed eyelids, his cheeks, his mouth. "It's…unexpected. What are we going to do now?"

"Get married as soon as we can," he said simply. He smiled reluctantly at her expression. "Don't faint on me, Jessie."

"But you don't want to get married," she protested. "You said you never wanted to."

"Honey, do you think we could live together in Whitehorn without raising eyebrows?" he asked gently. He smiled. "Besides that, when my shoulder heals, I'm going to have you. It's inevitable. We want each other too badly to abstain for much longer. Let's do this thing properly, by the book."

She traced a pattern in the thick tangle of hair on his broad chest. All her dreams hadn't prepared her for the reality of this. She could hardly believe it. "Marriage," she whispered with aching hunger. She lifted her eyes to his lean, hard face. "Someone of my own," she added involuntarily.

"There's that, too. Belonging to another person." He brought her hand to his lips. His teeth nipped the soft palm and she laughed. The glitter in his eyes grew.

"You've never had a man, have you? Except for that one bad experience, you're untouched."

"Not anymore," she murmured demurely. "I've been all but ravished today."

He chuckled. "If you think that was ravishment, you've got a lot to learn."

She searched his eyes and sadness overlaid her joy. "It's a lovely dream. But it isn't realistic. It will matter to you one day, not being able to have a child of your own."

He touched her mouth and his face became as serious as hers. "Jessie, if you could have a child with another man, but not with me, would you marry him?"

She looked confused for a minute. "Well, no," she said.

"Why?"

"Because I lo…because I care for you," she corrected.

He pulled her close. "You're not getting away with that," he said. "Tell me. Say the words."

She gnawed at her lower lip, hesitating.

"All the way, Jessie," he coaxed. "Say it."

"You won't," she said accusingly.

"I don't need to," he asserted. "If sex was all I wanted from you, I could have seduced you long ago. If it isn't just for the sake of sex, what other reason would I have for wanting to marry you?"

He hadn't said it, but she looked at him and realized with a start that he was telling her he loved her with everything except words. He couldn't bear to be parted from her, he wanted to marry her even though she couldn't give him a child.…

"Of course I love you," she whispered softly. "I've

loved you from the first time I saw you, but I never dared to hope—"

The last of the sentence was lost under the soft, slow crush of his mouth on her lips. He drew her close and kissed her with tenderness and passion, savoring her mouth until he had to lift his head to breathe. Yes, it was there, in her eyes, in her face; she loved him, all right. He began to smile and couldn't stop.

"You're surprisingly conventional," she mused, staring at him with loving eyes.

"Depressingly so, in some ways. I want the trimmings. I've never had much tradition in my life, but it starts now. We get engaged, then we get married, in church, and you wear a white gown and a veil for me to lift up when I kiss you."

She sighed. "It sounds lovely."

"It's probably Victorian." He chuckled. "Abstinence until the event and all. But a little tradition can be beautiful. All that separates people from animals, I read once, is a sense of nobility and honor. These days people want instant satisfaction. They don't believe in self-denial or self-sacrifice, or patience. I do. Those old virtues had worth."

"Indeed they did. I'm just as old-fashioned at heart as you are," she said gently. "I believe in forever, Sterling."

He drew her close and held her, hard. "So do I. We'll have differences, but if we compromise and work at it, we can have a long and happy life together." He kissed her forehead with breathless tenderness, grimacing, because holding her pulled the stitches and made his arm throb. But it was a sweet pain, for all that.

"My job..." she began.

He smoothed her hair away from her face. "I work.

You work. We won't have to worry about someone staying home with a child."

Her face contorted.

"Don't," he said gently. He scowled with concern. "Don't. We'll be happy together, I promise you we will. It's all right."

She had to fight down the tears. She pressed against him and closed her eyes. She would never stop regretting her condition. But perhaps Sterling was right. There would be compensations. First and foremost would be having this man love her as she loved him.

It took several weeks for McCallum's arm to heal completely, but they announced their wedding plans almost immediately. No one was really surprised, especially not Bess.

"When I saw how you looked at him that day, it didn't surprise me when I heard the news," Bess said with a grin. "I'm happy for both of you, honestly. I hope I get that lucky someday."

"Thanks," Jessica said warmly.

The office staff gave her an engagement party, complete with necessary household goods to start out— even though she'd accumulated a lot of her own. It was the thought that counted, and theirs were warm and pleasant.

An invitation to the wedding of Mary Jo and Dugin was forthcoming. It would take place in late June, about a month before Jessica and Sterling's. They decided to go together.

Meanwhile, another problem cropped up quite unexpectedly.

Keith Colson had finally done something that landed

him in the purview of the county sheriff and not the juvenile authorities. He held up a small car dealership out in the country.

The pistol he used was not loaded, and he didn't even run. They picked him up not far away, walking down a lonely highway with his sack of money. He even smiled at the sheriff's deputy—not McCallum— who arrested him.

He was brought into the sheriff's office for questioning, with new marks on his face.

This time McCallum wasn't willing to listen to evasions. He sat Keith down in the interrogation room and leaned forward intently.

"I've been too involved in my own life lately to see what was going on around me," he told Keith. "I meant to check on you again when the juvenile authorities released you, but I got shot and I've been pretty well slowed down. Now, however, I'm going to get to the root of this problem before you end up in federal prison." He looked the boy straight in the eye. "Your father is beating you." He watched Keith's eyes dilate. "And probably hitting your grandmother, too. You're going to tell me right now exactly what he's done to you."

Keith gaped at him. He couldn't find words. He shifted nervously in the chair. "Listen, it's not that—"

"Loyalty is stupid after a certain point," McCallum said shortly. "I was loyal to my mother, but when she broke my arm, I decided that my own survival was more important than the family's dark secret."

Keith's expression changed. "Your mother broke your arm?"

McCallum nodded curtly. "She was an alcoholic. She couldn't admit that she had a problem and she couldn't stop. It just got worse, until finally I realized that if she really cared about me, she'd have done something to help herself. She wouldn't, so I had to. I had her arrested. It was painful and there was a lot of gossip. Afterwards, I had no place to go, so I got shuffled around the county, to whichever farm needed an extra hand in exchange for bed and board. She died of a heart attack in jail when I was in my early teens. I had a hell of a life. But even then it was better than having to fend her off when she came at me with bottles or knives or whatever weapon she could lay her hand on."

Keith seemed to grow taller. He let out a long sigh and rubbed the arms of the old wooden chair. "You know all about it then."

"Living with an alcoholic, you mean? Yes, I know all about it. So you won't fool me anymore. You might as well come clean. Protecting your father isn't worth getting a criminal record that will follow you all your life. You can't run away from the problem by getting thrown in jail, son. In fact, you'll find people worse than your father there."

Keith leaned forward and dangled his hands between his knees. "He says it's because he lost his job and nobody else will hire him, at his age. But I don't believe it anymore. He hits my grandma, you see. Mostly he hits her, and I can't stand that, so I try to stop him. But he hits me when I interfere. Last time I landed a couple of shots, but he's bigger than I am. Whenever he sobers up, he says he'll quit. He always says he'll quit, that it will get better." He shook his head and smiled with a cynicism beyond his years. "Only it doesn't. And I'm scared he'll really hurt Grandma one day. But if I left, she could, too. She only stays to try and make some sort of home for me, and cook and clean for us. She can't talk to him. Neither can I. He just doesn't hear us."

"He'll hear me," McCallum said, rising.

"What will you do?" Keith asked miserably.

"I'll pick him up for assault and battery, and you'll sign a warrant," he told the boy. "He may go to jail, but they'll help him and he'll dry out. Meanwhile, we'll place you in a foster home. Your grandmother is too old to look out for you, and she's got a sister in Montana who'd enjoy her company."

"Miss Larson told you, I guess," he mused, smiling sheepishly.

"Yes. Jessica and I are getting married."

"I heard. She's a nice lady."

"I think so."

"You won't hurt my dad?"

"Of course not."

The boy got to his feet. "There's this robbery charge...."

"I'll talk to Bill Murray," McCallum said. "When he knows the circumstances, he won't press charges. The money was all recovered and he knows the gun wasn't loaded. He's a kind man, and not vindictive."

"I'll write him a note and tell him how sorry I am. I didn't want to do it, but I couldn't turn Dad in," he added, pleading for understanding.

McCallum clapped him on the back. "Son, life is full of things we can't do that we have to do. You'll learn that the hard part is living with them afterward. Come on. Let's go see the magistrate."

A warrant was sworn out and signed, and McCallum went to serve it. He felt sorry for Terrance Colson, but sorrier for the boy and his grandmother, who were practically being held hostage by the man.

He found Terrance sitting on his front porch, and obviously not expecting company, since he had a bottle of whiskey in one hand.

"What the hell do you want?" he demanded belligerently. "If it's that damned boy again, you can lock him up and throw away the key. I've had it with him!"

"He's had it with you, too, Terrance," McCallum replied, coming up onto the porch. "This is a warrant for your arrest, for assault and battery. Keith signed it."

"A…what?"

He stumbled to his feet, only to have McCallum grab him and whirl him around to face the wall, pinning him there while he cuffed him efficiently.

"You can't do this to me," Terrance yelled, adding a few choice profanities to emphasize his anger.

The door opened timidly and little Mrs. Colson peered out. Her eyes were red and there were bad bruises on one cheek and around her mouth.

"Are you…gonna take him off?" she asked McCallum.

He had to fight for control at the sight of the bruises on that small, withered face. "Yes, ma'am," he said quietly. "He won't be home for a while. The very least that will happen to him is that he'll be sent off to dry out."

She slumped against the door facing. "Oh, thank God," she breathed, her voice choked. Tears streamed down her face. "Oh, thank God. I've always been too weak and afraid to fight back, and Terrance takes after his daddy—"

Terrance glared at her. "You shut your mouth…!"

McCallum jerked him forward. "Let's go," he said

tersely. "Mrs. Colson, Jessica will be out this afternoon to talk to you when I tell her what's happened. I have an idea about where we can place Keith, but we'll talk about that later. Are you all right? Do you need me to take you to the doctor?"

"No, thank you, sir," she replied. "If you'll just carry him off, that's all I need. That's all I need, yes, sir."

Terrance yelled wild, drunken threats at her, which made McCallum even angrier. But he was a trained law-enforcement officer, and didn't allow his fury to show. He was polite to Terrance, easing him into the patrol car with a minimum of fuss. He called goodbye to Mrs. Colson and took Terrance off to jail.

Later, Jessica went with Sterling and Keith to talk to Mrs. Colson.

"This is short notice, but I called Maris Wyler before I came out here. She needs a good hand out at her ranch, and when I explained the circumstances, she said she'd be happy to have Keith if he wanted to come."

"Do I ever!" Keith interjected. "Imagine, Gram, a real ranch! I'll learn cowboying!"

"If that's what you want, son," Mrs. Colson said gently. "Heaven knows, it's about time you had some pleasure in life. I know how you love animals. I reckon you'll fit right in on a ranch. It's very nice of Maris to let you come."

"She's a good woman. She'll take care of Keith, and he'll be somewhere he's really needed," McCallum told the old woman. "He and I have had a long talk about it. The judge has offered to let him plead to a lesser charge in exchange for a probationary sentence in Maris's custody. He'll have a chance to change his whole life and get back on the right track. She's even going to arrange for the homebound teacher to come out and give him his lessons so he won't have to go to school and face the inevitable taunting of the other students."

Mrs. Colson just nodded. "That would be best, Keith," she told her grandson. "I tried to help you as much as I could, but I couldn't fight your father when he was drinking."

"It's all right, Gram," Keith said gently. "You did all you could. I wish you could stay."

"I do, too, but this is your father's house and I could never stay here again."

"Yeah, neither could I," Keith replied. "It wouldn't ever be the same again, even if he does dry out. He talked about moving, and maybe he will. But I won't go with him. The way he's gotten, I'm not sure he wants to change. I'm not sure he can."

"The state will give him the opportunity to try," McCallum told them. "But the rest is up to him. If you want to see him, I can arrange it."

Keith actually shivered. "No, thanks," he said with a laugh. "When can I go and see this lady who says she'll take me in?"

"Right now, I guess," McCallum said with a grin. "We'll take Jessica with us, in case we need backup."

Keith frowned. "This sounds serious."

"Maris is a character," he replied. "But she's fair and she has a kind heart. You'll do fine. Just don't get on the wrong side of her."

"What he means," Jessica said, with a pointed glance at McCallum, "is that Maris is a strong and capable woman who can run a ranch all by herself."

McCallum started to open his mouth.

"You can shut up," Jessica interrupted him deftly.

"And you'd better not swagger in front of Maris, or she'll cut you off at the ankles. She isn't the forgiving, long-suffering angel of mercy that I am."

"And not half as modest." McCallum grinned.

Jessica made a face at him, but love gleamed out of her soft brown eyes—and his, too. They had a hard time separating work from their private lives, but they managed it. They lived in each others' pockets, except at night. The whole town looked at them with kind indulgence, because they were so obviously in love that it touched people's hearts.

Even old Mrs. Colson smiled at the way they played. It took her back fifty years to her own girlhood and her late husband.

"Well, we'd better be on our way. I'll drive you to the bus station when you're packed and ready to leave," McCallum told her. "And if there's anything we can do, please let us know."

"All I need is to leave here," she replied, touching her swollen cheek gingerly. "Thank you for trying to help me, son," she told Keith. "You were the only reason I stayed at all. I was scared of what he'd do to you if I left."

"I kept trying to find ways to get out," Keith confessed, "so that you could leave. But they kept sending me home again."

"Well, nobody's perfect, not even the criminal-justice system," McCallum said, tongue-in-cheek.

They left Mrs. Colson with an ice bag on her cheek and drove to the No Bull Ranch. Maris Wyler came out to meet them.

She was tall and lean, very tan from working outdoors, her long golden hair pulled back into a ponytail.

She wore jeans and boots and a faded long-sleeved shirt, but she looked oddly elegant even in that rig.

"You're Keith. I'm Maris," she said forthrightly, introducing herself to the boy with a smile and a firm handshake. "Ever work with cattle?"

"No, ma'am," Keith shook his head.

"Well, you'll learn quickly. I can sure use a hand out here. I hope you like the work."

"I think I will," he said.

"That's good, 'cause there's plenty of it." Maris replied with a grin.

"He'll be fine here," Maris assured Jessica.

"I knew that already," Jessica replied. "Thanks, Maris. I hope someone does something as kind for you one day."

"No problem. Come on, Keith, grab your gear and let's get you settled. So long, McCallum, Jessica. Feel free to come out and see him whenever you like. Just call first and make sure we're home."

"I will," Jessica replied.

She watched the two walk off toward the neat, new bunkhouse. The ranch, originally called the Circle W, had been in Maris's husband's family for years. Ray hadn't been the sort of man a woman like Maris deserved. He was a heavy drinker like Keith's father, as well as a gambler and womanizer. Nobody had been surprised when he'd recently come to a bad end—running his pickup into a cement bunker on the highway in a drunken state one night. Maris had been doing all the work on the ranch for years while her lazy husband spent money on foolish schemes and chased the rodeo. It was poetic justice that she ended up with the ranch.

"Hensley's always been a little sweet on her, you

know," McCallum confided to Jessica as he drove them back to her place. "It was hard for him to tell her about Ray's death."

"Really? My goodness, she's nothing like his ex-wife."

"Men don't always fall for the same type of woman," he teased. "He called her for me when I approached him about someplace for Keith to go, besides into foster care."

"I'm glad Maris was willing," she said quietly. "Keith's not a bad boy, but he could have ended up in prison so easily, trying to get away from his father."

"It's a hell of a world for kids sometimes," he said.

She straightened the long denim skirt she was wearing with a plaid shirt and boots. "Yes."

He reached over and clasped her hand tightly in his. "I've been thinking."

"Have you? Did it hurt?" she teased.

He chuckled. "Not nice."

"Sorry. I'll behave. What were you thinking?"

His grip eased and he slipped his fingers in between hers. "That Baby Jennifer needs a home and we need a baby."

Chapter 13

Jessica had thought about that a lot—that Baby Jennifer needed someone to love her and take care of her. McCallum had been firm about the improbability of a court awarding the baby's care to a single woman. But that situation had changed. She and McCallum were engaged, soon to be married. There was every reason in the world to believe that, under the circumstances, a judge might be willing to let them have custody.

She caught her breath audibly. Bubbles of joy burst inside her. "Oh, Sterling, do you think…!"

His hand grasped hers. "I don't know, but it's worth a try. She's a pretty, sweet baby. And I agree with you—I think our lives would be enriched by having a child to love and raise. There's more to being a mother and father than just biology. It takes love and sacrifice and day-to-day living to manage that." He glanced at her gently. "You aren't the sort of woman who will ever be happy without a baby."

She smiled sadly. "I would have loved to have yours."

"So would I," he replied, his tone as tender as his eyes, which briefly searched hers. "But this is the next best thing. What do you think? Do you want to petition the court for permission to adopt her?"

"Yes!"

He chuckled. "That didn't take much thought."

"Oh, yes, it did. I've thought of nothing else since she was found."

"The judge may say no," he cautioned.

"He may say yes."

He just shook his head. That unshakable optimism touched him, especially in view of all the tragedy Jessica had had in her life. She was amazing. A miracle. He loved her more every day.

"All right, then," he replied. "We'll get a lawyer and fill out the papers."

"Today," she added.

He smiled. "Today."

Their wedding took place just a few weeks later, in July. They were married in the Whitehorn Methodist Church, with a small group of friends as witnesses. Jessica wore a simple white wedding dress. It had a lace bodice and a veil, and it was street length. After their vows, Sterling lifted the veil to kiss her. The love they shared was the end of the rainbow for her. When his lips touched hers, she laid her hand against his hard, lean cheek and felt tears sliding down her face. Tears of joy, of utter happiness.

Their reception was simplicity itself—the women

at the office had baked cookies and a friend had made them a wedding cake. There was coffee and punch at the local community hall, and plenty of people showed up to wish them well.

Finally, the socializing was over. They drove to Jessica's house, where they would have complete privacy, to spend their wedding night. Later, they planned to live at McCallum's more modern place.

"Your knees are shaking," he teased when they were inside, with the door locked. It had just become dark, and the house was quiet—even with Meriwether's vocal welcome—and cozy in its nest of forestland.

"I know," she confessed with a shy smile. "I have a few scars left, I guess, and even now it's all unfamiliar territory. You've been…very patient," she added, recalling his restraint while they were dating. Things had been very circumspect between them, considering the explosive passion they kindled in each other.

"I think we're going to find that this is very addictive," he explained as he drew her gently to him. "And I wanted us to be married before we did a lot of heavy experimenting. We've both suffered enough gossip for one lifetime."

"Indeed we have," she agreed. She reached up to loop her arms around his neck. Her eyes searched his. "And now it's all signed and sealed—all legal." She smiled a little nervously. "I can hardly wait!"

He chuckled softly as he bent is head. "I hope I can manage to live up to all those expectations. What if I can't?"

"Oh, I'll make allowances," she promised as his mouth settled on hers.

The teasing had made her fears recede. She relaxed

as he drew her intimately close. When his tongue gently penetrated the line of her lips, she stiffened slightly, but he lifted his head and softly stroked her mouth, studying her in the intense silence.

"It's strange right now, isn't it, because we haven't done much of this sort of kissing. But you'll get used to it," he said in a tender tone. "Try not to think about anything except the way it feels."

He bent again, brushing his lips lazily against hers for a long time, until the pressure wasn't enough. When he heard her breathing change and felt her mouth start to follow his when he lifted it, he knew she was more than ready for something deeper.

It was like the first time they'd been intimate. She clung to him, loving his strength and the exquisite penetration of his tongue in her mouth. It made her think of what lay ahead, and her body reacted with pleasure and eagerness.

He coaxed her hands to his shirt while he worked on the buttons that held her lacy bodice together. Catches were undone. Fabric was shifted. Before she registered the fact mentally, his hair-roughened chest was rubbing gently across her bare breasts and she was encouraging him shamelessly.

He picked her up, still kissing her, and barely made it to the sofa before he fell onto it with her. The passion was already red-hot. She gave him back kiss for kiss, touch for touch, in a silence that magnified the harsh quickness of their breathing.

When he sat up, she moaned, but it didn't take long to get the rest of the irritating obstacles out of the way. When he came back to her, there was nothing to separate them.

Loyal Readers
FREE BOOKS Voucher

We're giving away **THOUSANDS** of **FREE BOOKS**

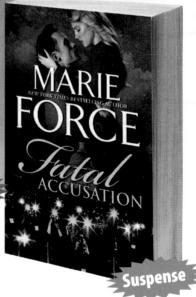

Romance

Suspense

Don't Miss Out! Send for Your Free Books Today!

Get up to 4
FREE FABULOUS BOOKS
You Love!

To thank you for being a loyal reader we'd like to send you up to 4 FREE BOOKS, absolutely free.

Just write "YES" on the Loyal Reader Voucher and we'll send you up to 4 Free Books and Free Mystery Gifts, altogether worth over $20, as a way of saying thank you for being a loyal reader.

Try **Essential Suspense** featuring spine-tingling suspense and psychological thrillers with many written by today's best-selling authors.

Try **Essential Romance** featuring compelling romance stories with many written by today's best-selling authors.

Or **TRY BOTH!**

We are so glad you love the books as much as we do and can't wait to send you great new books.

So don't miss out, return your Loyal Reader Voucher Today!

Pam Powers

LOYAL READER
FREE BOOKS VOUCHER

YES! I Love Reading, please send me up to 4 FREE BOOKS and Free Mystery Gifts from the series I select.

Just write in "YES" on the dotted line below then return this card today and we'll send your free books & gifts asap!

➡ _ YES _ _ ⬅

Which do you prefer?

☐ **Essential Suspense**
191/391 MDL GNR4

☐ **Essential Romance**
194/394 MDL GNR4

☐ **BOTH**
191/391 & 194/394 MDL GNSG

FIRST NAME

LAST NAME

ADDRESS

APT.#

CITY

STATE/PROV.

ZIP/POSTAL CODE

ST-220-OMLR20

▼ If offer card is missing write to: Reader Service, P.O. Box 1341, Buffalo, NY 14240-8531 or visit www.ReaderService.com ▼

BUSINESS REPLY MAIL
FIRST-CLASS MAIL   PERMIT NO. 717   BUFFALO, NY

POSTAGE WILL BE PAID BY ADDRESSEE

READER SERVICE
PO BOX 1341
BUFFALO NY 14240-8571

NO POSTAGE
NECESSARY
IF MAILED
IN THE
UNITED STATES

Her body was so attuned to his, so hungry for him, that she took him at once, without pain or difficulty, and was shocked enough to cry out.

His body stilled immediately. His ragged breathing was audible as he lifted his head and looked into her eyes, stark need vying with concern.

"It didn't hurt," she assured him in a choked voice.

"Of course…it didn't hurt," he gasped, pushing down again. "You want me so badly that pain wouldn't register now… God!"

She felt the exquisite stab of pleasure just as he cried out, and her mouth flattened against his shoulder as he began to move feverishly against her taut body.

"I love you," he groaned as the rhythm grew reckless and rough. "Jessie, I love you…!"

Her mouth, opened in a soundless scream as she felt the most incredible sensation she'd ever experienced in her life. It was like a throbbing wave of searing heat that suddenly became unbearable, pleasure beyond pleasure. Her body shuddered convulsively and she arched, gasping. He stilled just a minute later, and his hoarse cry whispered endlessly against her ear.

He collapsed then, and she felt the full weight of him with satisfied indulgence. She was damp with sweat. So was he. She stroked his dark hair, and it was damp, too. Wonder wrapped her up like a blanket and she began to laugh softly.

He managed to lift his head, frowning as he met her dancing eyes.

"You passed," she whispered impishly.

He began to laugh, too, at the absurdity of the remark. "Lucky me."

"Oh, no," she murmured, lifting to him slightly but deliberately. "Lucky *me!*"

He groaned. "I can't yet!"

"I have plenty of time," she assured him, and kissed him softly on the chin. "I can wait. Don't let me rush you."

"Remind me to have a long talk with you about men."

She locked her arms around his neck with a deep sigh. "Later," she said. "Right now I just want to lie here and look at my husband. He's a dish."

"So is my wife." He nuzzled her nose with his, smiling tenderly. "Jessie, I hope we have a hundred more years together."

"I love you," she told him reverently. Her eyes closed and she began to drift to sleep. She wondered how anything so delicious could be so exhausting.

The next morning, she awoke to the smell of bacon. She was in her bedroom, in her gown, with the covers pulled up. The pillow next to hers was dented in and the sheet had been disturbed. She smiled. He must have put her to bed. Now it smelled as if he was busy with breakfast.

She put on her jeans and T-shirt and went downstairs in her stocking feet to find him slaving over a hot stove.

"I haven't burned it," he said before she could ask. "And I have scrambled eggs and toast warming in the oven. Coffee's in the pot. Help yourself."

"You're going to be a very handy husband," she said enthusiastically. She moved closer to him, frowning. "But can you do laundry?"

He looked affronted. "Lady, I can iron. Haven't you noticed my uniform shirts?"

"Well, yes, I thought the dry cleaners—"

"Dry cleaners, hell," he scoffed. "As if I'd trust my uniforms to amateurs!"

She laughed and hugged him warmly. "Mr. McCallum, you're just unbelievable."

"So are you." He hugged her back. "Now get out of the way, will you? Burned bacon would be a terrible blot on my perfect record as a new husband."

"You fed Meriwether!" she gasped, glancing at her cat, who was busy with his own breakfast.

"He stopped hissing at me the second I picked up the can opener," Sterling said smugly. "Now he's putty in my hands. He even likes Mack!"

"Wonderful! It isn't enough that you've got me trained," she complained to the orange cat lying on the floor beside the big dog. Mack was already his friend. "Now you're starting on other people!"

"Wait until Jenny is old enough to use the can opener," he said. "Then he'll start on her!"

Jessica looked at him with her heart in her eyes. She wanted the baby so much.

"What if the judge won't let us have her?" she asked with faint sadness.

He took up the bacon and turned off the burner, placing the platter on the table.

"The judge *will* let us have her," he corrected. He tilted up her chin. "You have to start realizing that good times follow bad. You've paid your dues, haven't you noticed? You've had one tragedy after another. But life has a way of balancing the books, honey. You're about due for a refund. And it's just beginning. Wait and see."

"How in the world did a cynic like you learn to look

for a silver lining in storm clouds?" she asked with mock surprise.

He drew her close. "I started being pestered by this overly optimistic little social worker who got me by the heart and refused to let me go. She taught me to look for miracles. Now I can't seem to stop."

"I hope you find them all the time now," she said. "And I hope we get Jennifer, too. That one little miracle would do me for the rest of my life. With Jennifer and you, I'd have the very world."

"We'll see how it goes. But you have to have faith," he reminded her.

"I have plenty of that," she agreed, looking at him with quiet, hungry eyes. "I've lived on it since the first time I looked at you. It must have worked. Here you are."

"Here I stay, too," he replied, bending his head to kiss her.

Chapter 14

The petition was drawn up by their attorney. It was filed in the county clerk's office. A hearing was scheduled and placed on the docket. Then there was nothing else to do except wait.

Jessica went to work as usual, but she was a different person now that she was married. Her delight in her new husband spilled over into every aspect of her work. She felt whole, for the first time.

They both went out to the No Bull Ranch to see Maris Wyler and Keith Colson. The young man was settled in very nicely now, and was working hard. The homebound teacher who had been working with him since the summer recess was proud of the way he'd pulled up his grades. He was learning the trade of being a cowboy, too, and he'd gone crazy on the subject of wildlife conservation. He wanted to be a forest ranger, and Maris encouraged him. He was already talking about college.

"I couldn't be more delighted," Jessica told McCallum when they were driving back to town. "He's so different, isn't he? He isn't surly or uncooperative or scowling all the time. I hardly knew him."

"Unhappy people don't make good impressions. If you only knew how many children go to prison for lack of love and attention and even discipline.... Some people have no business raising kids."

"I think you and I would be good at it," she said.

He caught the note of sadness in her voice. "Cut that out," he told her. "You're the last person on earth I'd ever suspect of being a closet pessimist."

"I'm trying not to be discouraged. It's just that I want to adopt Jennifer so much," she said. "I'm afraid to want anything that badly."

"You wanted me that badly," he reminded her, "and look what happened."

She looked at him with her heart in her eyes and grinned. "Well, yes. You were unexpected."

"So were you. I'd resigned myself to living alone."

"I suppose we were both blessed."

"Yes. And the blessings are still coming. Wait and see."

She leaned back against the seat with a sigh, complacent but still unconvinced.

They went to court that fall. Kate Randall was the presiding judge. Jessica knew and liked her but couldn't control her nerves. Witness after witness gave positive character readings about both Jessica and McCallum. The juvenile authorities mentioned their fine record with helping young offenders, most recently Keith Colson. And through it all Jessica sat gripping McCallum's hand under the table and chewing the skin off her lower lip with fear and apprehension.

The judge was watching her surreptitiously. When the witnesses had all been called and the recommendations—good ones—given by the juvenile authorities, she spoke directly to Jessica.

"You're very nervous, Mrs. McCallum," Kate said with teasing kindness and a judicial formality. "Do I look like an ogre to you?"

She gasped. "Oh, no, your honor!" she cried, reddening.

"Well, judging by the painful look on your face, you must think I am one. Your joy in that child, and your own background, would make it difficult for even a hanging judge to deny you. And I'm hardly that." She smiled at Jessica. "The petition to adopt the abandoned Baby Jennifer is hereby approved without reservation. Case dismissed." She banged the gavel and stood up.

Jessica burst into tears, and it took McCallum a long time to calm and comfort her.

"She said yes," he kept repeating, laughing with considerable joy of his own. "Stop crying! She may change her mind!"

"No, she won't," the judge assured them, standing patiently by their table.

Jessica wiped her eyes, got up and hugged the judge, too.

"There, there," she comforted. "I've seen a lot of kids go through this court, but I've seen few who ended up with better parents. In the end it doesn't matter that your child is adopted. You'll raise her and be Jennifer's parents. That's the real test of love, I think. It's the bringing up that matters."

She agreed wholeheartedly. "You can't imagine how I felt, how afraid I was," she blurted out.

Kate patted her shoulder. "Yes, I can. I've had a steady stream of people come through my office this past week, all pleading on your behalf. You might be shocked at who some of them were. Your own boss," she said to McCallum, shaking her head. "Who'd have thought it."

"Hensley?" McCallum asked in surprise.

"The very same. And even old Jeremiah Kincaid," she added with a chuckle. "I thought my eyes would fly right out of my head on that one." Kate checked her watch. "I've got another case coming up. You'd better go and see about your baby, Jessica." She dropped the formal address since the court had adjourned. "I expect you new parents will have plenty of things to do now."

"Oh, yes!" she exclaimed. "We'll need to buy formula and diapers and toys and a playpen—"

"We already have the crib," McCallum said smugly, laughing at Jessica's startled reaction. "Well, I was confident, even if you weren't. I ordered it from the furniture store."

"I love you!" She hugged him.

He held her close, shaking hands with the judge.

From the courthouse they went around town, making a number of purchases, and Jessica was in a frenzy of joy as they gathered up all the things they'd need to start life with a new baby.

But the most exciting thing was collecting Baby Jennifer from a delighted Mabel Darren, the woman who'd been keeping her, and taking her home.

Even Meriwether was a perfect gentleman, sniffing the infant, but keeping a respectful distance. Jessica and McCallum sat on the sofa with their precious treasure, and didn't turn on the television at all that night.

Instead they watched the baby. She cooed and stared at them with her big blue eyes and never cried once.

Later, as Jessica and McCallum lay together in bed—with the baby's bed right next to theirs instead of in another room—they both lay watching Jennifer sleep in the soft glow of the night-light.

"I never realized just how it would feel to be a parent," McCallum said quietly. "She's ours. She's all ours."

She inched closer to him. "Sterling, what if her mother ever comes back?"

His arms contracted around her. "If her mother had wanted and been able to keep her, we wouldn't have her," he said. "You have to put that thought out of your mind. Sometimes there are things we never find out about in life—and then there are mysteries that are waiting to be solved just around the corner. We may solve it, we may not. But we've legally adopted Jennifer. She belongs to us, and we to her. That's all there is to it."

Jessica let out her breath in a long sigh. After a minute she nodded. "Okay. Then that's how it will be."

He turned her to face him and kissed her tenderly. "Happy?" he whispered.

"So happy that I could die of it," she whispered back. She pushed her way into his arms and was held tight and close. As her eyes closed, she thought ahead to first steps and birthday parties and school. She'd thought she'd never know those things, but life had been kind. She remembered what McCallum had said to her—that bad times were like dues paid for all the good times that followed. And perhaps they were. God knew, her good times had only just begun!

* * * * *

Books by Maisey Yates

Harlequin Desire

Copper Ridge

Take Me, Cowboy
Hold Me, Cowboy
Seduce Me, Cowboy
Claim Me, Cowboy
Want Me, Cowboy
Need Me, Cowboy

HQN Books

Gold Valley

Cowboy Christmas Blues
Smooth-Talking Cowboy
Mail Order Cowboy
Untamed Cowboy
Hard Riding Cowboy
Good Time Cowboy
Snowed in with the Cowboy
A Tall, Dark Cowboy Christmas
Unbroken Cowboy
Cowboy to the Core
Lone Wolf Cowboy
Cowboy Christmas Redemption

Visit her Author Profile page on Harlequin.com,
or maiseyyates.com, for more titles!

NEED ME, COWBOY

Maisey Yates

Prologue

Levi Tucker
Oregon State Penitentiary
2605 State St., Salem, OR 97310

Dear Ms. Grayson,
Due to certain circumstances, my prison sentence
is coming to its end sooner than originally scheduled. I've been following your career and I'd like
to hire you to design the house I intend to have
built.
Sincerely,
Levi Tucker

Dear Mr. Tucker,
How nice that you're soon to be released from
prison. I imagine that's a great relief. As you can

imagine, my work is in very high demand and I doubt I'll be able to take on a project with such short notice.
Regretfully,
Faith Grayson

Dear Ms. Grayson,
Whatever your usual fee is, I can double it.
Sincerely,
Levi Tucker

Dear Mr. Tucker,
To be perfectly frank, I looked you up on Google. My brothers would take a dim view of me agreeing to take this job.
Respectfully,
Faith Grayson

Dear Ms. Grayson,
Search again. You'll find I am in the process of being exonerated. Also, what your brothers don't know won't hurt anything. I'll triple your fee.
Sincerely,
Levi Tucker

Dear Mr. Tucker,
If you need to contact me, be sure to use my personal number, listed at the bottom of this page.

I trust we'll be in contact upon your release.
Faith

Chapter 1

Levi Tucker wasn't a murderer.

It was a fact that was now officially recognized by the law.

He didn't know what he had expected upon his release from prison. Relief, maybe. He imagined that was what most men might feel. Instead, the moment the doors to the penitentiary had closed behind him, Levi had felt something else.

A terrible, pure anger that burned through his veins with a kind of white-hot clarity that would have stunned him if it hadn't felt so inevitable.

The fact of the matter was, Levi Tucker had always known he wasn't a murderer.

And all the state of Oregon had ever had was a hint of suspicion. Hell, they hadn't even had a body.

Mostly because Alicia wasn't dead.

In many ways, that added insult to injury, because
he still had to divorce the woman who had set out to
make it look as though he had killed her. They were
still married. Of course, the moment he'd been able to,
he'd filed, and he knew everything was in the process
of being sorted out.

He doubted she would contest.

But then, how could he really know?

He had thought he'd known the woman. Hell, he'd
married her. And while he'd been well aware that everything hadn't been perfect, he had not expected his
wife to disappear one hot summer night, leaving behind
implications of foul play.

Even if the result hadn't been intentional, she could
have resurfaced at any point after she'd disappeared.

When he was being questioned. When he had been
arrested.

She hadn't.

Leaving him to assume that his arrest, disgrace and
abject humiliation had been her goal.

It made him wonder now if their relationship had
been a long tail game all the time.

The girl who'd loved him in spite of his family's
reputation in Copper Ridge. The one who'd vowed to
stick with him through everything. No matter whether
he made his fortune or not. He had, and he'd vowed to
Alicia he'd build her a house on top of a hill in Copper
Ridge so they could look down on all the people who'd
once looked down on them.

But until then he'd enjoyed his time at work, away
from the town he'd grown up in. Alicia had gotten more
involved in the glamorous side of their new lifestyle,

while Levi just wanted things to be simple. His own ranch. His own horses.

Alicia had wanted more.

And apparently, in the end, she had figured she could have it all without him.

Fortunately, it was the money that had ultimately been her undoing. For years prior to her leaving she'd been siphoning it into her own account without him realizing it, but when her funds had run dry she'd gone after the money still in his accounts. And that was when she'd gotten caught.

She'd been living off of his hard-earned money for years.

Five years.

Five hellish years he'd spent locked up as the murderer of a woman. Of his wife.

Not a great situation, all in all.

But he'd survived it. Like he'd survived every damn thing that had come before it.

Money was supposed to protect you.

In the end, he supposed it had, in many ways.

Hell, he might not have been able to walk out of that jail cell and collect his Stetson on his way back to his life if it wasn't for the fact that he had a good team of lawyers who had gotten his case retried as quickly as possible. Something you would've thought would be pretty easy considering his wife had been found alive.

The boy he'd been…

He had no confidence that boy would have been able to get justice.

But the man he was…

The man he was now stood on a vacant plot of land that he owned, near enough to the house he was renting, and waited for the architect to arrive. The one who would design the house he deserved after spending five years behind bars.

There would be no bars in this house. The house that Alicia had wanted so badly. To show everyone in their hometown that he and Alicia were more, were better, than what they'd been born into.

Only, she wasn't.

Without him, she was nothing. And he would prove that to her.

No, his house would have no bars. Nothing but windows.

Windows with a view of the mountains that overlooked Copper Ridge, Oregon, the town where he had grown up. He'd been bad news back then; his whole family had been.

The kind of guy that fathers warned their daughters about.

A bad seed dropped from a rotten tree.

And he had a feeling that public opinion would not have changed in the years since.

His reputation certainly hadn't helped his case when he'd been tried and convicted five years ago.

Repeating patterns. That had been brought up many times. An abusive father was likely to have raised an abusive son, who had gone on to be a murderer.

That was the natural progression, wasn't it?

The natural progression of men like him.

Alicia had known that. Of course she had. She knew him better than any other person on earth.

Yet he hadn't known her at all.

Well, he had ended up in prison, as she'd most likely

intended. But he'd clawed his way out. And now he was going to stand up on the mountain in his fancy-ass house and looked down on everyone who'd thought prison would be the end of him.

The best house in the most prime location in town. That was his aim.

Now all that was left to do was wait for Faith Grayson to arrive. By all accounts she was the premier architect at the moment, the hottest commodity in custom home design.

Her houses were more than simple buildings, they were works of art. And he was bound and determined to own a piece of that art for himself.

He was a man possessed. A man on a mission to make the most of everything he'd lost. To live as well as possible while his wife had to deal with the slow-rolling realization that she would be left with nothing.

As it was, it was impossible to prove that she had committed a crime. She hadn't called the police, after all. An argument could be made that she might *not* have intended for him to be arrested. And there was plausible deniability over the fact that she might not have realized he'd gone to prison.

She claimed she had simply walked away from her life and not looked back. The fact that she had been accessing money was a necessity, so she said. And, proof that she had not actually been attempting to hide.

He didn't believe that. He didn't believe *her*, and she had been left with nothing. No access to his money at all. She had been forced to go crawling back to her parents to get an allowance. And he was glad of that.

They said the best revenge was living well.

Levi Tucker intended to do just that.

* * *

Faith Grayson knew that meeting an ex-convict at the top of an isolated mountain could easily be filed directly into the Looney Tunes Bin.

Except, Levi Tucker was only an ex-convict because he had been wrongfully convicted in the first place. At least, that was the official statement from the Oregon State District Attorney's office.

Well, plus it was obvious because his wife wasn't dead.

He had been convicted of the murder of someone who was alive. And while there was a whole lot of speculation centered around the fact that the woman never would have run from him in the first place if he hadn't been dangerous and terrifying, the fact remained that he *wasn't* a killer.

So, there was that.

She knew exactly what two of her brothers, Isaiah and Joshua, would say about this meeting. And it would be colorful. Not at all supportive.

But Faith was fascinated by the man who was willing to pay so much to get one of her designs. And, maybe her ego was a little bit turbocharged by the whole thing. She couldn't deny that.

She was only human, after all.

A human who had been working really, really hard to keep on top of her status as a rising star in the architecture world.

She had designed buildings that had changed skylines, and she'd done homes for the rich and the famous.

Levi Tucker was something *else*. He was infamous.

The self-made millionaire whose whole world had come crashing down when his wife had disappeared more than five years ago. The man who had been tried and convicted of her murder even when there wasn't a body.

Who had spent the past five years in prison, and who was now digging his way back out...

He wanted her. And yeah, it interested her.

She was getting bored.

Which seemed...ungrateful. Her skill for design had made her famous at a ridiculously young age, but, of course, it was her older brothers and their business acumen that had helped her find success so quickly.

Joshua was a public-relations wizard, Isaiah a genius with finance. Faith, for her part, was the one with the imagination.

The one who saw buildings growing out of the ground like trees and worked to find ways to twist them into new shapes, to draw new lines into the man-made landscape to blend it all together with nature.

She had always been an artist, but her fascination with buildings had come from a trip her family had taken when she was a child. They had driven from Copper Ridge into Portland, Oregon, and she had been struck by the beauty that surrounded the city.

But in the part of the city where they'd stayed, everything was blocky and made of concrete. Of course, there were parts of the city that were lovely, with architecture that was ornate and classic, but there were parts where the buildings had been stacked in light gray rectangles, and it had nearly wounded her to see the mountains obscured by such unimaginative, dull shapes.

When she had gotten back to their hotel room, she had begun to draw, trying to find a way to blend function and form with the natural beauty that already existed.

It had become an obsession.

It was tough to be an obsessed person. Someone who lived in their own head, in their dreams and fantasies.

It made it difficult to relate to people.

Fortunately, she had found a good friend, Mia, who had been completely understanding of Faith and her particular idiosyncrasies.

Now Mia was her sister-in-law, because she had married Faith's oldest brother, something Faith really hadn't seen coming.

Devlin was just…so much older. There was more than ten years between he and Faith, and she'd had no idea her friend felt that way about him.

She was happy for both of them, of course.

But their bond sometimes made her feel isolated. The fact that her friend now had this *thing* that Faith herself never had. And that this *thing* was with Faith's brother. Of all people.

Even Joshua and Isaiah had fallen in love and gotten married.

Joshua had wed a woman he had met while trying to get revenge on their father for attempting to force him into marriage, while Isaiah married his personal assistant.

Maybe it was her family that had driven Faith to the top of the mountain today.

Maybe her dissatisfaction with her own personal life was why it felt so interesting and new to do something with Levi Tucker.

Everything she had accomplished, she had done with the permission and help of other people.

If she was going to be a visionary, she wanted—just this once—for it to be on her terms.

To not be seen as a child prodigy—which was ridiculous, because she was twenty-five, not a child at all—but to be seen as someone who was really great at what she did. To leave her age out of it, to leave her older brothers—who often felt more like babysitters—out of it.

She let out a long, slow breath as she rounded the final curve on the mountain driveway, the vacant lot coming into view. But it wasn't the lot, or the scenery surrounding it, that stood out in her vision first and foremost. No, it was the man standing there, his hands shoved into the pockets of his battered jeans, worn cowboy boots on his feet. He had on a black T-shirt, in spite of the morning chill, and a black cowboy hat was pressed firmly onto his head.

Both of his arms were completely filled with ink, the dark lines of the tattoos painting pictures on his skin she couldn't quite see from where she was.

But in a strange way, they reminded her of architecture. The tattoos seemed to enhance the muscle there, to draw focus to the skin beneath the lines, even while they covered it.

She parked the car and sat for a moment, completely struck dumb by the sight of him.

She had researched him, obviously. She knew what he looked like, but she supposed she hadn't had a sense of…the scale of him.

Strange, because she was usually pretty good at picking up on those kinds of things in photographs. She had a mathematical eye, one that blended with her artistic sensibility in a way that felt natural to her.

And yet, she had not been able to accurately form a picture of the man in her mind. And when she got out of the car, she was struck by the way he seemed to fill this vast empty space.

That also didn't make any sense.

He was big. Over six feet and with broad shoulders, but he didn't fill this space. Not literally.

But she could feel his presence like a touch as soon as the cold air wrapped itself around her body upon exiting the car.

And when his ice-blue eyes connected with hers, she drew in a breath. She was certain he filled her lungs, too.

Because that air no longer felt cold. It felt hot. Impossibly so.

Because those blue eyes burned with something.

Rage. Anger.

Not at her—in fact, his expression seemed almost friendly.

But there was something simmering beneath the surface, and it had touched her already.

Wouldn't let go of her.

"Ms. Grayson," he said, his voice rolling over her with that same kind of heat. "Good to meet you."

He stuck out his hand and she hurriedly closed the distance between them, flinching before their skin touched, because she knew it was going to burn.

It did.

"Mr. Tucker," she responded, careful to keep her voice neutral, careful, when she released her hold on him, not to flex her fingers or wipe her palm against the side of her skirt like she wanted to.

"This is the site," he said. "I hope you think it's workable."

"I do," she said, blinking. She needed to look around them. At the view. At the way the house would be situated. This lot was more than usable. It was inspirational. "What do you have in mind? I find it best to begin with customer expectations," she said, quick to turn the topic where it needed to go. Because what she didn't want to do was ponder the man any longer.

The man didn't matter.

The house mattered.

"I want it to be everything prison isn't," he said, his tone hard and decisive.

She couldn't imagine this man, as vast and wild as the deep green trees and ridged blue mountains around them, contained in a cell. Isolated. Cut off.

In darkness.

And suddenly she felt compelled to be the answer to that darkness. To make sure that the walls she built for him didn't feel like walls at all.

"Windows," she said. That was the easiest and most obvious thing. A sense of openness and freedom. She began to plot the ways in which she could construct a house so that it didn't have doors. So that things were concealed by angles and curves. "No doors?"

"I live alone," he said simply. "There's no reason for doors."

"And you don't plan on living with someone anytime soon?"

"Never," he responded. "It may surprise you to learn that I have cooled on the idea of marriage."

"Windows. Lighting." She turned to the east. "The sun should be up here early, and we can try to capture the light there in the morning when you wake up, and then..." She turned the opposite way. "Make sure that we're set up for you to see the light as it goes down here. Kitchen. Living room. Office?"

Her fingers twitched and she pulled her sketchpad out of her large, leather bag, jotting notes and rough lines as quickly as possible. She felt the skin prickle on her face and she paused, looking up.

He was watching her.

She cleared her throat. "Can I ask you...what was it that inspired you to get in touch with me? Which building of mine?"

"All of them," he said. "I had nothing but time while I was in jail, and while I did what I could to manage some of my assets from behind bars, there was a lot of time to read. An article about your achievements came to my attention and I was fascinated by your work. I won't lie to you—even more than that, I am looking forward to owning a piece of you."

Something about those words hit her square in the solar plexus and radiated outward. She was sweating now. She was not wearing her coat. She should not be sweating.

"Of me?"

"Your brand," he said. "Having a place designed by you is an exceedingly coveted prize, I believe."

She felt her cheeks warm, and she couldn't quite figure out why. She didn't suffer from false modesty. The last few years of her life had been nothing short of extraordinary. She embraced her success and she didn't apologize for it. Didn't duck her head, like she was doing now, or tuck her hair behind her ear and look up bashfully. Which she had just done.

"I suppose so."

"You know it's true," he said.

"Yes," she said, clearing her throat and rallying. "I do."

"Whatever the media might say, whatever law enforcement believes now, my wife tried to destroy my life. And I will not allow her to claim that victory. I'm not a phoenix rising from the ashes. I'm just a very angry man ready to set some shit on fire, and stand there watching it burn. I'm going to show her, and the world, that I can't be destroyed. I'm not slinking into the shadows. I'm going to rebuild it all. Until everything that I have done matters more than what she did to me. I will not allow her name, what she did, to be the thing I am remembered for. I'm sure you can understand that."

She could. Oddly, she really could.

She wasn't angry at anyone, nor did she have any right to be, but she knew what it was like to want to break out and have your own achievements. Wasn't that what she had just been thinking of while coming here?

Of course, he already had so many achievements. She imagined having all her work blotted out the way that he had. It was unacceptable.

"Look," she said stashing her notebook, "I meant what I said, about my brothers being unhappy with me for taking this job."

"What do your brothers have to do with you taking a job?"

"If you read anything about me then you know that I work with them. You know that we've merged with the construction company that handles a great deal of our building."

"Yes, I know. Though, doesn't the construction arm

mostly produce reproductions of your designs, rather than handling your custom projects?"

"It depends," she responded. "I just mean... My brothers run a significant portion of our business."

"But you could go off and run it without them. They can't run it without you."

He had said the words she had thought more than once while listening to Joshua and Isaiah make proclamations about various things. Joshua was charming, and often managed to make his proclamations seem not quite so prescriptive. Isaiah never bothered. About the only person he was soft with at all was his wife, Poppy, who owned his heart—a heart that a great many of them had doubted he had.

"Well, I just meant... We need to keep this project a secret. Until we're at least most of the way through. Jonathan Bear will be the one to handle the building. He's the best. And since you're right here in Copper Ridge, it would make sense to have him do it."

"I know Jonathan Bear," Levi said.

That surprised her. "Do you?"

"I'm a couple years older than him, but we both grew up on the same side of the tracks here in town. You know, the wrong side."

"Oh," she said. "I didn't realize."

Dimly, she had been aware, on some level, that Levi was from here, but he had left so long ago, and he was so far outside of her own peer group, that she would never have known him.

If he was older than Jonathan Bear, then he was possibly a good thirteen years her senior.

That made her feel small and silly for that instant response she'd had to him earlier.

She was basically a child to him.

But then, she was basically a child to most of the men in her life, so why should this be any different?

And she didn't even know why it was bothering her.

She often designed buildings for old men. And in the beginning, it had been difficult getting them to take her seriously, but the more pieces that had been written about her, the more those men had marveled at the talent she had for her age, and the more she was able to walk into a room with all of those accolades clearly visible behind her as she went.

She was still a little bit bothered that her age was such a big deal, but if it helped…then she would take it. Because she couldn't do anything about the fact that she looked like she might still be in college.

She tried—*tried*—to affect a sophisticated appearance, but half the time she felt like she was playing dress-up in a much fancier woman's clothes.

"Clandestine architecture project?" he asked, the corner of his lips working up into a smile. And until that moment, she realized she had not been fully convinced his mouth could do that.

"Something like that."

"Let me ask you this," he said. "Why do you want to take the job?"

"Well, it's like you said. I—I feel like I'm an important piece of the business. And believe me, I wouldn't be where I am without Isaiah and Joshua. They're brilliant. But I want to be able to make my own choices. Maybe I want to take on this project. Especially now that you've said…everything about needing it to be the opposite of a prison cell. I'm inspired to do it. I love this location. I want to build this house without Isaiah hovering over me."

Levi chuckled, low and gravelly. "So he wouldn't approve of me?"

"Not at all."

"I am innocent," he said. His mouth worked upward again. "Or I should say, I'm not guilty. Whether or not I'm an entirely innocent person is another story. But I didn't do anything to my wife."

"Your ex-wife?"

"Nearly. Everything should be finalized in the next couple of days. She's not contesting anything. Mostly because she doesn't want to end up in prison. I have impressed upon her how unpleasant that experience was. She has no desire to see for herself."

"Oh, of course you're still married to her. Because everybody thought—"

"That she was dead. You don't have to divorce a dead person."

"Let me ask you something," she said, doing her best to meet his gaze, ignoring the quivering sensation she felt in her belly. "Do I have reason to be afraid of you?"

The grin that spread over his face was slow, calculated. "Well, I would say that depends."

Chapter 2

He shouldn't toy with her. It wasn't nice. But then, he wasn't nice. He hadn't been, not even before his stint in prison. But the time there had taken anything soft inside of him and hardened it. Until his insides were a minefield of sharpened obsidian. Black, stone-cold, honed into a razor.

The man he'd been before might not have done anything to provoke the pretty little woman in front of him. But he could barely remember that man. That man had been an idiot. That man had married Alicia, had convinced himself he could have a happy life, when he had never seen any kind of happiness come from marriage, not all through his childhood. So why had he thought he could have more? Could have something else?

"Depends on what?" she asked, looking up at him,

those wide brown eyes striking him square in the chest…and lower, when they made contact with his.

She was so very pretty.

So very young, too.

Her pale, heart-shaped face, those soft-looking pink lips and her riot of brown curls—it all appealed to him in an instant, visceral way.

No real mystery, he supposed. He hadn't touched a woman in more than five years.

This one was contraband. She had a use, but it wouldn't be *that* one.

Hell, no.

He was a hard bastard, no mistake. But he wasn't a criminal.

He didn't belong with the rapists and murderers he'd been locked away with for all those years, and sometimes the only thing that had kept him going in those subhuman conditions—where he'd been called every name in the book, subjected to threats that would make most men weep with fear in their beds—was the knowledge that he didn't belong there.

That he wasn't one of them.

Hell, that was about the only thing that had kept him from hunting down Alicia when he'd been released.

He wasn't a murderer. He wasn't a monster.

He wouldn't let Alicia make him one.

"Depends on what scares you," he said.

She firmed those full lips into a thin, ungenerous line, and perhaps that reaction should have turned his thoughts in a different direction.

Instead he thought about what it might take to coax those lips back to softness. To fullness. And just how much riper they might become if he was to kiss them. To take the lower one between his teeth and bite.

He really wasn't fit for company. At least not delicate, female company.

Sadly, it was delicate female company that seemed appealing.

He needed to go to a bar and find a woman more like him. Harder. Closer to his age.

Someone who could stand five years of pent-up sexual energy pounded into her body.

The sweet little architect he had hired was not that woman.

If her brothers had any idea she was meeting with him they would get out their pitchforks. If they had any idea what he was thinking now, they would get out their shotguns.

And he couldn't blame them.

"Spiders. Do you have spiders up your sleeves?"

"No spiders," he said.

"The dark?"

"Well, honey, I can tell you for a fact that I have a little bit of that I carry around with me."

"I guess as long as we stay in the light it should be okay."

He was tempted to toy with her. He didn't know if she was being intentionally flirtatious. But there was something so open, so innocent, about her expression that he doubted it.

"I'm going to go sketch," she said. "Now that I've seen the place, and you've sent over all the meaningful information, I should be able to come up with an initial draft. And then I can send it over to you."

"Sounds good," he said. "Then what?"

"Then we'll arrange another meeting."

"Sounds like a plan," he said, extending his hand.

He shouldn't touch her again.

But he wanted to touch her again.

Pink colored her cheeks. A blush.

Dammit all, the woman had blushed.

Women who blushed were not for men like him.

That he had a sense of that at all was a reminder. A reminder that he wasn't an animal. Wasn't a monster.

Or at least that he still had enough man in him to control himself.

"I'll see you then."

Chapter 3

Faith was not hugely conversant in the whole girls'-night-out thing. Mia, her best friend from school, was not big on going out, and never had been, and usually, that had suited Faith just fine.

Faith had been a scholarship student at a boarding school that would have been entirely out of her family's reach if the school hadn't been interested in her artistic talents. And she'd been so invested in making the most of those talents, and then making the most of her scholarships in college, that she'd never really made time to go out.

And Mia had always been much the same, so there had been no one to encourage the other one to go out.

After school it had been work. Work and more work, and riding the massive wave Faith had somehow managed to catch that had buoyed her career to nearly absurd levels as soon as she'd graduated.

But since coming to Copper Ridge, things had somehow managed to pick up and slow down at the same time. There was something about living in a small town, with its slower pace, clean streets and wide-open spaces all around, that seemed to create more time.

Not having to commute through Seattle traffic helped, and it might actually be the sum total of where she had found all that extra time, if she was honest.

She had also begun to make friends with Hayley Bear, formerly Thompson, now wife of Jonathan. When Faith and her brothers had moved their headquarters to Copper Ridge, closer to their parents, Joshua had decided it would be a good idea to find a local builder to partner with, and that was how they'd met Jonathan, and merged their businesses.

And tonight, Faith and Hayley were out for drinks.

Of course, Hayley didn't really drink, and Faith was a lightweight at best, but that didn't mean they couldn't have fun.

They were also in Hayley's brother's bar.

They couldn't have been supervised any better if they tried. Though, the protectiveness was going to be directed more at Hayley than Faith.

Faith stuck her straw down deep into her rum-and-Coke and fished out a cherry, lifting it up and chewing it thoughtfully as she surveyed the room.

The revelers were out in force, whole groups of cheering friends standing by Ferdinand, the mechanical bull, and watching as people stepped up to the plate—both drunk and sober—to get thrown off his back and onto the mats below.

It looked entirely objectionable to Faith. She couldn't imagine submitting herself to something like that. A ride you couldn't control, couldn't anticipate. Where the only way off was to weather the bucking or get thrown to the mats below.

No, thanks.

"You seem quiet," Hayley pointed out.

"Do I?" Faith mused.

"Yes," Hayley said. "You seem like you have something on your mind."

Faith gnawed the inside of her cheek. "I'm starting a new design project. And it's really important that I get everything right. I mean, I'm going to be collaborating with the guy, so I'm sure he'll have his own input, and all of that, but…" She didn't know how to explain it without giving herself away, then she gave up. "If I told you something…could you keep it a secret?"

Hayley blinked her wide brown eyes. "Yes. Though… I don't keep anything from Jonathan. Ever. He's my husband and…"

"Can Jonathan keep a secret?"

"Jonathan doesn't really do…*friends*. So, I'm not sure who he would tell. I think I might be the only person he talks to."

"He works with my brothers," Faith pointed out.

"To the same degree he works with you."

"Not really. A lot more of the stuff filters through Joshua and Isaiah than it does me. I'm just kind of around. That's our agreement. They handle all of the… business stuff. And I do the drawing. The designing. I'm an expert at buildings and building materials, aesthetics and design. Not so much anything else."

"Point taken. But, yes, if I asked Jonathan not to say something, he wouldn't. He's totally loyal to me." Hayley looked a little bit smug about that.

It was hard to have friends who were so happily…

relationshipped, when Faith knew so little about how that worked.

Though at least Hayley wasn't with Faith's *brother*.

Yes, that made Faith and Mia family, which was nice in its way, but it really limited their ability to talk about boys. They had always promised to share personal things, like first times. While Faith had been happy for her friend, and for her brother, she also had wanted details about as much as she wanted to be stripped naked, had a string tied around her toe and be dragged through the small town's main street by her brother Devlin's Harley.

As in: not at all.

"I took a job that Joshua and Isaiah are going to be really mad about…"

Just then, the door to the bar opened, and Faith's mouth dropped open. Because there he was. Speaking of.

Hayley looked over her shoulder, not bothering to be subtle. "Who's that?" she hissed.

"The devil," Faith said softly.

Hayley blinked. "You had better start at the beginning."

"I was about to," Faith said.

The two of them watched as Levi went up to the counter, leaned over and placed an order with Ace, the bartender and owner of the bar, and Hayley's older brother.

"That's Levi Tucker," Faith said.

Hayley narrowed her eyes. "Why do I know that name?"

"Because he's kind of famous. Like, a famous murderer."

"Oh, my gosh," Hayley said, slapping the table with

her open palm, "he's that guy. That guy accused of murdering his wife! But she wasn't really dead."

"Yes," Faith confirmed.

"You're working with him?"

"I'm designing a house for him. But he's not a murderer. Yes, he was in prison for a while, but he didn't actually do anything. His wife disappeared. That's not exactly his fault."

Hayley looked at Faith skeptically. "If I ran away from my husband it would have to be for a pretty extreme reason."

"Well, no one's ever proven that he did anything. And, anyway, I'm just working with him in a professional capacity. I'm not scared of him."

"Should you be?"

Faith took in the long, hard lines of his body, the dark tattoos on his arms, that dark cowboy hat pulled low over his eyes and his sculpted jaw, which she imagined a woman could cut her hand on if she caressed it...

"No," she said quickly. "Why would I need to be scared of him? I'm designing a house for the guy. Nothing else."

He began to scan the room, and she felt the sudden urge to hide from that piercing blue gaze. Her heart was thundering like she had just run a marathon. Like she just might actually be...

Afraid.

No. That was silly. Impossible. There really wasn't anything to be afraid of.

He was just a man. A hard, scarred man with ink all over his skin, but that didn't mean he was bad. Or scary.

Devlin had tattoos over every visible inch of his body from the neck down.

She didn't want to know if they were anywhere else.

There were just some things you shouldn't know about your brother.

But yeah, tattoos didn't make a man scary. Or dangerous. She knew that.

So she couldn't figure out why her heart was still racing.

And then he saw them.

She felt a rush of heat move over her body as he raised his hand and gripped the brim of his cowboy hat, tipping his head down slowly in a brief acknowledgment.

She swallowed hard, her throat sticky and dry, then reached for her soda, feeling panicky. She took a long sip, forgetting there was rum in it, the burn making her cough.

"This is concerning," Hayley said softly, her expression overly sharp.

"What is?" Faith asked, jerking her gaze away from Levi.

"You're *not* acting normal."

"I'm not used to subterfuge." Faith sounded defensive. Because she felt a little defensive.

"The look on your face has nothing to do with the fact that he's incredibly attractive?"

"Is he?" Faith asked, her tone disingenuous, but sweet. "I hadn't noticed."

Actually, until Hayley had said that, she hadn't noticed. Well, she had, but she hadn't connected that disquiet in her stomach with finding him...*attractive*.

He was out of her league in every way. Too old for her. Too hard for her.

Levi was the deep end of the pool, and she didn't know how to swim. That much, she knew.

And she wouldn't… He was a client. Even if she was a champion lap swimmer, there was no way.

He was no longer acknowledging her or Hayley, anyway, as his focus turned back to the bar.

"What's going on with you?" Faith asked, very clumsily changing the subject and forcing herself to look at Hayley.

She and Hayley began to chat about other things, and she did her best to forget that Levi Tucker was in the bar at all.

He had obviously forgotten she was there, anyway.

Then, for some reason, some movement caught her attention, and she turned.

Levi was talking to a blonde, his head bent low, a smile on his face that made Faith feel like she'd just heard him say a dirty word. The blonde was looking back at him with the exact same expression. She was wearing a top that exposed her midriff, which was tight and tan, with a little sparkling piercing on her stomach.

She was exactly the kind of woman Faith could never hope to be, or compete with. And she shouldn't want to, anyway.

Obviously, Levi Tucker was at the bar looking for a good time. And Faith wasn't going to be the one to give it to him, so Blondie McBellyRing might as well be the one to do it.

It was no skin off Faith's nose.

Right then, Levi looked up, and his ice-blue gaze collided with hers with the force of an iceberg hitting the *Titanic*.

And damn if she didn't feel like she was sinking.

He put his hand on the blonde's hip, leaning in and saying something to her, patting her gently before moving away…and walking straight in Faith's direction.

Chapter 4

Levi had no idea what in the hell he was doing.

He was chatting up Mindy—who was a sure thing if there ever was one—and close to breaking that dry spell. He'd watched the little blonde ride that mechanical bull like an expert, and he figured she was exactly the kind of woman who could stay on his rough ride for as long as he needed her to.

A few minutes of banter had confirmed that, and he'd been ready to close the deal.

But then he'd caught Faith Grayson staring at them. And now, for no reason he could discern, he was on his way over to Faith.

Because it was weird he hadn't greeted her with more than just a hat tip from across the room, he told himself, as he crossed the roughhewn wood floor and moved closer to her.

And not for any other reason.

"Fancy meeting you here," he said, ignoring the intent look he was getting from Faith's friend.

"Small towns," Faith said, shrugging and looking like she was ready to fold in on herself.

"You're used to them, aren't you? Aren't you originally from Copper Ridge?"

She nodded. "Yes. But until recently, I haven't lived here since I was seventeen."

"I'm going to get a refill," her friend announced suddenly, sliding out of her seat and making her way over to the bar.

Faith was looking after her friend like she wanted to punch the other woman. It made him wonder what he'd missed.

"She leaving you to get picked up on?" he asked, snagging the vacant seat beside her, his shoulder brushing hers.

She went stiff.

"No," Faith said, lowering her head, her cheeks turning an intense shade of pink.

Another reminder.

Another reminder he should go back over and talk to Mindy.

Faith was *young*. She blushed. She went rigid like a nervous jackrabbit when their shoulders touched. He didn't have the patience for that. He didn't want a woman who had to be shown what to do, even if he didn't mind the idea of corrupting her.

That thought immediately brought a kick of arousal straight to his gut.

All right, maybe his body didn't hate the idea of corrupting her. But he was in control of himself, and whatever baser impulses might exist inside of him, he had the final say.

"She vacated awfully quickly."

"That's Jonathan Bear's wife," she said conversationally, as if that was relevant to the conversation.

Well, it might not be relevant. But it was interesting.

His eyebrows shot up, and he looked back over at the pretty brunette, who was now standing at the counter chatting with the bartender. "And that's her brother," Faith continued.

"I didn't pick Jonathan Bear for a family man."

"He wasn't," Faith said. "Until he met Hayley."

Hayley was young. Not as young as Faith, but young. And Jonathan wasn't as old as Levi was.

That wasn't relevant, either.

"I haven't been to the bar since it changed ownership. Last I was here was…twenty years ago."

"How old are you?"

"Thirty-eight. I had a fake ID."

She laughed. "I didn't expect that."

"What? That I'm thirty-eight or that I had a fake ID?"

"Either."

Her pink tongue darted out and swept across her lips, leaving them wet and inviting. Then she looked down again, taking a sip of whatever it was in her glass. He wondered if she had any idea what she was doing. Just how inviting she'd made her mouth look.

Just how starving he was.

How willing he would be to devour her.

He looked back at Mindy, who was watching him with open curiosity. She didn't seem angry or jealous, just watching to see how her night was going to go, he imagined.

And that was exactly the kind of woman he should be talking to.

He was still rooted to the spot, though. And he didn't make a move back toward her.

"Are you going to be too hungover after tonight to come over to my place and discuss your plans?"

She looked behind him, directly at Mindy. "I figure I should ask you the same question."

"I'm betting I have a lot more hard-drinking years behind me than you do."

"I'm twenty-five," she said. Like that meant something.

"Oh, nothing to worry about, then."

"Four whole years of drinking," she said.

"Did you actually wait to drink until you were twenty-one?"

She blinked. "Yes."

"You know most people don't."

"That can't be true."

He didn't bother to hold in his laugh. "It is."

"I'm sure the…" She frowned. "I was about to say that I'm sure my brothers did. But… I bet they didn't."

She looked comically shocked by that. Who was this girl? This girl who had been lauded as a genius in a hundred articles, and designed the most amazing homes and buildings he'd ever seen. And seemed to know nothing about people.

"You know the deal about the Easter Bunny, too, right?" he asked.

She twisted her lips to the side. "That he has a very fluffy tail?"

He chuckled. "Yeah. That one."

He didn't know why it was difficult to pull himself away. It shouldn't be.

Dammit all, it shouldn't be.

"How about we meet up after lunch?" he asked, pushing the subject back to the house.

"That sounds good to me," she said, her tone a little bit breathless.

"You have the address where I'm staying?"

"Text it to me."

"I will."

He stood and walked away from her then, headed back toward the woman who would have been his conquest. He had another drink with Mindy, continuing to talk to her while she patted his arm, her movements flirtatious, her body language making it clear she was more than ready to have a good time. And for some reason, his body, which had been game a few moments earlier, wasn't all that interested anymore. He looked back over to where Faith and her friend had been sitting, and saw that the table was empty now.

He didn't know when she had left, and she hadn't bothered to say goodbye to him.

"You know what?" he said to Mindy. "I actually have work tomorrow."

She frowned. "Then why did you come out?"

"That's a good damn question." He tipped back his drink the rest of the way, committed now to getting a cab, because he was getting close to tipsy. "I'll make it up to you some other time."

She shrugged. "Well, I'm not going home. Tonight might not be a loss for me. Enjoy your right hand, honey."

If only she knew that his right hand was even a luxury. In shared living quarters with all the stuff that went down in prison, he'd never had the spare moment or the desire.

There was shame, and then there was the humiliation of finding a quiet corner in the dirty cell you shared with one or two other men.

No thank you.

He would rather cut off his right than use it to add to all that BS.

It was better to just close off that part of himself. And he'd done it. Pretty damn effectively. He'd also managed to keep himself safe from all manner of prison violence that went on by building himself a rather ruthless reputation.

He had become a man who felt nothing. Certainly not pleasure or desire. A man who had learned to lash out before anyone could come at him.

The truly astonishing thing was how easy that had been.

How easy it had been to find that piece of his father that had probably lived inside of him all along.

"Maybe I will," he responded.

"So, are you really working early?" Mindy asked. "Or are you intent on joining that little brunette you were talking to earlier?"

Fire ignited in his gut.

"It'll be whatever I decide," he said, tipping his hat. "Have a good evening."

He walked out of the bar with his own words ringing in his head.

It would be what he would decide.

No one else had control over his life. Not now. Not ever.

Not anymore.

Chapter 5

The next morning, Faith's body was still teeming with weird emotions. It was difficult to untangle everything she was feeling. From what had begun when Hayley had called him attractive, to what she'd felt when she'd watched him continue to chat with the blonde, to when she had ultimately excused herself because she couldn't keep looking at their flirtation.

She realized—when she had been lying in her bed— that the reason she had to cut her girls' night short was that she couldn't stand knowing whether or not Levi left the bar with the pretty blonde.

She was sure he had. Why wouldn't he? He was a healthy, adult man. The kind who had apparently had a fake ID, so very likely a bad-boy type. Meaning that an impromptu one-night stand probably wouldn't bother him at all.

Heck, it had probably been why he was at the bar.

Her stomach felt like acid by the time she walked into the GrayBear Construction building.

The acidic feeling didn't improve when she saw that Joshua was already sitting there drinking a cup of coffee in the waiting room.

"What are you doing here?" she asked, then kicked the door shut with her foot and made her way over to the coffeemaker.

"Good morning."

"Shouldn't you be home having breakfast with your wife and kids?"

"I would be, but Danielle has an OB appointment later this morning." Joshua's wife was pregnant, and he was ridiculously happy about it. And Faith was happy for him. Two of her sisters-in-law were currently pregnant. Danielle very newly so, and Poppy due soon. Mia and Devlin seemed content to just enjoy each other for now.

Her brothers were happy. Faith was happy for them.

It was weird to be the last one so resolutely single, though. Even with her dating life so inactive, she had never imagined she would be the last single sibling in her family.

"I need to be at the appointment," he said. "She's getting an ultrasound."

"I see. So you came here to get work done early?"

"I've been here since six."

"I guess I can't scowl at you for that."

"Why are you scowling at all?"

She didn't say anything, and instead, she checked her buzzing text. It was from Levi. Just his address. Nothing more. It was awfully early. If he had a late night, would he be up texting her?

Maybe he's just still up.

She wanted to snarl at that little inner voice.

"You busy today?" Joshua asked casually.

"Not really. I have some schematics to go over. Some designs to do. Emails to send." She waved a hand. "A meeting later."

He frowned. "I don't have you down for a meeting."

Great. She should have known her PR brother would want to know what meeting she would be going out for.

"It's not like a work meeting. It's like, for…a school talk." She stumbled over the lie, and immediately felt guilty.

"No school contacted me. Everything is supposed to go through me."

"I can handle community work in the town of Copper Ridge, Joshua. It's not like this is Seattle. And there's not going to be press anywhere asking me stupid questions or trying to trip me up. It's just Copper Ridge."

"Still."

The door opened and Isaiah came in, followed by his wife, Poppy, who was looking radiant in a tight, knee-length dress that showed off the full curve of her rounded stomach. They were holding hands, with their fingers laced together, and the contrast in their skin tones was beautiful—it always ignited a sense of artistic pleasure in Faith whenever she saw them. Well, and in general, seeing Isaiah happy made her feel that way. He was a difficult guy. Hard to understand, and seemingly emotionless sometimes.

But when he looked at Poppy… There was no doubt he was in love.

And no doubt that his wife was in love right back.

"Good morning," Isaiah said.

"Did you know Faith had a meeting with one of the

schools today to give some kind of community-service talk?" Joshua launched right in. The dickhead.

"No," Isaiah said looking at her. "You really need to clear these things with us."

"Why?"

"That's not on my schedule," Poppy said, pulling out her phone and poking around the screen.

"Don't start acting like my brothers," Faith said to her sister-in-law.

"It's my job to keep track of things," Poppy insisted.

"This is off the books," Faith said. "I'm allowed to have something that's just me. I'm an adult."

"You're young," Joshua said. "You're incredibly successful. Everyone wants a piece of that, and you can't afford to give out endless pieces of yourself."

She huffed and took a drink of her coffee. "I can manage, Joshua. I don't need you being controlling like this."

"The company functions in a specific way—"

"But my life doesn't. I don't need to give you an accounting of everything I do with my time. And not everything is work-related."

She spun on her heel and walked down the hall and, for some reason, was immediately hit with a flashback from last night. Levi didn't talk to her like she was a child. Levi almost…flirted with her. That was what last night had been like. Like flirting.

The idea gave her a little thrill.

But there was no way Levi had been flirting with… her. He had been flirting with that pretty blonde.

Faith made sure the door to her office was shut, then she opened up her office drawer, pulling out the mirror she kept in there, that she didn't often use. Just quick checks before meetings. And not to make sure she looked attractive—to make sure she didn't look twelve.

She tilted her chin upward, then to the side, examining her reflection. It was almost absurd to think of him wanting to flirt with her. It wasn't that she was unattractive, it was just that she was...plain.

She had never really cared. Not really.

She could look a little less plain when she threw on some makeup, but then, when she did that, her goal was to look capable and confident, and old enough to be entrusted with the design of someone's house. Not to be pretty.

She twisted her lips to the side, then moved them back, making a kiss face before relaxing again. Then she sighed and put the mirror back in her drawer. It wasn't that she cared. She was a professional. And she wasn't going to...act on any weird feelings she had.

Even if they were plausible.

It was just... When she had talked to Levi last night she had left feeling like a woman. And then she had come into work this morning and her brothers had immediately reset her back to the role of little girl.

She thought about that so effectively that before she knew it, it was time for her to leave to go to Levi's place.

She pulled another bag out of her desk drawer—her makeup bag—and made the snap decision to go for an entirely different look, accomplished with much internet searching for daytime glamour and an easy tutorial. Then she fluffed her hair, shaking it out and making sure the curls looked a little bit tousled.

She threw the bag back into her desk and stood, swaggering out of her office, where she was met by Isaiah, who jerked backward and made a surprised sound.

"What?" she asked.

"You look different."

She waved a hand. "I thought I would try something new."

"You're going to give a talk at one of the…schools?"

"Yes," she said.

"Which school?" he pressed.

She made an exasperated sound. "Why do you need to know?" He said nothing, staring at her with his jaw firmed up. "You need to know because you need it to be in Poppy's planner, because if it's not in Poppy's planner it will feel incomplete to you, is that it?"

She'd long since given up trying to understand her brother's particular quirks. He had them. There was no sense fighting against them. She was his sister, so sometimes she poked at them, rather than doing anything to help him out. That was the way the world worked, after all.

But she'd realized as she'd gotten older that he wasn't being inflexible to be obnoxious. It was something he genuinely couldn't help.

"Yes," he responded, his tone flat.

If he was surprised that she had guessed what the issue was, he didn't show it. But then, Isaiah wouldn't.

"Copper Ridge Elementary," she said, the lie slipping easily past her lips, and she wondered who she was.

A *woman*. That's who she was.

A woman who had made an executive decision about her own career and she did not need her brothers meddling in it.

And her makeup wasn't significant to anything except that she had been sitting there feeling bad about herself and there was no reason to do that when she had perfectly good eyeliner sitting in her desk drawer.

"Thank you," he said.

"Are we done? Can you add it to the calendar and pacify yourself and leave me alone?"

"Is everything okay?" he asked, the question uncharacteristically thoughtful.

"I'm fine, Isaiah. I promise. I'm just… Joshua is right. I've been working a lot. And I don't feel like the solution is to do less. I think it might be…time that I took some initiative, make sure I'm filling my time with things that are important to me."

Of course, she was lying about it being schoolchildren, which made her feel slightly guilty. But not guilty enough to tell the truth.

Isaiah left her office then, to update the planner, Faith assumed. And Faith left shortly after.

She put the address to Levi's house in her car's navigation system and followed the instructions, which led her on much the same route she had taken to get up the mountain to meet him the first time, at the building site. It appeared that his rental property was on the other side of that mountain, on a driveway that led up the opposite side that wound through evergreen trees and took her to a beautiful, rustic-looking structure.

It was an old-fashioned, narrow A-frame with windows that overlooked the valley below. She appreciated it, even if it wasn't something she would ever have put together.

She had a fondness for classic, cozy spaces.

Though her designs always tended toward the open and the modern, she had grown up in a tiny, yellow farmhouse that she loved still. She loved that her parents still lived there in spite of the financial successes of their children.

Of course, Levi's house was several notches above

the little farmhouse. This was quite a nice place, even if it was worlds apart from a custom home.

She had been so focused on following the little rabbit trails of thought on her way over that she hadn't noticed the tension she was carrying in her stomach. But as soon as she parked and turned off the engine, she seemed to be entirely made of that tension.

She could hardly breathe around it.

She had seen him outside, out in the open. And she had talked to him in a bar. But she had never been alone indoors with him before.

Not that it mattered. At all.

She clenched her teeth and got out of the car, gathering her bag that contained her sketchbook and all her other supplies. With the beat of each footstep on the gravel drive, she repeated those words in her head.

Not that it mattered.

Not that it mattered.

She might be having some weird thoughts about him, but he certainly wasn't having them about her.

She could only hope that the blonde had vacated before Faith's arrival.

Why did the thought of seeing her here make Faith feel sick? She couldn't answer that question.

She didn't even *know* the guy. And she had never been jealous of anyone or anything in her life. Okay, maybe vague twinges of jealousy that her brothers had found people to love. Or that Hayley had a husband who loved her. That Mia had found someone. And the fact that Mia's someone was Faith's brother made the whole thing a bit inaccessible to her.

But those feelings were more like…envy. This was different. This felt like a nasty little monster on her back that had no right to be there.

She steeled herself, and knocked on the door. And waited.

When the door swung open, it seemed to grab hold of her stomach and pull it along. An intense, sweeping sensation rode through her.

There he was.

Today, he'd traded in the black T-shirt and hat from the last couple of days for white ones.

The whole look was…beautiful and nearly absurd. Because he was *not* a white knight, far from it. And she wasn't innocent enough to think that he was.

But there was something about the way the light color caught hold of those blue eyes and reflected the color even brighter that seemed to steal every thought from her head. Every thought but one.

Beautiful.

She was plain. And this man was *beautiful*.

Oh, not pretty. Scars marred his face and a hard line went through his chin, keeping him from being symmetrical. Another one slashed his top lip. And even then, the angles on his face were far too sharp to be anything so insipid as pretty.

Beautiful.

"Come on in," he said, stepping away from the door.

She didn't know why, but she had expected a little more conversation on the porch. Maybe to give her some time to catch her breath. Sadly, he didn't give it to her. So she found herself following his instructions and walking into the dimly lit entry.

"It's not that great," he said of his surroundings, lifting a shoulder.

"It's cozy," she said.

"Yeah, I'm kind of over cozy. But the view is good."

"I can't say that I blame you," she said, following his

lead and making her way into the living area, which was open. The point from the house's A-frame gave height to the ceiling, and the vast windows lit the entire space. The furniture was placed at the center of the room, with a hefty amount of space all around. "That must've been really difficult."

"Are you going to try to absorb details about my taste by asking about my personal life? Because I have to tell you, my aesthetic runs counter to where I've spent the last five years."

"I understand that. And no, it wasn't a leading question. I was just…commenting."

"They started the investigation into my wife's disappearance when you were about eighteen," he said. "And while you were in school I was on house arrest, on trial. Then I spent time behind bars. In that time, you started your business and… Here you are."

"A lot can happen in five years."

"It sure can. Or a hell of a lot of nothing can happen. That's the worst part. Life in a jail cell is monotonous. Things don't change. An exciting day is probably not a good thing. Because it usually means you got stabbed."

"Did you ever get—" her stomach tightened "—stabbed?"

He chuckled, then lifted up his white T-shirt, exposing a broad expanse of tan skin. Her brain processed things in snatches. Another tattoo. A bird, stretched across his side, and then the shifting and bunching of well-defined muscles. Followed by her registering that there was a sprinkling of golden hair across that skin. And then, her eye fell to the raised, ugly scar that was just above the tattooed bird's wing.

"Once," he said.

He pushed his shirt back down, and Faith shifted uncomfortably, trying to settle the feeling that the bird had peeled itself right off his skin and somehow ended up in her stomach, fluttering and struggling for freedom.

She looked away. "What happened?"

She put her hand on her own stomach, trying to calm her response. She didn't know if that intense, unsettled feeling was coming from her horror over what had happened to him, or over the show of skin that had just occurred.

If it was the skin, she was going to be very disappointed in herself and in her hormones. Because the man had just told her he'd been stabbed. Responding to his body was awfully base. Not to mention insensitive.

"I made the man who did it regret that he'd ever seen me." Suddenly, there was nothing in those ice-blue eyes but cold. And she didn't doubt what he said. Not at all.

"I see."

"You probably don't. And it's for the best. No, I didn't kill him. If I had killed him, I would still be in prison." He sat down in a chair that faced the windows. He rested his arms on the sides, the muscles there flexing as he moved his fingers, clenching them into fists. "But a brawl like that going badly for a couple of inmates? That's easy enough to ignore. I got a few stitches because of a blade. He got a few more because of my fists. People learned quickly not to mess with me."

"Apparently," she said, sitting down on the couch across from him, grateful for the large, oak coffee table between them. "Is any of this furniture yours?"

"No," he responded.

"Good," she replied. "Not that there's anything wrong with it, per se. But—" she knocked on the table "—if you were married to a particular piece it might make it more difficult, design-wise. I prefer to have total freedom."

"I find that in life I prefer to have total freedom," he said, the corner of his mouth quirking upward.

A rash of heat started at Faith's scalp and prickled downward. "Of course. I didn't mean… You know that I didn't…"

"Calm down," he said. "I'm not that easily offended. Unless you stab me."

"Right," she responded. She fished around in her bag until she came up with her notepad. "We should talk more about what you have in mind. Let's start with the specifics. How big do you want the house to be?"

"Big," he replied. "It's a massive lot. The property is about fifty acres, and that cleared-out space seems like there's a lot of scope there."

"Ten thousand square feet?"

"Sure," he responded.

She put her pen over the pad. "How many bedrooms?"

"I should only need one."

"If you don't want more than one, that's okay. But… guests?"

"The only people who are going to be coming to my house are going to be staying in my bed. And even then, not for the whole night."

She cleared her throat. "Right." She tapped her pen against the side of her notebook. "You know, you're probably going to want more bedrooms."

"In case of what? Orgies? Even then, we'd need one big room."

"All right," she said. "If you want an unprecedented one-bedroom, ten-thousand-square-foot house, it's up to you." She fought against the blush flooding her cheeks, because this entire conversation was getting a little earthy for her. And it was making her picture things. Imagining him touching women, and specifically the blonde from last night, and she just didn't need that in her head.

"I wasn't aware I had ordered judgment with my custom home. I thought I ordered an entirely custom home to be done to my specifications."

She popped up her head. Now, this she was used to. Arrogant men who hired her, and then didn't listen.

"You did hire me to design a custom home, but presumably, you wanted my design to influence it. That means I'm going to be giving input. And if I think you're making a decision that's strange or stupid I'm going to tell you. I didn't get where I am by transcribing plans that come from the heads of people who have absolutely no training. If there's one thing I understand, it's buildings. It's design. Homes. I want to take the feeling inside of you and turn it into something concrete. Something real. And I will give you one bedroom if that's what you really want. But if you want a computer program to design your house, then you can have no feedback. I am not a computer program. I'm an…artist."

Okay, that was pushing it a lot further than she usually liked to go. But he was annoying her.

And making her feel hot.

It was unforgivable.

"A mouthy one," he commented.

She sniffed. "I know my value. And I know what I do well."

"I appreciate that quality in…anyone."

"Then appreciate it when I push back. I'm not doing it just for fun."

"If it will make you feel better you can put a few bedrooms in."

"There will definitely be room," she said. "Anyway, think of your resale value."

"Not my concern," he said.

"You never know. You might care about it someday." She cleared her throat. "Now, bathrooms?"

"Put down the appropriate number you think there should be. Obviously, you want me to have multiple bedrooms, I would assume there is an appropriate bathroom number that coincides with that."

"Well, you're going to want a lot. For the orgies." She bit her tongue after she said the words.

"Yeah, true. The last thing you want is for everyone to need a bathroom break at once and for there not to be enough."

She took a deep breath, and let it out slowly. The fact of the matter was, this conversation was serving a bigger purpose. She was forming a lot of ideas about him. Not actually about orgies, but about the fact that he was irreverent. That there was humor lurking inside him, in spite of the darkness. Or maybe in part because of it. That he was tough. Resilient.

That things glanced off him. Like hardship, and knife blades.

A small idea began to form, then expanded into the sorts of things she had been thinking when they had first met. How she could use curves, angles and lines to keep from needing doors, but to also give a sense of privacy, without things feeling closed off.

"Can you stand up?" she asked.

She knew it was kind of an odd question, but she wanted to see where his line of sight fell. Wanted to get an idea of how he would fill the space. He wasn't a family man. His space was going to be all about him. And he had made it very clear that was what he wanted.

She needed to get a sense of him.

"Sure," he responded, pushing himself up onto his feet, arching an eyebrow.

She walked around him, made her way to the window, followed where she thought his line of sight might land. Then she turned to face him, obscuring his view.

"What are you doing?"

"I'm just trying to get a sense for how a room will work for you. For where your eye is going to fall when you look out the window."

"I can send you measurements."

She made a scoffing sound. "You're six-foot-three."

"I am," he said. "How did you guess?"

"I can visualize measurements pretty damn accurately. I'm always sizing up objects, lots, locations. That's what I do."

"It's still impressive."

"Well, I did have to see you stand before I could fully trust that I was right about your height."

"And how tall are you?"

She stretched up. "Five-two."

A smile curved his lips. "You wouldn't even be able to reach things in my house."

"It's no matter. I can reach things in mine."

"How would you design a house for two people with heights as different as ours?"

She huffed out a laugh, her stomach doing an uncomfortable twist. "Well, obviously when it comes to space, preference has to be given to the taller person so they don't feel like things are closing in on them."

He nodded, his expression mock-serious. "Definitely."

"Mostly, with a family," she said, "which I design for quite a bit, I try to keep things mostly standard in height, with little modifications here and there that feel personal and special and useful to everyone."

"Very nice. Good deflection."

"I wasn't deflecting."

He crossed his arms, his gaze far too assessing. "You seemed uncomfortable."

"I'm not."

"You would want space for a big bed."

"I would?" Her brain blanked. Hollowed out completely.

"If you were designing a room for a man my size. Even if the woman was small."

She swallowed, her throat suddenly dry. "I suppose so."

"But then, I figure there's never a drawback to a big bed."

"I have a referral I can give you for custom furniture," she said, ignoring the way her heart was thundering at the base of her throat, imagining all the things that could be done in a very large bed.

In gauzy terms. Seeing as she had no actual, real-world experience with that.

"I may take you up on that offer," he said, his words like a slow drip of honey.

"Well, good. That's just…great. It's a custom…sex palace." She pretended to write something down, all while trying to hide the fact her face was burning.

"No matter what it sounds like," he said, "I'm not actually asking you for a glorified brothel. Though, I'm not opposed to that being a use. But I want this house to be for me. And I want it to be without limits. I'm tired of being limited."

Her heart twisted. "Right. I—I understand."

She sucked in a sharp breath, and went to move past him, but he spoke again, and his voice made her stop, directly in front of him. "I shared a cell with, at minimum, one other person for the last five years. Everything was standard. Everything. And then sized down. Dirty. Uncomfortable. A punishment. I spent five years being punished for something I didn't do."

She tilted up her face, and realized that she was absurdly close to him. That she was a breath away from his lips. "Now you need your reward."

"That I do."

His voice went low, husky. She felt…unsteady on her feet. Like she wanted to lean in and press her lips to his.

She should move. She was the one who had placed herself right there in front of him. She was the one who had miscalculated. But she wasn't moving. She was still standing there. She couldn't seem to make herself shift. She licked her lips, and she saw his gaze follow the motion. His eyes were hot again.

And so was she. All over.

She was suddenly overcome by the urge to reach out her hand and touch that scar that marred his chin. The other one that slashed through his lip.

To push her hand beneath his shirt and touch that scar he had shown her earlier.

That thought was enough to bring her back to earth. To bring her back to her senses.

She took a step back, a metallic tang filling her mouth. Humiliation. Fear.

"You know," he said slowly. "They lock men like me up. That's a pretty good indication you should probably keep your distance."

"You didn't do anything," she said.

"That doesn't mean I'm not capable of doing some very bad things." His eyes were hot, so hot they burned. And she should move away from him, but she wasn't.

Heaven help her, she wasn't.

She tried to swallow, but her mouth was so dry her tongue was frozen in place. "Is that a warning? Or a threat?"

"Definitely a warning. For now." He turned away from her and faced the window. "If you listen to it, it'll never have to be a threat."

"Why?"

What she felt right now was a strange kind of emotion. It wasn't anger; it wasn't even fear. It was just a strange kind of resolve. Her brothers already treated her like a child who didn't know her own mind—she wasn't about to let this man do the same thing. Let him issue warnings as if she didn't understand exactly who she was and what she wanted.

She might not know who he was. But she damn well knew who she was.

And she hadn't even done anything. Maybe she wouldn't. Maybe she never would.

But maybe she wanted to, and if she did, the consequences would be on her. It wouldn't be for anyone else to decide.

Least of all this man. This stranger.

"Little girl," he said, his voice dripping with disdain. "If you have to ask why, then you definitely need to take a step back."

Little girl.

No. She wouldn't have this man talk down to her. She had it all over her life, from well-meaning people who loved her. People whose opinions she valued. She wasn't going to let him tell her who she was or what she wanted. To tell her what she could handle.

She didn't step back. She stepped forward.

"I have a feeling you think you're a singular specimen, Levi Tucker. You, with your stab wound and your rough edges." Her heart was thundering, her hands shaking, but she wasn't going to step away. She wasn't going to do what he wanted or expected. "You're not. You're just like every other man I've ever come into contact with. You think you know more than me simply because you're older, or maybe because you have a—a *penis*."

She despised herself for her stutter, but as tough as she was trying to be, she couldn't utter that word a foot away from a man. Not effortlessly. She sucked in a sharp breath. "I'm not exactly sure what gives men such an unearned sense of power. But whatever the reason, you think it's acceptable to talk down to me. Without acknowledging the fact that I have navigated some incredibly difficult waters. They would be difficult for *anyone*, much less someone my age. I'm a lot harder and more filled with resolve than most people will ever be. I don't do warnings or threats. *You* might do well to remember that."

He reached out, the move lightning-fast, and grabbed hold of her wrist. His grip was strong, his hands rough. "And I don't take lectures from prim little misses in pencil skirts. Maybe you'd do well to remember that."

Lightning crackled between them, at the source of his touch, but all around them, too. She was so angry at him. And judging by the fire in his eyes, he was mad at her, too.

She arched forward, and he held her fast, his eyes never leaving hers.

"Do they offer a lot?" she asked. "Prim little misses, I mean. To lecture you?"

"I can't say any of them have ever been able to bring themselves to get this close to me."

She reached out, flexing her fingers, then curled them into a fist, before resting her fingers flat onto his chest. She could feel his heartbeat raging beneath her hand. She could feel the rhythm echoed in her own labored breathing.

This was insane. She'd never...*ever* touched a man like this before. She'd never wanted to. And she didn't know what kind of crazy had taken over her body, or her mind right then.

She only knew that she wanted to keep touching him. That she liked the way it felt to have him holding tightly to her wrist.

That she relished the feeling of his heartbeat against her skin.

He smelled good. Like the pine trees and the mountain air, and she wondered if he'd been outside before she'd come over.

A man who couldn't be contained by walls. Not now.

And her literal job was to create a beautiful new cage for him.

She suddenly felt the urge to strip him of everything. All his confines. All his clothes. To make him free.

To be free with him.

The urge was strong—so strong—she was almost shocked to find she hadn't begun to pull at his T-shirt.

But what would she even do if she...succeeded?

He released his hold then, but she could still feel his touch lingering long after he'd taken away his hand. She felt dazed, thrown.

Stunned to discover the world hadn't collapsed

around them in those moments that had seemed like hours, but had actually been a breath.

"You should go."

She should. She really, really should.

But she didn't want him to know he'd scared her.

It's not even him that scares you. You're scaring yourself.

"I'm going to go sketch," she said, swallowing hard. "This has been very enlightening."

"If your plan is to go off and design me a prison cell now..."

"No," she said. "I'm a professional. But trust me, I've learned quite a bit about you. And my first question to you wasn't leading, not necessarily. But everything that we've discussed here? It will definitely end up being fodder for the design. You're truly going to be in a prison of your own making by the time I'm through, Levi. So you best be sure you like what you're using to build it."

She didn't know where she got the strength, or the wit for all of that. And by the time she turned on her heel and walked out of the A-frame, heading back to her car, she was breathing so hard she thought she might collapse.

But she didn't.

No, instead she got in her car and drove away, that same rock-solid sense of resolve settling in her stomach now as had been there only a moment before.

Attraction.

Was that what had just happened back there? Attraction to a man who seemed hell-bent on warning her off.

Why would he want to warn her off?

If he really did see her as a little girl, if he really did

see her as someone uninteresting or plain, he wouldn't need to warn her away.

What he'd said about threats...

By the time she pulled back into GrayBear Construction, she wasn't hyperventilating anymore, but she was certain of one thing.

Levi Tucker was attracted to her, too.

She was not certain exactly what she was supposed to do with that knowledge.

She felt vaguely helpless knowing she couldn't ask anyone, either.

Her brothers would go on a warpath. Hayley would caution her. Mia would...well, Mia would tell Devlin, because Devlin was her husband and she wouldn't want to keep secrets from him.

Faith's network was severely compromised. For one moment that made her feel helpless. Then in the next...

It was her decision, she realized.

Whatever she did with this... It was her decision.

She wasn't a child. And she wasn't going to count on the network of people she was used to having around her to make the choice for her.

And she wasn't going to worry about what they might think.

Whatever she decided...

It would be her choice.

And whatever happened as a result... She would deal with the consequences.

The resolve inside of her only strengthened.

Chapter 6

He was back at the bar. Because there was nothing else to do. As of today, he was officially a divorced man, and he'd been without sex for five years.

And earlier today he had been about a breath away from taking little Miss Prim and Proper down to the ground and screwing them both senseless.

And he had already resolved that he wouldn't do that. He wouldn't *be* that.

His post-divorce celebration would not be with Faith Grayson. With her wide eyes and easy blush. And uncommon boldness.

He couldn't work out why she wasn't afraid of him. He had thought... A little, soft thing like her... The evidence of a knife fight and talk of prison, jokes about orgies... It all should have had a cowering effect on her.

It hadn't.

No, by the end of the interaction she'd only grown bolder. And he couldn't for the life of him figure out how that worked.

She was fascinated by him. That much was clear. She might even think she wanted to have a little fun with some kind of bad-boy fantasy, but the little fool had no idea.

He was nobody's fantasy.

He was a potential nightmare, but that was it.

He flashed back to the way it had felt to wrap his hand around her wrist. Her skin soft beneath his. To the way she'd looked up at him, her breath growing choppy and fast.

Those fingertips on his chest.

Shit, he needed to get laid.

He ordered up a shot of whiskey and pounded it down hard, scanning the room, looking for a woman who might wipe the image of Faith Grayson from his mind.

Maybe Mindy would be back. Maybe they could pick up where they left off.

But as he looked around, his eye landed on a petite brunette standing in line for the mechanical bull. She was wearing a tight pair of blue jeans, and a fitted T-shirt, and when she turned, he felt like he'd been punched in the stomach.

Faith Grayson.

With that same mulish expression on her face she'd had when she'd left his house earlier.

The rider in front of her got thrown, and Faith rubbed her hands together, glaring at the mechanical beast with intensity. Then she marched up to it, and took her position.

She thrust her hips forward, wrapping one hand

around the handle and holding the other up high over her head. She looked more like a ballerina than a bull rider. But her expression...

That was all fire.

He should look away. He sure as hell shouldn't watch as the mechanical bull began its forward motion, shouldn't watch the way Faith's eyes widened, and then the way her face turned determined as she gripped more tightly with one hand, and tensed her thighs around the beast, moving her hips in rhythm with it.

It didn't last long.

On the creature's second roll forward, Faith was unseated, her lips parting in an expression of shock as she flew forward and onto the mats below.

And before he could stop himself, he was on his feet, making his way across the space. She was on her back, her chin-length curls spread around her head like a halo on a church window. But her expression was anything but angelic.

"Are you okay?" he asked.

She looked up at him, and all the shock drained from her face, replaced instead by a spark of feral-looking rage. "What are you doing here?"

"What are you doing getting on the back of that thing?" He moved closer, ignoring the crowd of people looking on. "You clearly have no business doing it."

"It's not your business...what I have business doing or not doing. Stop trying to tell me what to do."

He put out his hand, offering to take hold of hers and help her up, but she ignored him, pushing herself into a sitting position and scrabbling to her feet.

"I'm fine," she said.

"I know you're fine," he returned. "It's not like I

thought the thing was going to jump off its post and trample you to death. But it's also clear you're being an idiot."

"Well, look at the whole line of idiots," she said, indicating the queue of people. "I figured I would join in."

"Why exactly?"

"Because," she said. "Because I'm tired of everyone treating me like a kid. Because I'm tired of everyone telling me what to do. Do you know, that it was almost impossible for me to sneak away to our meeting today because my brothers need to know what I'm doing every second of every day. It's like they think I'm still fifteen years old."

He shrugged. "As I understand it, that's older brothers, to a degree."

"Are you an older brother?"

"No," he said. "Only child. But still, seems a pretty logical conclusion."

"Well, whatever. I went to boarding school from the time I was really young. Because there were more opportunities for me there then here. I lived away from my family, and somehow... Everyone is more protective of me. Like I didn't have to go make my own way when I was a kid." She shook her head. "I mean, granted, it was an all-girls boarding school, and it was a pretty cloistered environment. But still."

"Let me buy you a drink," he said, not quite sure why the offer slipped out.

You know.

He ignored that.

"I don't need you to buy me a drink," she said fiercely, storming past him and making her way to the bar. "I can buy my own drink."

"I'm sure you can. But I offered to do it. You should let me."

"Yeah, you have a lot of opinions about what I should and shouldn't do in a given moment, don't you?"

Still, when he ordered her a rum-and-Coke, she didn't argue. She took hold of it and leaned against the bar, angling toward him. His eyes dropped down to her breasts, a hard kick of lust making it difficult for him to breathe.

"What are you doing here?" He forced his gaze away from her breasts, to her face.

She narrowed her eyes. "I'm here to ride a mechanical bull and make a statement about my agency by doing so. Not to anyone but myself, mind you. It might be silly, but it is my goal. What's yours?"

"I'm here to get laid," he said, holding her eyes and not blinking. That should do the trick. That should scare her away.

Unless…

She tilted her head to the side. "Is that what you were here for last night?"

"Yes, ma'am," he responded.

Her lips twitched, and she lifted up her glass, averting her gaze. "How was she?" She took a sip of the rum-and-Coke.

"As it happens," he said, "I didn't go home with her."

She spluttered, then set down the glass on the bar and looked at him. She didn't bother to disguise her interest. Her curiosity. "Why?"

"Because I decided at the end of it all I wasn't really that interested. No one was more surprised by that than I was."

"She was beautiful," Faith said. "Why weren't you... into her?"

He firmed his jaw, looking Faith up and down. "That is the million-dollar question, honey."

That same thing that had stretched between them back at the house began to build again. It was like a physical force, and no matter that he told himself she was all wrong, his body seemed to disagree.

You dumbass. You want something harder than she can give. Something dirtier. You don't want to worry about your partner. You want a partner who can handle herself.

But then he looked back at Faith again, her cheeks rosy from alcohol and the exertion of riding the bull, and maybe from him.

He wanted her.

And there wasn't a damn thing he could do to change that.

"I have a theory," Faith said.

"About?"

"About why you didn't want her." She sucked her straw between her lips and took a long sip, then looked up at him, as if fortified by her liquid courage. "Is it because...?" She tilted her chin upward, her expression defiant. "Are you attracted to me, Levi?"

He gritted his teeth, the blood in his body rushing south, answering the question as soon as she asked it. "You couldn't handle me, baby girl."

"That's not what I asked you."

"But it's an important thing for you to know."

She shrugged her shoulders. "That's what you think. Again, putting you on the long list of men who think they know what I should and shouldn't do, or want, or think about."

He leaned in and watched as the color in her cheeks deepened. As that crushed-rose color bloomed more fully. She was playing the part of seductress—at least, in her funny little way—but she wasn't as confident as she was hoping to appear. That much he could tell.

"Do you have any idea what I would do to you?" he asked.

She wrinkled her nose. "I would assume…the normal sort of thing."

He chuckled. "Sweetheart, I was locked up for five years. I'm not sure I remember what the normal sort of thing is anymore. At this point, all I have to go on is animal instinct. And I'm not totally sure you should feel comfortable with that."

She shifted, and he noticed her squeezing her thighs together. The sight sent a current of lust straight through his body. Dammit. He was beginning to think he had underestimated her.

"That still isn't what I asked you," she said softly. She looked up at him, her expression coy as she gazed through her thick lashes. "Do you want me?"

"I'd take you," he said through gritted teeth. "Hard. And believe me, you'd like it. But I don't want *you*, sweetheart. I just want. It's been a hell of a long time for me, Faith. I'm all about the sex, not the woman. I'm not sure that's the kind of man you should be with."

She squared her shoulders and looked at him full on, but the color in her cheeks didn't dissipate. "What kind of man do you think I should be with?"

He could see it. Like a flash of lightning across the darkness in his soul. A man who would get down on one knee and ask Faith to be his. Have babies with her. Live with her, in a house with a lot of bedrooms for all those babies.

A man she could take to family dinners. Hold hands with.

A man who could care.

That was what she deserved.

"One who will be nice to you," he said, moving closer. "One you can take home to your family." He cupped her cheek, swept his thumb over her lower lip and felt her tremble beneath his touch. "A man who will make love to you." She tilted her face upward, pressing that tempting mouth more firmly against his thumb. "All I can do is screw you, sweetheart."

She looked down, then back up. And for once, she didn't have a comeback.

"You deserve a man who will marry you," he continued.

That mobilized her. "Get married? And then what? Have children? I'm twenty-five years old and my career is just starting to take off. Why would I do anything to interrupt that? Why would you think that's what I'm looking for right now? I have at least ten years before worrying about any of that. A few affairs in the meantime…"

He snorted. "Affairs. That sounds a hell of a lot more sophisticated and fancy than what I've got in mind, princess."

"What have I ever done to make you think I'm a princess? To make you think I need you to offer more than what I'm standing here showing interest in? You don't have access to my secret heart, Levi."

"If you had any sense in your head, you would walk

out of this bar and forget we had this conversation. Hell, if you had any sense at all you would forget today happened. Just do the job I hired you to do and walk away. My wife let me go to jail for her murder while she was alive. And whatever the authorities think, whatever she says…"

He bit down hard, grinding his teeth together. "She was going to let me rot there, in a jail cell. While letting me think she was dead. Do you know… I grieved her, Faith. I didn't know she was in hiding. I didn't know she had left me on her own feet. All I knew was that she was gone, and that I hadn't killed her. But I believed some other bastard had. My motivation while I was in prison was to avenge my wife, and in the end? She's the one who did this to me." He laughed hard, the sound void of humor. "Love is a lie. Marriage is a joke. And I'm not going to change my mind about that."

"Marriage is an impediment to what I want," Faith said. "And I'm not going to change my mind about that. You're acting like you know what I want. What I should want. But you don't."

"What do you want, sweetheart? Because all I've got to give you is a few good orgasms."

She drew in a sharp breath, blinking a couple of times. Then she looked around the bar, braced herself on the counter and drew up on her toes as high as she could go, pressing a kiss to the lower corner of his mouth. When she pulled away, her eyes were defiant.

If she was playing chicken with him, if she was trying to prove something, she was going to regret it. Because he was not a man who could be played with.

Not without consequences.

He wrapped his arm around her waist, crossed her

to his chest and hauled her up an extra two inches so their mouths could meet more firmly.

And that's when he realized he had made a mistake.

He had been of a mind that he would scare her off, but what he hadn't anticipated was the way his own control would be so tenuous.

He had none. None at all.

Because he hadn't been this close to a woman in more than five years. And he'd imagined his wife a victim. Kidnapped or killed. And when he'd thought of her his stomach had turned. And not knowing what had happened to Alicia…

It hadn't felt right to think of anyone else.

So for most of those five years in prison he hadn't even had a good go-to fantasy. It had been so long since he'd been with a woman who hadn't betrayed him, and it was hard for him to remember a woman other than his wife.

But now… Now there was Faith.

And she burned brighter, hotter, than the anger in his veins. He forgot why he had been avoiding this. Forgot everything but the way she tasted.

It was crazy.

Of all the women he could have touched, he shouldn't touch her. She worked for him. He had hired her to design his house and he supposed that made this the worst idea of all.

But she was kissing him back as though it didn't matter.

Maybe he was wrong about her. Maybe she made a habit of toying with her rich and powerful clients. Maybe that was part of why she'd gotten to where she was.

No skin off his nose if it was true. And it suited him

in many ways, because that meant she knew the rules of the game.

Because you need justification for the fact that you're doing exactly what you swore to yourself you wouldn't?

Maybe his reaction had nothing to do with his ex-wife making him into a monster. Maybe it had everything to do with Faith making him a beast.

Uncontrolled and ravenous for everything he could get.

He cupped her chin, forcing her lips apart, and thrust his tongue deep. And she responded. She responded beautifully. Hot and slick and enthusiastic.

"You better give an answer and stick to it," he said when they pulled away, his eyes intent on hers. "Say yes or no now. Because once we leave this bar—"

"Yes," she said quickly, a strange, frantic energy radiating from her. "Yes. Let's do it."

"This isn't a business deal, honey."

"That's why I didn't shake your hand." She sounded breathless, and a little bit dazed, and damn it all if it wasn't a thousand times more intoxicating than Mindy's careful seduction from last night.

"Then let's go." Now he was in a damn hurry. To get out of here before she changed her mind. Before he lost control completely and took her against a wall.

"What about my car?" she asked.

"I'll get you back to it."

"Okay," she said.

He put down a twenty on the bar, and ignored the way the bartender stared at him, hard and unfriendly-like, as though the man had an opinion about what was going on.

"Tell the man you're with me," he said.

Faith's eyes widened, and then she looked between him and the bartender. "I'm with him," she said softly.

The bartender's expression relaxed a fraction. But only a fraction.

Then Levi took her hand and led her out into the night. The security lights in the lot were harsh, bright blue, and she still looked beautiful beneath them. That was as close to poetry as he was going to get. Because everything else was all fire. Fire and need, and the sense that if he didn't get inside her in the next few minutes, he was going to explode.

"Levi…"

He grabbed her and pulled her to him, kissing her again, dark and fierce and hard. "Last chance," he said, because he wasn't a gentleman, but he wasn't a monster, either.

"Yes."

Chapter 7

Faith felt giddy. Drunk on her own bravery. Her head was swimming, arousal firing through her veins. She had never felt like this before. Ever. She had gone on a couple of dates, all of which had ended with sad, sloppy kisses at the door and no desire at all on her part for it to go any further.

She had begun to think the only thing she was really interested in was her career. That men were irrelevant, and if men were, then sex was, too. She had just figured that was how she was. That maybe, when the time came, and she was ready to settle down, or ready to pull back on her career, she would find her priorities would naturally restructure and sex would suddenly factor in. But she hadn't worried about it.

And now… It wasn't a matter of making herself interested. No. It was a matter of life and death. At least it felt like it might be.

He took her hand to his heart, and helped her into his truck. She didn't say a word as he started the engine and they pulled out of the parking lot.

Her heart was thundering, and she was seriously questioning her sanity. To go from her first make-out session to sex in only a few minutes might not be the best idea, but it might also be…the only way. She was half out of her mind with desire, just from feeling his lips on hers. Even so, she honestly couldn't imagine wanting more than sex.

This man, her secret.

It had been almost funny when he had said something about taking a man home to meet her family. There would be no way she could ever take him home to meet her parents.

His frame would be so large and ridiculous in that tiny farmhouse. The ice in his veins, the scars on his soul, so much more pronounced in that warm, sweet kitchen of her mother's.

No, Faith didn't want to take him home. She wanted him to take her to bed.

And maybe it was crazy. But she had never intended to save herself for anything in particular. Anything but desire, really.

And this was the first time she had ever felt it.

What better way to get introduced to sex, really? An older man who knew exactly what he was doing. Because God knew she didn't.

And for once, she wasn't going to think. She wasn't going to worry about the future, wasn't going to worry about anyone else's opinion, because no one was ever going to know.

Levi Tucker was already her dirty secret in her professional life. Why couldn't he be her personal one, too?

Suddenly, he jerked the car off the highway, taking it down a narrow, dirt road and into the woods. "This isn't the way to your house."

"Can't wait," he growled.

"What's this?" she asked, her heart pounding in her chest.

"A place I know about from way back. Back when I used to get in trouble around these parts."

Get in trouble.

That's what she was about to do. Get in trouble with him.

She felt…absolutely elated. She had gone out to the bar tonight to do *something.* To shake things up. She had seen riding the bull as a kind of kickoff tour for her mini Independence Day.

Oh, it wasn't one she was going to flaunt in front of her brothers or anything like that. It was just acknowledging that sense of resolve from earlier. She was going to have something that was just hers. Choices that were hers.

It had all started with taking this job, she realized. So, it was fitting that the rest of it would involve Levi, too.

"Okay," she said.

"Still good?"

She gritted her teeth, and then made a decision, feeling much bolder than she should have. She moved her hand over and pressed it against his thigh. He was hard, hot. Then she slid her hand farther up, between his legs, capturing his length through denim. He was big. Oh, Lord, he was big. She hadn't realized… Well, that just went to show how ignorant she was. Maybe he was average, she didn't know. But it was a hell of a lot bigger than she had imagined it might be.

It was going to be inside her.

Her internal muscles clenched, and she realized that rather than fear, she was overcome completely by excitement. Maybe that was the perk of waiting twenty-five years to lose your virginity. She was past ready.

He growled, jerking his car off the road and to a turnout spot next to the trees. Then he unbuckled his seat belt and moved over to the center of the bench seat, undoing her belt and hauling her into his lap. He kissed her, deep and hard, matching what had happened back at the bar.

Her head was spinning, her whole body on fire.

He stripped off her T-shirt, quickly and ruthlessly, his fingers deft on her bra. She didn't even have time to worry about it. Didn't have time to think. Her breasts were bare, and he was cupping them, sliding calloused thumbs over her nipples, teasing her, enticing her.

She felt like she was flying.

She wanted him to take her wherever this was going. She wanted him to take control. She was used to being the one in control. The one who knew what she was doing. She was a natural in her field, and that meant she always walked in knowing what she was doing. Being the novice was a strange, amazing feeling, and she had the sense that if she'd been with a man any less masterful, it might feel diminishing.

Instead it just felt like—like a weight on her shoulders suddenly lifted. Because he was bearing responsibility for all these feelings of pleasure in her body. He was stoking the need, and soothing it just as quickly. But all the while, a deep, endless ache was building between her legs and she wanted… She needed… She didn't know.

But she knew that he knew. Oh, yes, he did.

He kissed her neck, cupping her head as he moved lower, as he captured one nipple between his lips and sucked her in deep. It was so erotic, so filthy, and she couldn't do anything but arch into his touch as he moved his attention to her other breast. He was fulfilling fantasies she hadn't even known she'd had.

She had just never…thought about doing such a thing. And here he was, not only making it seem appealing, but it was also as if she might die if she didn't have it.

He pulled his own shirt over his head, tugging her heart against his chest, his muscles, the hair there, adding delicious friction against her nipples, and she squirmed. He wrapped his arm tightly around her waist, cupped her head and laid her back, somehow managing to strip her of her jeans and panties in record time in the close confines of the truck. Then he took hold of the buckle on his belt, and she heard the rasp of fabric and metal as he worked the leather strap through, as he undid the zipper on his jeans.

She jumped when he pressed his hand between her thighs, moved his fingers through her slickness, drawing the moisture up over that sensitized bundle of nerves, then slid his thumb expertly back and forth, creating a kind of tension inside her she wasn't sure she could withstand.

"I'll make it last longer later," he said gruffly. "Promise."

But she didn't really understand what he meant, and when she heard the tearing of a plastic packet, she only dimly registered what was about to happen. Then he was kissing her again, and she didn't think. Until the blunt head of his arousal was pushing into her body, until he thrust hard and deep, a fierce, burning sensation claiming any of the pleasure she had felt a moment before.

She cried out, digging her fingernails into his shoulders, trying to blot out the pain that was rolling through her like a storm.

"Faith…"

She tensed up, turning her head away, freezing for a moment. "Don't say anything," she whispered.

"Sorry," he said, sinking more deeply into her, a groan on his lips. "You feel so damn good."

And that tortured admission did something to her, ignited something deep inside her that went past pain. That went past fear. The scary part was over. It was done. And the pain was already beginning to roll itself back.

"Don't stop," she whispered, curling her fingers around his neck and holding on as she shifted beneath him.

It was strange, this feeling. His body inside hers. How had she not realized? How intimate something like this would be?

Everybody talked about sex at university. Gave great proclamations about what they liked and what they didn't, had endless discussions about the *when*, the *why* and the *with who*. But no one had ever said sex made you feel like someone hadn't just entered your body, but your whole soul. No one had said that you would want to run away and draw closer at the same time.

No one had said that it would be a great, wrenching pain followed by a deep, strange sense of connection that seemed to bloom into desire again as he shifted his hips and arched into her.

She tested what it might feel like if she moved against him, too, and found that she liked it. With each and every thrust that he made into her body, animalistic sounds coming from deep inside of him, she met him. Until her body was slick with sweat—his or hers, she didn't know. Until that fierce need she had felt the first time he had kissed her was back. Until she thought she might die if she didn't get more of him.

Until she no longer wanted to run at all.

He growled, his hardness pulsing inside her as he froze above her, slamming back into her one last time. And then, a release broke inside her like a wave, and she found herself drowning. In pleasure. In him.

And when he looked at her, she suddenly felt small and fragile. Any sense of being resolute crumbled.

And much to her horror, a tear slid down her cheek.

She was crying. God in heaven, the woman was crying.

No. He wasn't going to think about God. Not right now. Because God had nothing to do with this. No, this was straight from hell, and he was one of the devil's chosen. There was no other way to look at it.

Not only had he taken her in his truck like a beast— a fancy justification for sidestepping the word *monster* if ever there was one—but she had also been a virgin.

And he hadn't stopped.

When he had hit that resistance, when he had seen that flash of pain on her face, he had waited only a moment before he kept on going. She'd lifted her hips, and he hadn't been able to do anything but keep going. Because she was beautiful. And he wanted her. More than beautiful, she was soft and delicate, and an indulgence.

And he hadn't had any of that for more than five years.

Sinking into her tight body had been a revelation. As much as a damnation.

"Damn it to hell," he muttered, straightening and pulling his pants back into place. He chucked the condom out the window, not really giving a damn what happened to it later.

"What?" she asked, her petite frame shivering, shaking, her arms wrapped tightly around her body, as though she was trying to protect herself.

Too little, too late.

"You know."

"I don't," she said, shrinking more deeply into the far corner of the truck, her pale figure cast into a soft glow by the moonlight. "I don't... I thought it was good."

Her voice was trembling, watery, and he could hear the sigh that she breathed out becoming a sob.

"You didn't tell me you were a virgin," he said, trying to keep the accusation out of his voice, because dammit, he had known. On some level, he had known. And he hadn't been put off by it all.

No, he had *told* himself to be put off by it. By her obvious innocence and inexperience. He had commanded himself not to be interested in it. To chase after someone more like him. Someone a little bit dark. Someone a little bit craven. But his body didn't want that.

Because his soul was a destroyer. A consumer of everything good and sweet.

Hadn't Alicia been sweet when he'd met her? Hadn't she transformed into something else entirely over their time together? How could he ignore the fact that he was the common denominator at the center of so many twisted scenarios in his life.

Him.

The one thing he could never fully remove from the equation unless he removed himself from the world.

"So what?" she asked, shuffling around in the car, undoubtedly looking for her clothes. "I knew that."

"I damn well didn't."

"What does it have to do with anything?"

"You told me you knew what you were doing."

"I did," she said, her voice shrinking even smaller. "I knew exactly what we were going to do." She made a soft, breathy laugh. "I mean, I didn't know that we were going to do it in the truck. I expected it to take a little bit...longer. But I knew we were going to have sex."

"You're crying."

"That's my problem," she said.

"No," he said, reaching across the space and dragging her toward him. He gripped her chin between his thumb and forefinger and gazed into her eyes. It was dark, but he could see the glitter in her gaze. Like the stars had fallen down from the sky and centered themselves in her. "Now it's my problem."

"It doesn't have to be. I made a choice. My lack of experience doesn't make it less my choice."

"Yes, it does. Because you didn't really know. I hurt you. And because you didn't tell me, I hurt you worse than I would have."

"Again, that's on me. I wanted to have sex with an older guy. One who knew what he was doing. I'm way too old to be a virgin, Levi. I never found someone I wanted to change that with, and then I met you and I wanted you. It seems simple to me."

"Simple."

The top of his head had just about blown off. Nothing about this seemed simple to him.

"Yes," she said.

"Little girl, I haven't had sex in more than five years. You don't want a man like me in bed with you. You want a nice man who has the patience to take time with your body."

"But I like *your* body. And I like the way it made mine feel."

"I hurt you," he pointed out.

She lifted a pale shoulder. "It felt good at the end."

"Doesn't matter. That's all I have. Rough and selfish. That's what I am. It's all I want to be."

"Well, I want to be my own person. I want to be someone who makes her own choices and doesn't give a damn what anyone else thinks. So maybe we're about perfect for each other right now."

"Right now."

"Yes," she said. "I don't know why you find it so hard to believe, but I really do know what I want. Do you think I'm going to fall in love with you, Levi?"

She spoke the words with such disdainful incredulity, and if he was a different man, with a softer heart—with a heart at all—he might've been offended. As it was, he found her open scorn almost amusing.

"Virgins fall in love with all kinds of assholes, sweetheart."

"Have you deflowered a lot of them?"

"No. I haven't been with a damn virgin since I was one."

"Then maybe calm down with your pronouncements." She was wiggling back into her jeans now, then pulling her top over her head. She hadn't bothered to put her bra back on. And he was the perverse bastard who took an interest in that.

"I'm a lot more experienced than you. Maybe you should recognize that my pronouncements come from a place of education."

"It's done," she said. "And you know what? It was fine. It was fine until this."

"I'll take you home."

"Take me back to my car," she said.

"I'd rather not drop you back in the parking lot at this hour."

"Take me back to my damn car," she said. "I don't want to arrange a ride later. I don't need my car sitting in the parking lot all night, where people can draw conclusions."

"You didn't mind that earlier."

"Well, earlier I didn't feel bad or ashamed about my choices, but you've gone and made that…it's different now. It's different."

If he had a conscience, he would have felt guilt over that. But it wasn't guilt that wracked his body now. It was rage.

Rage that the monster had won.

The rage had nothing to do with her. Nothing about the way it might impact her life. It was about him.

Maybe that was selfish. He didn't really know. Didn't really care, either.

"If you'd like to withdraw from the job, I understand," he said when they pulled back into the parking lot of Ace's bar.

"Hell, no," she said, her tone defiant. "I'm not losing this job. You don't get to ruin that, too."

"I wouldn't figure you'd want to work with me anymore."

"You think you know a lot about me. For a man who knows basically nothing. The whole…intimacy-of-sex thing is a farce. You have no idea who I am. You have no idea what I want, what I need. I will finish this job because I took it on. And when I said that I wanted you, when I said I wanted this, I knew we were going to continue working together."

"Suit yourself."

"None of this suits me."

She tumbled out of the truck and went to her car, and he waited until she was inside, until she got it started and began to pull out of the space, before he started heading back toward his place.

But it wasn't until he parked in front of his house that he realized she had left her bra and panties behind.

The two scraps of fabric seemed to represent the final shreds of his humanity.

He reached out and touched her bra, ran his thumb over the lace.

And he asked himself why the hell he was bothering to pull away now. She had been…a revelation. Soft and perfect and everything he'd ever wanted.

He wondered why the hell he was pretending he cared about being a man, when being a monster was so much easier.

Chapter 8

One thought kept rolling through Faith's mind as she sat at her desk and tried to attend to her work.

She wasn't a virgin anymore.

She had lost her virginity. In the back of a pickup truck.

Of all the unexpected turns of events that had occurred in her life, this was inarguably the *most* unexpected. She surely had not thought she would do that, ever.

Not the virginity thing. She had been rather sanguine about that. She had known sex would happen eventually, and there was no point in worrying about it.

But the pickup truck. She had really not seen herself as a do-it-in-a-pickup-truck kind of girl.

With a man like that.

If she actually sat and broke down her thoughts on

what kind of man she had imagined she might be with, it wasn't him. Not even a little bit. Not even at all.

She had imagined she would find a man quite a bit like herself. Someone who was young, maybe. And understood what it was like to be ambitious at an early age. Someone who could relate to her. Her particular struggles.

But then, she supposed, that was more relationship stuff. And sex didn't require that two people be similar. Only that they ignited when they touched.

She certainly hadn't imagined it would be an ex-convict accused of murder who would light her on fire.

Make her come.

Make her cry.

Then send her away.

It had been a strange twelve hours indeed.

"Faith?" She looked up and saw Isaiah standing in the doorway. "I need estimates from you."

"Which estimates?" She blinked.

"The ones you haven't sent me yet," he said, being maddeningly opaque and a pain in the ass. He could just tell her.

She cleared her throat, tapping her fingers together. Hoping to buy herself some time. Or a clue. "Is there a particular set of estimates that you're waiting on?"

"If you have any estimates put together that I don't have, I would like them."

She realized that she didn't have any for him. And if she should…

That meant she had dropped the ball.

She never dropped the ball.

She had been working, full tilt, at this job for enough years now that she had anticipated the moment when she might drop the ball, but she hadn't. And now she had taken on this extra project, this work her brothers didn't know about, and she was messing up.

That isn't why...

No, it wasn't.

She was messing up because she felt consumed. Utterly and completely consumed by everything that was happening with Levi.

Levi Tucker was so much more than just an interesting architecture project.

It was the structure of the man himself that had her so invested. Not what she might build for him.

She wanted to see him again. Wanted to talk to him. Wanted to lie down in a bed with him, with the lights on so she could look at all his tattoos and trace the lines of them.

So she could know him.

Right. That makes sense. He's nothing like you thought you wanted. Why are you fixating?

A good question.

She didn't want him to be right. Right about virgins and how they fell in love as easy as some people stumbled while walking down the street.

"Faith?"

Isaiah looked concerned now.

"I'm fine," she said.

"You don't look fine."

"I am." She shifted, feeling a particular soreness between her legs and trying to hide the blush that bled into her cheeks. It was weird to be conscious of that while she was talking to her brother.

"Faith, no one has ever accused me of being particularly perceptive when it comes to people's emotions. But I do know you. I know that you're never late with project work. If all of this has become too much for you..."

"It isn't," she insisted. "I love what we do. I'm so proud of what we've built, Isaiah. I'm not ever going to do anything to compromise that. I think I might have overextended myself a little bit with…extra stuff."

"What kind of extra stuff?"

"Just…community work."

Getting screwed senseless for the first time in my life…

"You don't need to do that. Joshua can handle all of that. It's part of his job. You should filter it all through him. He'll help you figure out what you should say yes to, what you can just send a signed letter to…"

"I know. I know you'll both help me. But at some point… Isaiah, this is *my* life." She took a breath. "We are partners. And I appreciate all that you do. If I had to calculate the finances like you, I would go insane. My brain would literally leak out of my ears."

"It would not literally leak out of your ears."

She squinted. "You don't know that."

"I'm pretty confident that I do."

She shook her head. "Just don't worry about me. You have a life now. A really good one. I'm so happy for you and Poppy. I'm so excited for your baby, and for… everything. You've spent too many years working like a crazy person."

"Like a robot," Isaiah said, lifting his brow. "At least, that's what I've been told more than once."

"You're not a robot. You came here to check on me. That makes it obvious that you aren't. But, you also can't carry everything for me. Not anymore. It's just not… I don't need you to. It's okay."

"You know we worry. We worry because you're right. If it weren't for us…then you wouldn't be in this position."

She made a scoffing sound. "Thanks. But if it weren't for me you wouldn't be in this position, either."

"I know," he returned. "I mean, I would still be working in finance somewhere else. Joshua would be doing PR. And you would no doubt be working at a big firm somewhere. But it's what we could do together that has brought our business to this level. And I think Joshua and I worry sometimes that it happened really quickly for you and we enabled that. So, we don't want to leave it all resting on your shoulders now."

She swallowed hard. "I appreciate that. I do. But I can handle it."

Isaiah nodded slowly and then turned and walked out of her office.

She could handle all of this.

Her job, which encouraged her to open up some files for her various projects and collect those estimates Isaiah was asking for, and this new turn of events with Levi.

She was determined to finish the project. The idea of leaving it undone didn't work for her. Not at all. Even if he was being terrible.

And you think you can be in the same room with him and not feel like you're dying?

She didn't know. She had just lost her virginity twelve hours ago, and she had no idea what she was supposed to do next.

Sitting at her desk and basking in that achievement was about all she could do. It was lunchtime when she got into her car and began to drive.

She had spent the rest of the morning trying to catch up, and as soon as she got on the road her thoughts began to wander. Back to what Levi had said to her last night. All the various warnings he had given. About how rough he was. How broken. And in truth, he had not been gentle. But none of it had harmed her. It might have hurt her momentarily, but that pain wasn't something she minded.

Maybe…

Maybe he had been right.

Maybe the whole thing was something she'd been ill-prepared for. Something she shouldn't have pushed for. Because, while physically she had been completely all right with everything that had happened, emotionally she wasn't okay with being pushed away.

And maybe that was the real caution in this story.

He had gone on and on about all that he believed she could handle and she had imagined he meant what she could handle from a sexual-sophistication standpoint. Moves and skills and the knowledge of how things went between men and women.

But that had been the easy part. Following his lead. Allowing his hands, his mouth, his… All of him, to take her on a journey.

But afterward…

She frowned, and it was only then that she realized which direction she was driving.

And she knew she had a choice.

She could keep on going, or she could turn back.

But even as she thought it, she knew the truth. It was too late.

She couldn't go back.

She might have a better understanding of things after last night, and with everything she knew now, she might have made a different decision in that bar.

But she had to go forward.

With that in mind, she turned onto the winding road that led up to Levi's house.

And she didn't look back.

* * *

When Levi heard the knock on his door, he was less than amused. He was not in the mood to be preached at, subjected to a sales pitch or offered Girl Scout cookies. And he could legitimately think of no other reason why anyone would be knocking on his door. So he pulled it open on a growl, and then froze.

"You're not a Jehovah's Witness."

Faith cleared her throat. "Not last I checked." She lifted a shoulder. "I'm Baptist, but—"

"That's not really relevant."

Her lips twitched. "Well… I guess not to *this* conversation, no."

"What are you doing here?"

"I felt like I was owed a chance to have a conversation with you when I wasn't naked and waiting to be returned to my car."

When she put it like that… He felt like even more of a dick. He hadn't thought that was possible.

"Go ahead," he said, extending his hand out.

"Oh. I didn't think… Maybe you should invite me in?"

"Should I?"

"It would be the polite thing to do."

"Well, you'll have to forgive me. In all the excitement of the last few years of my life, I've forgotten what the polite thing is."

"Oh, that's BS." And she breezed past him, and stamped into the house. "I understand that's your excuse of choice when it comes to all of your behavior. But I don't buy it."

"My excuse?" he asked. "I'm glad to know you consider five years in prison to be an excuse."

"I'm just saying that if you know you're behaving badly you could probably behave *less badly*."

He snorted. "You have a lot of unearned opinions."

"Well, maybe help me earn some of them. Stop making pronouncements at me about how I don't know what I'm doing and help me figure out what I'm doing. We had sex. We can't change that. I don't want to change it."

"Faith…"

"I don't see why we can't…keep having sex. I'm designing a house for you. There's a natural end to our acquaintance. It's…" She laughed, shaking her head. "You know, when my brother Isaiah proposed to his wife he told her it made sense. That it was logical. And I was angry at him because it was the least romantic thing I'd ever heard."

"I'm not sure I follow you."

"They weren't dating. She was his assistant. He was looking for a wife, and because he thought she was such a good assistant it meant she would likely make a good wife."

"And that went well for him?"

"Well, not at first. And I was angry at him. I hated the fact that he was turning something personal into a rational numbers game. It didn't seem right. It didn't seem fair. But now it kind of makes sense to me. Not that we are talking about marriage, but…an arrangement. Being near each other is going to be difficult after what we shared."

"I'm fine," he lied, taking a step away from her and her far too earnest face.

If *fine* was existing in a bad mood with a persistent hard-on, yeah, he was fine.

"I'm not," she said softly.

She took a step toward him, just like she had done on

those other occasions. Like a kid who kept reaching her hand toward the stove, even though she'd been burned.

That he thought of that metaphor should be the first clue he needed to take a step away. But he didn't.

It's too late.

The damage had already been done.

The time in prison had already changed him. Hell, maybe the damage had been done when he was born. His father's genes flowing through his veins were far too powerful for Levi to fight against.

"Until you're done designing the house," he said, his voice hard. "Just until then."

Her shoulders sagged in relief, and the look of vulnerability on her face would have made a better man rethink everything.

But Levi wasn't a better man. And he had no intention of attempting to be one at this point.

"I'm supposed to be at work," she said. "I really should get back."

He reached out and grabbed the handle on the front door, shutting it hard behind her. "No," he said. "Baby, you stepped into the lion's den. And you're not leaving until I'm good and ready for you to leave."

"But work," she said, her voice small.

"But this," he responded, wrapping his hand around her wrist and dragging her palm toward him. He pressed it against that hard-on making itself known in the front of his jeans.

"Oh," she said, pressing her palm more firmly down and rubbing against him.

"You want to do this, we're doing it my way," he said. "I didn't know you were a virgin the first time, but now it's done. Taken care of. I'm not going to go easy on you just because you're inexperienced, do you understand?"

And he wasn't sure she had any idea at all what she was agreeing to. She nodded again.

If he was a better man, that, too, might have given him pause.

But he wasn't. So it didn't.

"I like to be in charge. And I don't have patience for inhibition. Do you understand me?" She looked up at him, those eyes wide. He didn't think she understood at all. "That means if you want to do it, you do it. If you want me to do it, you ask for it. Don't hide your body from me, and I won't hide mine from you. I want to see you. I want to touch you everywhere. And there's no limit to what I'm going to do. That means the same goes for you. You can do whatever you want to me."

"But you're in charge," she said faintly.

"And that's my rule. If you think it'll feel good, do it. For you, for me." He leaned in, cupping her head in his hand and looking at her intently. "Sex can be a chore. If you're in a relationship with someone for a long time and there's no spark between you anymore—which doesn't happen on accident, you have to stop caring— then it can be perfunctory. Lights off. Something you just do. Like eating dinner.

"Now, if there's no emotional divide I don't mind routine sex. There's a comfort in it. But I haven't had sex in five years. There is no routine for me. That means I want raw. I want dirty. Because it can be that, too. It can be wild and intense. It can be slow and easy. It can be deliciously filthy. Sex can make you agree to things, say things, do things that if you were in your right mind you would find…objectionable. But when you're turned on, a lot of things seem like a good idea when they wouldn't otherwise. And that's the space I want to go to with you. That means no thinking. Just feeling."

Then he lifted her up and slung her over his shoulder. She squeaked, but she didn't fight his hold as he carried her out of the entry and up the stairs.

"You don't have your custom orgy bed yet."

He chuckled as they made their way down the hall, and he kicked open the door with his foot. "Well, we're not having an orgy, are we? This is a party for two."

"How pedestrian. It must be so boring for you."

"No talking, either."

He laid her down on the bed and she looked up at him, mutinous.

"Did you have a bra to wear today?"

"Yes."

"I have your other one."

She squinted. "I have more than one. I have more than *two*."

"Let me see this one."

She shifted, sat up and pulled her top over her head, exposing the red lace bra she had underneath. Then she reached behind herself, unzipped her pencil skirt and tugged it down, revealing her pair of matching panties.

"Damn," he said. "Last night, before we started, I'd planned on that side-of-the-road stuff being just the introduction."

"Yes, and then you got ridiculous."

"I *tried*," he said, his voice rough. "I tried not to be a monster, Faith. Because I might not have known you were a virgin, or at least I didn't admit it to myself, but I knew that…my hands are dirty. I'm just gonna get you dirty."

She looked up at him, and the confusion and hope in her eyes reached down inside him and twisted hard. "You said sex was fun when it was dirty."

"Different kinds of dirty, sweetheart."

She eased back, propping herself up on her forearms. It surprised him how bold she was, and suddenly, he wanted to know more. About this little enigma wrapped in red lace. An architectural genius. So advanced in so many ways, and so new in others.

"Take your bra and panties off," he commanded.

She reached back and unclipped her bra, pulling it off quickly. There was a slight hesitation when she hooked her thumbs in the waistband of her panties and started to pull them down. But only a slight one.

She wiggled out of them, throwing them onto the floor.

She kept the same position, lying back, not covering herself. Exposing her entire, gorgeous body.

Small, perfect breasts with pale pink nipples and a thatch of dark curls between her legs.

"I wanted to do the right thing. Just once. Even if I'd already done the wrong thing. But I give up, babe. I give the hell up."

He moved toward the edge of the bed, curved his arms up around her hips and dragged her toward him, pressing a kiss to her inner thigh. She made a small, kittenish sound as he moved farther down, nuzzled her center and then took a leisurely lick, like she was the finest dessert he'd ever encountered. She squirmed, squeaking as he held her more tightly, and he brought her fully against his face and began to devour her.

It had been so long. So long since he'd tasted a woman like this, and even then…

Faith was sweeter than anyone.

Faith wiped away the memory of any previous lover. Doing this for her was like a gift to himself.

He brought his hand between her legs and pressed two fingers deep inside her, working them in and out, in time with his tongue. He could feel her orgasm winding up tight inside of her. Could feel little shivers in her internal muscles, her body slippery with need. He drew out that slickness, rubbing two fingers over her sensitive core before bringing his lips back down and sucking that bundle of nerves into his mouth as he plunged his fingers back in. She screamed, going stiff and coming hard, those muscles like a vise around his fingers now as her climax poured through her.

By the time she was finished, he was so damn hard he thought he was going to break in two.

He stood up, stripped his shirt over his head and came back down on the bed beside her.

She was looking at him with a kind of clouded wonder in her eyes, delicate fingertips tracing over the lines on his arms. "These are beautiful," she said.

"You want to talk about my tattoos now?"

"That was great," she said, breathless. "But I was waiting to see these."

"Celtic knot," he said, speaking of the intricate designs on his arms. That wasn't terribly personal. He'd had it done when he was eighteen and kind of an idiot. He'd hated his father and had wanted to find some identity beyond being that man's son. Inking some of his Irish heritage on his skin, making it about some long-dead ancestors, had seemed like a way to do that at the time.

Or at least that's what he'd told himself.

Now Levi figured it was mostly an attempt at looking like a badass and impressing women.

"And the bird?" she pressed.

Freedom. Simple as that. Also not something he was going to talk about with a hard-on.

"I like bird-watching," he said, his lips twitching slightly. "Now, no talking."

He gripped her chin and pulled her forward, kissing her mouth and letting her taste her own arousal there.

He took her deeper, higher, playing between her legs while he reached into his bedside table to get a condom.

Her head was thrown back, her breasts arched up toward him. Her lips, swollen from kissing, parted in pleasure. She was his every dirty dream, this sweet little angel.

He kept on teasing her, tormenting her with his fingers while he lifted the condom packet to his lips with his free hand and tore it with his teeth. Then he rolled it onto his length, slowly, taking his position against the entrance of her body.

She was so hot. So slick and ready for him. He couldn't resist the chance to tease them both just a little bit more.

He held himself firmly at the base and arched his hips forward, sliding through those sweet folds of hers, pushing down against her sensitive bundle of nerves and reveling in her hoarse sound of pleasure.

He wasn't made for her. There was no doubt about that. He was hard, scarred and far too broken to ever be of any use to her. But as he pressed the thick head of his erection against her, as he slid into her tight heat, inch by agonizing inch, he wondered if she wasn't made for him.

She gasped, arching against him, this time not in pain. Not like the first time.

She held onto his shoulders, her fingertips digging into his skin as he thrust into her, pulling out slowly before pressing himself back home.

Again. And again.

Until they were both lost in the fog of pleasure. Until she was panting. Begging.

Until the only sound in the room was their bodies, slapping against each other, their breathing, harsh and broken. It was the middle of the day, and he hadn't taken her on a date. Hadn't given her anything but an orgasm. And he couldn't even feel guilty about it.

He had spent all those days in the dark. Counting the hours until nothing. Until the end. He had been given a life sentence. And with that there was almost no hope. Just a small possibility they'd find a body—as horrendous as that would be—and exonerate him. He had felt guilty hoping for that, even for a moment. But something. *Anything* to prove his innocence.

That had been his life. And he had been prepared for it to be the rest of his life.

And now, somehow, he was here. With her.

Inside Faith's body, the sunlight streaming in through the windows.

Blinded by the light, by his pleasure, by his need.

This was more than he had imagined having a chance to feel ever again. And he wasn't sure he'd ever felt anything like this. Like this heat and hunger that roared in his gut, through his veins.

He opened his eyes and looked at her, forced himself to continue watching her even as his orgasm burst through him like a flame.

It was like looking at hope.

Not just a sliver of it, but full and real. Possibilities he had never imagined could be there for him.

He had come from a jail cell and had intended to ask this woman to build a house for him, and instead...

They were screwing in the middle of the afternoon.

And something about it felt like the first real step

toward freedom he'd taken since being released from prison.

She arched beneath him, gasping at her pleasure, her internal muscles gripping him as she came. He roared out his own release, grasping her tightly against his body as he slammed into her one last time.

And as he held her close against his chest, in a bed he should never have taken her to, he let go of the ideas of right and wrong. What she deserved. What he could give.

Because what had happened between them just now was like nothing he'd ever experienced on earth. And it wouldn't be forever. It couldn't be.

But if it was freedom for him, maybe it could be that for her, too.

Maybe...

Just for a little while, he could be something good for her.

And as he stared down at her lovely face, he ignored the hollow feeling in his chest that asked: even if he knew he were bad for her, would he be able to turn away now?

He knew the answer.

He held her close, pressed her cheek against his chest, against his thundering heartbeat.

And she pressed her hand over the knife wound on his midsection.

Oh, yes. He knew the answer.

Chapter 9

By the time Faith woke up, the sun was low in the sky, and she was wrapped around Levi, her hand splayed on his chest. He was not asleep.

"I was wondering when you might wake up."

She blinked sleepily. "What time is it?"

"About five o'clock."

"Shit!" She jerked, as if she was going to scramble out of bed, and then she fell back, laying down her head on his shoulder. "I'm supposed to have dinner with my parents tonight."

"What time?"

"Six. But Isaiah and Levi are going to pester me about where I was. Poppy probably won't let me off, either. My sister-in-law. She works in the office. She's the one who—"

"Former assistant," Levi said.

"Yes. Also, she's pregnant right now and you know how pregnant women have a heightened sense of smell?" she asked.

"Um…"

"Well, she does. But I think more for shenanigans than anything else."

"Shenanigans?" he repeated, his tone incredulous. "Are we engaging in shenanigans?"

"You know what I mean," she huffed.

"When are you going to tell them?"

She blinked. "About…this?"

"Not this specifically," he said, waving his arm over the two of them to indicate their bodies. "But the design project. They're going to have to know eventually."

"Oh, do they?" She tapped her chin. "I was figuring I could engage in some kind of elaborate money-laundering situation and hide it from them forever."

"Well, that will impact on my ability to do a magazine spread with my new house. My new life as a non-convict. As a free man."

"Right. I forgot."

"The best revenge is living well. Mostly because any other kind of revenge is probably going to land me back in prison."

"Isn't that like…double jeopardy at this point?"

"Are you encouraging me to commit murder?"

"Not encouraging you. I just… On a technicality…"

"I'm not going to do anything that results in a body count," he said drily. "Don't worry. But I would really like my ex to see everything I'm buying with the money that she can't have. If she can't end up in prison, then she's going to end up sad and alone, and with nothing. That might sound harsh to you…"

"It doesn't," Faith said, her voice small. "I can't imagine caring about someone like that and being betrayed. I can't imagine being in prison for five days, much less five years. She deserves…" She looked down, at his beautiful body, at the scar that marred his skin. "She deserves to think about it. What she could have had. What she gave away. Endlessly. She deserves that. I am so…sorry."

"I don't need your pity," he said.

"Just my body?" She wiggled closer to him, experimenting with the idea that she, too, could maybe be a vixen.

"I do like your body," he said slowly. "When are you going to tell your brothers about the job?"

"You know what? I'll do it tonight."

"Sounds pretty good. Do it when you have your parents to act as a buffer."

She grinned. "Basically."

She didn't want to leave him. Didn't want to leave this. She hesitated, holding the words in until her heart was pounding in her ears. Until she felt light-headed.

"Levi… We have a limited amount of time together. It will only be until the design project is finished. And I don't want to go all clingy on you, but I would like to… Can I come back tonight?"

He sat up, swinging his legs over the side of the bed, his bare back facing her. Without thinking, she reached out, tracing the border of the bird's wing that stretched around to his spine.

"Sure," he said. "If you really want to."

"For sex," she said. "But it might be late when we're finished. So maybe I'll sleep here?"

"If you want to sleep here, Faith, that's fine. Just don't get any ideas about it."

"I won't. I'll bring an overnight bag and I won't unpack it. My toothbrush will stay in my bag. It won't touch your sink."

"Why the hell would I care about that?"

He looked almost comically confused. On that hard, sculpted face, confusion was a strange sight.

"I don't know. There were some girls in college who used to talk about how guys got weird about toothbrushes. I've never had a boyfriend. I mean... Not that you're my boyfriend. But... I'm sorry. I'm speaking figuratively."

"Calm down," he said, gripping her chin and staring her right in the eyes. He dropped a kiss on her mouth, and instantly, she settled. "You don't need to work this hard with me. What we have is simple. We both know the rules, right?"

"Yes," she said breathlessly.

"Then I don't want you to overthink it. Because I definitely don't want you overthinking things when we're in bed together."

She felt a weight roll off her shoulders, and her entire body sagged. "Sometimes I think I don't know how to...not overthink."

"Why is that?"

She shrugged. "I've been doing it for most of my life."

He looked at her. Not moving. Like a predator poised to pounce. Those blue eyes were far too insightful for her liking. "Does it ever feel like prison?"

She frowned. "Does what ever feel like prison?"

"The success you have. You couldn't have imagined

that you would be experiencing this kind of demand at your age."

"I really don't know how to answer that. Nobody sentenced me to anything, Levi, and I can walk away from it at any time."

"Is your family rich, Faith?"

She laughed. "No. We didn't grow up with anything. I only went to private school because I got a scholarship. Joshua didn't even get to go to college. He didn't have the grades to earn a scholarship or anything. My parents couldn't afford it—"

"All the money in your family—this entire company—it centers around you."

"Yes," she said softly.

He made a scoffing sound. "No wonder you were a virgin."

"What does my virginity have to do with anything?"

"Have you done something for yourself? Ever?"

"I mean, in fairness, Levi, it's my…gift. My talent. My dream, I guess, that made us successful. It centers around me. Isaiah and Joshua fill in the holes with what they do well, but they could do what they do well at any kind of company. The architectural aspect… That's me. They're enabling me to do what I love."

"And you're enabling everyone to benefit from your talents. That they're supporting your talent doesn't make them sacrificial. It makes them smart. I'm not putting your brothers down. In their position I would do the same. But what bears pointing out is that whether you realize it or not, you've gotten yourself stuck in the center of a spider's web, honey. No wonder you feel trapped sometimes."

They didn't speak about anything serious while she

got ready. She dodged a whole lot of groping on his end while she tried to pull on her clothes, and ended up almost collapsing in a fit of giggles as she fought to get her skirt back on and cover her ass while he attempted to keep his hand on her body.

But she thought about what he said the entire time, and all the way over to her parents' house. His observation made it seem… Well, like she really should fight harder for the things she wanted. Should worry less about what Joshua and Isaiah felt about her association with Levi. Personally or professionally.

Though, she wasn't going to bring up any of the personal stuff.

Levi was right. The business, her career—all of this had turned into a monster she hadn't seen coming. It was a great monster. One that funded a lifestyle she had never imagined could be hers. Though, it was a lifestyle she was almost too busy to enjoy. And if that was going to be the case…

Why shouldn't she take on projects that interested her?

That was the thing. Levi had interested her from the beginning, and the only reason she had hesitated was because Joshua and Isaiah were going to be dicks about her interest and she knew it.

She pulled up to her parents' small, yellow farmhouse and sat in the driveway for a moment.

She wished Levi was with her. Although she had no reason to bring him. And the very idea of that large, hard man in this place seemed…impossible. Like a god coming down from Mount Olympus to hang out at the mall.

She got out of the car and walked up to the front

porch, opened the door and walked straight inside. A rush of familiarity hit her, that familiar scent of her mother's pot roast. That deep sense of home that could only ever be attached to this place. Where she had grown up. Where she'd longed to be while at boarding school, where she had ached to return for Christmases, spring breaks and summers.

Everyone was already there. Devlin and his wife, Mia. Joshua, Danielle and and their son Riley. Isaiah and Poppy.

Faith was the only one who stood alone. And suddenly, it didn't feel so familiar anymore.

Maybe because she was different.

Because she had left part of herself in that bed with Levi.

Or maybe because everyone else was a couple.

All she knew was that she felt like a half standing there and it was an entirely unpleasant feeling.

"Hi," Faith said.

"Where have you been?" Joshua asked. "You left the office around lunchtime the other day and I haven't seen you since."

"You say that like it's news to me," she said drily. "I had some things to take care of."

Her mom came out of the kitchen and wrapped Faith in a hug. "What things? What are you up to?" She pressed a kiss to Faith's cheek. "More brilliance?"

Her dad followed, giving Faith a hug and a kiss and moving to his favorite chair that put him at the head of the seating arrangement.

"I don't know." Faith rubbed her arm, suddenly feeling like she was fifteen and being asked to discuss her report card. "Not especially. Just... I picked up another project."

"What project?" Isaiah asked, frowning.

"You didn't consult me about the schedule first," Poppy said.

"I can handle it," Faith said. "It's fine."

"This is normally the kind of thing you consult us on," Joshua said, frowning.

"Yes. And I didn't this time. I took a job that interested me. And I had a feeling you wouldn't be very supportive about it. So I did it alone. And it's too late to quit, because I already have an agreement. I'm already working on the project, actually."

"Is that why you were behind on sending me those estimates?" Isaiah asked. As if this error was proof positive they were actually correct, and she couldn't handle all this on her own.

"Yes," she said. "Probably. But, you know, I'm the one who does the design. And I should be able to take on projects that interest me. And turn down things that don't."

"Are we making you do things you don't like?"

"No. It's just... The whole mass-production thing we're doing, that's fine. But I don't need to be as involved in that. I did some basic designs, but my role in that is done. At this point it's standardized, and what interests me is the weird stuff. The imaginative stuff."

"I'm glad you enjoy that part of it. It's what makes you good. It's what got us where we are."

"I know. I mean..." Everyone was staring at her and she felt strange admitting how secure she was in her talent. But she wasn't a fifteen-year-old explaining a report card. She was a grown woman explaining what she

wanted to do with the hours in her day, confident in her
area of expertise. "You can't get where I'm at without
being confident. But what I'm less confident about is
whether or not you two are going to listen to me when
I say I know what I want to do."

"Of course we listen to you."

She sucked in a sharp breath and faced down Joshua
and Isaiah. "I took a design job for Levi Tucker."

Isaiah frowned. "Why do I know that name?"

It was Devlin who stood up, and crossed large, tattooed arms over his broad chest. "Because he's a con-
vict," he said. "He was accused of murdering his wife."

"Who isn't dead," Faith pointed out. "So, I would
suggest that's a pretty solid case *against* him being a
murderer."

"Still."

Mia spoke tentatively. "I mean, the whole situation
is so…suspicious, though," she said softly. "I mean…
what woman would run from her husband if he was a
good guy?"

"Yes," Faith said, sighing heavily, "I've heard that
line of concern before. But the fact of the matter is, I've
actually met him." She felt like she did a very valiant job
of not choking on her tongue when she said that. "And
he's…fine. I wouldn't say he's a nice guy, but certainly
he's decent enough to work with."

"I don't like it," Devlin said. "I think you might be
too young to fully understand all the implications."

Anger poured into her veins like a hot shot of whiskey, going straight to her head. "Do not give me that
shit," she said, then looked quickly over at her mother
and gave her an apologetic smile for the language. "Your
wife is the same age as I am. So if I'm too young to

make a business decision, your wife is certainly too young to be married to you."

Mia looked indignant for a moment, but then a little bit proud. The expression immediately melted into smugness.

"I like his ideas." Faith didn't say anything about his house being a sex palace. "And it's a project I'm happy to have my name on."

Joshua shook his head. "You want to be associated with a guy like that? A young, powerful woman like yourself entering into a business agreement with a man who quite possibly has a history of violence against women…"

She exploded from the table, flinging her arms wide. "He hasn't done anything to anyone. There have been no accusations of domestic violence. He didn't… As far as anyone knows, he never did anything to her. She disappeared and he was accused of all manner of things with no solid evidence at all. And I think there was bias against him because he comes from…modest beginnings."

"It's about the optics, Faith," Joshua pointed out. "You're a role model. And associating with him could damage that."

Optics. That word made her feel like a creature in a zoo instead of a human. It made her feel like someone who was being made to perform, no matter her feelings.

"I don't care about *optics*, Joshua. I'm twenty-five years old and I have many more years left in this career. If all I ever do is worry about optics and I don't take projects that interest me—if I don't follow my passion even a little bit—then I don't see the point of it."

"The point is that you are going to be doing this

for a long time and when you're more well-established you can take risks. Until then, you need to be more cautious."

She looked around the room at her family, all of them gazing at her like she had grown a second head. Suddenly she did feel what Levi had described earlier.

This was, in its way, a prison.

This success had grown bigger than she was.

"I'm not a child," she said. "If I'm old enough to be at the center of all this success, don't you think I should follow my instincts? If I...burn out because I feel trapped then I won't be able to do my best work. If I burn out, I won't be able to give you all those years of labor, Joshua."

"Nobody wants that," her mother said. "Nobody expects you to work blindly, Faith. No one wants you to go until you grind yourself into the ground." She directed those words at Joshua and Isaiah.

"You think it's a good idea for her to work with an ex-con?" Joshua directed *that* question at their father.

"I think Faith's instincts have gotten all of you this far and you shouldn't be so quick to dismiss them just because it doesn't make immediate sense to you," her father responded.

Right. This was why she had confessed in front of her parents. Because, while she wanted to please them, wanted all their sacrifices to feel worth it, she also knew they supported her no matter what. They were so good at that. So good at making her feel like her happiness mattered.

A lot of the pressure she felt was pressure she had put on herself.

But every year when there was stress about the scholarship money coming through for boarding school, every year when the cost of uniforms was an issue, when a school trip came up and her parents had to pay for part of it, and scraped and saved so Faith could have every opportunity... All of those things lived inside her.

She couldn't forget it.

They had done so much for her. They had set her out on a paved road to the future, rather than a dirt one, and it hadn't been a simple thing for them.

And she couldn't discount the ways her brothers had helped her passiona for architecture and design become a moneymaking venture, too.

But at the end of the day, she was still owed something that was *hers*.

She still deserved to be treated like an adult.

It was that simple.

She just wanted them to recognize that she was a grown woman who was responsible for her own time, for her own decisions.

"I took the project," she said again. "It's nonnegotiable. He's going to publicize it whether you do or not, Joshua. Because it's part of his plan for...reestablishing himself. He's a businessman, and he was quite a famous one, for good reasons, prior to being wrongfully accused."

"Faith..." Joshua clearly sounded defeated now, but he seemed to be clinging to a last hope that he could redirect her.

"You don't know him," Faith said. "You just decided he was guilty. Which is what the public did to him. What the justice system did to him. And if he's innocent, then he's a man who lost everything over snap judgments and bias. You're in PR, maybe you can work with that when the news stories start coming out—"

"Dinner will be ready soon," her mother interrupted, her tone gentle but firm. "Why don't we table talk of business until after?"

They did that as best they could all through the meal, and afterward Faith was recruited to help put away dishes. She would complain, or perhaps grumble about the sexism of it, but her mother had only asked for her, and Faith had a feeling it was because her mother wanted a private word with her.

"How well do you know Levi Tucker?" her mother asked gently, taking a clean plate from the drying rack and stacking it in the cupboard.

"Well enough," Faith answered, feeling a twist of conviction in her chest as she plunged her hands into the warm dishwater.

"You have very strong feelings about his innocence."

"There's nothing about him that seems...bad to me."

Rough, yes. Wounded, yes. Stabbed through the rib cage because of his own wife, sure. But not bad.

"Be careful," her mother said gently. "You've seen more of the world than I ever will, sweetheart. You've done more, achieved more, than I could have ever hoped to. But there are some things you don't have experience with... And I fear that, to a degree, your advancement in other areas is the reason why. And it makes me worry for you."

"You don't have to worry for me."

"So your interest in him is entirely professional?"

Faith took a dish out of the soapy water and began to scrub it. "You don't have to worry about me."

"But I do," her mother said. "Just like I worry about your brothers sometimes. It's what parents do."

"Well, I'm fine," Faith said.

"It's okay to make mistakes," her mother said. "You know that, don't you?"

"What are you talking about?"

"Just, forget about Levi Tucker for a second. It's okay for you to make mistakes, Faith. You don't have to be perfect. You don't have to be everything to everyone. You don't have to make Isaiah happy. You don't have to make Joshua happy. You certainly don't have to make your father and I happy."

Faith shifted uncomfortably. "It's not a hardship to care about whether or not my family is happy. You did so much for me..."

"Look at everything you've done for *us*. Just having you as my daughter would have been enough, Faith. It would have always been enough."

Faith didn't know why that sat so uncomfortably with her. "I would rather not make mistakes."

"We would all rather not make them," her mother said. "But sometimes they're unavoidable. Sometimes you need to make them in order to grow into the person you were always supposed to be."

Faith wondered if Levi could be classified as a mistake. She was going into this—whatever it was—knowing exactly what kind of man he was and exactly when and how things were going to end. She wondered if that made her somehow more prepared. If that meant it was a calculated maneuver, rather than a mistake.

"I can see you, figuring out if you're still perfect."

Her mother's words were not spoken with any sort of unkindness, but they played at Faith's insides all the same. "I don't think I'm perfect," Faith mumbled, scrubbing more ferociously at the dish.

"You would like to be."

She made a sound that landed somewhere between a scoff and a laugh, aiming for cool and collected and achieving neither. "Who doesn't want to be?"

"I would venture to say your brothers don't worry very much about being perfect."

Sure. Because they operated in the background and worried about things like *her* optics, not their own. Isaiah somehow managed to go through life operating as if everything was a series of numbers and spreadsheets. Joshua treated everything like a PR opportunity. And Devlin… Well, Devlin was the one who had never cared what anyone thought. The one who hadn't gone into business with the rest of them. The one who had done absolutely everything on his own terms and somehow come out of it with Faith's best friend as a bonus.

"I like my life," Faith insisted. "Don't think that I don't."

"I don't think that," her mother said. "I just think you put an awful lot of pressure on yourself."

For the rest of the evening, Faith tried not to ruminate on that too much, but the words kept turning over and over in her head on the drive back to Levi's. She swung by her house and put together a toiletries bag, throwing in some pajamas and an outfit for the next day. And all the while she kept thinking…

You're too hard on yourself. You can make mistakes.

And her resistance to those words worried her more than she would like to admit.

Logically, she was completely all right with this thing with Levi being temporary. With it being a mistake, in many ways. But she was concerned that there was something deep inside her that believed it would become something different. That believed it might work out.

Beneath her practicality she was more of a dreamer than she wanted to acknowledge.

But how could she be anything but a dreamer? It was her job. To create things out of thin air. Even though another part of her always had to make those dreams a practical reality. It wasn't any good to be an architect if you couldn't figure out how to make your creations stand, make them structurally sound.

She didn't know how to reconcile those two halves of herself. Not right now. Not in this instance.

Now she had just confused herself. Because sex with Levi was not designing a house. Not even close.

She needed to stop trying to make sense of everything.

Maybe there were some things you couldn't make sense of.

She was having a just-physical relationship with the man. She nodded her head resolutely as she pulled up to the front of his house and put the car in Park. Then she shut off the engine decisively.

She knew exactly what was happening between them, and she was mature enough to cope with it.

He wasn't a mistake. He was an experience.

So there. She didn't need to make mistakes.

Satisfied with that, Faith grabbed her overnight bag, got out of her car and went to Levi's house.

Chapter 10

Faith had only left his house once in the past two days. On Friday she went to work. But on Friday evening she returned, and stayed the night again. Now it was deep into Saturday, a gloomy, rainy day, and she was loitering around his kitchen wearing nothing but a T-shirt and a smile.

He didn't mind.

"I've got some horses coming later today," he commented, looking over at her lithe, pale form.

She hauled herself up onto the counter, the T-shirt riding up, nearly exposing that heaven between her thighs. She crossed those long, lovely legs at the ankles, her expression innocent, her hair disheveled from their recent activities.

The woman managed to look angelic and completely

wicked all at once, and it did things to him he couldn't quite explain.

She wasn't for him. He had to remind himself. Because the things he liked about her... They didn't say anything good about him.

He had practically been born jaded. His vision of the world had been blackened along with his mother's eye the first time he had seen his father take his fists to her when he had been... He must've been two or three. His earliest memory.

Not a Christmas tree or his mother's smile. But her bruises. Fists connecting against flesh and bone.

That was his world. The way he had known and understood it from the very start.

He had never been able to see the world with the kind of unspoiled wonder Faith seemed to.

He had introduced her to dirty, carnal things, and had watched her face transform with awe every time he'd made her come. Every time he'd shown her something new, something illicit. She touched his body, his tattoos, his scars, like they were gifts for her to discover and explore.

There was something intoxicating in that.

This woman who saw him as *new*.

He had never had that experience with a woman before.

His high-school girlfriend had been as jaded and damaged as he was, and they might have experienced sex for the first time together, but there was no real wonder in it. Just oblivion. Just escape. The same way they had used drugs and alcohol to forget what was happening in their homes.

Sex with Faith wasn't a foggy escape. It was sharp

and crisp like crystal, and just as able to cut him open. He had never felt so present, so in his own body, as he was when he was inside her.

He didn't know what the hell to make of it, but he didn't have the strength to turn away from it, either.

"Horses?"

"There's a small stable, and some arenas and pastures on this property. Of course, when I move to the other one…"

"You didn't tell me you needed a riding facility."

"I figured that's pretty standard, isn't it?"

"It doesn't have to be. It can be whatever you want it to be."

"Well, maybe I'll have you sketch that out for me, too."

"Can I meet the horses?" She looked bright and happy at the idea.

"Sure," he said. "You like to ride?"

"I never did as much of it as my brothers. I did a little bit when I was away at school, but I didn't spend as much time doing the farm-life thing as they did. I know how to ride, obviously. We always had a couple horses. It's just been a while. That was actually one of my brothers' priorities, when we moved back here." She blinked. "You know, to get a ranching operation up and running."

He frowned. "Where do you live?"

She laughed. He realized that although the woman designed houses for a living, they had never discussed her own living situation. "Okay. You know how they say contractors are notorious for never finishing the work in their own houses? Or how mechanics always have jacked-up cars? I am an architect who lives above a coffeehouse."

"No shit."

"None at all. It's too much pressure. Think of designing a place for myself. I haven't done it. I was living in this great, modern, all-glass space up in Seattle. And I loved it. But I knew that I wasn't going to stay there, so I didn't do anything else. When we moved back to Copper Ridge... I didn't really know what I wanted to do here, either. So I haven't designed a house. And the vacancy came up above The Grind in town and I figured an old building like that, all redbrick and right there in the center of things, was the perfect place for me to get inspiration. I was right. I love it. It works for me."

"That's disappointing. I thought you lived in some architectural marvel. Like something made entirely out of cement shaped like the inside of a conch shell."

"That's ridiculous."

"Is it?"

"Okay, it's not that insane. I've definitely seen weirder. How did you learn to ride?"

This was skating close to sharing. Close to subjects he didn't want to go into. He hesitated.

"I got a job on a ranch. I was a kid. Twelve. Thirteen. But it's what I did until I went away to school. Until I got into manufacturing. Until I made my fortune, I guess. There was an older guy, by the name of Bud. He owned a big ranching spread on the edge of Copper Ridge. He passed on a couple years ago now. He took me on, and let me work his land. He was getting old, he was downsizing, but he didn't have the heart to get rid of everything. So... I got to escape my house and spend my days outdoors. Earn a little money doing it. My grades suffered. But I was damn happy.

"Ranch work will always be that for me. Freedom. It's one of the things I hated most about being in prison. Being inside. Four walls around you all the time. And... Nothing smells like a ranch does. Like horses. Hay, wood chips. Even horse piss. It's its own thing. That stuff gets in your blood. Not being around it at all was like sensory deprivation. My assets were liquified when I went to prison. Not frozen, though, which was convenient for Alicia. Though, in the end less convenient."

"Of course," she said testily.

"So, my horses were taken and sold, and the money was put into an account. I was able to get two of them back. They're coming today."

"Levi... That's... I mean... I can't believe you lost your ranch? Your animals?"

"It doesn't matter."

"It does. She took... She took everything from you." Faith blinked. "Do you think she did it on purpose?"

"I think she did," he said, his voice rough.

"Why? Look, I don't think that you did anything to her. But I..."

"The life I gave her wasn't the life she wanted," he said.

"Well, what life did she think she would be getting?"

"She—she was just like me. Poor and hating every minute of it. I was twenty-one. She was eighteen. She thought I might be on my way to something, and I swore to her I was. I thought she had hearts in her eyes, but they were just dollar signs. I loved her. We forged a path together, I thought. Were working toward a future where we could both look down on everyone who'd ever looked down on us."

"From a house on a hill?" Faith asked, softly.

"Yeah. From a house on a hill. But Alicia wanted more than that. She wanted to be something other than country, and I was never going to be that. Galas and all that crap. Designer clothes and eating tiny portions of food standing up and pretending to care about what strangers have to say about anything—it wasn't me. But I thought we were weathering those differences, I really did."

He shook his head. "When she went missing, it was the worst night of my life. She didn't take anything with her, not that I could see. I thought for sure something had happened to her. She had her purse, but that was it. It looked like she'd been snatched walking between a grocery store and her car. I lost sleep wondering what was happening to her. Dammit, I was picturing her being tortured. Violated. Terrified. I've never been so afraid, so sick to my stomach, in my whole life. We might not have been in the best space right then, but I didn't want anything to happen to my wife, Faith. Hell, I didn't even think it was so bad that we would get divorced. I figured we needed to work on some things, but we could get around to it."

Faith bit her lip. "I can't imagine. I can't imagine what you went through."

"It was awful. And then they came and arrested me. Said they had reason to believe I'd done something to her. And later…that there was evidence I'd killed her and made sure the body wouldn't be found. The body. My wife was a body at that point. And they were accusing me of being responsible for that." He shook his head. "And what an ass I was. I grieved for her."

"Do you—do you think she ever loved you?" Faith asked. "I can't imagine doing that to someone I hated, much less—"

"I think she did in the beginning. But everything got twisted. She thought wealth and success meant something to me that it didn't. I wanted a ranch, and I wanted to go to fewer parties. I was fine with her going by herself. She didn't like that. She wanted me to be on her arm. She wanted a very specific life, and it was one she didn't inform me she wanted until it was too late. And I"—

"You weren't willing to give it."

He felt like he'd been punched in the chest.

Faith shrugged. "It's still no excuse to go framing you for murder," she said. "Or, whatever she intended to frame you for. But I just mean… There were maybe one or two things you could have given her to make her happier. If she weren't a psycho."

He chuckled hollowly. "I expect you're right. If she weren't a psycho. But that's why I don't ever intend to get married again."

"Honestly, I can't blame you." Faith looked down, a dark curl falling into her face.

"Do you want to go for a ride later today?"

She looked at him, her whole face bright, her expression totally different from the way it had been a moment before. "Yes."

"Well, cowgirl, I hope you brought your jeans."

Chapter 11

Faith sat on the top of the fence while she watched the horses circle the paddock. They seemed content in their new surroundings. Or maybe, it was the presence of Levi. Watching as he had greeted the horses, pressing his hand to their velvet soft noses, letting them take in his scent had been...

Her chest felt so full she thought it might burst.

He was such a hard man. And yet... It was that hardness that made the soft moments so very special. She didn't know why she was thinking about him in those terms. Why she wanted special moments. Why she cared.

But seeing him like that, even now, out in the paddock, as the horses moved around him, and he stood in that black Stetson, black T-shirt and tight jeans...

She ached.

She had been outside of so many things. There, but not quite a part of them.

The only single person at dinner last night. A prodigy in architecture, but so much younger than everyone else, seemingly someone people couldn't relate to. The poor girl at boarding school, there on a scholarship. The smart kid who would rather escape into books and her imagination than go to a party.

That had been fine. It had been fine for a long time. But it wasn't fine now.

She wanted to meld herself with him. Mold herself into his life. Melt against him completely. She didn't know what that meant. But the urge tugged at her, strongly. Made it so she could hardly breathe.

She hopped down off the fence, her boots kicking up dust as she made her way across the arena and toward him.

"What are you doing?" he asked.

"I just… They're beautiful horses." And he was beautiful. With them, he was stunning. It was like watching him be right where he belonged. At ease for the first time since she'd met him.

Like a bird spreading his wings.

A smile tipped up the corners of his lips. "I'm glad to have them back."

"The others?"

"It's not possible to track all of them down. It's okay. For now, this is enough."

"And then what?"

"They'll make a great story," he said, his expression suddenly shuttered. "When we do that big magazine spread. Showing my new custom home, and the equestrian facility you're going to build me. A big picture of me with these horses that Alicia took from me."

"Is that what everything is about?"

"My entire life has been about her for seventeen years, Faith. In the last five years of that all I could do was think about…" He gritted his teeth. "That is the worst part. I worried about her. All that time. And she was fine. Off sipping champagne and sitting on a yacht. Screwing who the hell knows. While I sat in prison like a monk. An entire life sentence ahead of me. And I was worried about her. She knew I was in prison. She knew. She didn't care. That's the worst part. How much emotional energy I wasted worrying about the fate of that woman when…"

She stepped forward, put her fingertips on his forearm. "This isn't emotional energy?"

He looked down at her. "How would you feel? How would you feel in my position?"

"I don't know. Possibly not any better. I don't know what I would do. You're right. I can't comment on it."

"Stick to what you do, honey. Comment on the design work you can do for me."

She took a step back, feeling like she had overstepped. That little bubble of fantasy she'd had earlier, that need to get closer to him, had changed on her now. "I will. Don't worry."

"How did you realize you were an architecture prodigy?" he asked suddenly.

"I don't know," she said, lifting a shoulder. "I mean, I drew buildings. I was attracted to the idea of doing city design in a slightly more…organic way. I was fascinated by that from the time I was a kid. As for realizing I was good… I was naturally good at art, but I've always been good at math and science as well. History. Art history."

"So you're one of those obnoxious people who doesn't have a weakness."

"Well, except for...social stuff?" She laughed. "Academically, no. Not so much. And that opened a lot of doors for me. For which I will always be grateful. It was really my brothers who helped me focus. Because, of course, Isaiah being a numbers guy, he wanted to help me figure out how I could take what I did and make money with it. My education was paid for because I was brilliant, but that comes to an end eventually. You have to figure out what to do in the real world. Architecture made sense."

"I guess so."

"Why...manufacturing? And what did you make?"

"Farm equipment," he said. "Little generic replacement parts for different things. A way to do it cheaper, without compromising on quality."

"And what made you do that?"

"Not because I'm an artist. Because there are a lot of hardworking men out there, pleased as hell to replace the parts themselves if they can. But often things are overcomplicated and expensive. I wanted to find a way to simplify processes. So it started with the basic idea that we can get around some of the proprietary stuff some of the big companies did. And it went from there. Eventually I started manufacturing parts for those big companies. It's a tricky thing to accomplish, here in the United States, but we've managed. And it served me well to keep it here. It's become part of why my equipment is sought after."

She giggled. "There's a double entendre."

"It's boring. That was another thing my wife objected to. She wanted me to get into real-estate investing. Something more interesting for her to talk about with her friends. Something a little bit sexier than gaskets."

"A gasket is pretty sexy if it's paying you millions of dollars, I would think."

"Hell, that was my feeling." He sighed heavily. "It's not like you. Mine was a simple idea."

"Sometimes simplicity is the better solution," she said. "People think you need to be complicated to be interesting. I don't always think that's true, in design, or in life. Obviously, in your case, the simple solution was the revolutionary one."

"I guess so. Are you ready to go for a ride?"

"I am," she said.

And somehow, she felt closer to him. Somehow she felt…part of this. Part of him.

She wanted to hold onto that feeling for as long as it would last, because she had a feeling it would be over a lot sooner than she would like.

But then, that was true of all of this. Of everything with him.

She was beginning to suspect that nothing short of a lifetime would be enough with Levi Tucker.

Chapter 12

Levi had missed this. He couldn't pretend otherwise. Couldn't pretend that it hadn't eaten at him, five years away from the ranch.

The animals were in his blood, in his bones. Had been ever since he had taken that job at Bud's ranch. That experience had changed him. Given him hope for the future. Allowed him to see things in a different way. Allowed him to see something other than a life filled with pain, fear.

The other kids at school had always avoided him. He was the boy who came to school with bruises on his face. The boy whose family was whispered about. Whose mother always looked sallow and unhappy, and whose father was only ever seen at night, being pulled drunkenly out of bars.

But the horses had never seen him that way. He had earned their trust. And he had never taken it for granted.

The back of a horse was the one place he had ever felt like he truly belonged. And things hadn't changed much. Twenty-three years—five of them spent behind bars—later, and things hadn't changed much.

He looked back from his position on the horse, and the grin on Faith's face lit up all the dark places inside him. He hadn't expected to enjoy sharing this with her. But then, he hadn't expected to share so much with her at all.

There was something about her. It was that sense of innocence.

That sense of newness.

A sense that if he could be close enough to her he might be able to see the world the way she did. As a place full of possibility, rather than a place full of pain. Betrayal. Heartbreak.

Yes, with her, he could see the scope of so much more. And it made him want to reach out to her. It made him want to...

He wanted her to understand him.

He couldn't remember ever feeling that way before. He hadn't wanted Alicia to understand him.

He hadn't cared. He'd loved her. But that love had been wrapped up in the life he wanted to build. In the vision of what they could be. He'd been focused on forward motion, not existing in the moment.

And maybe, there, Faith was right. Maybe that was where he had failed as a husband.

Though, he still hadn't failed so spectacularly that he'd deserved to be sent to prison, but he could acknowledge that some of the unhappiness in his marriage had come down to him.

"It's beautiful out here," Faith said.

"This is actually part of the property for the new house," he said. He glanced up at the sky, where the dark gray clouds were beginning to gather, hanging low. "It's starting to look stormy, but if you don't mind taking a chance on getting caught in the rain, I can show you where we might put the equestrian facility."

"I'd like that," she said.

He urged his horse on, marveling at how quickly he had readjusted to this thing, to horsemanship, to feeling a deep brightness in his bones. If that wasn't evidence this was where he belonged, in the woods on the back of a horse, he didn't know what was.

They came through a deep, dark copse of trees and out into a clearing. The clouds there were layers of patchwork gray, moving from silver to a kind of menacing charcoal, like a closed fist ready to rain down judgment on the world below.

And there was the clearing. Overlooking the valley below.

The exact positioning he wanted, so he could look down on everyone who had once looked down on him.

"You think you can work with this?" he asked.

"Definitely," she responded. She maneuvered her horse around so she was more fully facing the view before them. "I want to make it mirror your house somehow. Functional, obviously. But open. I know the horses weren't in prison for the last five years, but they had their lives stolen from them, too, in a way. I want it all connected. And I want you to feel free."

Interesting that she had used that word. A word that had meant so much to him. One he had yearned for so much he'd traded cigarettes to have a symbol of it tattooed on his body.

It was a symbol he was deeply protective of. He wasn't a sentimental man, and his tattoos were about the closest thing to sentiment he possessed.

"I like the way you think," he said.

He meant it. In many ways. And not just this instance.

She tilted her head, scrunching her nose and regarding him like he was something strange and fascinating. "Why do you like the way I think?"

"Because you see more than walls, Faith. You see what they can mean to people. Not just the structure. But what makes people feel. Four walls can be a prison sentence or they can be a refuge. That difference is something I never fully appreciated until I was sent away."

"Homes are interesting," she said. "I design a lot of buildings that aren't homes. And in those cases, I design the buildings based on the skyline of the city. The ways I want the structure to flow with the surroundings. But homes are different. My parents' house, small and simple as it is, could not feel more like home to me. Nothing else will ever feel like home in quite the same way it does. It's where I grew up. Where the essential pieces of myself were formed and made. That's what a home is. And every home you live in after those formative years…is not the same. So you have to try and take something from the life experience people have had since they left their parents and bring it all in and create a home from that."

He thought of his own childhood home. Of the way he had felt there. The fear. The stale scent of alcohol and sadness. The constant lingering threat of violence.

"Home to me was the back of a horse," he said. "The mountains. The trees. The sky. That's where I was made. It's where I became a person I could be proud of, or at the very least, a person I could live with. My parents' place was prison."

He urged his horse forward, moving farther down

the trail, into the clearing, before he looped around and headed back toward the other property. Faith followed after him.

And the sky opened up. That angry fist released its hold.

He urged the horse into I canter, and he could hear Faith keeping pace behind him. As they rode, the rain soaked through his clothes. All the way through to his skin. It poured down his face, down his shirt collar.

Rain.

It had been five years since he had felt rain on his skin.

Hell.

He hadn't even known he'd missed it until now. And now he realized he was so thirsty for it he thought he might have been on the brink of death.

He released his hold on the reins and let his arms fall to his sides, spread his hands wide, keeping his body movements in tune with the horse as the water washed over him.

For a moment. Then two.

He counted the raindrops at first. Until it all blended together, a baptism out there in the wilderness.

He finally took control of the animal again. By then, the barn was back in view.

The horse moved with him as Levi encouraged him into a gallop. The rain whipped into his eyes now, but he didn't care. He brought the horse into the stable and looped the lead rope around a hook, then moved back outside and stripped off his shirt, letting the rain fall on his skin there, too.

If Faith thought it was strange, she didn't say anything. She went into the barn behind him and disappeared for a few moments. Leaving him outside, with the water washing over him. When she returned she was without her horse, her chin-length dark hair wet and clinging to her face.

"Are you okay?" she asked.

"I just realized," he said, looking up above, letting the water drops hit him square on the face. "I just realized that it's the first time I've felt the rain since before I was in jail."

Neither of them said anything. She simply closed the distance between them and curved her fingers around his forearm.

They stood there for a while, getting wet together.

"Tell me about your family," she said softly.

"You don't want to hear the story."

"I do," she said.

"Maybe I don't feel like telling it," he responded, turning to face her.

She looked all around them, back up at the sky, and then back at him. "We're home," she said. "It's the best place to tell hard stories."

And he knew exactly what she meant. They were home. They were free. Outside and with no walls around them. In the exact kind of place he had found freedom for himself the first time.

"My very first memory is of my father hitting my mother in the face," he said. "I remember a bruise blooming there almost instantly. Blood. Tears. My home never felt safe. I never had that image of my father as a protector. My father was the enemy. He was a brutal man. He lived mean, and he died mean, and I've never mourned him. Not one day."

"How did he die?" she asked softly.

"Liver failure," he said. "Which is kind of a mundane way to die for a man like him. In some ways, it would've been better if he'd died in violence. But sometimes I take comfort in the fact that disease doesn't just come for good people. Sometimes it gets the right ones."

"Your mother?"

"Packed up and left Oregon the minute he died. I send her money sometimes. At least, I did before..."

"Obviously you couldn't send money when you were in prison."

He shook his head. "No. I don't think you understand. She didn't want anything from me after that. She didn't believe me. That I didn't have something to do with Alicia's disappearance. She figured I was cut from the same cloth as my old man."

"How could she think that?" Faith asked. "She was your mother."

"In the end, she was a woman standing with another woman. And part of me can't blame her for that. I think it was easier for her to believe that her worst nightmare had come true. That I had fully become the creation of my genetics. You can understand why she would have feared that."

He had feared it, too. Sometimes he still did.

Because that hate—that hard, heavy fist of rage living in his chest—felt far too evil to have been put there recently. It felt born into him. As much a part of him as that first memory.

He swept her up into his arms then and carried her toward the house, holding her tightly against his chest. She clung to him, her fingers slick against his skin, greedy as they trailed over him.

"That's who I am," he said, taking her hand and pressing it against the scar left by the knife. "And that's why I told you I wasn't the right man for you. That's why I told you to stay away from me."

She shifted her hand, moving her fingertips along the scarred, raised flesh. The evidence of the day he'd been cut open and left to bleed. He'd considered lying down and dying. A damn low moment. He had been sentenced to life in prison, he'd thought. Why not let that sentence be a little shorter?

But his instincts, his body, hadn't let him give up. No. He'd gotten back up. And hit the man who'd come after him. And then hit him again, and again.

No one had come for Levi after that.

She made a soft sound as she shifted, letting her fingers glide over to the edge of the bird's wing. She traced the shape, its whole wingspan.

"No," she said, shaking her head. "*This* is who you are. This," she said. "This scar... You didn't choose that. You didn't choose to be born into a life of violence. You didn't choose your father. You didn't choose that time in prison. Didn't choose to get in a fight that day and have your body cut open. You chose *this*. These wings. This design. Whatever it means to you, you chose that. And it's more real than anything that was inflicted on you could ever be."

He stopped her from talking then, captured her mouth with his and silenced her with the fierceness of his kiss.

He wanted everything she said to be real. He wanted her words to matter, as much as everything that had come before them. As much as every blow he'd witnessed, every blow he'd been subjected to, every vile insult.

He wanted her kiss to mean more than his past.

He smoothed his hands down her body, his touch filled with reverence, filled with awe.

This woman, so beautiful and sweet, would touch *him*. Would give herself to *him*.

Yes, he wanted to believe what she said. He did. But he could see no way to do that. Couldn't find it in himself.

He could only be glad that somehow, he had found her.

He wanted to drown in her, as much as he had wanted to drown in the rain. To feel renewed. Clean. If only for a moment. She was like that spring rain. Restorative. Redemptive. More than he deserved, and essential in ways he wouldn't let himself think about.

She moved her hands over his body, over his face, pressing kisses to the scar on his ribs, to the tattoo, lower. Until she took him into her mouth, her tongue swirling in a torturous pattern over the swollen head of his erection. He bucked up, gripping her hair even as a protest escaped his lips.

"Let me," she said softly.

And then she returned her attention to him, this beautiful woman who had never done this for a man before. She lavished him with the kind of attention he didn't deserve, not from anyone, least of all her.

But he wanted it, wanted her. He wanted this in a way he hadn't wanted anything for longer than he could remember. He *wanted*, and it was because of her.

He *wanted*, and he would never forget her for it.

He *wanted*, and he would never forgive her for it.

She was hope. She was a promise of redemption he could never truly have.

She was *faith*, that's what she was. Believing in something you couldn't see or control. Until now, he had never wanted any part of something like that.

But here he was, drowning in it. In her.

A missing piece. To his life.

To his heart.

His vision began to blur, his body shaking, wracked

with the need for release as Faith used her hands and her mouth on him. As she tempted him far beyond what he could handle.

He looked down at her, and their eyes met. He saw desire. Need.

And trust.

She trusted him. This beautiful angel trusted him like no one ever had.

And it pushed him right over the edge.

He didn't pull away from her, and she didn't stop, swallowing down his release before moving up to his mouth again, scattering kisses over his abs and his chest as she went. He claimed her lips, pressing his hands between her thighs, smoothing his fingers over her and pushing two deep inside her as he brought her to her own climax.

She clung to him, looking dazed, filled with wonder.

Yet again, because of him. She was a gift. Possibly the only gift he'd ever been given in all his life.

But Faith should have been a gift for another man. A man who knew how to treasure her.

Levi didn't know how to do that.

But he knew how to hold on.

She clung to him, breathing hard, her fingernails digging into his shoulders. "I don't want to go home," she said softly.

"Then stay with me."

She looked up at him, her face questioning.

"Yes," he confirmed. "Stay with me."

Chapter 13

It was easy to let time slowly slip by, spending it in a bubble with Levi. It was a lot less easy for Faith to hide where she was spending all her nights and, frankly, half her days. If her brothers weren't suspicious of her behavior, Poppy certainly was.

There was no way she could get her unusual comings and goings past the eagle eye of her sister-in-law, and Poppy was starting to give Faith some serious side eye whenever Faith came into the office late, or left a little early.

Faith knew the reckoning was coming. She was going to have to deal with whatever was between her and Levi, and soon. Because the fact of the matter was, whatever they had agreed on in the beginning, she no longer wanted this relationship to be temporary.

The two of them had lapsed into a perfect routine

over the past few weeks. When she wasn't at work, she was at his house, and often sketching.

Working sometimes late into the night while she watched him sleep, more and more ideas flowing through her mind.

She had begun to think of his new house like a bird's nest.

To go with the bird that he'd tattooed on his body. A place for that soaring creature to call home. A home that rested effortlessly in the natural environment around it, and seemed to be made from the materials of the earth.

Of course, maybe she was pondering all of that to the detriment of her other work. And that was a problem. She felt...so removed from her life right now. From everything she was supposed to care about.

She cared about Levi.

About what lay on the other side of all of this. About the changes taking place inside of her.

She should care more about her upcoming interview with *Architectural Digest.* She should care more about a television spot she was soon going to be filming in the office. One that was intended as a way to boost the participation of young girls in male-dominated fields, like architecture.

Instead, Faith was fixating on her boyfriend.

Immediately, her heart fell.

He wasn't her boyfriend. He was a man she had a temporary arrangement with, and she was becoming obsessed. She was becoming preoccupied.

Even so, she wasn't sure she cared. Because she had never been preoccupied in her life. She had always been focused, on task. Maybe it was her turn to go off the trail for a little while.

Need Me, Cowboy

Maybe it was okay.

You don't have to be perfect.

Her mother's words rang in her ears, even as Faith sat there at her desk. She wasn't sure what perfect even looked like for her anymore and the realization left her feeling rocked.

Poppy was going to appear in a moment to film the television spot they were sending in, and Faith knew she needed to pull herself together.

She wasn't sure if she could.

The door cracked open and Poppy came in, a smile on her perfectly made-up face, her figure—and her growing baby bump—highlighted by the adorable retro wiggle dress she was wearing.

Poppy was always immaculate. The only time she had ever seemed frazzled in any regard was when she had been dealing with issues in her relationship with Isaiah. So maybe—*maybe*—Poppy would be the ally Faith needed.

Or at the very least, maybe she would be the person Faith could confide in. For all that they had married older men with their own issues, Hayley and Mia did not seem like they would be sympathetic to Faith's situation.

It was all very "do as I say and do" not "do the kind of man that I do."

"Are you ready?" Poppy asked.

Her skeptical expression said that Faith was not ready. Though, Faith wasn't sure why Poppy felt that way.

"I was going to say yes," Faith said slowly. "But you clearly don't think so."

Poppy frowned. "You look very pale."

"I *am* pale," Faith said drily.

"Well," Poppy said, patting her own glowing, decidedly *not* pale complexion, "compared to some, yes. But that isn't what I meant. You need some blush. And lipstick with a color. I don't support this millennial pink nonsense that makes your lips blend into the rest of your skin."

"I'm *not* wearing lipstick."

"Well, there's your problem."

Poppy opened the drawer where Faith normally kept her makeup, and that was when Faith realized her mistake. The makeup wasn't there. Because she had taken the bag over to Levi's.

Poppy narrowed her eyes. "Where is your makeup?"

Faith tapped her fingers on her desk. "Somewhere?"

"Honestly, Faith, I wouldn't have been suspicious, except that was a dumb-ass answer."

"It's at Levi Tucker's," Faith said, deciding right in that moment that bold and brazen was what she would go for.

Everything was muddled inside her in part because she hadn't been sure if she wanted to go all in here. Cash her chips in on this one, big terrible thing that might be the mistake to end all mistakes.

But she did. She wanted to.

She wanted to go all in on Levi.

That horrible ex-wife of his had done that. She had cashed in all her chips on a moment when she could take his money and have the life she wanted with absolutely no care about what it did to him.

Well, why couldn't Faith do the opposite? Blow her life up for him. Why couldn't she risk herself for him?

No one in his life ever had. Not his father, who was drunk and useless and evil. Not his mother, who had allowed the scars and pains from her past to blind her to her own son's innocence.

Not his wife, who had been so poisoned by selfishness.

And Faith… What would she be protecting if she didn't?

Her own sense of perfection. Of not having let anyone down.

None of that mattered. None of it was *him*.

"Because you were…working on a job?" Poppy asked, her expression skeptical, but a little hopeful.

Faith's lips twitched.

"Some kind of job," she responded, intentionally digging into the double entendre, intentionally meeting Poppy's gaze. "So, there you have it."

"Faith…" Poppy said. "I don't… With a *client*?"

"I know," Faith said. "I didn't plan for it to go that way. But it did. And… I only meant for it to be temporary. That's all. But… I love him."

The moment she said it, she knew it was true. All her life she had been apart. All her life she had been separate. But in his arms, she belonged. With him, she had found something in herself she had never even known was missing.

"Your brothers…"

"They're going to be mad. And they're going to be afraid I'll get hurt. I know. I'm afraid I'll get hurt. Which is actually why I said something to you. Isaiah is not an easy man."

Poppy at least laughed at that. "No," she said. "He isn't."

"He's worth it, isn't he?"

Poppy breathed out slowly, then took a few steps toward Faith's desk, sympathy and understanding crinkling her forehead. "Faith, I've loved your brother for more than ten years. And he was worth it all that time, even when he was in love with someone else."

"Levi's not in love with anyone else. But he's…angry. I'm not sure if there's any room inside him for any other emotion. I don't know if he can let it go."

"Have you told him that you love him?"

"No. You're the first person I've told."

"Why me?" Poppy asked.

"Well, first of all," Faith said, "Isaiah won't kill you."

"No," Poppy said.

"Second of all… I need to know what I should do. Because I've never loved anyone before and I'm terrified. And I don't want him to be a mistake, and that has nothing to do with wanting to be perfect. And everything to do with wanting him. I'm not hiding it anymore. I'm not."

"You never had to hide it. No one needed you to be perfect."

"Maybe I needed it. I can't let them down." Faith shook her head. "I can't let them down, Poppy. Isaiah and Joshua have poured everything into our business. I can't… I can't mess up."

"They would never look at it that way," Poppy said. "Isaiah loves you. So much. I know it's hard for him to show it."

"It's easy for me to forget that he struggles, too. He seems confident."

"He is," Poppy said. "To his detriment sometime. But he's also just human. A man who fell in love. When he didn't see it coming. So, he's not going to throw stones at you for doing the same."

"They're going to be angry about who it is. Levi's older than they are."

Poppy shook her head. "And Isaiah is my foster sister's ex-fiancé. We all have reasons things shouldn't be. But they are. And sometimes you can't fight it. Love doesn't ask permission. Love gets in the cracks. And it expands. And it finds us sometimes when we least expect it."

"So, you don't judge me?"

"I'm going to judge you if you don't put on a better lipstick color for the video. But I'm not going to judge you for falling in love with a difficult man who may or may not have the capacity to love you. Because I've been there."

"And it worked out."

"Yes," Poppy said, putting her hand on her stomach. "It worked out."

"And if it hadn't?" Faith asked.

Poppy seemed to consider that for a while, her flawlessly lipsticked mouth contorting. "If it hadn't, it would have still been worth it. In my case, I would still have the baby. And she would be worth it. But also… No matter what Isaiah was able to feel for me in the end, I never would have regretted loving him. In a perfect world, he would have always loved me. But the world isn't perfect. It's broken. I suspect it's that way for your Levi, too."

Faith nodded. "I guess the only question is…whether or not he's too broken to heal."

"And you won't know that unless you try."

"That sounds an awful lot like risk."

"It is. But love is like that. It's big, Faith. And you can't hold on to fear. Not if you expect to carry around something so big and important as love. Now get some lipstick on."

Chapter 14

She was finished designing the house.

That day had been inevitable from the beginning. It was what they had been moving toward. It was, in fact, the point. But still, now that the day had arrived, Levi found himself reluctant to let go. He found himself trying to figure out ways he might convince her to stay. And then he questioned why he wanted that.

The entire point of hiring her, building this house, had been to establish himself in a new life. To put himself on a new path. The point had not been to get attached to his little architect.

He was on the verge of getting everything he wanted. Everything he needed.

She should have nothing to do with that.

And yet, he found himself fantasizing about bringing her into his home. Laying her down on that custom bed he didn't really want or need.

He hadn't seen the designs yet. In fact, part of him wanted to delay because after he approved the designs, Jonathan Bear would begin work on the construction aspects of the job. Likely, any further communications on the design would be between her and Jonathan.

Levi should be grateful that once this ended, it would end cold like that. For her sake.

He wasn't.

It was a Sunday afternoon, and he knew that meant she had dinner with her parents later. But she hadn't left yet. In fact, she was currently lying across the end of his bed, completely naked. She was on her stomach, with her legs bent at the knees and crossed at the ankles, held up in the air, kicking back and forth. Her hair had fallen in her face as she sketched earnestly, full lips pursed into a delicious O that made him think of how she'd wrapped them around his body only an hour or so earlier.

"Don't you have to be at your parents' place soon?" he asked.

She looked over at him, her expression enigmatic. "Yes."

"But?" he pressed.

"I didn't say 'but.'"

"You didn't have to," he said, moving closer to the bed and bringing his hands down on her actual butt with a smack. "I heard it all the same."

"Your concern is touching," she said, shooting him the evil eye and rolling away from him. "It's complicated."

"I understand complicated family." He just didn't

want to talk about complicated family. He wanted to get his hands all over her body again. But he could listen to her. For a few minutes.

"No," she corrected. "You understand irredeemable, horrendous families. Mine is just complicated."

"Are you going to skip this week?"

"Why do you care?"

It was a good question. Whether or not she went to her family's weekly gathering was only his concern if it impacted his ability to make love with her.

Right. Because making love was what she's been doing all day, every day at your house.

Not living together. Not playing at domesticity.

Going out and riding on the trails. Cooking dinner. Eating dinner. Going to sleep, waking up, showering.

Hell, they had ended up brushing their teeth together.

He could suddenly see why—per her earlier concern—men got weird about toothbrushes.

There was something intimate about a toothbrush.

There was also something about knowing her so intimately that made the sex better. Everything that made the sex unique to her, made it better. Living with her, being near her, was foreplay.

He didn't have to understand it to feel it.

Faith cleared her throat. "I told Poppy about us."

He sat down on the edge of the bed. "Why?" He had never met Poppy, but he knew all about her. Knew that she had pretty recently become Faith's sister-in-law. But he hadn't gotten the impression they were friends in particular.

"It just kind of...came out." She shrugged, her bare breasts rising and falling. For the moment, he was too distracted to think about what she was saying. "And I didn't see the point in hiding it anymore."

"I thought you really didn't want your brothers to know."

"I didn't. But now…"

"You finished designing the house. We both know that."

She ducked her head. "I haven't shown it to you yet."

"That doesn't change the fact that you're done. Does it?"

"I guess not. It's not a coincidence that I went ahead and told her now. I needed to talk to her about some things."

"Don't you think that if it's about—" he hesitated over saying the word *us* "—this, that you should have talked to me?"

"Yes, I do need to talk to you." She folded her knees upward, pushing herself into a sitting position. "I just… I needed to get my head on straight."

"And?"

"I failed. So, this is the thing." She frowned, her eyebrows drawing tightly together. "I don't want us to be over."

Her words hit him with all the force of a blade slipping into his rib cage.

"Is that so?"

He didn't want it to be over, either.

That was the thing. *Not being over* was what he had been pondering just a few moments ago. They didn't have to be over yet.

He almost felt as if everything else was on pause. His revenge, his triumphant return back into Alicia's circles. His determination to make sure that she went to prison by proving what she had done to him.

All of that ugliness could wait. It would have to. It was going to start once the house was finished. And until then...

What was the harm of staying with Faith?

Right. Her brothers know. Soon, her parents will know. And you really want all of that to come down on you?

That's not simple. That's not casual.

That's complicated.

But still. The idea that he could have her, for a little while longer. That he could keep her, locked away with him...

It was intoxicating.

"You want more of this?" he asked, trailing his finger along her collarbone, down her rib cage, then skimming over her sensitized nipple.

"Yes," she said, her voice a husky whisper. "But not just more of this. Levi, you have to know... You have to know."

Her eyes shone with emotion, with conviction. His chest froze, his heart a block of ice. He couldn't breathe around it.

"I have to know what, little girl?" he asked, locking his jaw tight.

"How much I love you."

That wasn't just a single knife blade. That was an outright attack. Stabbing straight through to his heart and leaving him to bleed.

"What?"

"I love you," she said. She shook her head. "I didn't want it to be like this. I didn't want to be a cliché. I didn't want to be who you were afraid I would be. The virgin who fell for the first man she slept with. But I realized something. I'm not a cliché. I'm not a virgin who fell for the first man she slept with. I'm a woman who waited until she found something powerful enough to act on. Our connection came before sex. And I have to trust that. I have to trust myself. Until now, everything I've done has been safe."

"You went away to boarding school. You have excelled in your profession before the age of thirty. How can you call any of that safe?"

She clasped her hands in front of her, picking at her fingernails. "Because it made everyone happy. Not only that—for the most part, it made me happy. It was the path of least resistance. And it still is. I could walk away from you, and I could continue on with my plan. No love. No marriage. Until I'm thirty-five maybe. Until I've had more of a career than many people have in a lifetime. Until I've done everything in the perfect order. Until I'm a triumph to my brothers and an achievement to my parents. It will make me feel proud, but it will never make me...*feel*. Not really.

"A career isn't who you are. It can't be. You know that. Everything you accomplished turned to dust because of what your ex did to you. She destroyed it, because those things are so easily destroyed. When everything burns there's one thing that's left, Levi. And that's the love of other people."

"You're wrong about that," he said, his chest tightening into a knot. "There is something else that remains through the fire. That's hatred. Blinding, burning hatred, and I have enough of that for two men. I have too much of it, Faith. Sometimes I think I might have been born with it. And until I make that bitch pay for what she did to me, that's how it's going to be."

"I don't understand what that has to do with anything."

Of course she didn't understand. Because she couldn't fathom the kind of rage and darkness that lived inside him. She had never touched a fire that burned so hot. Had never been exposed to something so ugly.

Until now. Until him.

"Then choose something else," she said. "Choose a different way."

"I've never had a choice," he said. "Ever. My fate was decided for me before I ever took a breath in this world."

"I don't believe that. If people can't chose, what does that mean for me? Have I worked hard at any of this, or was it just handed to me? Did I ever have a choice?"

"That's different."

"Why?" she pressed. "Because it's about you, so that means you can see it however you want? You can't see how hypocritical that is?"

"Hypocrisy is the least of my concerns," he said.

"What *is* your concern then? Because it certainly isn't me."

"That's where you're wrong. I warned you. I told you what this could be and what it couldn't be. You didn't listen."

"It wasn't a matter of listening. I fell in love with you by being with you. Your beauty is in everything you do, Levi. The way you touch me. The way you look at me."

"What's love to you?" he asked. "Do you think it's living here in this house with me? Do you think it's the two of us making love and laughing, and not dealing with the real world at all?"

"Don't," she said, her voice small. "Don't make it like that."

He interrupted her, not letting her finish, ignoring the hurt on her face. "Let me tell you what love is to me. A continual slog of violence. Blind optimism that propels you down the aisle of a church and then into making vows to people who are never going to do right by you. And I don't even mean just my wife. I mean *me*. You said it yourself. I was a bad husband."

"Not on the same level as your father," she argued. "Not like your wife was a bad wife."

He shrugged. "What did she get from me? Nothing but my money, clearly. And what about in your family? They're normal, and I think they might even be good people, and they still kind of mess you up."

"I guess you're right. Loving other people is never going to be simple, or easy. It's not a constant parade of happiness. Love moves. It shifts. It changes. Sometimes you give more, and sometimes you take more. Sometimes love hurts. And there's not a whole lot anyone can do about that. *But it's worth it*. That's what it comes down to for me. I know this might be a tough road, a hard one. But I also know that love is important. It matters."

"Why?" he asked, the question torn from the depths of his soul.

He wanted to understand.

On some level, he was desperate to figure out why she thought he was worth all this. This risk—sitting before him, literally naked, confessing her feelings, tearing her chest open and showing those vulnerable parts of herself. He wanted to understand why he merited such a risk.

When no one else in his life had ever felt the same.

"All my life I've had my sketchpad between myself and the world," she said. "And when it hasn't been my sketchbook it's been my accomplishments. What I've done for my family. I can hold out all these things and use them to justify my existence. But I don't have to do that with you. I don't think I really have to do it with my family, but it makes me feel safe. Makes me feel secure. I don't have to share all that much of myself, or risk all that much of myself. I can stand on higher ground and be impressive, perfect even. It's easy for people to be proud of me. The idea of doing something just for myself, the idea of doing something that might make someone judge me, or make someone reject me, is terrifying. When you live like I have, the great unknown is failure. You were never impressed with me. You wanted my architecture because it was a status symbol, and for no other reason."

"That isn't true. If I didn't like what you designed, I would never have contacted you."

"Still. It was different with you. At first, I thought it was because you were a stranger. I told myself being with you was like taking a class. Getting good at sex, I guess, with a qualified teacher. But it wasn't that. Ever. It was just you. Real chemistry with no explanation for it."

"Chemistry still isn't love, Faith," he said, his voice rough.

She ignored him. "I want to quit needing explanations about something magical happening. I wanted to be close to you without barriers. Without borders. No sketchbook, no accomplishments. You made me want something flawed and human inside myself that scared me before."

"The idea of some flawed existence is only a fantasy for people who've had it easy."

She frowned. "It's not a fantasy. The idea that there is such a thing as perfect is the fantasy. Maybe it's the fantasy you have. But there is no perfect. And I've been scared to admit that."

Tucking her hair behind her ear, Faith moved to the edge of the bed and stood before continuing. "My life has been easy compared to yours. You made me realize how strong a person can be. I've never met someone like you. Someone who had to push through so much pain. You made yourself out of nothing. My family might come from humble beginnings, but it isn't the same. We had each other. We had support. You didn't have any of that.

"I don't want you to walk alone anymore, Levi. I want to walk with you. From where I'm sitting right now, that's the greatest accomplishment I could ever hope to have. To love and be loved by someone like you. To choose to walk our own path together."

"My path is set," he said. "It has been set from the beginning."

He looked down at her, at her luminous face. Her eyes, which were full of so much hope.

So much foolish hope.

She didn't understand what she was begging him to do. He had thought of it earlier. That he could pull her inside and lock her in this cage with him.

And he might be content enough with that for a while, but eventually... Eventually she wouldn't be.

Because this hatred, this rage that lived inside him, was a life sentence.

Something he had been born with. Something he feared he would never be able to escape.

And asking Faith to live with him, asking Faith to live with what he was—that would be letting her serve a life sentence with him. And if anyone on this earth was innocent, it was her.

Even so, it was tempting.

He could embrace the monster completely and hold this woman captive. This woman who had gripped him, body and soul, and stolen his sense of self-preservation, stolen his sense of just *why* vengeance was so important.

It was all he had. It consumed him. It drove him.

Justice was the only thing that had gotten him through five years in prison. At first, wanting justice for his wife, and then, wanting it for himself.

Somewhere, in all of that, wanting justice had twisted into wanting revenge, but in his case it amounted to more or less the same. And he would not bring Faith into that world.

She stood there, a beacon of all he could not have. And still he wanted her. With all of him. With his every breath.

But he knew he could not have her.

Knew that he couldn't take what she would so freely give, because she had no idea what the repercussions would be.

He knew what it was to live in captivity.

And he would not wish the same on her.

He had to let her go.

"No," he said. "I don't love you."

"You don't love me?" The question was almost skeptical, and he certainly hadn't cowed her.

He had to make her understand what he was.

"No."

It was easy to say the word, because what was love? What did it mean? What did it mean beyond violence and betrayal, broken vows and everything else that had happened in his life? He had no evidence that love was real. That there was any value in it. And the closest he had ever come to believing was seeing Faith's bright, hopeful eyes as she looked up at him.

And he knew he didn't deserve that version of love.

No. If there was love, real love, and it was that pure, it didn't belong with him.

Faith should give that love to someone who deserved it. A man who had earned the right to have those eyes look at him like he was a man who actually had the hope of becoming new, better.

Levi was not that man.

"I can't love you. You or anyone."

"That isn't true. You have loved me for weeks now. In your every action, your every touch."

"I haven't."

"Levi…" She pressed her hand to his chest and he wanted to hold it there. "You changed me. How can you look at me and say that what we have isn't love?"

He moved her hand away. And took a step back.

"If there is love in this whole godforsaken world, little girl, it isn't for me. You'll go on and you'll find a man who's capable of it. Me? I've chosen vengeance. And maybe you're right. Maybe there is another path I could walk on, but I'm not willing to do it."

She stared at him, and suddenly, a deep understanding filled her brown eyes. He was the one who felt naked now, though he was dressed and she was not. He felt like she could see him, straight to his soul, maybe deeper even than he had ever looked inside himself.

It was terrifying to be known like that.

The knowledge in Faith's eyes was deep and terrible. He wanted to turn away from it. Standing there, feeling like she was staring into the darkness in him, was a horror he had never experienced before.

"The bird is freedom. That's what it means," she said suddenly, like the sun had just risen and she could see clearly for the first time. She turned away from him, grabbing her sketchbook off the bed and holding it up in front of his face. "Look at this," she said. "I have the real plans on my computer, but look at these."

He flipped through the journal, until he found exactly what she was talking about. And he knew. The moment he saw it. He didn't need her to tell him.

It was a drawing of a house. An aerial view. And the way it was laid out it looked like folded wings. It wasn't shaped like a bird, not in the literal sense, but he felt it. Exactly what she had intended him to feel.

"I knew it was important to you, but I didn't know why. Freedom, Levi. You put it on your body, but you haven't accepted it with your soul."

"Faith…"

"You never left that prison," she said softly.

"I did," he said, his voice hard. "I left it and I'm standing right here."

"No," she responded. "You didn't. You're still in there." She curled her fingers into fists, angry tears filling her eyes. "That woman got you a life sentence, Levi. But it was a wrongful sentence. The judge released you, but you haven't released yourself. You don't deserve to be in prison forever because of her."

"It's not just her," he said, his voice rough. "I imagined that if I changed my life, if I earned enough money, if I got married and got myself the right kind of house, that I would be free of the fate everyone in my life thought I was headed for. Don't you think every teacher I ever had thought I was going to be like my father? Don't you think every woman in Copper Ridge who agreed to go on a date with me was afraid I was secretly a wifebeater in training? They did. They all thought that's how I would end up. The one way people could never have imagined I would end up was rich. I did it to defy them. To define my own fate, but it was impossible. I still ended up in prison, Faith. That was my fate, no matter what I did. Was it her? Or was it me?"

"It's not you," she said. "It isn't."

"I can't say the same with such authority," he said.

"You're not a bad man," she said, her voice trembling. "You aren't. You're the best man I've ever known. But you can tattoo symbols of freedom on your skin all you want, it won't make a difference. Revenge is not going to set you free, Levi. Only hope can do that. Only love can do that. You have to let it. You have to let me."

He couldn't argue, because he knew it was true. Because he had known that if he brought her into his life then he would be consigning her to a prison sentence, too.

And if it was true for her, it was true for him.

He was in prison. But for him there would be no escape.

She could escape.

"For my part," he said, his voice flat, as flat as the

beating of his heart and his ears, "I've chosen vengeance. And there's nothing you can do to stop it."

"Levi…" She blinked. "Can you just give us a chance? You don't have to tell me that you love me now. But can't you just—"

"No. We're done. The house is done, and so are we. It's already gone on too long, Faith, and the fact that I've made you cry is evidence of that."

"Please," she said. "I'll beg. I don't have any pride. I'm more than willing to fall into that virgin stereotype you are so afraid of," she reiterated. "Happily. Because there is no point to pride if I haven't got you."

He gritted his teeth, and took a step forward, gripping her chin between his thumb and forefinger. "Now you listen to me," he said. "There is every reason for you to have pride, Faith Grayson. Your life is going to go on without me. And when you meet the man who loves you the way you deserve to be loved, who can give you the life you should have, you'll understand. And you'll be grateful for your pride."

"I refuse to take a lecture on my feelings from a man who doesn't even believe in what I feel." She turned and began to collect her clothes. "I still want you to have my design. My house. Because when you're walking around in it, I want you to feel my love in those walls. And I want you to remember what you could have had." She blinked her eyes. "I designed it with so much care, Levi. To be sure that you never felt like you were locked in again. But you're going to feel like you're in prison. Whether you're inside or outside. Whether you're alone or with me or whether you're on the back of a horse or not. And it's a prison of your own making. You have to let go. You have to let go of all the hate you're carrying around. And then you might be surprised to find out how much love you can hold. If you decide to do that, please come and find me."

She dressed quietly, slowly, and without another word. Then she grabbed her sketchbook and turned and walked out of the bedroom.

He didn't go after her. He didn't move at all until he heard the front door shut, until he heard the engine of her car fire up.

He walked into the bathroom, bracing himself on the sink before looking up slowly at his reflection. The man he saw there...was a criminal.

A man who might not have committed a crime, but who had been hardened by years in jail. A man who had arguably been destined for that fate no matter which way he had walked in the world, because of his beginnings.

The man he saw there...was a man he hated more than he hated anyone.

His father. His ex-wife.

Anyone.

Levi looked down at the countertop again, and saw the cup by the sink where his toothbrush was. Where Faith's still was.

That damn toothbrush.

He picked up the cup and threw it across the bathroom, the glass shattering decisively, the toothbrushes scattering.

It was just a damn toothbrush. She was just a woman.

In the end, he would have exactly what he had set out to get.

And that was all a man like him could ever hope for.

Chapter 15

Faith had no idea how she managed to walk into her parents' house. Had no idea how she managed to sit and eat dinner and look like a normal person. Force a smile. Carry on a conversation.

She had no idea how she managed to do any of it, and yet, she did.

She felt broken. Splintered and shattered inside, and like she might get cut on her own damaged pieces. But somehow, she had managed to sit there and smile and nod at appropriate times. Somehow, she had managed not to pick up her dinner plate and smash it on the table, to make it as broken as the rest of her.

She had managed not to yell at Joshua and Danielle, Poppy and Isaiah, Devlin and Mia, and even her own parents for being happy, functional couples.

She felt she deserved a medal for all those things, and yet she knew one wasn't coming.

When the meal was finished, her mother and Danielle and Poppy stayed in the kitchen, working on a cake recipe Danielle had been interested in learning how to bake for Joshua's birthday, while Devlin and her father went out to the garage so that Devlin could take a look under the hood of their father's truck.

And that left Faith corralled in the living room with Joshua and Isaiah.

"Poppy told me," Isaiah said, his voice firm and hard.

"She's a turncoat," Faith said, shaking her head. Of course, she had known her sister-in-law would tell. Faith had never expected confidentiality there, and she would never have asked for it. "Well, there's nothing to tell. Not anymore."

"What does that mean?" Joshua asked.

"Just what it sounds like. My personal relationship with Mr. Tucker is no more, the design phase has moved on to construction and he is now Jonathan Bear's problem, not mine. It's not a big deal." She waved a hand. "So now your optics should be a little clearer."

"I don't care about my optics, Faith," Joshua said, his expression contorted with anger. "I care about you. I care about you getting hurt."

"Well," she said, "I'm hurt. Oh, well. Everybody goes through it, I guess."

"That bastard," Joshua said. "He took advantage of you."

"Why do you think he took advantage of me? Because I'm young?" She stared at her brother, her expression pointed. "Because I was a virgin?" She glared at them both a little bit harder, and watched as both expressions paled slightly, and they exchanged glances. "People who live in glass towers cannot be throwing stones. And I think the two of you did a pretty phenomenal job of breaking your wives' hearts before things all worked out."

"That was different," Isaiah said.

"Oh, really?"

"Yes," Joshua said. "Different."

"Why?"

"Because," Joshua said simply, "we ended up with them."

"But they didn't know that you would end up together. Not when you broke things off with them."

"Do you think you're going to end up with him?" Isaiah asked.

"No," she said, feeling deflated as the words left her lips. "I don't. But you can't go posturing about me not knowing what I want, not knowing what I'm doing, when you both married women closer to my age than yours."

"Poppy is kind of in the middle," Isaiah said. "In fairness."

"No," Faith said, pointing a finger at him. "No *in fairness*. She was in love with you for a decade and you ignored her, and then you proposed a convenient marriage to her with absolutely no emotion involved at all. You don't get any kind of exception here."

He shrugged. "It was worth a shot."

"I don't need a lecture," she said softly. "And I don't need you to go beat him up."

"Are you still going ahead with the project?" Joshua asked. "Because you know, you don't have to do that."

"I do," she said. "I want to. I want to give him the house. I mean, for money, but I want him to have it."

"Well, he's the asshole who has to live in the house designed by his ex, I guess," Joshua said.

She sighed heavily. "I know what you're thinking— you're thinking that you were right, and you warned me. But you *weren't* right. Whatever you think happened between Levi and I, you're wrong."

"So he didn't defile you?" Joshua asked.

"No," Faith said, not backing down from the challenge in her brother's eyes. "He definitely did. But I love him. And I don't regret what happened. I can't. It was a mistake. But it was my mistake. And I needed to make it."

"Faith," Joshua said, "I know it seems like it sometimes, but I promise, you don't have to justify yourself to me. Tell us. I know what I said about optics, but that was before I realized... Hell," he said, "it was before I realized what was going on. I'm sorry that you got hurt."

"I'll survive," she said, feeling sadly like she might not.

"Faith," Isaiah said, her older brother looking uncharacteristically sympathetic. "Whatever happens," he said, "sometimes a person is too foolish to see what's right in front of them. Sometimes a man needs to be left on his own to fully understand what it was he had. Sometimes men who don't deserve love need it the most."

"Do you mean you?" she asked.

He looked at her, his eyes clear and focused. And full of more emotion than she was used to seeing on him. "Yes. And it would be hypocritical of me to accept the love I get from Poppy and think Levi doesn't deserve the chance to have it with you. Or maybe *deserve* is the wrong word. It's not about deserving. I don't deserve what I have. But I love her. With everything. And it took me a while to sort through that. The past gets in the way."

"That's our problem," she said. "There's just too much of the past."

"There's nothing you can do about that," Isaiah said. "The choice is his. The only question is…are you going to wait for him to figure it out?"

"I vote you don't," Joshua said. "Because you're too good for him."

"I vote you decide," Isaiah added, shooting a pointed look at Joshua. "Because you probably are too good for him. But sometimes when a woman is too good for a man, that means he'll love her a hell of a lot more than anyone else will." He cleared his throat. "From experience, I can tell you, that if you're hard to love, when someone finally does love you, it's worth everything. Absolutely everything."

"You're not hard to love," she said.

"That's awfully nice of you to say, but I definitely have my moments. I bet he does, too. And when he realizes what it is you're giving him? He'll know what a damn fool he was to have thrown it away."

"I still disagree," Joshua said.

"And who are you going to listen to about interpersonal relationships? Him or me?"

Faith looked over at Isaiah, her serious brother, her brother who had difficulty understanding people, connecting with people, but no difficulty at all loving his wife. She smiled, but didn't say anything. She felt broken. But Isaiah had given her hope. And she would hold onto that with everything she had.

Because without it… All that stretched before her was a future without Levi. And that made all her previous perfection seem like nothing much at all.

Chapter 16

It had been two weeks since Levi had last seen Faith.

And in that time, ground had been broken on the new house, he'd had several intensive conversations with Jonathan Bear and he'd done one well-placed interview he knew would filter into his ex-wife's circles. He'd had the reporter come out to the house he was currently staying in, and the man had followed him on a trail ride while Levi had given his version of the story.

It had all gone well, the headline making national news easily, and possibly international news thanks to the internet, with several pictures of Levi and his horses. The animals somehow made him seem softer and more approachable.

And, of course, his alliance with Faith had only helped matters. Because she was a young woman and because the assumption was that she would have vetted him before working with him. What surprised him the most was the quote that had been included in the story from GrayBear Construction. Which, considering what Levi knew about the company, meant Faith's brother Joshua. It surprised him, because Joshua had spoken of Levi's character and their excitement about working on the project with him. On this chance for a new start.

For redemption.

Levi wasn't sure what the hell Faith had told her brother, but he was sure he didn't deserve the quote. Still, he was grateful for it.

Grateful was perhaps the wrong word.

He looked at the article, running his thumb over the part about his redemption.

And in his mind, he heard Faith's voice.

You never walked out of that prison.

She didn't understand. She couldn't.

But that didn't change the fact that he felt like he'd been breathing around a knife for the past two weeks. Faith—*his* Faith—had left a hole in his life he couldn't imagine would ever be filled. But that was…how it had to be.

He had his path, she had hers.

There was nothing to be done about it. His fate had been set long before he'd ever met her. And there was no changing it now.

He had gone out to the building site today, just to look around at everything. The groundwork was going well, as was the excavation over where he wanted to put the stables. She had been right about Jonathan Bear. He was the best.

Jonathan had assembled a crew in what seemed to be record time, especially considering that this particular project was so large. It looked like a small army working on the property. Jonathan was also quick and efficient at acquiring materials, and speeding through permits and inspections. He also seemed to know every subcontractor in the state, and had gotten them out to bid right away.

Levi had already built on a property where money was no object, but this was somewhere beyond that.

He turned in a circle, watching all the commotion around him, then stopped and frowned when he saw a Mercedes coming up the drive. Bright red, sporty. Not a car that he recognized.

The car stopped, and he saw a woman inside, large sunglasses on her face, hair long and loose.

Flames licked at the edge of his gut as a sense of understanding began to dawn on him.

The blonde got out of the car, and that was when recognition hit him with full force.

Alicia.

His ex-wife.

She was wearing a tight, black dress that looked ludicrous out here, and she at least had the good sense to wear a pair of pointed flats, rather than the spiked stilettos she usually favored. Still, the dress was tight, and it forced her entire body into a shimmy with each and every step as she walked over to meet him.

He'd loved her. For so many years. And then he'd hated her.

And now… His whole chest was full of Faith. His whole body. His whole soul. And he looked at Alicia and he didn't feel much of anything anymore.

"Are you really here?" he asked, not quite sure why those were the words that had come out of his mouth.

But… It was damn incredulous. That she would dare show her face.

"I am," she said, looking down and back up at him, her blue eyes innocent and bright. "I wasn't sure you would be willing to see me if I called ahead. I took a chance, hoping I would find you here. All that publicity for your new build… It wasn't hard to find out where it was happening."

"You're either a very brave woman or a very stupid one."

She tilted her chin upward. "Or a woman with a concealed-carry permit."

Suddenly, the little black handbag she was carrying seemed a lot less innocuous.

"Did you come to shoot me?"

She lifted a shoulder. "No. But I'm not opposed to it."

"Why the hell do you have the right to be angry at me?"

"I'm not here to be angry at you," she said. "But I didn't know how you would receive me, so self-defense was definitely on my mind."

He shook his head. "I never laid a hand on you. I never gave you a reason to think you would have to protect yourself around me. Any fear you feel standing in front of me? That's all on you."

"Maybe," she said. "I didn't really mean for them to think you killed me."

"Didn't you? You knew I went to prison. Hell, babe, you siphoned money off me for a couple of years to fund the lifestyle you knew you wanted to live out in the French Riviera, and you only got back on police radar when you had to dip into my funds. So I'd say you knew exactly what you were doing."

"Yes, Levi, I meant to steal money from you. But I didn't want you to go to jail. I wanted to disappear. And I needed the money to live how I wanted. When you got arrested, I didn't know what to do. At that point, there was such a circus around my disappearance that I couldn't come back."

"Oh, no, of course not."

"People like us, we have to look out for ourselves."

"I looked out for you," he said. "You were mine for twelve years, and even when I was in prison it was only you, so, for me, it was seventeen years of you being mine, Alicia. I worried about you. Cared for you. Loved you."

"I'm sorry," she said.

"You're sorry? I spent five years in prison and had my entire reputation destroyed, and you're sorry."

"I want you back." She shook her head. "I know it sounds insane. But I… I'm miserable."

"You're broke," he spat. "And you're afraid of what I'm going to do."

The way she looked up at him, the slight flash of anger in her eyes before it was replaced by that dewy innocence, told him he was definitely on the right track. "I don't have money, I'm not going to lie to you."

"And yet, that's a nice car."

She shrugged. "I have what I have. I can hardly be left without a vehicle. And I was your wife for all that time, you're right. And that's basically all I was, Levi. I enhanced your image, but being your wife didn't help me figure out a way to earn the kind of money you did, and now no one will touch me with a ten-foot pole. My reputation is completely destroyed."

"Forgive me for not being overly concerned that you faking your death has left you without a lot of options."

"In fairness, I didn't fake my death. I disappeared. That the police thought I was dead is hardly my fault."

"Alicia, are you honestly telling me you thought I would say I wanted you back?"

"Why not? You want a redemption story, and getting back with me would benefit us both. I don't think either of us were ever head over heels in love with each other. We both wanted things from the other. And you know it. Don't go getting on your high horse now. We can come back. You don't need to be vindictive," she said.

"I don't need to be vindictive?" He shook his head. "This, from you?"

She was standing in front of him, imploring him to rescue her. That was what she wanted. For him to reach down to lift her out of this hell of her own making.

It was this exact moment when he knew he had her under his heel. He could take her in, make her think he was going along with her plan, and maybe get some information about what exactly she had done that was illegal, and get the exact kind of revenge he wanted. Or, if not that, he could finish it now, devastate her.

And then what?

That question echoed inside him, hollow and miserable.

Then what?

What was on the other side of it? What was feeding all that anger, all that hatred?

Where was the freedom? Where was the reward? Nothing but an empty house filled with reminders of Faith, but without the woman herself inside it.

Somehow, he had a vision of himself standing by a

jail cell holding a key. And he knew that whatever he decided to do next was the deciding factor. Did he unlock the door and walk out, or did he throw the keys so far away from himself he would never be able to reach them again?

Faith was right.

He had been given a life sentence, but he didn't have to submit to it.

Faith.

He had been looking for satisfaction in this. Had been looking for satisfaction in revenge. In hatred.

And maybe there was satisfaction there. Something twisted and dirty, the kind of satisfaction his father would have certainly enjoyed.

But there was another choice. There was another path.

It was hope.

It was love.

But a man couldn't straddle two paths.

He had to choose. He had to choose hope over darkness, love over hate.

And right now, with dark satisfaction so close at hand, it was difficult. But on the other side...

Faith could be on the other side.

If he was strong enough to turn away from this now, Faith was on the other side.

"Go away," he said, his heart thundering heavily, adrenaline pulsing through his veins.

"What?"

"I don't ever want to see you again. I'm going to write you a check. Not for a whole lot of money, but for some. Trade in your car, for God's sake. Don't be an idiot. I'm not giving you money for *you*, I'm doing it for me. To clear this. Let it go. Whatever you think I did to you… Whatever you really wanted to do to me… It doesn't matter. Not anymore. We are done. And after you cash that check I want you to never even speak my name again. Do you understand me?"

"I don't want a check," she said, taking a step forward, wrapping her hands around his shirt. "I want you."

He jerked her hands off him, his lip curling. "You don't. You don't want me. And I sure as hell don't want you. But I'm also not going to let you suffer for the rest of your life. Do you know why not? Because everything in me, every natural thing in me, *wants* to. Wants to make you regret everything you've ever done, wants to make you regret you ever heard my name. But I won't do it. I won't let that part of myself with. Because I met a woman. And I love her. I love her, Alicia. You don't even know about the kind of love I found with her. The kind of love she has for me. I don't deserve it. Dammit, I have to try to be the kind of man that deserves it. So I want you to walk away from me. Because I'm choosing to let you go. I'm choosing to get on a different road.

"Don't you dare follow me."

"Levi…"

"Leave now, and you get your money. But if you don't…"

She stared at him. For a long time. As if he might change his mind. As if she had some kind of power over him. She didn't. Not over any part of him. Not his anger. Not his love. Not his future.

It was over, all of it. Her hold on him. The hold his childhood had over him.

Because love was stronger.

Faith was stronger.

"Okay," she said, finally. "I'll go."

"Good."

He watched her, unmoving, as she got back in her Mercedes and drove away. And as she did, he looked up into the sky and saw a bird flying overhead.

Free.

He was free.

Whatever happened next, Faith had given him that freedom.

But he wanted her to share it with him. More than his next breath, more than anything else.

He'd lived a life marked by anger. A life marked by greed. He'd been saddled with the consequences of the poison that lived inside other people, and he'd taken that same poison and let it grow and fester inside him.

But he was done with that now.

He was through letting the darkness win.

He was ready. He was finally ready to walk out of that cell and into freedom.

With Faith.

Chapter 17

It was Sunday again. It had a tendency to roll around with alarming regularity. Which was massively annoying for Faith because it was getting harder and harder to put on a brave face in front of her family.

Although, how brave her face was—that was up for debate.

Her brothers already knew exactly what had happened, and by extension so did their wives. And even though she hadn't spoken to her parents about it at all, she suspected they knew. Well, her mother had picked up on her attachment to Levi right away, so why wouldn't she have this figured out as well?

Faith sighed heavily and looked down at her pot roast. She just wasn't feeling up to it. You would think that after two weeks things would start to feel better. Instead, if anything, they were getting worse.

How was that supposed to work? Shouldn't time be healing?

Instead she was reminded that she had a lot more time without him stretching in front of her. And she didn't want that. No. She didn't.

She wished she could have him. She wished it more than anything.

The problem was, Joshua was right. She was kind of secretly hoping things would work out. That he would come back to her.

But he hadn't.

That was the problem, she supposed, about never having had a real heartbreak before.

She hadn't had all that hope knocked out of her yet.

Well, maybe this would be the thing that did it.

Not at all a cheering thought.

There was a knock on the door, and her parents looked around the table, as if counting everybody in attendance. Everyone was there. From Devlin on down to baby Riley.

"I wonder who that could be," her mother said.

"I'll check," said her father as he stood and walked out of the dining room, heading toward the entryway.

For some reason, Faith kept watch after him. For some reason, she couldn't look away, her entire body filled with tension.

Because she knew. Part of her knew.

When her father returned a moment later, Faith knew.

Because there he was.

Levi.

Levi Tucker, large and hard and absurd, standing in the middle of her parents' cozy dining room. It seemed...beyond belief. And yet, there he was.

"This young man says he's here to see you, Faith," her father said.

As if on cue, all three of her brothers stood, their height matching Levi's. And none of them looked very happy.

"If he wants to see Faith, he might need to talk to us first," Devlin said.

Those rat bastards. She hadn't told Devlin. That meant clearly they'd had some kind of older-brother summit and had come to an agreement on whether or not they would smash Levi's face if he showed up. And obviously, they had decided that they would.

"I can talk to him," Faith said.

Their father now looked completely concerned, like maybe he should be standing with his sons on this one.

But her mother stood also, her tone soft but firm. "If Faith would like to a chance to speak to this gentleman, then I expect we should allow it."

Her sons, large, burly alpha males themselves, did exactly as their mother asked.

"I'll just be a minute," Faith said, as she slipped around the table, worked her way behind all the chairs and met Levi in the doorway.

"Hi," she said.

"Why don't we go into the living room?" he asked.

"Okay."

They walked out into the living room, where his presence was no less absurd. Where, in fact, he looked even more ridiculous standing on the hand-braided rug that her grandmother had made years ago, next to the threadbare sofa where she had grown up watching cartoons.

She had known she wouldn't be able to bring this man home with her.

He had followed her home anyway.

"Is everything all right with the design?" she asked, crossing her arms to make a shield over her heart. As if she could ever hope to protect it from him.

As if there were any unbroken pieces that remained.

He tipped back his hat, his mouth set into a grim line. "If I needed to talk to you about your design work I would have come to the office."

"Well, you might have made less of a scene if you would have come to the office."

"I also would have had to wait. Until Monday. And I couldn't wait." He took off his hat and set it on the side table by the couch. And now she'd think of his hat there every time she looked at it.

This was the real reason he should never have come to her parents' house.

She'd never be in it again without thinking of him, and how fair was that? She'd grown up in this house. And Levi had erased eighteen years of memories without him here in one fell swoop.

He sighed heavily. "It took some time, but I got my thoughts sorted out. And I needed to see you right away."

"Yes?" She tightened her crossed arms and looked up at him. But this time she didn't let herself get blinded by all that rugged beauty. This time she looked at him. Really looked.

He looked...exhausted. His handsome face seemed to have deeper lines etched into the grooves by his mouth, by his eyes, and he looked like he hadn't been sleeping.

"Alicia came to see me," he said.

Her stomach hollowed out, sinking down to her toes. "What?"

"Alicia. She came to see me. She wanted us to get back together."

Faith's response was quick and unexpected. "How dare she? What was she thinking?" Even angry at him, that enraged her. The idea of that woman daring to show her face filled Faith with righteous fury. How dare Alicia speak to him with anything other than a humble apology as she walked across broken glass to get to him?

And if there had been broken glass he would have mentioned it.

"It was a perfect opportunity to find a way to make her pay for what she did to me, Faith. She handed herself to me. Told me her troubles. Told me she needed me to fix them. I wanted to destroy her, and she handed herself to me. Gave me all the tools to do that."

Ice seemed to fill her veins as he spoke those words. Those cold, terrifying words.

What had he done? What would he do?

"But you're right," he continued, his voice rough. "You were right all this time."

"About?" She pressed her hand to her chest, trying to calm her heart.

"I do have a choice. I have a choice about what kind of man I want to be, and about whether or not I choose to live my life in prison. I have a choice about what path I want to walk. I was worried I was on the same road as my father. That his kind of end was inevitable for me, but it was only ever inevitable if I embraced the hatred inside myself instead of the love. You showed me that. You taught me that. You gave me…something I didn't deserve, Faith. You believed in me when no one else did. When no one else ever had. You gave me a reason to believe I can have a different future. You gave me a reason to want a different future."

"I don't know how," she said. "I don't know how I could—"

"Sometimes looking at someone and seeing trust in their eyes changes everything. You looked at me and saw someone completely different than anyone else saw. I want to be that man. For you. The man you see. The man you care about. That you want."

"Levi, you are. You always were."

"No," he said, the denial rough on his lips. "No, I wasn't. Because I was too consumed with other things. You are right. To take hold of something as valuable as love there are other things that need to be set down. Because love is too precious to handle without care. It's far too precious to carry in the same arms as hate, as anger. I couldn't hate Alicia with the passion that I did and also give you the love you deserve. It would have been like locking you in a prison cell with me, and you don't deserve that, Faith. You deserve so much more. You deserve everything." He took a deep breath. "I love you. I gave Alicia money. And it took the past couple of days to get that squared away. But I also drafted some legal documents. And she is not going to ever approach us. She's not speaking about me in the media. Nothing. If she does, she's going to have to return what I gave her."

"Why?" Faith asked. "Why did you…give her money?"

"To make sure she stayed out of our lives. I don't ever want her touching you."

"You didn't have to do that, Levi…"

"I would do anything to protect you," he said. "And I don't trust her. I needed to at least hold some kind of card to keep her away from us. And I knew that if she was just out there, desperate and grasping, she could become a problem later."

"But to give money to a woman you hate..."

He shook his head. "You know, suddenly it didn't matter as much. Not when there is a woman I love. A woman I would die for. Laying all my anger down was a small thing when I realized I'd lay my life down for you just as easily."

"Levi..."

"That feeling, *this* feeling," he said, taking a step toward her and grabbing her hand, placing her palm flat on his chest. "It is so much bigger than hate. That's what I want. I don't want to be my father's son. I don't want to be my ex-wife's victim. I want to be your husband."

"Yes," Faith said, her heart soaring. Her arms went around his neck and she kissed him. Kissed him like she wasn't in her parents' living room. Like he wasn't absurd, and they weren't a ridiculous couple.

She kissed him like he was everything.

Because he was.

"What about your plan? I didn't think you were going to get married until you were at least thirty-five? And to be clear, Faith, I would wait for you. I would. I will. Whatever you need."

She shook her head. "I don't want to wait. I don't see why I can't have all my dreams. I'm an overachiever, after all."

"Yes, you are." He laughed and picked her up off the floor. "Yes, you are."

She heard a throat clear, and she turned, seeing her dad standing in the doorway. "I expected that the man who would ask my daughter to marry him would ask for my permission first."

Levi squared his shoulders, moved forward and extended his hand. "I'm Levi Tucker," he said. "I would like to marry your daughter. But, no disrespect, sir, she's already said yes. And strictly speaking, hers is the answer I need."

Her father smiled slowly, and shook Levi's hand. "That is correct. And I think...you just might be the one who can handle her."

"Handle me?" Faith said, "I'm not *that* hard to handle."

"Not hard to handle," her dad said. "You are precious cargo. And I think he knows that."

"I do," Levi said. "She's the most important thing in my life."

"I'm not that important," she said.

"No, you only saved me. That's all."

"That's all," Faith said, smiling up at him.

"It's good he proposed," her father said. "Now I probably won't have to stop my sons from killing you. Probably."

Her dad turned and walked back into the dining room, leaving Levi and Faith alone together.

"How badly do I really have to worry about your brothers?"

She waved a hand. "You're probably fine."

"Probably?"

"Probably," she confirmed.

She looked up into his eyes, and her heart felt like it took flight. Like a bird.

Like freedom.

And as he gathered her up in his arms, held her close, she knew that for them that was love.

Redemption. Hope. Freedom.

Always.

Epilogue

When the house was finished, he carried her over the threshold.

"You're only supposed to do that with your wife," she pointed out.

"You're going to be my wife soon enough," Levi said, leaning in and kissing her, emotion flooding his chest.

"Just a couple of months now."

"It's going to be different," he said.

"What is?"

"Marriage. For me. When I got married the first time… It wasn't that I didn't care. I did. But I thought I could prove something with that marriage. She wasn't the important thing—I was. No matter what I told myself, it was more about proving something to me than it was about being a good husband to her. And that isn't what I want with you. I love you. I don't want to

prove anything. I just want to be with you. I just want
to make you happy."

"And I want to make you happy. I think if both of us
are coming at our relationship from that angle, we're
going to be okay."

He set her down in the empty space, and the two of
them looked around. The joy in her eyes was unmistakable. The wonder.

"We're standing in a place you created. Does that
amaze you?"

It amazed him. She amazed him. He'd thought of
her as too innocent for him. Too young. Too a lot of
things. But Faith Grayson was a force. Powerful, cre-
ative. Beautiful.

Perfect for him.

She ducked her head, color flooding her cheeks. "It
kind of does. Even though I've made a lot of buildings
now. I've never…made one for me."

"You did this for *me*. I never asked you if that bothered you."

"Why would it bother me?"

"We talked about this. You haven't had a chance to
design your own house yet."

She looked down at her hands, and then back up at
him, sincerity shining from her brown eyes. "You know,
I've always thought a lot about homes. Of course I did.
How could I not, in my line of work? But I always felt
like home was the place where you grew up. I never
thought any place could feel like home to me more than
my parents' house. I took my first steps there. I cried
over tests, I was stressed about college admissions in
my little bed. I had every holiday, endless family discussions around the dinner table. I never thought any

place, even if it was custom-built for me, could ever feel more like home than there. I was wrong, though."

"Oh?"

She took a step toward him, pressing her fingers to his chest. "This is home."

"We don't even have any furniture."

"Not the house." She stretched up on her toes and kissed him on the lips. "You. You're my home. Wherever you are. That's my home."

* * * * *

We hope you enjoyed reading

Rogue Stallion

by *New York Times* bestselling author

DIANA PALMER

and

Need Me Cowboy

by *New York Times* bestselling author

MAISEY YATES.

Both were originally Harlequin series stories!

Harlequin Desire transports you to the worlds of the American elite—oil barons, family dynasties, business moguls and celebrities. Get ready for juicy plot twists, delicious sensuality and intriguing scandal.

Luxury, scandal, desire—welcome to the lives of the American elite.

Look for six *new* books every month!

Available wherever books are sold.

Adam leaned forward slightly, and his hands went with him, sliding over the countertop, and she watched them. The tips of his fingers were so close to hers.

It wouldn't take much. A slight shift, and their hands would touch.

"How are you?" His voice was low, and it skimmed over her skin in a way that made her feel edgy and uncomfortable.

She should move, because being close to him was making her uncomfortable, too.

But she didn't.

"Ugh. Don't ask me that." She looked up at his face. "I'm here asking you advice at 9:00 p.m. How do you think I am?"

"In general," he said.

"We don't talk about that stuff."

He shrugged. "We do now, I guess."

"I don't know. I don't know what to call how I am. Sad, and tired of being sad, because I feel like half of my life has been sadness for years. And it's all kind of bittersweet, because the end that I knew was coming came, and I don't know what to do with myself. Except…I have a date."

Adam's hands moved back a fraction. "Really?"

"Yes."

"With who?" Another fraction away.

"That is not your business." Her own hands slid back slightly.

"Why not? Do I know him?"

"Probably. Mark."

"Mark from the plumbing store?" They moved an inch.

"Yes. I went in to buy a pipe and he asked me on a date."

"Really?" His hands slid back with that repeated question.

"Yes. You asked me that already." She curled her hands into fists, still resting on the counter. "I mean, we're going out as friends. It's just…practice for being a human in the world. It's not a thing."

"Well, I guess that's the thing," he said. "You go out, you find yourself a guy. You go on dates. That's what you do while your daughter's at college. Because…you can. Isn't that kind of the point of empty nests?"

"I don't want one," she insisted. "Not really."

"Life doesn't tend to ask what you want. It's not a diner. Things aren't made to order."

"Neither is your food."

Their eyes caught. And then he quit moving away.

He leaned in just slightly, and she caught that scent again. His aftershave. His skin. Her stomach fluttered, just a little bit. And she was absolutely and totally taken aback by the sensation.

By her need to stay where she was, right in his orbit.

She had always felt drawn to him. From the moment they met. But it was different right now.

Don't miss
Secrets from a Happy Marriage
available May 2020 wherever
HQN books and ebooks are sold.

HQNBooks.com

HARLEQUIN
DESIRE

Luxury, scandal, desire—welcome to the lives of the American elite.

Save $1.00

on the purchase of ANY Harlequin Desire book.

Available wherever books are sold, including most bookstores, supermarkets, drugstores and discount stores.

Save $1.00

on the purchase of ANY Harlequin Desire book.

Coupon valid until June 30, 2020.
Redeemable at participating outlets in the U.S. and Canada only.
Not redeemable at Barnes & Noble stores. Limit one coupon per customer.

52616697

5 65373 00076 2   (8100)0 12455

® and ™ are trademarks owned by Harlequin Enterprises ULC.

© 2020 Harlequin Enterprises ULC

BACCOUP91529

Love Harlequin romance?

DISCOVER.

Be the first to find out about promotions,
news and exclusive content!

Facebook.com/HarlequinBooks

Twitter.com/HarlequinBooks

Instagram.com/HarlequinBooks

Pinterest.com/HarlequinBooks

ReaderService.com

EXPLORE.

Sign up for the Harlequin e-newsletter and
download a free book from any series at
TryHarlequin.com

CONNECT.

Join our Harlequin community to
share your thoughts and connect
with other romance readers!
Facebook.com/groups/HarlequinConnection